Destiny In Blood

A Vampire Novel

by

Karla J.M. Brading

GHP
Grosvenor House
Publishing Limited

This book is published by
Grosvenor House Publishing Ltd
28-30 High Street, Guildford, Surrey, GU1 3HY.
www.grosvenorhousepublishing.co.uk

A CIP record for this book
is available from the British Library

ISBN 978-1-906210-36-6

Printed by Biddles Ltd, King's Lynn, Norfolk

Acknowledgments

This book is dedicated to all the special people in my life- people I love, adore and cherish spending time with:

My three sisters, Emily, Nadine and Alice- the most interesting bunch of siblings you'll ever meet, and my beautiful mum, Denise.

My good and fabulous friend Angela Stanton, to whom I owe so much. Without her, this book would be full of mistakes! Thank you for all the praise and encouragement you've given me over the years. Words can't describe how much I appreciate everything you've ever done for me.

My Nan- Gloria Jean Musckat- who will no doubt kill me for using her full name.

The Trio- Steevie Organ and Laurie Birch (myself being the third in this team). Together we will conquer all!

The HQ Crew: Michaela Roberts, Michael Samuel, Kevin Davies, Leanne Campbell, Arran (Asran) Rees, Rhydian Jones, Kylie Picton, Sean Jenkins, Lili, Sars.

And to the friends that I no longer have the pleasure of seeing on a day to day basis: Melissa Edwards, Lauren Cusack, Rebecca Gay, Michelle Jones and Mikayla Mannion.

Prologue

The Stone Table

The Stone Table was positioned in the centre of the vast and crumbling city of Meridion, surrounded by twelve identical rocks, each placed in an upright position. Legend had it, if the Stone Table tasted a human's blood, their soul would remain imprisoned in the circle for all eternity.

The chance to bask in the light of God was abolished.

Kiya could see the Stone Table from the rooftop of Meridion's most impressive building, the Sun Tower. The sky was a beautiful combination of orange and pinks, with a spattering of thin white clouds in the distance. According to the weather forecast, the gentle heat they'd been having was about to waver into a few weeks of dark, discouraging rainy days.

But regardless of what was to come, Kiya was content. She couldn't think of a more perfect location to meet Rycan; high up and away from all the gloomy faces on the streets, with a breath taking view of the setting sun. Already, she could just make out the twinkling of stars overhead, pushing through the dying daylight.

Her shoulders relaxed as a pair of muscular arms circled her waist suddenly, drawing her into the warmth of a firm, toned body. She'd heard his footsteps long before he had touched her, so her composure remained cool and collected.

Rycan pushed Kiya's long brown hair aside and lightly kissed her neck in greeting.

"I missed you," she told him, turning without coming free from his hold. His blue-grey eyes observed her lips with longing, but he resisted the temptation to kiss them-teasing her to the extreme.

"I couldn't get away from work early like I'd hoped. We've had another large order for red-tang samurai swords and Jason was late getting the axes shipped to one of our best customers, so I've been up to my ears in it. Things were so hectic, I even burnt myself on the furnace."

"Again? That's the second time this week." Kiya touched Rycan's wrist where the skin appeared red and blistered. Affectionately, she kissed the wound, feeling the rough surface soften beneath her. The wound had healed to its former self.

"A Healing Kiss? For me?" he smiled widely. "If your mother saw you performing that magical crap on me she'd have both our heads."

"She can *try*," Kiya grinned playfully.

"So, how was work?"

"The usual. Kevin made you a painting of a dinosaur. At least, I think it's a dinosaur-"

Rycan chuckled. As darkness swallowed the city, he embraced his beautiful partner and gave her the kiss she'd been waiting for- sending her spirit to Heaven and back. She tasted of strawberries. He tasted of a ham sandwich.

"Eaten already, huh?" she asked accusingly.

Rycan failed to bite back a grin. "I grabbed something on the way over."

"You'll spoil your dinner."

"I've only got a chicken curry microwave meal left anyway. Nothing special."

She nodded in understanding. Since Rycan had asked her the 'big question'- to which she had said 'yes' a thousand times over- the couple had slowly transferred his belongings into her house, for it was the bigger of the two. Kiya wanted things to be perfect. They'd been together for two and a half years now and had never shared a bed more than two- maybe three- nights a week, due to the fact they both had very busy lives that required easy access to belongings. But at last, they felt ready to commit to each other *entirely*. Rycan was moving in at the weekend, and Kiya couldn't wait to start making plans for the wedding.

"You should get some rest," she suggested, touching the dark circles under his eyes. He didn't deny he was tired.

"But I only just got here."

Kiya kissed him tenderly on the cheek.

"I'll see you tomorrow-"

"Tomorrow's too far away." He lifted a palm and cupped her face. "I love you."

Kiya raised her hand and placed it over the top of his. "I love you too sweetheart, but you really look as if you need some sleep."

"Fine. You win," he sighed. "I'll be on my way then." He turned to leave, but halted when he noticed Kiya's absence. "You coming?"

She shook her head- hair blowing in the gentle breeze. "I'm going to stay here for a few more minutes. It's just so peaceful. You don't get much of that when you work in a nursery school."

Rycan didn't like the idea of her staying behind, but knew she was capable of looking after herself. They had met at a martial arts class, and had trained side by side for a few months before he'd finally worked up the guts to ask her out on a date. As well as combat skills, they had been trained to use swords- something their sensei had taught them in a secret night class he offered to only a select few.

"You be careful."

"I will."

He left apprehensively, knowing he was being silly to feel so worried. Before he disappeared out of Kiya's view, she waved goodbye and blew him a kiss, which he pretended to catch in the palm of his hand.

I'm so lucky, he thought. *She's the most beautiful creature on the planet and she's all mine- to love- forever.*

A scream pierced the night. High and distinctly feminine.

For a fleeting moment, Rycan thought it was Kiya, but as he plunged into the darkness consuming the circle of stones, he found the source to be a most unlikely character.

"Are you okay, Miss?"

She was blonde- the type of brilliant white-blonde that was likely to darken with age and her shoulders looked narrow in a little pink cardigan.

Rycan glanced around. The vicinity was deserted.

"It's Lydia right?"

The girl refused to answer as he advanced. She was seated on the edge of the Stone Table- her pale knees exposed under her black skirt. Shadows masked her face and chest, but Rycan could tell, from viewing her so often on the television, that it was the Mayor's daughter.

Her silence was unsettling.

"I heard a scream-"

Suddenly, Lydia flopped sideways, her body no longer capable of sitting upright. A soft 'thump' sounded as her right shoulder hit the stone and her feet lifted off the ground, hovering above the grass.

Rycan rushed forward instantly, placing a hand on the girl's face and looping an arm around her back. It was only as he turned her head into the light that he noticed the blood trickling from her parted lips. Lydia's brilliant green eyes were wide and lucid. He trailed a hand over her body in swift, panicked movements, checking for damage, and pulled away with a sharp hiss as something pricked his palm.

A jagged point, wet with blood.

"Oh *shit*. Shit, shit, shit," he cursed under his breath. Reaching behind her again, Rycan found the hilt of a long sword protruding from the centre of the teenage girl's back. "Oh, no. Oh, *shit-*"

From his pocket, he pulled out a silver coloured mobile and punched in the number for both the ambulance and police service, shaking from head to toe as he clutched the girl to his chest. He didn't want to think-just act. The voice on the end of the line promised to be with him as soon as possible, and as the night closed in around him, he felt the warm blood of the Mayor's daughter splash against his trembling hands.

"Don't die, girl. It's not your time," he whispered in her ear croakily. As he sat in wait, he threw a glance up towards the Sun Tower, but could see no sign of his partner. She probably hadn't heard the scream, being up so high, and had left none the wiser to his distressing plight.

The police arrived before the ambulance did. Two officers with round bellies waddled over- both male- one had a notebook and pen. They gave Rycan a once over, still holding the dead girl in his arms, his eyes red and watery.

"What seems to be the problem here?"

"The problem!?" Rycan exclaimed, a little louder than he'd expected. "She's been stabbed! Someone must have... she's been... Don't just stand there! She needs help!"

The officer lacking the most hair lazily crossed his arms over his ample breasts. He looked at his colleague with a rigid expression. "Name?" he asked monotonously.

"It's the Mayor's daughter. Lydia I think-"

"No. *Your* name."

"Rycan White."

The ambulance siren sounded in the distance.

"What were you doing out here?"

Rycan's mind was fuzzy. He couldn't understand why he was being interrogated.

"Shouldn't you be telling me everything's going to be okay?" he queried hopelessly, his eyes wide and pleading. Never in his life had he walked into such a horrific situation. The only time he'd ever seen this much blood was when he'd walked into the stables at his parents farmhouse a few years previously and discovered his horse- Night Ride- giving birth to a stillborn foal.

"I'm afraid you're going to have to come along with us pretty boy-" the officer with the pen informed him, a hint of excitement in his hoarse, aged voice.

That was when the nightmare began and all prospects of a happy future with Kiya faded to black.

"Hello Kiya."

The sound of that oily drawl made her stop in her tracks as she was about to push the key into her front door. Reluctantly, she rotated on the spot to face her stalker.

"Make it quick, Tristian," she sighed, keeping her fingertips on the key behind her.

Tonight, Tristian was the embodiment of darkness, dressed in a black coat and jeans with his greasy, thin black hair tied back in a low ponytail. It reminded Kiya of a rats tail- long and disgusting. His skin was the colour of ice, white and corpse like.

Kiya had no sympathy for this man, who claimed to love her more than words could describe. He'd been in a few of her classes during high school, always lurking in the shadows to watch her from afar and had lost his sanity after the long hard school years were over, having been left him with less opportunities to be near her.

"I wrote you a poem," he grimaced, edging closer. His footsteps made Kiya anxious.

"I told you if you came here again I'd phone the police."

Tristian chortled. "They won't come. Why would they want to spend their time arresting a love sick poet? *Hmm?*"

Jeez, this guy was insane.

"I'm tired. Just… mail it to me okay?" She left Tristian hurriedly, slamming her front door for effect. For a while, she watched him through the peep-hole as he stroked the door with thin, bony fingers. He then bent over to push a piece of paper through her letter box, where it fell at her feet. Without giving it much thought, she snatched it up and tossed it into the bin beneath the telephone in her front passageway.

The bedroom beckoned to her and she prayed for no more disturbances in the remaining hours of the night.

Kiya awoke to a knock at the door late the following morning to find a police officer- female, slim and attractive- standing on her doorstep with a grim expression. Solemnly, she informed her that Rycan had been taken into custody.

"I'm sorry," she apologised, with twinkling, sympathetic eyes. "But since the reports on the news this morning, people have burnt down your partner's business."

"Excuse me?" Kiya cried in surprise. She neglected pinching her white dressing gown together beneath her breasts, allowing her red and black heart-patterned pyjamas to fall on display.

Suddenly, a man with a camera crept out from behind the red brick wall that separated her small front garden from the street, and a light flashed, catching Kiya's tired face as she stood in complete disarray before the police officer.

"Get out of here!" the officer shouted, but the man refused to listen. She turned her head back to Kiya. "You're needed at the station. I'll wait in the car for you."

"Is he okay?" Kiya blurted out, grabbing the woman's arm before she could move away.

Her silence was enough to frighten her into realisation.

"Just hurry."

Kiya burst into tears when she was told that Rycan had been accused of murder. At the station, men stared at her grief stricken face as if she were a circus act, muttering amongst themselves instead of offering to make a distressed woman a hot drink. Kiya had to bite back the urge to scream in their faces. *Assholes.*

The female officer, who had first spoken with Kiya at her house, had explained that the Mayor wanted a detective from *outside* the city to deal with the case of his daughter's death and that she no longer had any influence over the matter.

"I spoke with Rycan in his cell late last night," she had said in the car on the drive over. "I believe he's innocent."

Kiya had been unable to thank her at that point.

"I'm praying for you both," the officer whispered, before directing her into a small room with a table and two chairs.

Kiya sat alone for about ten minutes, staring up at the camera with a tear streaked face and wishing she had Rycan to hold her hand. She couldn't believe this was happening. It was so wrong- so unfair!

When the detective arrived, she found her voice at last.

"He was with me! He can't have done it! We were on the roof top of the Sun Tower."

"Can anyone verify this?" The detective was hunched forward in his chair, hands pressed together as if in prayer. His dark brown eyes bit into Kiya like a wolf locked onto prey. She could tell that he was already under the impression that Rycan was guilty and that no matter what she said, *nothing* would change the detective's opinion.

"No-"

"Does Rycan own a sword?"

"He makes them for a living. Of course he fucking does!"

The detective raised a bushy brown eyebrow at the use of her foul language and flitted his gaze over the tape recorder to check it was still rolling.

"Are you aware that we found your partner's sword in the victim's back? His name engraved clearly in the steel?"

Her mouth opened and closed like a fish out of water.

"His fingerprints are all over it. He was found holding the girl at the scene of the crime. No one, other than yourself, can place him elsewhere."

"Isn't my word enough?"

"Do you love him?"

Kiya frowned. "What kind of a question is that?"

"Answer me."

Her eyes sparked with fury. "Yes."

"Then I know, from experience, that a person will say anything if it means saving their lover's life."

Kiya stood up suddenly, scraping her chair loudly across the polished floor. A guard from outside the room entered instantly, waiting for instruction from the old man who was sat at the table, staring at Kiya in amusement.

"I believe this interview is over. Please escort this woman off the premises."

Kiya shrugged the guys plump fingers off her shoulder as he tapped her sensitive flesh. He didn't try to manhandle her out because she wasn't the one being accused of murdering an innocent. Only the *bad* ones received mistreatment at the station.

"What's going to happen to him?"

The detective had turned his back on her now, scraping a hand through his bristly brown-grey hair. He then sparked up a cigarette and blew smoke upwards towards the ceiling.

"You know the rules."

"No-" Kiya yelled. "This is wrong! He's innocent!"

"Those who use a blade unjustly die upon one," the detective recited morosely. He paused. "Hey- I don't suppose Mr White was likely to have affairs, was he? Perhaps he was seeing young Lydia behind your back and now that you've agreed to marry him, he felt the need to silence her?"

Kiya ran over and slapped the detective across the face. *Hard*. His cigarette fell from between his fingers. The guard was between them before she could hurt him further.

"Thank you for your time." The detective smiled as she left, stomping out the cigarette with his boot.

Rycan was bound and gagged as two officers placed him on the Stone Table, dressed in a thick black shirt that came up tight around his neck and a pair of baggy black trousers that were far too loose around his thighs. His wrists hurt as the handcuffs grated against his raw flesh and his eyes stung from lack of sleep.

He didn't struggle. The faces surrounding him came for a show, but he refused to give them one.

How did his life become so plagued with injustice?

He wasn't a killer.

He was a good person- a hard working, law abiding citizen. Never disloyal. Never cruel. Just a genuine nice guy. And now, all the people who had once called him 'friend' were leering at him with accusing eyes behind camera-men and news reporters.

The world made him sick.

A few hours before the execution, the detective on Rycan's case had allowed him to spend a few hours with Kiya in his cell. She had been quiet at first- sick with fear for him and trying her hardest not to spend their last moments together crying hysterically.

Lovingly, he'd laced his fingers through hers, touching the engagement ring on her finger.

"We would have been so happy together," he'd said, keeping his eyes on the diamond as it sparkled in the light. "I bet you would have looked breath taking in your wedding dress."

At this, Kiya sobbed, clutching at his collar and pulling at clothes.

"Why did this have to happen!?" she shouted. "Why!?"

Rycan put a hand on either side of her arms and held her back. He hadn't known what to say to her. What *could* he say?

"I'm not afraid to die," was all he could manage, as if it would ease her pain.

"But you shouldn't *have* to die! Not yet! It's that detective and that *bastard* Mayor. They just want more blood shed-"

"His daughter died. Can you blame him?"

"So put some flowers on her grave and take a long vacation. Don't execute someone for it, for fuck sake-"

Rycan bowed his head. He didn't want to talk about it. Bad things happened to good people right? That's how the saying went. It was just his time.

"Please Kiya. Promise me you won't come to the execution."

She was silent, watching his eyes as if her own life depended on it. Her heart was pounding so hard and fast, she thought it would explode.

"I don't want you to see me go. It'll haunt you forever. You don't deserve to be tormented by it. Just stay home and go to sleep. Take a tablet if you have to. Just close your eyes and forget about everything."

Kiya shook her head. "I can't forget. I won't."

"Please Kiya-"

"I need to find him."

"Who?"

"The person who did this."

Rycan sighed. "Whoever it is, they're insane. Don't go looking for them, for God's sake. I want you to keep living, for the both of us."

On the hard, uncomfortable bed where they were sat together, Kiya placed her head on Rycan's lap. He could feel her tears soaking through the material of his trousers.

"Don't dwell on this. I love you too much to see you in so much pain."

She sniffed and cried even harder. He continued to talk to her, over the sound of her despair. One hand brushed her cheek, the other lay against her small waist.

"I'm sure we'll meet again, in the afterlife."

"The afterlife is too far away," she said, barely above a whisper.

She raised her head and sat up once more, kissing him passionately and under the thin, itchy sheets of the cell's bed, they made love one last time.

The execution came upon Rycan quicker than he'd expected and to his relief, Kiya was absent from the scrambling, nudge-happy crowd. He also noticed that the cowardly Mayor was missing, probably at home flicking through photo albums whilst getting drunk on a bottle of wine.

Police bellowed threats to the people of Meridion, but they paid the officers no heed. Things were getting out a hand, and Rycan overheard someone suggesting they hurry things up, as if he were a cockroach, not a human being.

When the executioner stood forth, clothed in a black mask and bearing a long silver sword encrusted with diamonds, the noise died instantaneously.

Rycan looked away, thinking only of Kiya. His beautiful, *perfect* Kiya.

She'll find someone new. Someone to care for her. And she'll be happy to the end of her days, he told himself comfortingly.

"May God have mercy on your soul," the executioner proclaimed, for everyone to hear. "That's if you ever manage to worm your way out of this place."

Of course, he thought miserably. *The legend. How could I have forgotten?*

But before he could address the matter further in the corners of his mind, the sword of the executioner separated his head from his neck.

Eternal darkness followed.

The brief trip to the nearest store was just another mind numbing activity for Kiya to try and ignore the fact that close by, her boyfriend was being beheaded.

She could feel the eyes of the young female shop attendant following her as she approached the brightly lit fridges and selected a pint of milk.

"On the house love," the lady had said with a weak grin as she plonked the carton down on the marble countertop. Her words shook Kiya from her trance.

"Oh...thanks," she mumbled, accepting the plastic bag that was being offered her way.

The walk home was a daunting task. She didn't much like the idea of crossing paths with people who might want to talk to her. All she wanted was to make a hot drink, curl up in bed and die- although she was aware the latter would fail to happen.

She felt like a lost soul. As if her purpose had been stolen from her. The idea of going back to work to teach little kids their ABC's was the last thing she wanted! How could she show her face in front of a class of impressionable young students ever again? It made her feel sick.

"Not sad are you?"

Her heart fluttered in her chest and she raised a hand in surprise as Tristian emerged from the shadows. He was wearing the same clothes as the last time she'd encountered him, but had his hair down for a change.

Kiya was too shattered to care about his presence as he joined her, although it agitated her that he thought himself worthy of her company. Especially right then.

"Lovers come and go," he consoled, to no affect. "Perhaps it just wasn't meant to be."

Finally, she mustered the strength to speak.

"Just go."

"But Kiya, my sweet, what kind of a vile creature would I be to leave a weeping lady walk the streets alone?"

"I don't need your help, *Tristian.*"

"My my, is that the thanks I get for caring about you?"

Kiya breathed a sigh of relief as her house came into view. All the curtains were closed and the lights off except for the front passageway. The thought of spending the rest of her life alone in that building made her shiver in misery.

"I don't need this right now," she told him gruffly.

"Of course you don't, my rose," he replied in understanding. "Just know that I'm only a whisper away if you need to mourn in someone's arms." He backed away at last, watching the woman he loved grit her teeth at him.

As she'd grown accustomed to doing, the door slammed in his face.

I really need to take out a restraining order on that guy, she thought. *He's insane!*

She paused beside her telephone and rubbish bin.

He's insane.

Rycan had said the person who killed the Mayor's daughter was probably insane. But just how insane about Kiya *was* Tristian? Enough to frame her lover for murder?

She acknowledged the flashing red number 'two' on her answering machine and disregarded listening to the voice mail completely- one each from her divorced parents she assumed. She then bent down to snatch up the crumpled piece of paper in the bottom of her bin, dropping the milk carelessly onto the carpet.

He was out the night Rycan was arrested. He caught up with me on my way home. Oh God-

Her eyes scanned his spidery scrawl.

It was I who kidnapped Lydia,
To lay her on a stone bed,
And by driving Rycan's sword into her heart,
I left her alone for dead.
My sweet delectable Kiya of Meridion,
You had left me NO choice,
I had to take such desperate measures
To silence Rycan's voice.

My love for you is eternal.
Always yours,
Tristian Raine

"No-" Kiya gasped. "No, no no-"

The poem that she held in her trembling hands had been just the evidence she'd needed to save Rycan from a horrible death. If she had just read the damn thing when Tristian had posted it through her door, she could have taken it to the police station and stopped the nightmare from happening.

Kiya placed a hand on the wall to support herself. She felt weak with sorrow and disappointment.

She re-read the poem through big fat tears, consumed by disbelief, then felt an unquenchable anger boiling beneath her breast.

"I'll fucking kill him," she vowed. "I'll see to it that he burns in Hell for this!"

And with that, she obtained her samurai sword from beneath her bed, and left for the man-hunt.

Chapter 1

The Lily

Kiya stood among the wreckage and felt a wave of emotion work its way up through her quivering body, until it found its release at her eyes. Finally, tears of sorrow poured down her pale cheeks.

She imagined there were no more tears left to summon as she had walked the short distance to Rycan's 'Weapons of War' shop, now lying in ruin, but the sight of its blackened walls, demolished roof and mutilated merchandise had ripped her heart to pieces, knowing that the cruel society had taken practically *everything* he had.

Miserably, she traced the front of her right boot through the ashes, making circular motions and marvelling at the way some of the embers still smouldered and flickered, before she stomped them out with her heel. Occasionally, there was the sound of steel clanking against steel as her foot disturbed some of the unfinished swords that the people of Meridion had left behind. There was nothing worth salvaging here. Nothing the fire had left untouched.

All had been lost.

Kiya fell to her knees, dirtying the black leather of her skin tight trousers, and wept into her hands, smearing mascara all around her face. At first, she was concerned that a passer-by might see her in such a state and felt a pang of embarrassment as noisy sobs escaped her mouth, but then another thought bit at her and she decided she didn't give a shit what people thought. If she wanted to lie in the ashes of her deceased fiancés family business, then by God, she would.

As if her deep despair affected the weather somehow, rain began to pour from the heavens like arrows slicing through the air in jagged wet lines. There came a harsh wind that lifted the ashes off the ground, blowing and buffeting them about and sending many of them floating into the tangled mess of long brown hair that Kiya had neglected to comb.

"Why did this have to happen?" she choked, knowing only too well that silence would ensue. "What kind of a God lets my fiancé take the blame for a murder committed by one Hell-bound rat, *huh*?" Her voice was growing more and more hysterical as she lifted her head to the skies. "What kind of a God has my fiancé *slaughtered* just *two* weeks after he proposed to me?" On shaking legs, Kiya rose. "And what kind of a *God* has my loving, pure-hearted fiancé mercilessly *executed* in front of every citizen in this shit-hole of a city, twenty seven hours before I discover I'm pregnant with his child?!"

Thunder crashed above her angrily, shaking the sodden earth and scaring an ebony coloured cat that had been prowling through the area.

Kiya was sure she had infuriated the Heavenly Father with her words, but stood her ground none the less, watching the lightning cut through the night and listening to the sound of the skies belly as it protested with more grumbling noises.

"I loved him," she cried, feeling more alone now than she ever had before. "I would have given my heart and soul to that man and you took him from me, and for what purpose?"

As the sky blackened completely to night, the lamps in the city flickered into life, illuminating shop windows and an empty road that ran down the centre of the shopping district, where Kiya had placed herself on this particular eve. Most of the stores sold clothes and shoes, but there were a few other businesses such as a little book shop, where both old and new novels could be purchased; a bicycle and motorcycle business, which was popular because most citizens had found the use of cars a less intriguing way to travel these days; three different grocery stores, all selling similar stuff, but each battling to keep the lowest prices without going bankrupt; a small stationary store, where mostly students went to buy supplies before the summer holidays ended and a new term began; a rather expensive hair dressers that offered just about every style you could think of, and finally, one of the more sanitary 'tattoo' parlours that was to be found situated in Meridion.

Rycan's store had been on the end of the street, next to the tattoo parlour. The people who had set fire to it hadn't been too concerned about setting the parlour alight too, but luckily for its owner, no damage had come to it. Now, the rain lashed against the roofs of the shops and splashed down drains set into the floor, soaking all the rats to their core as they ran about, scurrying along the gutters and weaving in and out of dark alley ways.

Kiya realised that future shoppers would look at that empty gap on the end of the well established row of stores, on a daily basis, and hoped they'd feel unimaginable guilt every time for what they'd done to an innocent man. *Her* innocent man.

In her hand was the crumpled piece of paper with Tristian's confession written on. She knew that by taking it to the authorities, they would have the evidence they needed to take Tristian to the 'Stone Table' where he would suffer the same fate Rycan had, only this time, it would taste the blood of a *real* murderer.

But Kiya wanted her revenge to be on *her* terms. She believed it would be less satisfying to see the executioner slicing that bastards head off; hidden under a black mask and sharing none of the overpowering emotions that she had chewing away inside of her. She craved an audience with the fiend who'd marred the name of her soul mate. She wanted to take her time, tying his disgusting little body to a chair, then merrily cut away at his putrid, oily flesh; generally torturing him for as long as his body could stay conscious. Oh how the thought made her beam inside.

Kiya had been a relatively calm and kind person all her life, but since Rycan was stolen from her, all that had changed *drastically*. She'd never before felt such an achingly *overwhelming* explosion of bloodlust coursing through her veins and muscles like she did now.

The Mayor's daughter. Her mind uttered the words in the shadows of her scheming thoughts, allowing ideas of torture to dissipate for a moment.

The Mayor's daughter had been a victim in all this. She had been an 'only' child, the news had previously mentioned, leaving her father with no one to watch grow and prosper in a society he tried his hardest to keep pleasant. Surely he deserved to know who the real killer of his daughter was? Surely the knowledge would encourage him to crack down on the increasing percentage of rebellious and more 'relaxed' police officers, who were trying to play by their own rules now?

Kiya lifted her dripping fingertips to her forehead and dragged the soggy strands of hair back from her eyes. Her body was protesting against the cold and the darkness was making it increasingly dangerous to be hanging around the streets.

I won't let myself be prey to the scum that lurks in this city, she thought determinedly. *I'll be the one who* they *fear, because if anybody tries fucking with me, there'll be hell to pay.*

With the tip of her index finger, she reached out and stroked the floor before her. The second she did so, she felt the natural vibrations run up her hand and arm; vibrations that most people had lost the ability to identify and control. Mother Nature was a mysterious thing and had probably suffered a great blow of distress when she discovered simple-minded humans could manipulate the elements she'd spent so many years nurturing and controlling. Kiya's finger had become warm to the touch and as she closed her eyes and pictured the earth and all its beauty, a single lily sprung from the ground; its white petals becoming instantly battered by large raindrops.

She cracked a tight lipped smile at her handiwork just as an unexpected bright white light flashed painfully in her eyes.

"Who goes there?" somebody yelled from the street.

Torchlight travelled over the length of her slim body, coming to rest on her beautiful, pale face. On a strap over her shoulder hung her samurai sword, glinting threateningly in the blinding glow that the stranger had cast upon her, but Kiya felt no need to hide it. Although the possession of swords and knives was frowned upon in Meridion, the strict laws had become lenient towards banning them completely. Kiya sickeningly thought perhaps the officers liked the idea of having 'potentials' to arrest, humiliate on public television and then execute. They had to get their jollies somehow.

"What's your business here, Miss?" asked the torch bearer, whose features remained hidden under a hooded green trench coat.

"What *business* is it of yours?" she replied, trying to keep her cool. The full extent of her wrath was on the brink, but she didn't feel it was necessary to unleash it on innocents who were probably just doing their jobs.

The man raised his hand. "I was merely asking. No need to be tetchy."

Kiya had no reason to further interact with the man that stood before her, but he seemed to be content in disturbing her even further. The torchlight remained on her face, making it difficult to see the man in his entirety.

"You're not one of them damned vampires are you, feasting on rats and what not?"

Kiya sighed. "No, but even if I was, do you think I'd tell *you*?"

"Well if you ain't a vamp, what's a lovely specimen like you doing out here? It's raining and you look pretty damn lonely. Don't you have some place to go? A family, or a boyfriend to go home to perhaps?"

"No," she hissed, standing up from her crouched position to face the man and hoping her forced answer would be sufficient enough to scare him away.

"Well I'll be damned," the man said in a sympathetic voice, which suddenly dripped away into something that suggested evil intent. "It's my lucky day."

Kiya found it hard to suppress the shock she felt as the trench coat-wearing stranger rushed at her, grabbing her by the shoulders and throwing her to the ground, crushing the lily she had moments ago summoned. She felt the rage inside her swell in her chest as she thought of how strenuous it had been, just to create the perfect flower in memory of her lost love.

The man had climbed on her chest after she'd hit the earth, pressing the length of her body into the ash strewn floor and pinning her arms down by her sides.

She couldn't believe the misfortune she had been plagued with as the man leaned closer and the torch rolled- neglected- against her right hip. Still the shadows masked his face, but she could just about make out the whites of his eyes with the dark pupils in their centre. They ripped into her; gawking at her beauty, observing the delicate lines of her nose and mouth and the amazing length of her long dark eyelashes that surrounded intense blue eyes.

"What a *very* lucky find," the man drooled, showing no sign of agitation as Kiya writhed and wriggled beneath him. He bent low and ran his tongue over her left cheek, making her squirm in disgust.

"Get the fuck off of me!" she yelled, but the weight of the man seemed to be increasing as his knees and thighs crushed her ribs. She cursed at the fact her samurai sword was pressed into her right shoulder- out of reach.

"I love it when they scream and beg." Excitement rose in the man's voice.

Kiya almost vomited as he placed his mouth against her lips, parting them with his tongue as she tried to prevent further access. When he eventually pulled away, she let out a gasp and spat at his face, hitting him directly on the chin. The man seemed unabashed by this action.

"It's such a shame you haven't cried," he muttered in disappointment. "I like it when they cry. *Hmmm...* perhaps I can do something about that..."

The moment he released her left hand, with a mind to unzip her leather trousers, Kiya pulled the samurai sword from its case as smoothly as possible and brought it up to the man's throat.

"I told you to get the fuck off of me," she said coolly, pressing the cold steel harder against his adams-apple, which rose as the man swallowed in fear. He freed her other hand and lifted his weight instantaneously.

"Bet you didn't expect *that* to happen, did you?"

The man was silent as Kiya shifted her position from lying down flat on her back to sitting up straight. By gently pushing the blade into the man's neck, she led him to his feet.

"Why so silent?" she queried, dropping the blade and circling the man. If he moved an inch, she'd slice him in half. "Don't you wanna talk dirty to me, *hmm*? Don't you wanna reach out and take all my clothes off? Play more of your sick fucking games perhaps? Dominate me *completely*?"

The man was making whimpering noises now. He could sense the fiery creature before him wasn't likely to let him go unpunished.

"What's your name?" Kiya demanded, jabbing the tip of her blade into his side, but not enough to penetrate the skin. It made the man jump in anticipation of the pain.

"C...Carl," he stuttered.

"Well Carl...," Kiya allowed her tone of voice to soften. "Guess what?"

She whirled around and faced him.

"I like it when they cry *too*,"

With her lines delivered, Kiya sliced Carl's right arm completely off and felt the red, hot blood splatter against her face, only to be washed away again by the rain. His screams pierced the night as he rolled around on the floor at her feet, crying tears of agony. The torch was conveniently illuminating the severed limb, that was amusingly twitching at the fingertips.

Kiya swung her sword around again and rested it against Carl's left shoulder.

"That'll teach you to keep your fucking hands to yourself," she said fiercely. "And if I find out you went to the police and told them about tonight, I swear to God, I'll hunt you down and cut the other one off too. Got that?"

Carl nodded in response and began dragging his body over to his detached body part, grasping it in his bloodied hand. He was making noises like nothing Kiya had ever heard before and she revelled in his pain as he caressed the useless limb in his remaining arm.

There was no use in staying there any longer. Kiya decided to make a hasty exit, just in case Carl's screams aroused other passers-by. It would not be wise to get caught and killed so early in the game.

Feeling the fire in the pit of her stomach douse out, she placed her sword back in its case and disappeared into the night, hearing the word '*Bitch!*' being carried on the wind, from where Carl sat in a pool of his own blood.

Chapter 2

The Factory

Eventually, the thunder and lightning ceased and a break in the clouds revealed twinkling stars scattered across the heavens. The rain however, continued to lash down, though Kiya was far too pissed off with the people of Meridion to give her cold and wet body too much thought.

The shopping district was far behind her now as she hastily moved down an empty road. She thought about heading straight home, but instead took a detour, for reasons that were unknown even to her.

She wanted to be home, warm in bed with a mug of tea steaming away on her bedside table and a trashy novel in hand, but something told her all those happy household experiences weren't likely to happen anymore. She'd just chopped a man's arm off for fuck sake! No doubt somebody would find out and that *someone* would probably come looking for her.

Shit, she thought. *What have I done?*

There was nothing for it. Kiya would have to move elsewhere if she wished to remain undiscovered and undisturbed. Her face had humiliatingly been plastered all over network television during Rycan's execution, which meant Carl would eventually realise who she was and where he could find her. Kiya couldn't let that happen.

On 'Dyer Street' there was an old factory, closed down years before she was even born. It was a hotspot for travellers because the area was pretty much derelict and nobody in Meridion could be bothered to chase them off the land once the travellers had set up camp. At this time of year, when winter was setting in and the winds were picking up, there weren't many 'happy campers' to be found, so access to the factory wouldn't be too complicated for her. Kiya decided this was her best chance at having a roof over her head for a few days. She'd have to gather a few belongings at home, leaving behind all her luxuries for basic survival items, and break her way into the building.

In all her frenzied arrangements to insure a future where her heart was *still* actually pumping and her soul still present beneath her flesh, Kiya still hadn't forgotten the reason why she'd gone out that night.

Tristian.

That little rat bastard was still out there, a free man. He made her blood simmer and her head pound painfully. No words could describe just how angry and disgusted she was by that revolting maggot. If he tried worming his way into her life again, he wouldn't even get the chance to open his mouth before she'd ripped his lips off his ugly face.

Turning back, Kiya made her way to her dwelling, sticking to the shadows to avoid confrontation. There weren't many people out at this hour, though it was still early evening, because the streets weren't as safe as they used to be. The only presence known to Kiya at that point in time were a few homeless people in doorways, or on benches, and an excruciating amount of cats stalking the streets, after a witch doctor had arrived in town and told the people of Meridion that his kittens had the power to protect families from danger. *Yeah right!* Kiya couldn't believe how *stupid* people could be. But then again, who wouldn't want to try *every* possible way to protect their loved ones? After the Slayers and Were-Hunters diminished in numbers, more demons rose out of the bowls of hell, tormenting the people of earth. There was once a plea to put a large wall around Meridion to protect its people within, and prevent the evil from terrorising the city, and the Mayor had been very reluctant to approve it. Taxes rose for the wall's purpose, but even with it there, it felt as if it were everyman for themselves. That's why there had been such a popular demand for weapons such as swords, axes and wooden or silver stakes. People were afraid, but having something sharp and pointy in their hands helped to decrease the fear in their hearts, even if they were unskilled in using them.

Werewolves were less of a threat than vampires because they tended to stay away from big cities. If a werewolf sought out human blood on a full moon, it usually found its way into the mountains, under the cover of trees and bushes, where it could pick people off in the quiet little villages that had developed up there. And if they couldn't have human flesh to feast on, the deer and other wildlife in the forests were sufficient for survival on the eve of their transformation from human to rabid dog.

The problem with *vampires* was, they looked just like human-beings twenty four seven, as long as they didn't open their mouths to reveal the sharp fangs within. They dressed like humans and moved like humans. The only 'un-human' quality, other than the fangs, was the rancid smell of blood on their breath. *Anybody* could mistake a vampire for a man or woman coming home from a late shift at work and feel the kiss of death on their neck as they past on the street, falling dead to the ground, or if they're lucky, waking up again in twenty four hours as one of 'them.' How could anyone tolerate being un-dead for eternity though? If you woke up to discover this was your fate, it made sense just to stake yourself and be done with it, surely?

Kiya thought about the beasts that roamed around at night and shuddered just as she turned onto Willow Street, where her home lay in wait for her arrival. As she approached it, she got the sense that something was wrong. She didn't remember leaving her bedroom light on, or the passage light for that matter. And why was the curtains pulled open in one of the rooms?

Fear gripped her throat as she picked up speed, sprinting up the steps leading to her doorway. It was slightly ajar with the key still placed in the lock. *How was this so*? With her foot, Kiya kicked over the plant pot that her spare key was usually hidden under for Rycan to use when he came over in the nights, and discovered it was missing. It must be the key in the door...

With her heart thumping loudly beneath her ribs, Kiya drew her samurai sword from its case and nudged the door open.

Everything in her passage-way seemed in order. The phone was still blinking with her parent's messages and there was nothing new in her waste-paper bin.

The darkness downstairs suggested the intruder had gone straight for the second floor, but Kiya checked the rooms below just to be sure. The backdoor was still locked, much to her relief and the kitchen and living room seemed untouched. So far so good.

Cautiously, she made her way up the stairs; each step drawing her closer and closer to someone who would no doubt taste her blade.

But when she reached her bedroom, it appeared to be empty of criminals or beasts. The bed was still made, just as it had been that morning; her jewellery was still in its decorative box on her dressing table; the wide screen television was still on the cupboard, with the DVD player and VCR present on two of the shelves and her laptop was still resting on her desk.

"What the hell is going on?" Kiya whispered, lifting up her bed sheets and dropping onto the floor to see if there was someone hidden underneath the bed. It was empty, besides the millions of dust mites that probably bred under there.

Perhaps, Kiya thought, *the burglar lost his nerve and left empty handed? Or, perhaps they didn't come with the intention of stealing?* Kiya shook the thought from her head and got to work. She grabbed a large bag from the next room, which was full of her junk and had potentially been a 'nursery' if she was ever to become a mother. The thought suddenly made Kiya freeze and clutch her stomach. She *was* with-child, but what kind of a life would they be able to lead now that she was running off with the intention of killing people along the way? *Maybe now isn't the time to think about it,* she decided, picking the bag up again and rushing back into her bedroom. *People tend to love the thing that's growing inside of them* far *too soon and then something terrible happens. You just end up being devastated over a life that wasn't even lived.*

Kiya's head reeled with lists of items she required, but once she'd thought of something new, the old list seemed to vanish completely. It became a matter of what she laid her hands on first. There was her second pair of black leather trousers as well as a blood red pair of the same design. She'd acquired them both on her birthday when Rycan had taken her shopping. When she couldn't decide which pair to buy, he had generously bought them both, "But this means you won't get anything for Christmas," he'd joked.

Next, Kiya reached into her underwear drawer, only to move back in alarm.

It was empty. All her undergarments were missing, except for a pair of Rycan's clean grey boxer shorts that must have gotten mixed up in her washing pile.

"This has Tristian written all over it," Kiya growled, slamming her cupboard drawer shut and checking the next one. The socks were still present, and luckily for her, a black bra had found its way into the back, which she uncovered with relief in her heart.

"I can't believe that *shit* would do something like this!" The thought of Tristian touching her things made her cringe. He was probably stroking her silk panties, whilst she fretted over finding outfits to wear, thinking quite happily that she'd have to go around wearing nothing under her trousers.

After selecting a couple of t-shirts, tank-tops, crop-tops, tight-fitting jeans, a leather *and* a denim jacket, her biker boots, a battered pair of white trainers, make-up and a few hair accessories to keep the strands out of her eyes if they became too rebellious; a flannel and soap from the bathroom, her toothbrush and toothpaste, a small pink comb and her stash of money in the pot labelled 'coffee,' Kiya *finally* checked her washing machine and discovered that Tristian had missed the underwear in there without realising it. Finding her sopping wet thongs was a blessing, but unfortunately, there was no time to dry them.

"I'm bound to have forgotten something," she said to herself, in the quiet gloominess of her living room. She thought perhaps she should call her parents, but decided against it. They could wait. She'd call them from a pay-phone in the near future, if she remembered.

All that was left to do was switch off all the lights and lock up.

It broke her heart, turning the key in her door for what felt like the last time. She knew she could come back if she needed to, but couldn't help feeling a wave of sadness splashing against her heated face.

How did things get this bad?

She uttered a silent prayer as she descended the steps to her sleeping house- a request for forgiveness after her impure thoughts regarding her revenge on Tristian, and also for slicing Carl's arm off.

I know I'm probably not your favourite person right now. I can't ask you to protect and watch over me because you know only too well that my intentions are evil. All I ask is that you understand the reason why *these things have happened and* will *happen in the future. I used to be a law-abiding citizen. I'm sorry I can't be that same, simple person. But as they say here on earth: 'life's a bitch' and nobody knows that better than you, God. So forgive me for my actions. Amen.*

Kiya met the surrounding night with feelings of being uplifted and invincible. Her feet pounded the sidewalk rhythmically and all the while she walked, her heart beat strong in time with her footfalls. The power she felt, with her sword on her back, made her crack a rare smile.

I'm gonna make Tristian wish he was never born, she thought, leaving Willow Street behind.

The factory was dank and miserable looking from the outside. It's red brick walls looked dull in the moonlight and its solid, metal, rusty double-doors were far from welcoming. All the windows were set high up around the building, a few inches below the flat metal roof, preventing access to anyone wishing to climb through one and they were all either dusty from neglect, or completely smashed through.

Kiya touched the hefty looking padlock and chain that held the doors together with the tip of her samurai sword. Then, standing a little to the left, at a rather jaunty angle, she lifted the blade above her head and brought it down hard, knocking the padlock clean off the handles it had been fastened to with a loud 'clank.'

Success!

Before entering her new domain, she glanced a suspicious eye around the deserted area. She felt pretty confident that she hadn't been followed. All that was left to do now was to set up camp. With her bag slung heavily over one shoulder, she dropped it onto the cold stone floor inside, which sent dust flying up into the air around her. The sound of the bag hitting the floor echoed all around.

The moonlight only illuminated a small portion of the room through one row of dusty, broken window panes and it was impossible to identify what had been left within the confines of the old building until morning came.

Kiya observed her new environment. One of the window panes cast a slither of light over what appeared to be a small sofa. It was burgundy in colour and capable of providing her with a bed for the night.

"Perfect," she said, not too sure whether she was being sarcastic or genuinely pleased to see a soft place to lie.

Closing the extremely heavy metal doors behind her seemed to cut out a large amount of light and Kiya found herself stumbling over to the sofa with short, baby steps. She yawned loudly, feeling the pull of sleep on her eyelids, and finally allowed her exhaustion to take control. The second she hit those burgundy coloured cushions, she was thrown into a world of nightmares that had her tossing and turning fitfully. At about two-thirty in the morning, the nightmares eased off and at last she slumbered soundly.

Chapter 3

Slayers

The warm kiss of morning brushed Kiya's cheek as she lay peacefully on the sofa, curled up tight in a ball, with one hand lolling over the edge and brushing the hilt of her sword that was resting on the floor. It was going to be an unusually bright day by the feel of those warm rays against her skin, and Kiya relished in the heat with her eyes closed, until something *extremely* cold splashed her in the face.

She woke instantly, snatching up her sword and extending it towards a group of unfamiliar faces she had *not* expected to encounter.

"I told you she *can't* be a vampire because she's lying in sunlight you fucking idiot! Now you've wasted half a bottle of holy water!"

Kiya's breathing was heavy. Her face was dripping wet.

Before her stood three men, and behind *them* was a young woman, all of whom were holding some form of weapon.

The man who spoke had the broadest shoulders Kiya had ever seen, with shoulder length, dark brown hair and dark brown eyes to match. His face looked rough with stubble, which suggested he was too busy to shave and possibly even wash, but his handsome features were far more distracting than the thought of whether or not this muscular warrior-type individual actually showered. He was dressed in tight black jeans and a white, sleeveless top that was marked with what looked like dirt and blood. Kiya guessed he must have been about six foot six- six foot seven- though his large black biker boots probably exaggerated his height a little. Over one shoulder, the man had rested a mighty big shotgun that looked shiny from regular polishing.

"I think you've got some explaining to do," the man spoke in a thick southern accent that gave Kiya chills. He didn't seem to be of Meridion. The next character in the group *definitely* wasn't either. He was a Chinese man, clutching an open bottle of clear liquid in his left hand- liquid that Kiya assumed was now glistening wet on her face- and was about six foot three in height. The belt he was wearing had shiny silver throwing-stars attached to it, a few of which looked blood stained. His black hair was thick and wavy and his eyes were a piercing blue that had Kiya enraptured as her own eyes travelled over him. In his right hand, he held a samurai sword, much like her own, only the tang of *his* blade was deep blue in colour.

The Chinese man *also* had some disconcerting blood stains spattered over his skin, though his outfit was made up of black items which hid most of the filth. He wore a similar pair of tight black jeans to the man who had spoken previously and a black silk shirt that was unbuttoned at the top to reveal part of his chest. A dark bead-necklace clung to his neck.

Kiya turned to examine the next man, who was standing a few steps behind the other two. He was far from muscular, in fact, he looked incredibly out of place with his pale white skin, limp brown hair, tall lanky features and dull grey eyes. In his hands was a wooden crucifix and pointy wooden stake, resting inside the waist of his denim jeans was a small handgun- easily accessible if things got heated.

"So little girl, you gonna talk to me, or am I gonna have to beat an explanation out of you?" the shotgun wielding warrior said.

Kiya's eyes darted from one man to the next, waiting for someone to make the first move, until the young woman, who had distanced herself from the group, spoke.

"Leave her alone, Kieran. I don't think she's a threat."

Kiya was taken aback by the remark.

"Come over here *little girl* and perhaps I can change your mind," she snarled.

The young woman remained unperturbed, making her way over to the men. She dropped Kiya's bag of belongings in front of them, kicking up the dust. Kiya was infuriated by the girl's actions. How dare she open it! All her half-dry undergarments were on display, having been placed at the top of the pile, as well as her make-up bag and clothes.

"She's clean. There's nothing here worth worrying about."

"Hey! Keep your fucking hands out of my stuff," Kiya cried, snatching it up by the handles and tossing it onto the sofa behind her. Again, she resumed her fighting position, with the tip of her samurai sword aimed at Kieran's face, because he appeared to literally be the biggest threat in her current situation.

"You're a fine one to talk," Kieran said. "How dare you park that toned little ass of yours on *my* sofa!"

The Chinese man had become bored with Kiya's display of uncertainty- should she stay and fight her ground or should she run and be deemed a coward? Instead of waiting for her to make a move, he lowered his sword and disappeared into the shadows, deeper into the old factory, where Kiya could hear him clinking away, playing with something metal. Perhaps cleaning his throwing stars?

Now Kiya had the opportunity to closely examine the other female on the premises.

She was a pretty specimen, who looked as if she had entered into adulthood with her head held high and had an attitude about her that suggested she took no shit from anyone. She must have been no older than eighteen; nineteen at a stretch. Her body was slim, her legs long and her arms noticeably muscular. On her back was strapped an ebony coloured case full of feather tipped arrows- Kiya deduced from this that the girl was skilled with a bow. Her make-up was immaculate. Each eyelash was extended to almost *three* times its natural length, surrounding bright green eyes that twinkled with deceptive innocence. The length of her hair was astounding. A long blonde plait ran all the way down her back, reaching well past her hips, swaying back and forth as she walked.

"Let's keep her as a pet," the pale skinny man suggested jokingly, looking to Kieran as he spoke. His hand was resting on his hand gun.

Kiya's eyes were still fixed on the girl. Her attire was blood red in colour: a corset that tied up with scarlet ribbons at the back and leather 'hipster' trousers, a lot like the ones Kiya had folded neatly in her bag. Her two inch heeled boots had buckles running up the length of them, a time consuming yet attractive feature. Kiya had always wanted a pair of boots like that.

"Talk to me," Kieran instructed.

"I have nothing to say," she replied.

"Zeke, chuck the kettle on and make me some tea. I'll handle the girl."

The pale man with the handgun nodded and left, heading towards a wall and flicking on a few light switches that Kiya had failed to notice. The old factory came alive instantly revealing quite a sight.

"Awesome ain't it?" Kieran said, admiring the way Kiya looked about in awe. "This is our Headquarters."

"Headquarters for what?" she asked curiously.

He let out a laugh.

"I ain't answering any of *your* questions until you start answering some of *mine*."

The old factory was a lot bigger than Kiya had anticipated. Towards the far end of the room was a row of white wooden doors, six in total, leading to God knows where. The sofa she had slept on appeared to be dumped in a randomly bare area, but further away was a rather spacious kitchen, complete with marble tabletops and plenty of storage cupboards set in the walls. In total there were two large silver fridge-freezers, which Zeke opened in turn in order to find a carton of milk, revealing a wide variety of foods and drinks. If only Kiya had known it had been there! She'd been *so* hungry as the night had progressed. Now she felt as if she were dying from starvation.

"The beers are mine sweet cheeks, so don't go getting any ideas."

Kieran could see Kiya's hungry expression and almost sympathized with the woman.

As well as kitchen table tops, there were work benches covered in all kinds of weaponry. It was certainly a treat for the eyes, if handling such things was a passion of yours. There were a lot of different guns hanging on one of the walls too, though Kiya had never been up to scratch on the types there were to offer. Give her a blade any day! She then noticed for the first time that a few metres ahead of the sofa, to the left a bit, was a television; its screen caked in dust.

"Why don't you sit down for a second?" Kieran pointed at the sofa.

Kiya raised a perfectly plucked eyebrow.

"I thought you said I wasn't allowed to park my 'toned little ass' on it?"

He shrugged smoothly and arched his brow.

"Fine, stand. See if I care."

With that, he edged around her and slumped into the seat beside her open bag, placing his gun on his lap. Kiya picked the bag up for what felt like the millionth time in the space of twenty four hours and zipped it up quickly, snapping back into an upright position as soon as she could. It was *so* hard keeping an eye on everyone in the factory. The Chincse man was at one of the work benches, completely focused on a weapon before him, and the man named 'Zeke' was filling two mugs with sugar in the distance. Kiya wasn't sure where the girl had disappeared to- how the hell did she manage to let that happen? She was letting her guard down for sure.

"You owe me a new padlock and chain missy," Kieran said, knocking Kiya from her thoughts. "I have to admit I was quite surprised to find my place being broken in to and I'd appreciate it if you paid for the damages-"

"Bite me," Kiya hissed.

A smile spread across Kieran's face.

"Love to."

He made a move to get up, making her flinch and as he sat back down in his chair, he laughed.

"You're too tense."

"And you're an asshole," she retorted.

He leant back and grinned up at her. "I try to be," he said airily.

The lights in the building flickered for a moment then returned to normal. In the split second it took for Kieran to be distracted by it, Kiya had kicked the shotgun off his lap and placed the base of her right foot against his crotch, holding the sword to his jugular.

"Damn woman, you're quick," he muttered, genuinely impressed.

"Quit the sweet talk and tell me, who are you people and what is this place for?"

"Honey...," Kieran said, without batting an eyelid, "If I was sweet talking you, you'd know about it."

Kiya could sense the other men in the factory were stirring from their routines and returning their attention to her. She wasn't sure what she was doing anymore. The dilemma she was in could well be the death of her if she didn't play it cool.

"Tell me!" she demanded.

Kieran could see the desperation in her eyes. She was beginning to perspire near her temples and the samurai sword shook ever-so slightly. She reminded him of a caged animal, trapped and scared of its ringmasters.

"Why is it so important that you know?"

It was Kiya's turn to shrug.

"I guess it's because I like to know my enemies before I hack them to pieces."

"Is that so?"

As Kiya was about to press the blade further into Kieran's neck, a cry rang out.

"Lower your sword or I put this arrow between your eyes!"

The eighteen- possibly nineteen- year old girl had her bow drawn back with a feather tipped arrow ready to release in Kiya's direction.

"Hold your horses, Roxy," Kieran said, lifting his hands up, "Kiya wasn't planning on hurting anyone. She's just scared is all-"

Kiya was sweating profusely now.

"How did you-?"

Kieran answered before she could finish.

"Are you shitting me? Your face has been on television, morning, noon and night. Your boyfriend killed the Mayor's daughter right? On the Stone Table? That's a Hell of a way to go if you ask me-"

Kiya couldn't control herself. She thrust the sword forward a millimetre or two, drawing blood from a small piercing she'd made in the man's skin.

"He didn't kill her! Tristian did! I have proof."

"All right," Kieran soothed her, "All right. I believe you. Nobody would go out hunting in the night and then find a dump like this to sleep in if they weren't *sure* they had good reason to."

Kiya was astounded that Kieran had believed her so easily, when her outcries *before* Rycan's execution had been absolutely futile. All it took was a sword to the throat and people would actually listen to what you had to say. Incredible.

"We aren't going to hurt you," Kieran continued reassuringly.

"What about her?" Kiya nodded towards Roxy.

"Roxy's just itching for some target practise after having so many uneventful nights, but don't fret over it. She won't kill an innocent woman, unless you give her reason to."

Kiya's pulse slowed a little and she dropped the blade completely, taking her foot off Kieran's sensitive 'area.' She almost jumped out of her skin when Zeke came up beside her, handing a steaming hot mug of tea over to his friend in silence.

"Thanks, bud."

Roxy had deserted her post now and joined the Chinese man at the work bench without even throwing a glance Kiya's way. Something told her that Kieran was the one to look out for and that the rest were just doing their duty.

Kiya's legs felt weak. She'd woken up too quickly and her head was beginning to pound after all the activity. Things were happening too fast and everything around her started to spin. Before she knew it, she was involuntarily dropping down onto the sofa next to Kieran whilst clutching her stomach in pain.

"You hungry?" Kieran asked. "Thirsty?"

Kiya nodded weakly in response.

"Tea would be great," she said, feeling pathetic for folding under the pressure. Maybe it was best if she gave these people a chance. Hear them out. Be civil.

"Zeke- tea!"

"Dude, why didn't you say about five minutes ago when I was making yours?"

"Quit whining, you pussy. It's not like you have anything better to do!"

"Whatever." Zeke shouted, then muttered, "Dick," as he walked back over to the kitchen area.

Silence fell between the two for a second. Kiya had her hands folded in her lap as she felt Kieran's eyes examining her every curve.

"You look a lot prettier in real life," he told her, thinking it would cheer her up a bit.

"Maybe because on television I had a tear-streaked face and was hysterical," she replied sarcastically.

"Aye, that's probably it."

Kiya didn't want to talk about the television or anything that had happened over the past few days. She didn't feel comfortable enough to open her heart to complete strangers just yet. Hell, her parents were still out of the loop! Heaven knows what state they were in with not knowing where she was and if she was out doing something stupid.

"Are you going to tell me who you are or am I going to have to pretend I can't see all those weapons lying on the table over there and act as if I can't see your blood drenched clothing?"

Kieran sighed.

"Well since you asked so nicely...," he broke off and looked up at the sunlight pouring through the windows. "We're Vampire Slayers."

Chapter 4

Employment

"That's funny-," Kiya said in an amused tone of voice, "I haven't heard of any registered Vampire Slayers in Meridion, and I've lived here my whole life."

Kieran slurped at his tea noisily. It was far too hot for his liking, but he insisted on sipping at the creamy brown liquid none the less, with its three large spoonfuls of sugar teasing his taste buds. Once he'd swallowed a few mouthfuls, he continued to converse with the curiously attractive female, whose hair looked tangled and unkempt from last nights downpour.

"We're not registered," he said breezily, studying her reaction.

"Well then, you're hunting illegally, surely?"

Kieran sighed. "Since when was hunting vermin an *illegal* activity? If I wanna shoot some blood suckers, I'll fucking do it- without signing any damned papers to say I'm *officially* a hunter. Last time I checked, vampires didn't need registering to kill *us*, so who gives a shit what I do with *them?*"

"But, don't you want to get paid for all your trouble? Slaying is dangerous. Nobody wants to fight evil to ensure the safety of mankind these days, unless there's a big pay-packet involved-"

Kieran looked surprised, "Hold on there, precious. Who gave you the right to start asking questions about my financial dealings?"

Kiya tensed a little. She didn't want to enrage Kieran, who was now dredging the last of his tea from his navy blue mug and placing it roughly down onto the dusty floor.

"I-"

Kieran raised a hand to her face, to still her lips, then dropped it as her vocal chords relaxed.

"I don't want paying." He spoke calmly to her once more. "Seeing vamps' dying in an explosion of blood is payment enough. Plus...," he added nonchalantly, "I'm rich and don't need no more cash."

Kiya stared into Kieran's eyes to see if there was any glint of a lie behind them.

"You're rich?" she asked sceptically.

"Sure! I said this was my place, didn't I? I bought it and made it our Slaying Headquarters. All the weapons you see on the walls and tables are mine. And I pay these fine gentleman-" he signalled his cohorts, "and the lovely Roxy over there a very generous sum of money to work alongside me, watching my back in battle."

The expressions on the other people's faces were wooden. Kieran had not told Kiya anything untrue or absurd. She couldn't believe that all the times she'd past the old factory, a team of vampire Slayers were inside, waiting for night to fall so that they could get out and kick vampire butt.

"Are there many?" she queried.

"Vamps?"

She nodded.

"Like you wouldn't believe! There's never been a dry night... until recently... but that's no thanks to us keeping the population down. But I believe they're up to something. They must be in hiding because we haven't seen any on the outskirts of Meridion for quite sometime and that ain't right."

Zeke had approached the two of them whilst Kieran had voiced his suspicions. In his hand was a fresh mug of tea, which he handed to Kiya. She noticed the way he held the mug for a second longer than necessary, as if trapped in thoughts that rendered him powerless. After the mug had left his fingers, he scratched the back of his head.

"I'm going to hit the showers," he informed them. His droopy eyes were a tell-tale sign of just how tired he felt, and as he walked away, Kiya noticed that he could barely lift his own feet. The Slayer's jobs must be highly strenuous and energy consuming, for they all looked as if they needed to sleep for an eternity, although Kieran looked extremely perky for a man who'd been out 'working' all night.

"You seem like an odd group of people." Kiya stopped and then tried to cover her tracks when she realised how insulting her comment had sounded. "I mean- you're an odd mix. Not what I'd imagined a group of Vampire Slayers to look like."

"Well... they can't *all* be as well tanned and handsome as me," Kieran joked, though it came across as arrogance. Kiya didn't want to judge him too much on it- she was just beginning to like the man.

Behind them, Zeke was lifting up a trapdoor that Kiya was not at all surprised to see, considering how mysterious this building actually was. It made a creaking noise as it rose then a loud 'crash' as it hit the floor, revealing a wide entrance into the ground. Zeke's tired legs carried him down the steps, out of her sight, until there was nothing to hold her interest further.

She had a fresh question on the tip of her tongue, but swallowed it as Kieran was advanced on again, this time by the Chinese man; his throwing stars now gleamed brightly on his belt- clean at last.

"I'm going to bed now," the man said, bowing in a short and sharp manner.

"Don't you want a bit of breakfast first?"

The man shook his head.

"I am quite fine for now."

"Okay." Kieran smiled jovially, "Sweet dreams, Siren."

The Chinese man laughed as he walked away, entering through one of the six doors towards the back of the factory. Roxy was the only one left now, other than Kiya and Kieran of course. She had a wig between her knees, for some strange reason, whilst she clipped her superb plait up into a messy bun on top of her head.

"Siren, ey?" Kiya said thoughtfully. She hadn't realised she had spoken allowed until Kieran responded.

"Yeah... he picked it himself. He says he chose it because he likes to sing, but I've never heard the guy even *whistle*, let alone sing, in the entire two years I've known him. He must do it when we're all sleeping."

"Or in the shower," Kiya offered, thinking of herself singing her heart out over the sound of water beating against her naked flesh. She loved singing in the shower. It was uplifting and meditative. Sometimes she even found herself swaying back and forth peacefully to the sound of her own music.

Silence followed. Kieran was leaning to the left with his front facing her slightly as she continued to sit in her hunched position. There was a strange glow about his face and an uncontrollable smirk that spread across his lips. He was infatuated with her. It wasn't just her natural beauty but the way she emanated such awesome power. This girl was angry with society. She was probably looking to snap some necks. She was perfect! Definitely his kind of girl.

It was only then that Kiya realised she had forgotten to drink any of her tea. Zeke hadn't even asked her how she took it. *Must be because he was so tired,* she thought. She brought the mug to her lips and tasted the warm liquid. There was no sugar in it and hardly enough milk and so she returned it to the floor, feeling guilty for not touching it again.

Roxy was in the kitchen area now, with an intense violet coloured wig on her head. It was short and spiky in style, with a long streak of brilliant white hair trailing down either side of her face. Briskly, she opened cupboards, taking out a green coloured bowl and a box of cereal. She then grabbed milk from the fridge, a spoon from a drawer and finally, leant on the counter top- which was detached from the wall- watching Kiya carefully.

"Nice wig," Kiya said sarcastically, trying to convince the girl that any looks she threw her way would not throw her off. She may be on Roxy's territory, but it wasn't going to make her sink into an inferior rank because of it.

Roxy wordlessly continued to crunch on her cereal.

Kieran noticed the heat between the women and decided to draw Kiya's attention away from the teenage girl and back to him.

"Say... I've been looking to recruit new members of the team, since I got that creepy feeling those vampires are plotting something *bad*." He paused to swallow. "How would you like to work for me?"

Kiya didn't look convinced. She looked as if she needed to hear more before she made a decision.

"I understand you've got commitments of your own. I respect that. But think about it... you have a roof over your head here, plenty of food, good company, all the weapons and ammunition you can lay your hands on and demons you can slaughter without facing execution afterwards." He bit his lip. *Shit*. What kind of a dumb-fuck mentions execution after your boyfriend just suffered the same hideous fate?! "I'm sorry," he apologised quickly, "I didn't mean to... what I meant was you can-"

"I'm in," Kiya agreed.

"Well ain't that just peachy," he said in satisfaction, breathing a sigh of relief. "The hours are pretty hard. We're talking dusk till dawn, unless you ain't feeling up to a hunt due to illness or injury, in which case you can stay behind. But I'll have you know, I don't employ slackers. You have to use all the anger inside of you to help pick those bastards off, and there's always that chance you might get bitten-"

"Have you?" she interrupted.

"Nope. Not even close."

"What about the others?"

Kieran shrugged, "Near misses."

"It gets really intense out there." Roxy had joined them, to both Kiya and Kieran's surprise. She was holding the half empty bowl of cereal in the palm of one hand with the spoon still balancing inside. "The night makes it hard to pin-point their locations and you have to be sure your target isn't one of *us* before you shoot. If you're not alert, accidents happen."

Kiya imagined a vampire coming her way as she aimed a gun at its head, then noticed something wrong with the picture.

"I thought vampires didn't die if they got shot."

Kieran nodded. "That's right. They don't, if you miss the heart. But it can still slow them down a considerable amount, which gives *you* the opportunity to sever its head off or stake it through the heart."

"I see."

"And another thing... don't go getting a guilty conscience. These things may look and sound human but at the end of the day, they're after one thing-*your* blood. Don't give them the opportunity. Just do what's necessary. So, do you still want to join my crew?"

"If you'll have me."

"Oh, I most certainly will," Kieran grinned flirtatiously.

Roxy hadn't budged since she came over. Now, she was looking at the sofa longingly.

"Hey Kieran... when the fuck do you plan on buying more sofa's for this dump?"

Kieran pointed a finger at her. "Watch what you're saying missy. I'll have you know I selected this dump out of a great many dumps in Meridion, so don't go slagging it off okay?" He didn't sound genuinely peeved. It was more of a play.

"It's about time his *royal highness* let his *slaves* put their feet up once in a while," Roxy teased, indicating Kieran's laidback posture.

"Fine. You win." Kieran said, getting up off the sofa and picking up his fallen shotgun. "Take the God damn seat. I was going for a shower anyway."

Kiya was curious as to how Kieran planned on having a shower when Zeke was still in there, but decided it was best not to think on it until she had a chance to check it out for herself. It wouldn't surprise her if there were cubicles.

Time seemed to stand still after Kieran's exit.

Kiya was sat alone with Roxy and felt stiff doing so. Roxy's spoon clinked noisily against the bowl as she swirled the food around absentmindedly, taking a bite every now and again. Finally, the silence was broken.

"I um... I'm sorry... about being such a bitch," she said nervously. "I didn't mean to make you feel unwelcome and I most definitely didn't want to have to point that arrow at you earlier."

Kiya felt herself relaxing. She hadn't expected an apology. With Roxy so close now, she could see just how young and pure the girl looked. There were no scars yet. No battle wounds. Just creamy skin and a fine figure. *How could this pale beauty slay vampires?*

"It's okay," she replied. "Really."

Roxy smiled back in a friendly manner.

"You know, I've waited for this day for quite some time."

This made Kiya confused, but she tried her hardest not to show it.

"The day Kieran employs another female, so I actually have somebody to talk to once in a while."

Kiya got the impression suddenly that the girl was extremely lonely, living in an old, filthy factory with a bunch of sweaty men who didn't understand her. She started to wonder how an eighteen/nineteen year old ended up in such a dangerous business, but thought it best to let themselves be better acquainted before she probed for answers.

"I'm really glad you're here," she continued. There was a sparkle in her eyes.

"Thanks." Kiya said appreciatively.

Roxy set the bowl down onto the floor and wiped her lips with the back of her hand. They were full red lips, the type you'd expect to see in a lipstick advert, covered in gloss. Kiya found her gaze being drawn once again to the peculiar wig on the girl's head. It didn't go particularly well with the scarlet corset, but Kiya wasn't about to tell her that.

Roxy noticed Kiya's eyes were fixed on the wig and quickly explained.

"It's er... it's my cover for when I go out."

Kiya raised an eyebrow.

"You guys all have to wear disguises when you leave Headquarters?"

Roxy was quick to correct her.

"No- no! Not at all. It's just because of my parents. They er... they don't know where I am or what I do after I ran away on my eighteenth birthday. They've got people out there looking for me so I have to lay low, you know. If they find me, they'll take me home and lock me up- and I'm not talking figuratively." The girl slipped into distant thoughts and spoke as if on auto-pilot. "I can't give up what I have now. I can't let them find me. I won't go back. I *won't* go back."

Kiya couldn't understand how living with parents, who cared for you, could be so hard. She knew from experience that the loving bond between mother, father and daughter could sometimes be too tight, until you feel as if they're cutting off your air supply, but it never occurred to her that a teenage girl would hate it *so* much that they would completely detach themselves from family and home life. Perhaps there was more to Roxy's story than met the eye.

"I'm sorry about that. Sometimes I get thinking about the past and it just makes me want to hurl! Can I ask you something?"

Kiya urged the girl on with a nod.

"Would you come shopping with me?"

It was strange thing to ask of her and so soon into any friendship that may have been developing between the two. But Kiya obliged.

Retail therapy. There's nothing quite like it.

"Sure thing," she agreed, not to give the impression she was grumpy or unkind. "I don't suppose you have a spare wig do you?"

Chapter 5

West Meridion Mall

Kiya immediately regretted her agreement to go shopping. She didn't feel like trawling through crowds of people- snatching up products before some other undeserving paws dirtied them- she just wasn't in the mood. The thought of shopping was starting to give her a headache as she fumbled with the blonde wig Roxy had leant to her. She had to acquire assistance in pinning back her long, dark, tatty locks of hair so that the wig would slide snugly into place on her scalp. Result. She then discovered blonde wasn't her colour, but that she would just have to make do.

Kiya felt dirty too. She'd never gone this long without showering and her paranoia about smelling terrible and looking unclean was making her uncomfortable around the young adult, whose smile was bigger than the South Meridion Bridge. If only she could use the bathroom to change her clothes and perhaps have a quick wash, then perhaps she'd stop sweating at the brow so much, but Kiya had to settle with brushing her teeth in the kitchen sink. Nothing more.

"Hey Roxy... when we go out today, do you mind if I run a little errand at some point?"

Roxy shrugged nonchalantly. "Whatever you want to do, I'm game." She certainly didn't seem bothered by anything that Kiya had up her sleeve. It was still shocking to see how friendly the girl was around her, after meeting in such an awkward and unusual situation. The girl was extremely perky, as if she was about to meet up with female friends at the mall, bearing 'Daddy's' credit card.

"How do you plan on getting there?" Kiya asked curiously. It was a hell of a long way to go on foot and she couldn't imagine the two of them on the local bus together. The people of Meridion *may* be petrified of practically everything that breathed, but they weren't too frightened to use their mobile phones in order to alert the police of her whereabouts *if* she was, by chance, recognised. And what of Roxy? Didn't she mention being 'looked' for by her parents? That couldn't be good.

"When his Lordship... Kieran the Great," Roxy said melodramatically, "was seated beside you on that there uncomfortable sofa, I swiped his keys without him knowing."

Kiya was impressed. She hadn't noticed Roxy's skill of theft and she'd been given a front row seat to the performance.

"Well I sure as hell know now!" came a voice from behind the two of them.

Kieran had emerged from the steps in the ground, rubbing a towel at the back of his head to dry the last of his hair and skin.

Roxy's triumphant expression crashed at the knowledge of being busted.

"You should never brag afterwards, Roxy. You never know who might be listening. Now hand the keys over."

"Oh shit," Roxy mumbled, placing the keys into his large outstretched palm and then dropping her arms to her side loosely.

"Here-" Kieran said, unexpectedly. He handed over a different set of keys. "Take Siren's truck instead."

After a rapid change of clothing on Roxy's behalf and the consumption of a banana on Kiya's, the pair left the factory, listening to the sound of Kieran laughing at something on the old television, as he wolfed down toast drenched in butter.

Kieran had given no warnings as they'd parted ways-just a wink, which he directed at his newest employee. He couldn't wait to take her out vampire slaying. By God he couldn't wait.

To be on the safe side, Kiya carried her samurai sword on her lap as she slipped smoothly into the passenger seat of the beaten up, dusty vehicle they'd been loaned, and stroked it lovingly, remembering the day Rycan had passed it to her with pride written in the depths of his eyes. She put a lot of faith in this particular blade, knowing that as long as she wielded it well, it would never shatter in combat, or bend like some knock offs did.

She almost bit her tongue clean off as Roxy put the truck in reverse, then slammed on the breaks too hard as they reached the road. For obvious reasons, the Slayers vehicles were all parked around the back of the old factory, under the shadows of some parched and very crispy looking trees. There was less chance people would spot them there, but even if they *were* noticed, people would just assume it was teenagers planning on trashing the factory or drug dealers undergoing some shady business.

"Sorry about that." Roxy noticed Kiya stroking the back of her neck in pain and changed gears quickly, speeding off in a flurry of dust clouds, which trailed behind them as a signature of their departure.

The further away from the old factory they got, the less comfortable Kiya felt. The first sign of civilisation made her snatch the sunglasses from her jacket pocket and slip them on protectively. The blonde wig was far from convincing, or at least she believed so.

"Relax. Relax. They don't want you. You've done nothing wrong."

Kiya felt anger stir within her. *What the hell did* she *know?* She glanced down at her fingernails in order to distract herself from retorting, noticing how mud and blood had buried its way underneath them. It made her feel even more disgusting, so she tried to forget about everything with the mellow tunes coming from the radio instead.

"This stuff isn't fast enough for me," Roxy informed her as they stopped at a set of traffic lights. She switched stations, picking up some disco shit that Kiya absolutely despised. Subconsciously she sunk into her seat, eyeing up the people walking past the car like zombies, all solemn and dead inside. *Was everyone's soul sucked out of them the day Rycan died?* she thought, though she knew perfectly well it was an unlikely concept.

"Roxy," Kiya said, her voice a little croaky, "Do you mind if we shop at the West Meridion Mall instead of the shopping district here?" It was quite a big request, considering the West Meridion Mall was a good forty to fifty minutes away. "I just don't want to see Rycan's store, you know?" All she needed was another run-in with Carl after last night's episode and her miserable life would be complete.

Roxy's brow lifted in realisation. "Of course," she smiled.

For an eighteen year old, who was pretty new to driving, Roxy knew her way around Meridion like the back of her hand. They reached the Mall in almost half the time Kiya had expected, using little roads through desolate streets instead of the main route that was always pretty busy in the mornings.

Instead of parking in the areas provided, Roxy parked outside someone's house, about five minutes walk away from their destination and as they left the truck, a figure appeared from a house, waving their arms about like a creature gone mad.

"No no no!" they wailed. It was a man, in his forties, with balding grey-brown hair and a distinct beer-belly under an old white t-shirt. The overhang of his gut could be seen pale and hairy above the waist line of his jeans and Kiya felt her nose wrinkle up at the sight of it. "No no no!" he repeated, coming face to face with Roxy as she turned the car key in the lock and stepped away from the vehicle.

"Is there a problem, Sir?" she said pleasantly, blinking more times than necessary.

"Yes there's a fucking problem! That's my space!"

"*Your* space?" Roxy replied dumbly.

"Yes. *My* space. Now get your fucking tin- can out of it!"

Roxy crossed her arms over her chest. She was wearing a violet coloured crop-top, revealing a smooth, flat stomach and the glint of a belly ring, even though the weather didn't look as if it would stay warm for much longer. Her trousers were jet black and silky, flaring out at the bottom, with violet coloured roses stitched up the length of both legs and her boots had killer heals. But apparently, her beauty wasn't enough to faze the man. He stared at her like a bug that needed to be exterminated.

"Do you own a vehicle?" she asked.

The man's face grew increasingly sweaty and red in the cheeks.

"Yes, as a matter of fact, I do. I have to pick it up in an hour and bring it back here because I'm having my brakes fixed. Now I don't want to ask you again, but, move your damn truck!"

Roxy cocked her head to the side innocently then feigned a look of surprise.

"Don't move, Sir. You have a *huge* spider on your shoulder-"

The man froze in fear.

"Get it! Get it!" he pleaded, trying to twist his neck so that he might catch a glimpse of the beast that dared to touch him.

Roxy reached out and pressed her fingers somewhere in the man's neck, much to Kiya's confusion. Less than a minute later, the man's eyes rolled up in his head and he crumpled to the floor like a soldier who'd been shot in the back. Hurriedly, Roxy grabbed the man's arms and signalled to Kiya to grab his legs.

"Quick, before someone sees us!"

Together they carried the great human bulk through a weed infested front garden and slung him into his house, on a dirty old green sofa in the living room.

"Don't look so worried," Roxy said, brushing her hands clean, "He'll wake up in about two to three hours wondering how the hell he ended up falling asleep on his couch and that's about it. Guess he'll be late picking up his car now though. Too bad. Asshole."

They left the man snoring soundly and closed the front door behind them without being met by hoards of unhappy neighbours who'd seen the previous event unfold. Kiya's eyes darted from left to right, trying to catch of glimpse of any faces in the windows. There was no one.

The West Meridion Mall was teeming with people when they arrived through its extravagant glass doors, with the initials W.M.M printed on in gold letters. It had six floors altogether, two of which were dedicated entirely to clothes and undergarments. It was the perfect place to blend into because nobody cared about faces, only sales.

Kiya thought about the folded up pound notes she'd tucked into her bra before leaving the factory. She should have learned her lesson in reality, after once concealing a fifty in there and losing it an hour or so later, but now she was confident her tight sports bra wouldn't let her down. Also, she always felt kind of sexy, teasing the young till operators as she reached in to pull the money from her cleavage. The expression on their faces said it all. Rycan had told her it was cruel to tease boys who were desperately in need of getting laid for the first time, but he usually cracked a smile afterwards.

"So...where to start?" Kiya glanced around at the first floor, with its water fountains running along the centre of the building at well measured points. Meridion may not have much, but it certainly made shopping for junk a beautiful occasion. The pillars that held up the floors above were all decorated with ivy and enchanted to look as if there were fairies sat on the leaves in various places. Kiya had read about it in a newspaper once. The floor manager had gone to great lengths to gain permission for such a spell. Magic was dangerous, which is why the practise of it was highly frowned upon- but what *wasn't* dangerous nowadays, was the argument of many witches and warlocks- a rare breed in these parts. They were only harmless 'fairy' illusions; spells that children used to conjure quite easily before the magic in the world started to die out. Eventually the manager was granted permission to decorate his magnificent store just so.

Kiya cast her eye upwards, past the balconies of each busy and equally extravagant floor to the glass ceiling above. Each panel was bigger than the length of your average car and they were separated by gold plated steel. It must have been horrible cleaning the bird crap off them and being able to see the ground floor so far below.

All of Meridion's money went into this place because of its popularity with people outside the city. Tourists from far and wide spent a bundle of cash here and left feeling just as empty as they did before. *You can't buy happiness*, Kiya believed, *but you* can *distract yourself from misery for about an hour or two before reality kicks in again.* This was something she planned on doing right now.

After passing an on-duty officer and not receiving a flinch, Kiya sighed and followed Roxy into a glass elevator with gold coloured rails to hold onto inside. She gripped the rail and watched the ground floor disappear from below her feet, feeling slightly queasy.

"It's pay day next week!" Roxy blurted out obscenely, showing the teenage girl in her. "But I still have a ton of cash left over from last month. Kieran is really generous you know- he hands out cash like it's sandwiches. You can borrow some of mine if you want, until we get you trained and you start earning cash yourself."

"I'm fine thanks." Kiya objected.

"Well, don't be afraid to ask if you're in a tight spot. Money doesn't mean all that much to me. Just the clothes I buy with it!" she laughed at herself. "There's this store I want to show you, where they have the coolest outfits you could imagine. They've got just about every outfit ever designed for the sexy 'warrior women' characters of the movies. They even sell shit like bullet proof bodices for, and I quote: 'The sexy but dangerous types.' Reckon you and I fit that description?"

"Sounds about right," Kiya grinned bleakly. Her head was beginning to sweat under the wig and itch a lot for that matter. It was the most uncomfortable thing she'd ever had to wear.

Roxy practically jumped out of the elevator as the door slid open on the fifth floor. Her boots glided smoothly over the shiny marble floors and Kiya had to pick up the pace in order the keep up with the girl's stride. It was a blessing when she finally stopped outside a store.

"Here we are!"

The brightly lit window had a whole array of outfits on display, including the familiar 'Lara Croft' hot pants and tight t-shirt, complete with gun holsters around the thighs, as well as the leather 'Cat Woman' get-up, equipped with a dangerous looking whip. The shop itself was called 'Bianca's.'

"This is wicked shit, man." Roxy clapped her hands together joyously and then grabbed Kiya by the elbow, dragging her inside.

"Hello ladies," came a rather seductive sounding voice. It was the lady herself, Miss Bianca Fox, greeting the pair with a glorious smile. "Welcome to my store."

"Hey," Roxy replied, already stroking a velvet dress hung on a rack next to her.

"Is that my favourite customer under that wig?" Bianca cooed, lifting Roxy's chin up to inspect her closer. Her cheeks went bright red in response.

"Sure is, B", Roxy grinned sheepishly.

"My my, how you've grown. You look an inch taller and a year older every time you walk through those doors. Such a beautiful young woman you have become!"

"It has been a while I guess...," Roxy murmured.

"And who is this fair lady?"

Bianca flexed her arms out before her, before crossing them over her large breasts. She wore a long blue-grey shawl over a black shirt and had a dark grey skirt on that brushed the floor, concealing her feet beneath the rippling material. Her hair was short and spiky, dyed brown to cover up the grey that poked through and her brown eyes were lined expertly with a dark eyeliner and mascara. Years ago, Bianca had had the body of a Goddess, or so she was told, and now she believed she had the body of a walrus. But she didn't let her weight get her down. She prided herself on creating beautiful and rather kinky outfits for the women who still had a sexy exterior and a fine ass to shake in front of the male species.

"This is a...friend," Roxy informed her, with a pause in her sentence.

Bianca lifted a thinly plucked eyebrow. "A 'friend' you say?" Kiya looked nervously away, knowing only too well she was being slightly rude in the presence of the eccentric fashion designer. She nudged Kiya gently in the ribs. "It took me a while to get Roxy to spill the beans about her true identity, but after a little prying she gave in to me. I always knew she didn't look anything like a 'Starla.' So, sweet heart, what's your name?"

Kiya remained wooden in facial expression. "Starla."

Bianca expressed surprise then realised Kiya was just fucking with her. Her sense of humour was of the malicious kind though- something she didn't like- and so she skulked off, looking quite offended.

"You didn't have to be so mean," Roxy hissed when Bianca was out of earshot. Kiya couldn't be bothered to move her tongue to create words for an answer and instead listened to Roxy whine, "Now we won't get discount."

Chapter 6

Logan

Kiya wrapped her fingers around the polystyrene cup and felt the warmth of her decaffeinated coffee soothe her tips. She'd always preferred to *purchase* hot drinks than make them because she could never quite get them to taste as good when she did it herself. Roxy was swirling the red ice of her 'slushy' around with a pink straw, taking little sips that chilled her sensitive teeth and tongue. The small café was thriving around them and as much as Kiya hadn't wanted to, they'd been shown a seat outside of the shop, at a round metal table, still sticky from its previous visitors.

They hadn't spent too much time at Bianca's place because it had been a little awkward when they'd gone to the counter to pay for their items, after the unfriendly conversation they'd had at the front of the store.

Kiya had found a sturdy knife pouch there that you could wrap around the lower part of your leg, to conceal a weapon under your trousers, as well as finding a decorative black strap-top which had a criss-crossed ribbon design running from the centre, near her cleavage, to the middle of her flat stomach, just below her belly button. It had a built-in bra, for maximum support when out slaying those demons, and was made from a mysteriously *tough* material, which was said to be 'scratch resistant'- in case a werewolf or vampire took a swipe at you. The price was pretty steep on both items, but Kiya didn't think it mattered. She had a feeling she'd be able to keep on buying whatever the hell she wanted as soon as she got cosy enough with the vampire slaying team and started bringing home the bacon- bacon being money of course.

Roxy was all for grabbing whatever she could lay her hands on as long as it was her size. She'd rushed to the fitting rooms, then decided she couldn't be bothered to change, and brought everything back out, dumping it on the counter top before returning to the racks of clothing and fetching more.

"I suppose its just as well we brought the truck instead of the motorbike with all this shopping," she'd giggled, holding up lace panties and passing them to Kiya when she had inspected them enough.

Roxy was carrying four large plastic bags with Bianca's logo plastered on them; the silhouette of a naked woman, sat cross-legged and holding two swords, which were crossed above her head. At the rate Roxy was buying, Kiya was sure they'd need to employ a bag-carrier boy.

They'd hit a few more clothes shops after that, but neither of them were particularly interested in anything they had to offer. Who needed a flowing, baby blue gown with silver sequins on, or a saucy black, figure-hugging dress that revealed a whole lot of leg? There wasn't time to go out gallivanting anymore in pretty clothes. Life was about to get hardcore.

"Would you like a refill?"

Kiya blinked up at the waitress who was lingering over her shoulder, bearing a pot of coffee. She noticed the dark circles under the girl's eyes and the way her dark brown hair had fallen out in places, from the clip that held it all back from her face. She was dressed in a white blouse and black trousers and from her apron pocket there peeked out a notebook to write orders in. She was too thin and too tired, Kiya thought, knowing only too well that the smile she bore was a false one.

"No thank you," she replied, noting that the girl was staring at her hair a little too much. Had the wig shifted, allowing her real hair to be on show? When the waitress had gone, Kiya turned back to Roxy.

"Is my hair okay?"

Roxy gave it a once over. "Sure." There was silence for about three minutes whilst Roxy drained the last of the slush from her plastic cup; *then* came the excited babbling of teenager. "Oh- I love the mall! There are hot guys *everywhere*! It's like they congregate here or something because everywhere I turn, there's a handsome guy strutting past and giving us both the eye." Coincidentally, a dark haired stranger strolled past their table, dressed in a black suit and carrying a leather briefcase. His eyes scouted out the area, paused on Roxy who was waving cutely, then walked off with a big smirk on his face. "See what I mean?" she gushed.

"I suppose."

"I have to admit, I was totally into Kieran when we first met," she started quite randomly. "I thought he was some sort of *god*, with that tight butt in those leather trousers and muscles to die for! I could hardly stop myself from drooling, and it made it worse when I noticed him staring at me from across the bar the first night I met him."

Kiya took a sip of her coffee. It was going cold already. *Yuk*. She should have had a refill after all.

"I left home the day I turned eighteen, which was hard, but definitely worth the price of freedom," Roxy reminisced. "At the time, I was seeing someone, but it turned out, so was *he*. It was the typical 'I get home from a hard day of looking for jobs and discover some bitch all wrapped up in my bed covers with my boyfriend,' scenario. Too bad for them that I caught them at it because I broke his arm in two places and gave her the bloodiest nose I've ever seen as a parting gift- and believe me, I've watched a *lot* of violent movies and this was right up there with Quentin Tarantino flicks."

"Did the police get involved?" Kiya asked, thinking about her own limb-severing evening.

"Nope. Well, not that I know of. So anyway- I got a job working behind a bar. It was shitty pay but the owner was kind enough to give me the work because I was *seriously* desperate. He said it was because I was 'beautiful' and that perhaps he'd get a few more customers with a pretty face like mine behind the counter," she smiled at the thought. "Unfortunately, I *did* attract a few more customers- most of them assholes."

"What do you expect?" Kiya said, "We live in Meridion."

"No shit." Roxy gave the perimeter a quick scan as she continued to speak. "Well, some dude, who looked seriously whacked out on drugs, was sat at the bar, getting drunker and drunker by the millisecond. When I told him he should go home and lie down, he refused loudly. I said he wasn't getting another drop of alcohol from me and all of a sudden, he lunged at me! He had my ponytail and was pulling my head forward, so I punched the fucker in the face a few times until he was flat on his back and crying for his mummy."

"I take it Kieran saw all this?"

Roxy nodded. "He was the one who helped to throw that grimy bastard out. I couldn't believe how strong he was! He picked the drunk up like he was a bag of feathers and tossed him onto the sidewalk with ease. It was bloody mesmerising. I gave him a drink on the house but he refused to take it without paying. I knew he was a cool guy as soon as he tipped me with a fifty. A *fifty*!"

Kiya listened with fascination at Roxy's banter. She hadn't been 'all there' when they'd first arrived at the Mall, but now she was showing signs of breaking free of that zombie mode she'd been stuck in for hours.

"At closing time, I left the pub feeling full of adrenaline. It was almost a welcoming sight, seeing that drunk in the street with a knife."

Kiya found this to be a particularly odd kind of statement. What teenage girl found knife bearing maniac's *welcoming*?

"I battered the shit out of him, without gaining a scratch myself, and left him lying in the gutter, with a few broken ribs. At that point, Kieran pulled out of the alley on his motorbike and offered me a job straight out. I met him at the factory the next day and *bang*, I was a Vampire Slayer!" She went droopy eyed for a moment. "I thought training with Kieran, with his perfect abs on display, was *heaven*. I couldn't take my eyes off him! And that voice of his sent shivers down my spine."

"So, you still dig him?" Kiya asked, trying to use adolescent slang, which didn't sound at all correct when she used it.

Roxy's dreamy expression melted. "Nah-" she said, changing her tone. "I've been with him for about ten months and see him as more of a father figure now. Anyway, I think he prefers brunettes."

Kiya thought perhaps Roxy was referring to her, but ignored the implication completely.

"Are we still good to run that errand later?" Kiya pressed, reminding Roxy that she had more than shopping to do.

"Yeah. No probs. I just need to-" Roxy paused. She'd noticed something in the distance. A young man. He was attending to some puppies in the window of a pet shop, just a few stores along from the café.

"Is everything okay?" Kiya queried, following Roxy's line of vision.

Roxy didn't answer. Instead, she got up, leaving her shopping bags under the table at Kiya's feet, and approached the pet shop in a daze. *Could it really be him?*

She tapped the window and grinned sheepishly at the boy, whose hand was sliding along the sleek, soft back of a small Dalmatian. He was wearing brown overalls, with his name stitched in gold on one of the pockets. His body looked thick and muscular and his nose showed signs of being broken once or twice, but there was no denying he was handsome, with that wavy blonde hair and piercing blue eyes.

"Logan?" she mouthed from the other side of the window.

The young man gave a slow nod, looking almost as shocked as she.

Roxy felt the adrenaline pumping wildly through her veins as she entered the pet shop. There were butterflies in her stomach and her cheeks were slowly turning a vibrant shade of red. She couldn't believe how fast her heart was beating as she drew nearer to the person she'd loved all through high school and still loved now, considering how her body was reacting to his presence.

Logan Price. Twenty in a few months time- she recalled- and still as sexy as ever. He had been the boy of Roxy's dreams, a couple of years ago and had raised a lot of arguments with her (now non-existent) best friend Shannon; Logan's younger sister.

Shannon didn't approve of Roxy's lust for her sibling, in fact, she'd even threatened to stop being her mate if she didn't get over him. But Roxy had ached for Logan. All those nights she'd spent watching television at his house or sitting in the bedroom next-door to his as Shannon painted her nails, she'd wanted to be with him and him *only*; breathing in his scent; getting lost in the warmth of his body.

Roxy had almost melted when Logan had escorted her home from school one day, leaving Shannon to catch the train with a group of gossiping females. He'd winked at her in greeting and taken her along a relatively unused path through the park, which had long since been turned into a miserable construction sight.

She'd kept her eyes to the floor, trying not to get sucked into that beautiful gaze of his, but it had become too much. She'd lost focus on her footing and tripped over a root that was poking out of the ground. Logan had been quick to catch her.

It had been a fairytale come true after that. He'd allowed her to catch her breath before trailing a hand over her thigh, under her grey school skirt, then up over her waist and breasts where it came to rest at her neck, tenderly caressing her skin.

The kiss that followed had been mind-blowing. She'd allowed Logan to make the first move, tasting her mouth with short sweet kisses then deepening each one with a fiery need in the pit of his stomach. She responded with equal passion, running her hands through his hair then daringly stroking him through his trousers. They'd stopped themselves before clothes parted with skin, much to Roxy's disappointment. People might catch them. Rumours would start. Arguments would follow. What was the point in spoiling it all?

Shannon had been devastated when she'd discovered a few months later that Logan had invited Roxy to the high school prom as his date. She'd pouted and moaned and stomped her feet, even when Roxy had arrived at her home in a glittering, green, velvet ball gown that trailed along the floor in a swish of glossy fabric and gave the impression she was floating, not walking, across the room. Her long blonde hair had been in springy, loose curls, pulled back with a silver butterfly clip to reveal cute ears bearing dangly silver earrings, like sparkling raindrops falling from her skin. The kiss Logan gave her as a welcoming 'hello' only infuriated Shannon further and she left in a rage, knocking over a vase of flowers in the process.

"You look breath taking," he'd whispered, kissing her neck gently.

"So do you," Roxy had replied, feeling faint with desire.

As the magnificent 'Prom' came to an end, Roxy had ended up at a hotel, paid for by her high school sweetheart. Logan was strong, even back then, and had carried her skinny frame through the door of their room, where he'd dropped her gently onto the double bed. After a few more shots of vodka and orange on Roxy's behalf and downing some Jack and Coke on Logan's, they'd started kissing and tugging at each other's expensive and glamorous outfits, until they were naked in front of each other for the first time.

Logan had thought Roxy perfect, with her slim figure, flat stomach and tight ass. Her hair had come free of its butterfly clip during the evening and had now fallen over her breasts, concealing them from his sight- making him even more desperate to go over and touch her. She was beautiful to him.

Roxy hadn't been at all shy in Logan's presence. She'd stripped quite willingly; even letting him help her to slide out of the black thong she was wearing, with its bows tied on either side of her hips. She'd loved the way Logan placed his hands on her hips, sliding them further down until they rested on her ass. He'd been so gentle and loving, taking everything slow and making her feel more alive than she'd ever felt in her entire life. She'd wished she could have been trapped in his warm embrace forever, lying on the bed underneath him.

She'd been hopelessly in love with him, but all good things usually came to an end in her life.

When exams had finished, Logan had left high school and was taken from Roxy by his extremely dominant father, who forced him to sort papers and make phone calls all day in their family business somewhere in the city of Karanthian. They'd lost touch pretty quickly because Logan was overworked and always too tired to respond to her letters. He'd tried coming to see her once, but had been caught up in a drugs-bust at a shady truck stop, where his father bailed him out of jail and took him straight back home again.

A year had past since she'd seen Logan. She'd been with another man since then; a lying, cheating rat. But she had always hoped that someday he'd return to her.

"Sonja...," he said, using her real name. "I've been looking for you. But you left home and... and I couldn't find anyone who knew where you were staying. I thought you might be-"

"Dead?" Roxy whispered. "No. Not dead. And please, don't call me that. I go by Roxy now."

"Roxy? Doesn't sound like the type of name for a sweet little thing like you."

"A lot has changed in the past year. As you know, I don't flounce around in school skirts anymore. I have an identity to keep secret now."

"Are you're parents taking over *your* life too?"

"They tried," she said, "And failed."

He was silent for a moment, his eyes twinkling in the dim lighting of the shop.

"I can't believe I found you," Roxy muttered. "I mean, why are you here, in the West Meridion Mall?"

"I quit working at my Dad's firm and came back here in hope of finding you. I couldn't stop thinking about you when I was stuck in Karanthian, being so far away. It drove me insane. I thought the best chance of me ever seeing you again was to get a job in a shopping complex like this and hope to hell you'd come here someday."

"Boy am I glad we didn't go to the other shopping district," Roxy sighed, thinking about Kiya's suggestion of heading to the Mall in order to avoid Rycan's burnt down shop.

"We?" Logan looked at her quizzically. "Are you with somebody else?"

Roxy could see fear etched into the creases of his handsome face.

"A friend. She's watching my shopping. I probably should get back to her"

Logan grabbed her hand all of a sudden. "Don't leave me," he stopped to compose himself. "Let's talk, out back. *Please*?"

She glanced over at Kiya, through the clear glass of the pet shop window, and gave a little wave; not entirely positive Kiya had noticed it.

"Of course," she breathed, thinking about his hand latched onto her arm, "Let's go."

Chapter 7

Love Renewed

Kiya hadn't spotted Roxy disappearing into the back of the store with love-sick eyes. She'd spotted someone she knew from the Nursery school instead and had ducked her head low, to avoid confrontation and dreary conversation, at the time Roxy had waved her way. From Kiya's position, it had seemed as if Roxy was there one second, and gone the next; without warning her of her whereabouts.

Kiya strained her neck desperately to catch a glimpse of that wild purple wig, but saw nothing that resembled the teenage girl. The pet shop window was now empty out front *and* inside.

"Shit," she cursed under her breath.

Roxy's heart fluttered as Logan took her hand and led her to the back of the shop. A man, in his late thirties, was buried in a newspaper, behind the counter, and gave Logan a short, sharp nod as he strolled past with her in tow. For a second, the man's bushy uni-brow lifted in bewilderment, then dropped back down after he got a good look at Roxy's ass. *Boys will be boys,* he thought.

That kid is one lucky son of a bitch. Logan had forgotten to close the door behind him, so as a favour, the man reached out a podgy hand and nudged it shut. *Let them have some privacy*, he decided, thinking wickedly of all the naughty things Roxy might be doing in the next room with that amazing body he had glimpsed. His groin tightened for a moment, until his eye found its focus on the Mayor's sad face, on the left page of his newspaper. *Yeesh*, he thought, returning to his reading.

In the back room, there were a few empty cages stacked up on tables, minus their animals. Some still had faeces inside, or shredded newspapers, but most were fresh and ready to be inhabited again. Roxy glanced around nervously at the pictures of neglected and mistreated animals tacked to the walls, but was too energised by the warmth of Logan's hand to feel any pang of guilt for the poor beasts.

"Is business good?" she asked casually, thinking of anything to break the silence.

"Who cares?" Logan said suddenly, whirling her around to face him and forcing his mouth to hers in a long-awaited kiss. He sighed contentedly as he parted. "Still taste as good as you did before I left you, Sonja."

Her heart jolted at the sound of her real name again. He couldn't keep calling her that. It was too risky. Anyone could be an employee of her mother and father's and then she'd be screwed if they caught wind of her. Sonja was an old name. Dying out like many others. It wasn't very popular in Meridion, which heightened her parents chances of finding her.

"Lay off the Sonja shit, okay?" she said, wiping her lips with the back of her hand. They were still tingling pleasantly.

"But it's who you are. You can't run from that. Since when did you start hiding from people anyway? You didn't have to leave your parents you know."

"Hey!" Roxy shouted, feeling slightly embarrassed about the magnitude of her voice in such a small room, "You know as well as I do what its like to have parents that want to control your life. So back off."

Logan looked taken aback. "I'm sorry. I didn't mean to upset you."

"I'm not upset," she insisted, looking down at the floor and kicking the front of her right shoe against the table leg absentmindedly. "It's just, after a year or so of not being able to speak to you, my parents and my history with them is the last thing I want to be thinking about okay?"

Logan managed a smile and patted the table. "Take a seat," he offered. She took his hand again willingly and lifted herself onto the counter top, feeling its cold surface through her trousers. He remained standing, facing her, breathing in her scent and applauding himself on gaining the perfect position to check out her cleavage. It was almost too much, having her so close to him after such a long time. That violet coloured crop-top was just begging to be ripped off.

"Where have you been?" he asked, biting back the urge to sink his teeth into her neck lustfully and put his mark on her creamy skin. She'd liked to be bitten he recalled- within reason.

"I had a few jobs," she explained, brusquely.

"And?"

"And what?"

"Where were you staying all this time?"

She thought briefly about her boyfriend, the one she'd started seeing after Logan had become lost to her. They'd shared a small apartment, until she'd found out about the affair of course. After that, she didn't return, not even for her underwear.

"I had a place, but moved out."

"Where are you staying now?" Logan asked, his eyes piercing into her.

"An old factory with some friends," she bit her lip when she saw his bemused expression. "We're not drug addicts if that's what your thinking. Or into massive orgies either. It's just a quiet place in a quiet area where we can get some shut eye before work."

"Where do you work now?"

"I'm a waitress," she lied quickly. Logan looked pressingly at her, wanting to know more about this 'waitressing' she spoke of. But she decided to change the subject quickly. "So what about you? Where are you staying?"

"Here and there," he said mysteriously. "I move around a lot."

"Oh, I see." She didn't see, but she believed him none-the-less.

Roxy glanced down for a moment, feeling something in her eye. A lash maybe? But she was alert again as Logan's hand came to rest on the top of her head, tugging the wig off her scalp. Her blonde hair was all sweaty underneath, with tiny strands poking up messily. She looked terrible compared to him.

"Logan!" she objected, swinging her arm out to snatch the wig back. He threw it out of her reach and pressed in closer to her. Automatically, her legs lifted and wrapped around him. He wasted no time in leaning in, stroking her through her trousers and kissing her neck. She grabbed his head, digging her nails into his skin as she forced him to her lips.

Logan pulled back suddenly, both of them breathing heavily in the brief silence.

"Did you fuck anyone else while I was gone?"

Roxy shuddered under him. She didn't want to say. But why not? He left her right?

"I was... with someone else when I thought you weren't coming back."

Logan ran a hand over her thigh. "Did he treat you like the Goddess you are?"

A tear sprung to Roxy's eye unexpectedly. She didn't like talking about *him*- that wanker from a past best forgotten. "No," she whispered, feeling both eyes watering uncontrollably.

Logan started to unbutton her trousers, then fumbled with the zip. "I forgive you for seeing another man," he said, between ragged breaths of excitement, "I forgive you because it was my fault I left all of you here alone. I'm sorry I wasn't here to be the boyfriend you trusted and relied on once. But now I'm going to remind you what it's like to fuck someone who loves you more than anyone else in the world,"

Roxy was faint from the heat between them both.

Logan was battling with the animal inside him.

Hastily, he slipped his hand into her open trousers...

Kiya was tense. She scraped her nails across the table top but stopped when she noticed an old couple giving her an angry look.

The first ten minutes were a worry. When it neared twenty five, she jumped up from her seat, swung her samurai sword over her shoulder, grabbed her own shopping bag- but left Roxy's- and strode briskly over to the pet shop, where she'd last seen her standing.

There was a man inside; your average fat bastard like the one Roxy had knocked out on a doorstep a few hours ago.

When she entered the store, the man rustled his paper, but refused to look at her. Puppies barked happily. Cats brushed their lean, furry bodies against the bars of their enclosures. Birds squawked and flapped their wings. A small monkey bounced up and down noisily in a cage suspended from the ground.

She didn't ask for permission. Instead, she walked straight past the man, pushing him back down into his chair as he rose in protest.

"I wouldn't go in there if I was you!" he exclaimed.

She ignored him.

Logan leapt away from Roxy the second he heard the door handle click from its original position. Roxy looked stunned at the absence of his touch for a moment, then almost choked in embarrassment when Kiya walked in, looking red in the face with annoyance.

"Who the hell do you think you are, barging in here like this?" Logan yelled, whilst doing his overalls back up.

"Kiya, I was just-" Roxy tried explaining, feeling her brow becoming increasingly wet with moisture. She zipped up her trousers with shaking fingers and pulled her crop-top back over her head as fast as she could.

"Save the explanations," Kiya suggested bitterly. "I'm fed up of shopping. Let's get out of here."

"Can... can I have five minutes to say good bye?" Roxy requested. She was almost too afraid to speak after catching a glimpse of that terrifying fire in Kiya's eyes.

"Two minutes," she replied dryly, and left without shutting the door.

The old man had laid down his newspaper now and was peeking through curiously, showing disappointment at the sight of Roxy's clothed body. *Too bad.*

"I am so s-" Roxy began to apologise, but Logan stopped her by pressing a finger to her lips.

"We will continue this another time, I promise. I want to see you again, *soon*, if that's okay with you?"

"Of... of course," Roxy nodded.

"Next Friday night."

"I can't do evenings," she replied gloomily.

"I didn't ask you," he said powerfully, "I'm telling you. I work all day long here, from dawn until dusk, cleaning the third and fourth floor, then working here in between. I have to see you Friday. I can't wait any longer than that."

"Logan," she spoke calmly, "I have responsibilities. A job that really needs me there-"

"Pretend you're feeling ill."

"Maybe...," she whispered.

"No maybes. Say yes."

Roxy sighed. "Yes."

"That's my girl," he kissed her on the forehead. "Wait for me by the Stone Table. You know where that is in the city, right?"

She rolled her eyes playfully. "Everyone knows where that is."

"Good. I'll meet you there at seven thirty. *Don't* be late."

"I won't," she promised. "But where are we going?"

Logan grinned cheekily. "That's for me to know, and for you to find out."

Chapter 8

The Errand

Kiya's mood showed no signs of breaking as the pair waltzed through the exits with no respect for the other shoppers; pushing and shoving their way through. The sunlight was bright, though the air chilled, and the people around them were looking eager to step into the warmth of the West Meridion Mall, still gleaming with its silver, gold and white marble colouration.

"I'm sorry, okay?" Roxy assured her, talking to Kiya's back, for it was all she could reach. Her bags were flapping around hopelessly in her waving hands and her hair, which had been hurriedly tucked away under the purple wig, had little strands dangling loose that tickled her nose distractingly. "I couldn't help myself! He's like... my soul mate... and I *had* to speak to him."

Kiya was tempted to draw her blade, but found the necessary patience to hold back before someone got hurt. "That didn't look like *speaking* to me," she hissed in response, making a point of keeping her eyes forward and her expression stiff.

"Well... we *were*... but we-" Roxy tried grimly, then stopped. "Oh... fuck this! I don't have to explain myself to *you*. I love that guy and I wanted to remember what it felt like to be loved back after all the shit I've gone through this past year or so. I'm not gonna let you ruin that for me just because you had to sit on your own for five fucking minutes."

Kiya rounded on her in a flash. "It was a *lot* longer than that, and you had me worried."

Roxy arched her brow. "You were worried?"

"Yeah... because you have the key to the truck and I need to get a ride home somehow," she said, feeling her explanation was adequate enough. The sight of Roxy's intrigue melting away led her to add, "And I was worried for you too. I thought somebody had led you off somewhere against your will. I was preparing myself for bloody combat!"

"Really?" Roxy asked in amusement. "You'd do that?"

Kiya shrugged. "Like I said, I need a ride home."

"Sure thing." Roxy said, trying hard to hold back a grin.

"Now about my errand..."

Their dangerous looking heels pounded the sidewalk as they went in pursuit of their borrowed truck, parked precariously outside the angry man's house. They both sent out silent prayers that he would still be trapped in an unconscious state of mind when they approached, but unfortunately, he was ready and waiting on the doorstep, yelling abuse like a madman until Kiya drew her sword and told him to back off. He did so without back-chat, and took to glaring at them from the living room window of his home, until they were on the road and out of sight. That was one guy they hoped never to encounter again.

Roxy put her headache inducing music on the tape player and nodded her head along to the beat, tapping her fingernails against the steering wheel. Each 'tap' bit into Kiya, but she resisted the urge to moan. What was wrong with her? She felt so full of anger all the time and if she kept it up, she'd have permanent creases in her face from all the frowning. And nobody liked a frowner.

But maybe it was part of her new identity; not being liked. She didn't feel like she wanted to share a few laughs with people like she used to. But this was probably the depression part of losing her lover. She'd get over it. If she could just have her revenge on Tristian.

When she finally instructed Roxy to pull up alongside a particular house, the teenage girl gave her a suspicious look.

"What are we-?"

"Just keep your head down, okay? I don't want this guy harassing you too. He's sly as fuck," Kiya ordered suddenly. The street was empty, which probably had something to do with the fact they were in a hotspot for drug dealing and fighting in this particular neighbourhood. "Wait here."

She swept along the garden path and banged on the entrance of the small house with a solid, clenched fist. Each bang reverberated through the building and she could just make out the sound of stray cats hissing and slinking away inside. Paint was peeling and chipping away from the door and its handle had succumbed to rust. It almost brought up bile, thinking about the greasy hands that had touched it. Every window-sill was infested with bugs and every window looked grimy. It was hardly a Barbie Dream-House like this guy had once told her it was. She wouldn't want to be seen dead in a dump like this.

Nobody came to answer her persistent bangs, which was rather disappointing. *At least I can do some damage inside*, she thought, bringing a smile back on her lips. With a solid kick, she bust the rotten door through and squeezed inside the gap, dragging her samurai sword through after her.

She paused and smelt the stale air.

"Tristian, you pig," she muttered, examining the stains on the cream carpet, sticking out like a sore thumb, and all the cups and plates left lying around in random places, covered in old food and mould. No wonder the cats had found sanctuary here. His house was a wreck. If she wasn't so afraid she'd catch a disease from it, she would have torn the place down with her bare hands.

Carefully, she made her way up into the bedroom where she found a double bed with some disconcerting red marks over its messy sheets and pillows. At first glance, it looked like spilt wine, but on closer inspection, one could see it was more likely blood. Innocent blood.

On a bedside table sat a small metal cage with a dead pixie lying naked inside. It's blue skin had dulled to grey and its little black eyes were being eaten by tiny maggots. One small hand dangled from between two of the bars, stretching towards an apple core that was rotting away a few inches out of its reach. *Poor thing*, Kiya thought, thinking how rare pixies were in this area. They weren't meant to be house-hold pets. They belonged in woods or by waterfalls, not in the dusty wasteland of Meridion, with its dirty streets and eroding buildings.

"Now then-" Kiya said, tearing her eyes away from the dead creature, "Let's take a good look around."

She didn't know exactly what she was looking for. Receipts maybe, so she could figure out where he did his shopping? A diary would be perfect, so she could surprise him at a rendezvous point and rip his little head off. There had to be something. *Anything*. But this house was blatantly a no-go for him now, so where was the little prick hiding instead?

In the top drawer of his desk, she found a copy of her front door key- dirty from the grubby touch of Tristian's fingertips now.

"Slimy asshole," she mumbled, pocketing it.

As well as the key, she found her missing underwear, which she refused to re-claim because of the cockroaches nesting in them; a pile of poems sickeningly dedicated to her; a picture of her when she was eighteen, stolen from one of her albums in the attic of her house no doubt; a pair of her shoes tucked away in a box in his closet and her grandmother's ring, which she'd cried over *so* many nights, thinking she'd lost it when Rycan and herself had gone for a meal, followed by a jam-packed evening of dancing and drinks.

One of her more disturbing discoveries was a doll perched on Tristian's radiator. It was clearly a female doll that he had given a short hair cut and also, he'd jaggedly cut away the lower part of the dolls red dress to make it into a t-shirt. In black marker, the name Rycan was scrawled onto its front and the finishing touch: pins sticking through its eyes, mouth, nose, ass and groin.

Kiya dropped the doll with shaking fingers. Although the doll did not resemble Rycan in anyway, the letters of his name made her upset.

Eventually, she came to the conclusion that there was nothing of interest in Tristian's dwelling, except for the rather upsetting artefacts linked to her own life. Most of the house had been cleared out, but it seemed odd that Tristian would leave her things behind after going through all the trouble of stealing them. Perhaps he had finally gotten over her? Perhaps the house was empty because the sad bastard had never owned any belongings in the first place? And where the fuck did this guy work for a living? He had no friends she could interrogate really… unless you could call that dead pixie a deceased comrade?

"There's nothing here," she told herself, feeling like she'd wasted an hour of her life. "How the hell am I gonna find that slippery fucker now?"

There was only one thing she could do. Wait for Tristian to come to her.

Chapter 9

Sundown

The old factory was her home now, Kiya realised quite drearily as Roxy followed her inside, shifting the large metal doors and letting the sunlight fall onto a disgruntled, half-asleep Kieran. He showed first signs of life by lifting a hand to his squinting eyes, peering tiredly over at the two girls as they sauntered in, rustling shopping bags. *Women.*

"How'd it go?" he asked both in general. Kiya was standing rather awkwardly nearby, observing Roxy as she slung the bags down on the kitchen counter top and headed towards one of the many doors at the other end of the factory. On passing Kieran, she waved a hand, thinking only of bed before the night's hunt began. Man, she was exhausted.

Kiya caught a glimpse of a small bedroom as Roxy pushed the rickety door open. The light inside was limited, and the size of the room tiny, but it was sufficient enough to hold a bed and two wardrobes- full of clothes no doubt.

"At the rate she buys, I'm going to have to build her a walk-in closet, or perhaps a shed," Kieran commented. He watched Kiya glance around, pretending like she *wanted* to be standing in the middle of the large workshop floor. "Roxy's right," he mumbled casually, "I really do need to buy more sofas for this joint. Guess I can't be the only one with the privilege of lying on his ass all day long, watching television or catching some z's. It ain't fair on the rest of you."

Kiya remained silent.

"Don't just stand there, girl. This is your home now. If you wanna sit down, just say 'Kieran, get the fuck out of that seat,' and I will gladly oblige." He successfully brought a smile to her lips. Score one. "Say, I hope you don't mind sleeping on this couch for a few days- just until Zeke and I can clear out one of our storage rooms for you. I'm gonna have to go into the city and pick up a bed and something to keep your clothes-"

"That's fine," Kiya replied, a little croakily. Why did voices sound broken and shaky when you start using them for the first time in ages? She guessed she was thirsty. "The couch is great, for now."

"Oh- and each month we draw up a food list, then someone heads out to pick it all up, so you'll have to start thinking about what food you want us to grab for you. It's not often we all sit down for a proper meal, to be honest. Most of the guys just eat microwave meals or eat whatever they can throw in a frying pan, though occasionally Siren will rustle up something half-decent for everyone to enjoy. But when I say 'occasionally,' I mean it, so don't go getting your hopes up. We're always too tired, you see. Nobody can be fucked to lift a finger because fighting takes a lot out of you."

"I can imagine it would-"

"I bet you can tell just by looking at the state of this place," he added, indicating the clumps of dust, hair and pigeon feathers on the floor. "Roxy sweeps up every now and again mind you."

Kiya found that hard to believe. What teenage girl, in their right mind, cleaned up after people *willingly*? She knew from her own childhood that she'd tried to make plans to go out everyday with friends so that she wouldn't be around when her mother dragged the vacuum and duster out.

"Do you think you're ready to fight?" Kieran queried, noticing how Kiya kept her samurai sword within reach at all times. She had it across her lap again, perching anxiously on the edge of the sofa.

"I'm ready," she told him coolly.

"We head to the border at six."

"That's fine. But I was wondering… could I have shower, like, now?"

Kieran smiled, "Of course, follow me."

The showers were made of white tile, with shiny silver heads and knobs poking out, but unfortunately, there were no cubicles and *no* separate rooms for different genders. Kieran had mentioned Roxy showering in a bikini because Siren had waltzed in wearing next to nothing one morning and scared the crap out of her, but there was nothing Kiya could do about her nakedness. If she'd known this, she would have picked up a bikini when she'd been at the mall.

Timidly she stripped as Kieran closed the double doors behind her and felt sure he was still standing on the other side, wishing he had an excuse to walk in as she undressed. She could tell he wanted to catch a glimpse of skin by the way he'd dithered through his speech.

"I'll let the others know your down here," he'd said pleasantly, "And if you want, I can stand outside to make extra sure nobody disturbs you?"

"That's quite all right," she assured him, noting the disappointment in his eyes.

"All righty then. Oh- you might want to take that thing off before you shower too-" he reached out and pulled the blonde wig off her head with a solid tug. At last, her scalp could breathe again!

The water wasn't particularly warm, but it got pretty steamy in there never the less. It made her clothes damp and she soon realised, with a pang of fear, that she'd left her bag upstairs out of reach. Sure, the clean towel Kieran had given her was suitable and Roxy's shampoo did the trick, making her hair smell like wild flowers, but she needed a change of underwear and something clean to slip into. Slowly, she wrapped the cream coloured, cotton towel around her dripping wet body and peeked outside.

"Oh!" came a highly surprised cry from Kieran, "I... er... I thought I'd keep watch anyway... you know... for your sake-"

"Shut up a moment," Kiya demanded between his bumbling. He stopped instantly. "I need my bag-"

"Sure. Sure thing. I'll just go get it." His eyes were transfixed on the area where she was clutching the towel to her breasts, turning away only when it became necessary to. He dashed out of the hatch and back down again before Kiya could mutter 'typical' and thanked him kindly as he handed her belongings over.

Kieran was hoping Kiya would let the towel slip a little as she took the bag from him, but she was holding it far too tight to let any skin peek through. She was too smart to let something like that happen in the presence of a blatantly horny bloke.

When five thirty came, Kiya was brimming with eagerness, but tried her hardest not to show it. She wasn't a school kid, waiting for mummy's cookies to finish baking so she could sample their sweet delights. She was a warrior, or soon to be one at least.

She was feeling a lot happier with her hair combed and dried and her face clear of oil and grit. She'd even spent quarter of an hour applying eyeliner, mascara, a thin layer of foundation and a touch of gloss- though it did become annoying every time her hair clung to it. She eventually wiped it away with tissue taken from the magnificently huge bathroom- another non-gender facility that had to accommodate both species- and applied vibrant red lipstick that emphasized her perfect pout. *That should give Kieran something to think about for a bit*, she thought.

Roxy joined her a while later. With tired eyes, she scraped her hair into neat strands with a pink brush and began the long process off tying and plaiting it all to keep it out of her eyes. She then persisted to prepare herself, bringing a large make-up bag into the vicinity and tidying up her face whilst Kiya slipped into clean panties and a fresh outfit in one of the many toilet cubicles.

"I really am sorry about today," Roxy said, her voice echoing off the white tile walls and the big silver mirrors that were lazily wiped clean with a fist only in the centre of each piece of glass.

Kiya was struggling to get one leg into her leather trousers as she replied with, "If it was someone I loved,

I'd probably have done the same. Let's just forget it ever happened."

"Are we definitely cool though?" the teenage girl pressed.

"Of course."

In the remaining half an hour, Roxy gave Kiya an introduction to each weapon the vampire hunters had to offer. She brandished a stake at her and insisted she keep one nearby at all times because staking often came in handy when an individual got into cramped situations.

"You could have hundreds of them pressing in on you and all it takes is a quick stab to the heart and they're dust. Saves you swinging your sword around and tiring yourself out."

"Maybe," Kiya said, thinking that if she were in a life or death situation, she'd find the strength to swing her blade no matter what. She took the stake anyway- noticing that all the slayers had them concealed somewhere.

"I have a spare bow if you wanna try your hand at archery? I tend to hang back and let the guys kick vampire ass. It's less work for me if I just pick them off with arrows from a safe distance." Roxy handed over the spare bow, stroking it caringly and handing Kiya an arrow.

"I think I'll stick with my sword," she objected, putting her hands up.

"Suit yourself."

Each gun was a mystery to Kiya. She didn't care about their uniqueness or their size and capability. The only thing she found of any use to her were the knives, which she selected to fit in her new pouch under her trouser leg. The steel was cool against her flesh at first, and the hairs stood on end where she'd neglected to shave them since Rycan's arrest and execution. It would be time consuming to reach for it when in danger, but she liked knowing it was there if her sword was out of reach.

Kieran brushed past her during Kiya's briefing and offered her a sharpening utensil for her blade. She declined politely, however. Her blade edge was pretty damn sharp. Rycan had made sure of that. It wouldn't need sharpening for quite some time.

"Okay, as soon as you're geared up lets head out. Kiya... you might want to wear this-" Kieran held a shiny black motorcycle helmet out towards her and gave it a little shake with his hand so that the dying sun glinted off the visor. "You're with me."

"Can't I just sit in the truck with those guys?" she asked, feeling as if Kieran had planned to have her clutching onto his back all along.

"It's a three-seater. No room for the new girl I'm afraid. But don't sweat it baby. You'll be safe with me." He winked mischievously and slipped into a leather jacket that made his body look even burlier. *Damn him and his exquisite physique*, Kiya thought testily. It was literally impossible not to gawk at.

He left without a word, pounding the floor in his biker boots and leaving swirls of dust behind him. On one shoulder he balanced his shotgun; on his belt were three wooden stakes and on his hands he wore leather gloves with dangerous, jagged spikes protruding from each knuckle. *That'll crack some heads.*

Kiya felt ready and hesitant both at the same time. She watched Roxy check her arrows before placing them into their container strapped tightly to her back and then noticed the way Siren lit some incense near his weapons of choice and prayed softly to himself in Chinese. Zeke was putting bullets in his hand gun and then rifled through the box of stakes, looking for the sharpest he could find. They were all fixated on their routines and she'd never felt more out of place.

She couldn't take the build in tension anymore and with a swish of her jacket, she left the group in pursuit of her motorcycle buddy, leaving the helmet purposely behind. Nobody stopped her. There were no more words of wisdom. She had her sword, knife and stake. There was nothing else to it.

"Kiya- I was just gonna have a smoke," Kieran said as she approached. He was holding a cigarette between his lips and cupping a hand around a lighter. "You never know when it could be your last in this business."

She stood a few feet away, admiring the Harley Davidson parked next to him. It was a little bit grubby from the desert dust but shiny enough to show Kieran had paid a pretty penny for the thing.

"Beautiful ain't it?" he spoke between drags, blowing smoke up into the air. "Here-" he held the box out towards her.

"Thanks," she smiled, taking one of the 'coffin nails' before realising her mistake. *Smoking when pregnant can damage the baby. Hell, so can fighting vampires you silly bitch.* With Kieran's eyes still on her, she tucked the cigarette down her cleavage quickly. "I'll save it for later... if I survive of course." It was her attempt at a joke, but a weak one at that. Kieran had returned to savouring the taste of his cigarette, trailing his eyes over Kiya's body as he did so.

"Is there something wrong?" she asked, almost annoyed with the audacity of this stunningly handsome, vampire slaying, motorcycle riding man.

"With you baby... not a damn thing." He chuckled as she rolled her eyes then stomped the last of his cigarette out on the floor. "Okay. Hop on. We'll head out now."

"But what about the others-?" she queried.

"They'll follow when they're ready. I need to show you a few things first." He swung a long leg over the bike and started up the engine noisily.

"If one of those things is in your pants-" Kiya whispered in his ear as she jumped on behind him, "I'll rip said thing off,"

"What do you take me for?" Kieran asked light heartedly. "I'm a gentleman. I never kiss on a first date, let alone get out anything in my pants."

Kiya's words of scepticism that followed were lost by the sound of wind in their ears as they tore away from the factory. On the horizon was painted a beautiful pink and blue sunset, that made shimmering heat lines in the distance as the bike spun across the desert road and into the first signs of civilisation. Luckily the rain clouds from earlier in the day had evaporated before any water could lash down on them.

They had to pass through some of the suburban homes of Meridion in order to reach the South Meridion Bridge, which provided access out of the city. Underneath the bridge was a massive dip in the earth, where Meridion's dead were buried in very shallow graves. This was because nobody in Meridion was employed to dig holes in the ground- a loved one to the deceased had to do it themselves out of respect.

The graveyard spread out for miles and miles, encircling a good third of the large city. It was often a dark and miserable place and provided the perfect backdrop for wrong-doers and evil creatures to hide out or meet up. There *were* fences around the perimeter, but only a simple mesh design that could be broken if someone was strong or determined enough. After all, once vampires or werewolves got inside, it was hard to tell them apart from regular humans as long as they played their cards right. Your average demon was much easier to spot because it bore the physical features of your stereo-typical 'Satan' image. Nobody was likely to invite *him* into their homes, were they? But most of Meridion's enemies could blend in well. *Really* well.

With Rycan's execution, Kiya had not been granted permission to dig his grave. The body had probably been robbed of its organs and blood as soon as his head left his body and the remains later burnt at a crematorium. There was no service to help grieving loved ones. His parents had died many years ago, but Kiya would have liked to have said a few words, and perhaps played a song for him. Instead, she had to wait for the delivery of his ashes in nothing but a simple tin can so that she may whisper a few words and dispose of them somewhere special- like the equally burnt shop he once owned or from the top of the Sun Tower where they usually met, just for the sake of its beautiful view perhaps?.

"You okay back there?" Kieran yelled. His long hair was hitting her in the face as she leant into him, burying her head into his back and holding onto his waist with an iron grip. At one point, she thought her Samurai sword was slipping off her shoulder, but she was too scared to reach up and grab it. To her relief, it stayed there the entire journey, though next time she might not be so lucky. She made a mental note to ask Kieran if she could strap it to the back of the bike next time, with his shotgun- if he'd permit it.

"I'm good," Kiya shouted back, feeling her nose sting as the cold wind hit her. The sun finally disappeared out of sight.

Sundown, she thought, *when all the nasties come out to play.*

Chapter 10

Blood and Ash

Kieran squeezed the brake gently as he pulled up beside the South Meridion Bridge toll booth, where a couple inside stood wrapped up in each others' arms behind the glass. The clueless pair were both teenagers; the female's hair blonde, almost pure white in colour and the boy's a faded red with dark brown roots showing through.

"Sean my boy, let me the fuck through. I haven't got all night!" Kieran exclaimed, tapping loudly on the glass with the metal spikes of one gloved hand.

The boy looked dazed for a moment, wiping the remains of his girlfriend's gloss off the corner of his lips, where it was smeared and glistening wetly. The girl was smiling timidly at Kieran; dressed in her leather mini skirt, boots and a low-cut burgundy top. She kept one hand resting on Sean's shoulder as he nodded Kieran through, pushing a red button on his control panel so that the impenetrable metal gates swung open enough for Kieran to fit his bike through.

"Cheers-" Kieran thanked him, though futilely, for the boy was attached to the young girl's lips once again.

"How come he didn't ask any questions?" Kiya queried from the back seat as they took the turning to the left, just before the bridge itself. The image of Sean's uncaring expression was imprinted in her mind.

"He knows me. He knows what we're all about and he likes knowing I'm out here with my crew, stopping the bad guys from forcing their way through. Otherwise he'd have to explain a whole lot of shit to his father- who covers the toll booth in the daytime- if the vampire population got too high behind the city's walls."

They descended a hill slowly for quite sometime before hitting the flat again, where the first gravestones poked out from the ground at jaunty angles. Most people couldn't be bothered to pay for gravestones in this city because they didn't intend on returning to the sight unless *they* were the ones being buried. Meridion's border was prone to stories of hideous murders- which Kiya thought were just as likely to occur within the city, not just surrounding it- so nobody risked visits unless it was completely necessary these days.

It was extremely dark now, except for the lampposts situated at strategic points along the little pathways that led off in all directions, weaving through the resting places of the dead. Kiya decided she preferred the idea of cremation after spending just five minutes in this dank and bleak pit. *How depressing it would be, knowing you'd end up here.*

"How the fuck do you guys spot the enemy in this light?" she asked as Kieran pulled into one of a few small parking areas that could be found all over the graveyard.

"We're used to it. Our eyes have learnt to adjust over time. I wouldn't worry too much about it. As long as your hearing is adequate, the sound of them coming at you is usually what you notice first, before you can pinpoint what you're dealing with."

Kiya's body felt like jelly as she slid off the seat and her ass was unnaturally numb. The ride had been smooth, but still achingly so, which was making it hard for her to prepare for combat. As life gradually returned to her, she stretched her legs elegantly, feeling the muscles strain, then relax. Her arms felt tired, but she relentlessly pulled and twisted them until they were ready for her to swing the Samurai sword without any threat of aching limbs in the morning.

"When you're ready, Angelina Ballerina, I'd like to take you to a nest we cleared out three days ago, just to make sure nobody has returned-"

"What about backup?"

"They'll be here soon enough. You're not afraid are you?"

"If I said I was, would you think any less of me?"

Kieran grinned. "You've every right to be, but I don't think you've anything to worry about. Just chill out and let the night embrace you. Enjoy the wind on your face and the bloodlust in your soul. I know you've got it in there somewhere."

"Wow, Kieran," Kiya mocked after a moment of feigned reflection on his words. "That was almost poetic- for a biker."

"Har-de-har-har," he said coolly, his boots crunching in the gravel. He untied his shotgun from the back of the bike and balanced it in its usual spot, against one broad shoulder. "Shall we?"

Kieran was confident in his step, trudging through the overgrown blades of grass and crushing the weeds beneath his heavy boots. The moon was bright tonight, casting an eerie glow over everything, including Kiya's ice cold face. She kept her eyes on Kieran's ass, being the most prominent part of his body in the mild beams of starlight from above, and tried her best not to stumble through the thick greenery that had been long ago neglected. The graveyard was the greenest part of Meridion, Kiya reflected as she walked. Most of Meridion was made up of wasteland and desert sands. It was almost a nice change, seeing plant life for miles around.

She soon shook thoughts of mother nature from her head as Kieran made a signal with his hand to halt. He pointed silently towards a mausoleum decorated grandly with what looked like angles with silver horns to blow on. The door to the tomb was ajar, with a hint of pure darkness within.

"You first-" Kieran mouthed. "They have no where to run once you're inside."

Kiya gave a curt nod and drew her blade. She inhaled ceremoniously and exhaled seconds before kicking the doors open with her foot, throwing herself inside. She didn't have time to think. There was a dark figure in the corner, hiding behind a pillar, peering out and then hiding away again. Just as Kiya was sure it would strike, another figure came from behind, kicking her in the back of her leg until she buckled and fell forward. With speed, she turned her fall into a forward roll, springing back up until she was situated in the centre of the room, next to the containment area for the dead person the mausoleum belonged to. Silence fell.

One scuffle of a shoe was enough to give Kiya a basic location of her attacker and with a fluid motion, she was driving a sword in the direction of its heart, only to have it deflected by a blade equal in shape and size to her own.

She almost lost her cool at the sound of metal scraping cold hard metal. Sparks lit up the room and she spotted another figure moving behind another of the pillars to her left, but first she had to deal with attacker number one, who was lashing its blade down in violent swoops towards her skull, before she could take on any of her inactive opponents.

Forgetting her blade, Kiya kicked the attacker in the stomach as they just missed her right shoulder with their sword. The creature fell to the floor, but rolled aside in time to avoid Kiya's plunging weapon.

"Shit," she hissed as her sword became wedged between two slabs of stone. She almost lost her head as the creature arced its weapon through the air before her, trying to slice her head off.

She had to leave the sword and seek other means of defence before it was too late. With her heart beating wildly, she grabbed a stake from the inside of her jacket pocket and blindly swung out, hoping to catch the creature that stalked her and injure it enough so that she may finish the job cleanly and professionally.

"Come on asshole," she enticed.

It was at this point she realised something was out of the ordinary. Why wasn't Kieran helping her in all this? She was almost getting slaughtered in here!

Her thinking cost her a blow to her side, feeling the point of someone's boot collide with her hip. *Damn that hurt*. But why didn't they use their sword when they had the chance?

"Okay, time out. Time out!" Kiya screamed. Surprisingly, no more blows followed and suddenly, lights appeared from two points in the room, one held by Zeke, the other by Roxy. On his knees before her was Siren, panting slightly and using his Samurai sword for support.

"Why'd you guys stop? I was enjoying it!" Zeke whined in the direction of his Chinese friend.

"She called a time out," Siren explained indifferently.

"KIERAN!" Kieran blundered forward at the sound of his name, showing great concern. His eyes flickered from Kiya, to Siren, and then back to Kiya, who was approaching him quickly. With one sudden movement, Kiya slapped him hard in his stubble coated face.

"What the fuck are you playing at?"

"Tr...Training," he sputtered, putting a palm to his red-raw cheek.

"You had me fighting someone I'm meant to be working alongside, without fucking telling me. Are you a maniac? I could have killed him-"

"Or him, you." Kieran added, unhelpfully.

Roxy was moving closer, cupping a hand around her flickering candle.

"We needed you to get a feel for the darkness and how to sense the enemy. Siren isn't an enemy, yet you fought him without question. The good thing was that you realised it was a set up. All of us carried on fighting our partners until sun-up during *our* training- when we could finally see who it was terrorising us all night. So you did good, Kiya!"

"Did I do good?" she asked Kieran, coming right up into his face. "Did I play the game well, Kieran? Did you find it fun watching me make a fucking fool of myself?"

"You didn't make a fool of yourself, Kiya. You fought well for a first-timer and you'll find that most vampires aren't as fast as Siren here, so when you really face them bloodsuckers, it'll be over with a lot swifter."

"What makes you think I still want this job?"

"Because I know you enjoyed it just now."

Kiya pretended to be aghast, then bit her lip. He was right, in a way. It was a great way to let off steam, *true*, but she had genuinely thought she might be the one who'd lose her life at the end of it. Nobody likes staring death in the face, even if it is a Chinese man who prays over incense and rustles up great meals for friends when he can be bothered.

"I'm sorry if I harmed you, but I was just following orders." Siren bowed and backed away, joining Roxy.

"Don't take this to heart," Roxy said encouragingly from the sidelines. "We all go through it. Now you're officially ready to slay demons- by our standards anyway."

"I'm not finished with the Chinese guy yet," Kiya said, breaking the ice a little as each member of the group smirked.

"Anytime you want a rematch, I am ready," he offered.

Kieran was looking slightly less relaxed as Roxy left the mausoleum with her two male friends in tow, leaving him behind with Kiya. Zeke put a comforting hand on his best friend's shoulder on passing, but said nothing to boost his morale.

"I don't want to scare you off-" Kieran said calmly, "but life isn't fair Kiya."

"You don't have to tell me that," she retorted with undertones of ice.

"I did what I always do to a new employee so that I can get an idea of your technique and where you need to improve. If you hadn't thought this was real, you might have held back and then I'd have fired you for not being as good as I'd thought you'd be."

"Was I?"

"Were you what?"

"As good as you thought I'd be?"

Kieran suppressed a grin. "Better," he replied simply. "Although you might want to analyse where you're about to stick your sword before you drive it into places you can't get it back out of in a hurry," with that, he pulled her Samurai sword free a lot easier than she'd expected.

"Now let's go find some *real* bad-guys," he suggested enthusiastically, holding her sword out towards her.

"I'm beginning to wonder if there's one standing before me now," Kiya teased, feeling the anger washing away from her as she exited the mausoleum behind him. He chuckled in response to her words.

"You won't think so once you get to know me better."

Strangely enough, Kiya liked the idea of doing so.

"I hope so, for your sake."

If it hadn't been for the clouds of mist escaping the mouths of the Slayers, Kiya would have thought them all dead and frozen from the cold as they crouched behind the wall of another mausoleum, not too far from the one she'd just suffered her first battle in.

Roxy was on the roof of the small building, using binoculars to slowly observe the graveyard for any immediate danger.

"It's been too quiet for too long," Zeke whispered to Kieran, who nodded in agreement. Kiya thought they had meant the evening was going slow, but what the men *really* meant was that they had had very little action- fighting wise- for over a week now. "Something is cooking though. I can smell it."

Kieran chuckled. “Hope it’s a Sunday roast. I’m starving-”

Suddenly, a loud animal noise split through the night air like a police siren. It made Kiya jump and blush with embarrassment, especially when Kieran put a hand on her knee to still her. “Roxy?” he asked, glancing up to the roof where the girl was perched.

“Nothing, boss man. I can’t find the bastards-”

Kiya heard the shrill cry of a bird again, and looked to Kieran for an explanation.

“Big birds don’t roost in these parts,” he said, barely above a whisper. “Have you noticed the animal life in Meridion is limited? It’s because there’s no food or shelter for any of them and the graveyard, being the only place to provide those things, is too eerie even for the birds to be around. They just die here.”

“So that noise-” Kiya asked, “It’s something else?”

“If you mean it’s a vampire communicating with another, then, “yes.”

Siren was shifting uneasily all of a sudden, turning so that his back was pressed against the wall in order to face the way the Slayers had just walked. He had a throwing star in one hand and a stake in the other, while his fabulous blade rested in a double-strap shoulder carrier, so that it lay against his spine- not just over one side of his back like Kiya’s was. It made it a lot easier for him to fight this way.

“Got one-” came Roxy’s gleeful announcement, though in a trained undertone. “I can try and take it out with an arrow, but it might scare the rest off before we get the chance to see who we’re dealing with and how many.”

“Keep an eye on it,” Kieran instructed. “Zeke, get up there with her and scan the rest of the area near the target. It won't be alone. Male or female, Rox?" he asked quickly, whilst Zeke scrambled up the side of the wall, using a crumbling gargoyle for support.

Kiya's hands were freezing and her ears and nose felt as if they were about to fall off. She would have welcomed a hot drink right then, in the darkened ditch she found herself crouched in, amongst hungry spiders and frosted grass-blades. She'd catch a cold and maybe her death if there wasn't some action soon.

"It's one of those half and half types. Extremely short bleached blonde hair, slightly muscular build, snazzy sneakers. Could have tits concealed under that out-of-date jumper or firm 'pecs'. Who knows?"

"Position?"

"Heading in our general direction. Strolling actually, along one of the walkways. It doesn't look too concerned that we're here and it's not like the underground would expect us to have a day off because you'd never let that happen, would you K?"

"Hell no I wouldn't."

"Maybe its- FUCK!" Roxy failed to finish her sentence as something hit her. She crumpled limply, caught just in time by Zeke, before she fell head first off the roof of the mausoleum. A dart, poisoned with a sleeping draught, which vampires were using these days to knock their victims out, protruded from her neck. In order to sample human blood without the relentless screaming that alerted slayers to their presence, poisoned darts were becoming more and more popular in these parts. Roxy was very much inactive now because of it.

"Roxy's been hit. It's an ambush-" Zeke cried, laying her down and using his jacket to support her head.

Kieran swore. "Here they come. Draw your weapons."

"Is it too late to say I'm having second thoughts about vampire slaying?" Kiya asked quizzically. In answer to her question, a shadow to her right darted towards her like a cheetah locked onto its prey and tried to hit her in the face with a clenched fist. Just milliseconds before it could collide with her cheek, Zeke put a bullet between its eyes, spraying blood across her face and knocking it backwards to the floor.

"Stake it!" he screamed, before shooting his pistol in the general direction of their enemies.

Kiya was lost in the glistening silver eyes of her attacker, lying twitching on the ground and leaking blood from a hole in its head. It was a male, young and handsome with jet black hair and a light wash of stubble over its paper white cheeks. From its gaping mouth shone two huge fangs, itching to penetrate someone's throat.

Her hands shook as she stepped over the creature, examining its navy silk shirt and black trousers. In its agony, the vampire could hardly bring itself to respond as she unbuttoned the shirt, revealing its chest, accept for giving off a feeble hiss in her general direction.

This thing was human once, Kiya realised with rising guilt. It probably went to high school and had a girlfriend it cared for. Now it was dribbling scarlet blood from its open mouth and curling up in a frenzy as its brain tried to repair the bullet hole that had sliced its way through its un-dead corpse of a body. There was no fight in it as she lifted the stake high and plunged it down, ripping into its skin and piercing its heart mercilessly.

The explosion of smoke and ash that followed was a startling sight to witness as the creature convulsed and finally disintegrated into nothingness. The thin gold necklace that had laced around the guy's neck fell to the grass, glinting dully in the moonlight as a pathetic reminder that this un-dead *thing* once existed. Kiya was in half a mind to claim it but was brought back instantly to her terrible situation.

There was more than one of these things and she was letting her guard down.

Chapter 11

The Healer

Kieran blasted one blood-sucker in the stomach and marvelled as its guts splattered over the vampire that was flanking him. "Beautiful!" There was no need to stake the big pile of mushy entrails he'd created because there was no *way* it could pull itself together after an injury that huge. With a round house kick to the head, he took down the other creature that was bearing its fangs at him and staked it fast, emerging from the smoke and ash in time to see Kiya stake her first vampire attacker. *Most people miss the heart on their first go*, he mused.

Siren was fighting with smooth and incredibly quick swipes of his sword, forced into combat with a she-bitch-biter with crazy, pink, punk-style hair and a black one-piece outfit that looked dreadful on her bony body. She was trying to slash at Siren with her talons, but ended up losing both hands as he brought the sword across her wrists, spilling blood all over her bright pink trainers.

The shrill cries that escaped the girl's mouth made Kieran shudder. They could be unnaturally loud and ear-drum destroying bastards at times, leaving his head ringing for hours afterwards. "Would you shut that bitch up?" he yelled, moving towards Kiya to start regrouping.

Zeke was still on the mausoleum rooftop, checking Roxy's pulse and lifting her eyelids to examine her pupils. All he could do for now was remove the dart from her neck. She was likely to have a fever before showing any signs of recovery and in order to help the poor girl, they needed to return to the base camp- meaning the comforting solid metal walls of the old factory, where his medical supplies were to be found.

Siren dropped his sword and did a back flip as the she-vampire crouched low and cut her foot across his shins, only to have him avoid her blow at the last second. He'd lost his sword- yes- but he still had his stars, and with a swish of his wrist, he released one in her general direction, cutting the tip of her nose off.

"Would you *please* finish her already?" Kieran begged, whilst reloading his gun and clicking it back into place.

The ash and smoke that followed was the result of Siren throwing three stars at the vampire. Two embedded themselves into her silver eyes. The third hit her in the chest and just managed to pierce her heart.

"*Thank you.*" Kieran sighed.

There was silence at last, broken only by the sound of Zeke jumping off the rooftop with Roxy in his arms. His landing was impressive, but Kiya could see he was suffering pain, running through his feet and legs, after the impact with the earth.

"How many was that?" he asked, clutching Roxy's limp frame to his chest. Her long blonde plait was scraping the floor as her head lolled loosely in his hold.

"I nailed two. Siren hit two and Kiya bagged one."

"Thanks to Zeke," she said modestly and nodded in thanks to him

"I don't know about you guys, but I think we should head back and tell Sean not to let anyone through the gate tonight- not even travellers with official papers. I'll come back for Roxy's bow later. We need to give her a shot before this poison throws her into a fever," Zeke suggested, almost frantic to leave.

"Fine," Kieran said. "Early night guys."

Zeke was already walking away.

"If only Roxy was conscious to hear you say those words," Siren said, to lighten the mood. He retrieved his throwing stars from the small pile of ash then left without another word, pursuing his friend.

Kiya coughed unexpectedly and smiled at Kieran, who was wiping blood from his brow.

"You good?" she asked him.

He laughed. "*I* should be the one asking *you* that question."

"That's not an answer," she replied smartly.

"This is what I do."

"Again," Kiya said, "That's *not* an answer."

"You're right, princess. It isn't."

He said nothing more on the matter and left her standing stupidly for a moment. There was an odd feeling in the pit of her stomach as he did so, for she had sensed a change in his attitude. But why? Perhaps he was worried about Roxy? Or maybe he was disappointed they had to go back so soon?

Kiya shook the thoughts from her head and followed, feeling increasingly tingly. Something was wrong. Her gut was quivering and her heart was jolting in fear.

She stopped in her tracks.

It was as if everything had slowed down as she focused all her energy on listening to the world around her.

"The decoy," she whispered to herself.

Reality hit.

Kiya's legs slid apart into 'the splits' as the 'questionable gender' decoy vampire, first spotted by Roxy, dove for her back. As Kiya dodged the ravenous beast, it automatically tumbled forward and felt the cold, hard burn of steel slice its ugly head off in one fluid motion.

"And the prize for the weirdest looking vampire goes to..." she mumbled.

Kieran came to investigate at the sound of vampire flesh sizzling and expanding into ash and smoke clouds. He ran to Kiya's aid, lifting her from her 'splits' position and patted the dust off her back with a solid slap.

"Are you going to tell me you left that one to me for training purposes?" she inquired with a parched throat. *Fighting was thirsty work.*

"Nope. I genuinely forgot about the decoy. You're lucky she didn't rip your head off before you could turn it."

"Luck has nothing to do with it,"

"Oh I'm sorry," Kieran said, dripping with mild sarcasm, "I must have mistook you for a newcomer in all this. My mistake."

Now it was her turn to use the phrase: "Har de har har."

He grinned at her beautiful face, taking in the arch of her eyebrows and the outline of her lips. She was covered in blood, but still managed to look sexy in that tight little black bodice of hers and her expensive designer jacket. If she weren't in such a delicate mental-state, he'd sweep her off her feet and fuck her right there and then, making sure to keep her naked flesh warm in the cruel bed of dew-kissed grass. There was something about starlight and full moons that made Kieran want to do the romantic thing- set a blanket on the floor and open a bottle of wine; sweet talk and caress her; rip her clothes off and screw her. Okay- he was bullshitting about the romance thing. He just wanted to bury his head between her legs and hope she'd return the favour.

"Shit," he grumbled, feeling the stirring of a hard-on.

"What is it?" Kiya asked, showing concern. His eyes lit up with panic.

"Oh... nothing. I er... forgot it was my mother's birthday yesterday. Need to send a card..." His voice trailed off. If he didn't look at her, he could focus on something else and perhaps tame the beast in his trousers when he got home, locked safely away in his bedroom.

"You think about your mother after slaughtering demons?" she asked incredulously.

"*No-*" he stressed, realising how dumb he was beginning to sound. "Just this once. It had slipped my mind... her birthday that is, not my mother in her entirety."

"*Right*," Kiya said, with a tone that suggested she was thinking him a '*weirdo*.'

"Let's just get out of here."

Cold hard soil was a vampire's least favourite thing to be beneath when it lusted for the blood of humans, but for now it was sufficient for the purposes of their plan. *His* plan. A plan to rise and take anyone and anything he wanted and nobody in Meridion would have the strength to stop him.

Right now, his minions were giving the meddlesome Slayers a run for their money; ambushing them in the graveyard from all angles. He knew his people would fail to harm any of them greatly, for they were his least credible fighters- all adrenaline and no real talent. But killing wasn't on his agenda, strangely enough. He just needed to keep them busy for a few more days. A week at the most.

Lucky for him, his minions would run at a brick wall, or jump off the highest mountain if he asked them too, which made his life easier when he needed something done. The problem was, he needed things done right. That's why he left the mindless killing to everyone else and the tactful luring to himself. As long as the blood flow kept coming and their numbers kept rising, everything would be ready for the final move. War. War on Meridion. The un-dead versus everything else that dared to breathe. And he would own it all when the human race suffered defeat.

"I have returned," came a voice from the mouth of his cave suddenly, loosening soil from the ceiling and bringing it down in small dusty waterfalls.

"Lower your voice!"

The man in the opening cowered. He was an older vampire, compared to the majority of his clan. His hair was grey and his clothes consisted of a horrid looking knitted cream and brown jumper, with faded blue denim jeans. This guy was pretty useless in most departments, but was a damn good shot with the dart gun he'd designed.

"Report?"

"Our people were wiped out."

He shrugged nonchalantly. "That was to be expected."

"I hit one of them with a dart, but couldn't reach the rest. They were moving too fast-"

"Which one?" he demanded.

"A girl-"

With an explosion of anger, he punched the old vampire in the face, whipping the guys head back so far it almost snapped at the neck.

"I told you to leave the female Slayers alone you fucking imbecile!"

The old vampire sniffed and grumbled in pain, pouring blood from his brittle, broken nose. He was tempted to argue, but didn't feel like losing his head completely.

"I specifically asked you to hit the males with the dart. I want the females alive and well."

"Sorry, sir."

"You'd better fucking be. Now give me the dart gun and get out of my sight."

The old vampire dropped the weapon into his palm begrudgingly and left, trying not to hurry too much to reveal how frightened he was. And he had every right to be too, for the vampire behind him lifted the gun and shot a dart at the departing vampire's head.

"Don't fail me again or it'll be a silver stake next time."

"I broke a nail out there," Kiya complained as she hopped onto the seat with Kieran, wrapping her arms around his waist without putting too much thought into it. She was feeling far too cold to care about what *he* was thinking and welcomed the warmth of his back

"You may end up breaking a lot more than that in future," he told her, kicking the motorcycle into life with his heavy boot.

Zeke, Siren and an unconscious Roxy had already left, for their vehicle was in a separate parking lot- something Kieran had asked for, for the purposes of Kiya's test in the mausoleum.

Sean wasn't too happy that the Slayers were finishing early for the night, as Kieran explained through the voice box at the side of the gate what had happened. He was threatening to leave the pair of them out there all evening and mumbled something about 'slackers' even though at the time, he was enjoying caresses from his girlfriend who had been sliding her hand down his trousers.

"You suck, you know that?" he grumbled to the biker, clicking the red button to open the gates.

There was no talk on the way home, mainly because the wind made it challenging to hear one another's words. Kiya felt happy- almost jubilant. She'd proven herself worthy of the vampire slaying team and was sinfully proud of herself for slaughtering the decoy when it finally caught up with them. The first time she'd staked one of them, she'd felt sorry for the thing. She had to keep telling herself: *This is not a human life you're taking. There's no human left. It's just a shell. A soulless shell that harms innocents.* After that, it became easier. One could even say 'fun.'

Unfortunately, the merriment wore off when they parked up and found Zeke and Siren hunched over Roxy on Kieran's couch with worried expressions. Roxy's skin was the same mottled white and grey as the moon and her veins were looking darker and more emphasized.

"You're positive she's breathing, right?" Kieran asked, and in response, Zeke held a small mirror to Roxy's parted lips. It misted instantly. "Fair enough."

Kiya watched Kieran's face as he touched Roxy's cheek with the backs of his fingers, gently stroking her skin. He looked lost for a moment, contemplating her well being and wishing the warmth from his hand were enough to stir her back into life. Siren disappeared and returned again with a soft pink blanket, which he'd taken from Roxy's bedroom. Dropping it over her lightly, she looked at peace.

"When do you think it'll wear off?"

"Could take anything up to twenty four hours," Zeke informed him. "I've given her one of my medicine shots-"

"Which would be?" Kieran urged him on with a pressing glare.

"Just something I created to give you a kick. It's not an outlawed drug if that's what your getting at. It's compiled of caffeine pills mostly."

"I don't think you should be trying to counteract that shit they put in her," Kiya perked up, drawing all eyes on her. "It's probably as bad as mixing drinks. If she's in no immediate danger- as in, knocking on Death's door- then you should have just let her sleep it off."

"And when the fuck did you become a doctor?" Zeke spat.

"Lay off her would you?" Kieran snapped. "We've got our youngest recruit injured and your trying to start a fight. Make yourself useful and put the kettle on."

Zeke looked at Kiya. She scoffed. "I didn't think dogs-body and housekeeper was in the job description."

"Neither did I," Zeke moaned, leaving the group with a sigh.

Quiet reflection time followed, in which Siren left the group to have a shower, leaving Zeke to slam cups around in the kitchen area and Kieran and Kiya to watch over Roxy.

Kiya was absentmindedly giving her cuts and grazes a once-over, when an idea sparked in her head. How could she forget the 'Healers' blood she had in her veins? Her grandmother had been a Healer; using magic to close wounds and cure sickness, but her mother had been very much against it. When she would spend Sunday's at her Gran's house, they'd sit and practice the ancient art of 'Healing Kisses' on whatever they could find- mice, cats, Grandfather etc. Kiya became pretty good at it, but not half as good as her Grandmother, who could fuse broken bones together without working up a sweat.

The question was, would a Healing Kiss work on poison? There had never been an incident in Kiya's life when her Grandmother had needed to rid something of a sleeping draught...

"Let me get to her for a moment," she said, giving Kieran's shoulder a slight nudge. She pulled the blanket down to reveal Roxy's neck and examined the red area where the dart had penetrated her skin. "I think I can help her." Before Kieran could inquire into her actions, she leant forward and kissed the wound, drawing on the ancient magic in her blood to drain the poison from Roxy's veins.

"You turning lesbian on her or somethin'- because I don't think Roxy swings that way-" Kieran stopped talking as she slugged him hard in the stomach, still keeping her lips to Roxy's skin. She could taste the poison, feel its powerfully drowsy effect. It took about five minutes, giving off a warm yellow glow as the wound finally healed over. Kieran was in awe when he saw Roxy's eyes shoot open in fear. Even more disturbing was the price

Kiya paid to help the girl, for as she moved away, a thick black fluid- like tar- dripped disgusting from her mouth.

"I'm okay," she tried to reassure him as more of the gunk poured from her parted lips.

"What the hell is *that* shit?" Roxy gasped, bolting upright and staring open-mouthed at her new friend.

As the last of the liquid fell to the floor in disturbingly loud 'plops,' Kiya wiped her mouth with the arm of her jacket. It tasted like bile had coated her throat and mouth, but she continued to wave Kieran off her, claiming she was fine in incoherent moans.

The tar-like substance was a consequence of getting bad things out of someone else's system. It couldn't just be annihilated. Instead, it took another form and could often exit the 'healer' instead of the 'healed.' These consequences to healing were the reason why nobody practised the magic anymore. Who wanted to suffer pain or discomfort for the purposes of someone else? Only those who really cared enough, she believed.

"Are you *sure* you're okay?"

"Water-" she said simply.

"I'm on it." Kieran ran over to Zeke, who had poured hot water all over the countertop as he'd watched the mess fall out of Kiya's mouth in bewilderment. Only when he'd scorched his leg did he realise what he was doing and noticed with fury that he had to fill the kettle again.

Kiya snatched the water out of Kieran's hand when he returned and swallowed as much as she could before she choked. She could still taste the poison in her mouth- thick and vile.

"If that hadn't resulted in the ultimate grossness- I would have found that kiss you gave Rox' a real turn on."

"Shut up Kier."' Roxy hit him in the stomach.

"Hey, what's with all the hitting tonight? I'm merely sharing my sexual desires with the two of you."

"Yeah- well now isn't the time." Roxy shifted and patted the sofa cushion, urging Kiya to join her. She was still trapped in a state of confusion and numbness, after waking up to the strangest sight she had ever seen. Her eyes still felt droopy and her brain a little fuzzy, but she was awake enough to stay that way for another few hours.

"If you want, I can try and perform a Healing Kiss on you-" Kieran offered with a playful grin. "I'm not very good with magic, but it might take your mind off things. Hell, you may even like it-"

Roxy hit him again for Kiya's sake.

"Okay! Okay! I'll be in my bunk. If you need anything, get Zeke to do it."

Zeke protested from the kitchen, holding up Kieran's cup of tea and swearing loudly as his friend waved it away. *What an asshole*, Zeke moaned inwardly.

Chapter 12

Aching

Zeke had kindly tended to Kiya after the horrific mess that had been the result of her breathing life back into Roxy, which proved he did have a soft spot for Kieran's new 'favourite' on the premises. He'd thrown Kieran's tea down the sink and made a cup of hot chocolate instead, offering it to Kiya with an apprehensive smile. He then fetched his medical supplies, found some headache tablets for the both of them and used a clean cloth- dampened with tap water- to wipe the remaining black stains from Kiya's pale skin.

"So you're a Healer, huh?" he asked lamely, searching for the right kind of small talk.

Roxy had left the room to lie down in her bedroom, feeling too hazy to sit and talk. She couldn't thank Kiya enough for neutralising the poison, telling her how she had thought herself as good as dead when the dart had hit her. *I can't die yet*, she'd thought. *I have unfinished business with Logan*. Just by mentally mentioning his name it had her squirming with excitement in the bed.

Kiya felt like a child with chocolate smeared around its mouth as Zeke cleaned her face, wiping most of her make-up off with it. "I'm not a Healer. Well I *am*. It was my Grandmother... she taught me the basics. I can do enough, you know?"

Zeke nodded. "I always wanted to be a doctor when I was young, but couldn't raise enough money for the schooling."

"That's a shame," Kiya said, wondering how a guy interested in doctoring ended up as a vampire hunter. She hadn't expected Zeke to start sharing memories with her all of a sudden.

"I did manage to go to high school, like all the other adolescents in Meridion are forced to," he informed her casually. "They were the best days of my life too. Kieran was my best mate even then-"

"You knew Kieran from school?" she interrupted.

"Yup. And we went *everywhere* together. People thought we were brothers! I wrote his essays and he hooked me up with chicks in return."

"That sounds kind of unfair."

Zeke shook his head. "Not really. I was an ugly kid."

Kiya blushed at the man's brutal honesty. "I see." She took a nervous sip of her hot chocolate. It was warm and creamy, but most importantly, it masked the horrid taste of the black tar-like substance that still coated her throat. *Delicious.*

"I won't show my nostalgia by reiterating all of my crappy past, but I'll tell you one thing. It takes a lot for me to trust women."

Kiya frowned. "Why are you telling me this?"

Zeke was frowning too. "I was engaged once. Fell in love. Wanted a family. Went down on one knee to someone I thought was destined to be my wife. But on my wedding day, she left me standing there with Kieran-who was naturally my best man- at the front of the church, watching the slow, daunting hours slip us by.

"The guests eventually took what food they could and left when it became obvious the bride wasn't going to show. Some bastard from *her* side of the family even stole the top half of our fucking wedding cake!

"It turns out, she'd packed her bags and run off with a 'door to door' salesman, who she'd stumbled upon one day as he visited our home selling bath plugs. The day they met, she took him straight upstairs and fucked him in *my* double bed- at least that's what her goodbye note said. That bitch even pawned the engagement ring I'd bought her, to pay for the fuel in the bloody getaway car."

Kiya was silent. She could see Zeke's face getting blotchy with anger as all the memories came rushing back. She wanted to make him stop. She wanted to clamp a hand over his mouth and overpower his words with her own screaming. But instead, she let him ramble on- to make worse a heart that had broken long ago, without knowing how to prevent it from happening.

"I didn't see her again after that. She thought it would be funny to send a postcard from the Island of Liantia one time, but that was it really. So as you can imagine Kiya, I don't like your species very much."

"We're not all alike," she argued, in her own defence and the defence of all woman-kind. This asshole barely knew her! Who did he think he was telling her this?

"Whatever," he said crisply. "I can pretend to be like Kieran; chatting up the ladies as if I care about them; take a couple out for drinks then take one home to do the dirty with. I can be a smooth talker if I try hard enough and I can be all nicey-nice to a lady when there's something in it for me, but I swore the day my wife-to-be left me that I wouldn't let another woman fuck me around *ever* again."

"What makes you think *I* will? We've only just met for crying out loud!" Kiya questioned in confusion, wondering what the hell she'd done to deserve all this. She hadn't given this guy any hint of being sexually attracted to him, yet he seemed to be warning her away. What was his problem?

Zeke finally took a deep breath and sighed. "You won't mess me around, I know. You probably think I'm crazy, talking like this to you and of course, you're probably right. It's just when I first laid eyes on you, you reminded me so much of *her*. I've wanted to say my piece *so badly* since then."

"Hope you feel better now," Kiya snapped sarcastically, snatching the cloth out of Zeke's limp hand to wipe her face completely clean of her make-up, without any help from *him*. "I didn't find that speech of yours the least bit enlightening. In fact, you've made me develop a great dislike for you."

Zeke looked taken aback then allowed his face to melt into solemnity. "I imagine it would have," he said weakly. "I'm sorry if I made you feel uncomfortable."

"You made me feel *more* than uncomfortable."

He was on his feet now, backing away gradually with his hands up. "I don't know what came over me. Once I start talking about *her* I can get kind of-"

"Nasty?" Kiya offered, refusing to feel intimidated.

"I guess. Yes." He was looking slightly ashamed of himself.

"Just because my face bears similar features to some bitch you slept with doesn't mean you can take your crappy life experiences out on me."

Anger sparked back up in Zeke's eyes, but he said nothing.

"Okay!" came a loud voice from behind them. Kieran reared his handsome head from the darkness that dwelled in the entrance to the hatch, clapping his hands together to alert them both to his presence. "I think someone here is over-tired. Zeke-Man, get an early night." Zeke opened his mouth to protest. Kieran raised a hand as he strutted over in nothing but a towel wrapped tightly around his waist. "Please, Zeke. You're not doing yourself any favours right now. Don't make me regret taking you under my wing. Just remember it was me who helped you get through Michelle's disappearance and I don't want to find out you've opened that ugly box again."

"Forgive me." Zeke said guiltily. "I'll be in my bunk."

As he left, Kiya rounded on Kieran.

"I didn't hear you leave your room to have a shower."

Kieran winked at her. "That's because I crept over to the hatch and decided to sit in the dark for a while- listening to you guys talking."

"If it had been a particularly private conversation, I would have been angry about what you just said, but as it is, I'm glad you were there to get rid of him."

Kieran was shaking his head now. "Zeke is strange."

"That's kind of a weird statement-" she replied.

"It's as simple as," he continued. "He's always been strange. The guy has mood swings like my mother did when I was sixteen years old! But I don't blame him for being that way. He did suffer, you know?"

"Hell- haven't we all?" she ventured.

There was silence for a while. Then Kieran slapped a strong hand down on Kiya's knee.

"Don't suppose you want to shower with me, do you? Maybe check out my bed after?"

"Oh, yes please, Kieran. Take me now!" she feigned desperation, deciding to play along with the flirting game. "I want to see what you look like under that towel! I want to brush my soft skin against your rock-hard abs! I want to feel you warm and hard inside me!"

"Okay! Okay! No need to be like that. I get the picture, Princess."

"Oh yes, yes! I'm the Princess to you, my Prince! Don't leave a poor damsel lying on your crappy sofa, completely gagging for it!" she exclaimed as he got up. Playfully, she tugged on Kieran's arm.

"Stop it," he moaned. "Your making me-"

"Ache?" she queried with a devilishly naughty grin. She could see Kieran was hard under his towel. "Come on, you know you want it."

Kieran was looking baffled, but greatly tempted by her false offers of sex. His arm was tingling where she was holding it and another part of his body was screaming for him to take her in his arms.

"Let go, Kiya"' he mumbled, half heartedly pulling his arm free.

"But you want me!" she pleaded.

Kieran couldn't take it anymore. He grabbed her by the shoulders and roughly kissed her mouth, feeling her tug free almost as soon as he'd managed to brush her lips.

"What are you doing?" she cried in astonishment, jumping to her feet so that the sofa separated them both.

Kieran scratched his head uneasily. "Shutting you up, is all."

Kiya was too shocked to speak. She only had herself to blame for what had just happened. She should have known it wasn't wise to tease Kieran like that. He was 'all man' and heartless- meaning, brainless sex was all you'd get.

"I, er-" Kieran couldn't bring himself to finish his sentence and instead left. He felt silly more than anything. Instead of being a gentleman, he had acted the fool. But what had she expected him to do, throwing herself at him like that?- even if it was all in the name of fun. He felt like a grade 'A' loser. A grade 'A' loser with a hard-on that wouldn't go away. He'd just have to deal with it in the showers, if he ever got there.

Kiya snapped out of her stunned state as soon as he vanished beneath the hatch. She didn't know what had come over her. Her emotions were all over the place and her behaviour unacceptable. She felt she had to ask herself: *Do I really want Kieran?* And as she did so, an angry fire burned inside her stomach. *My boyfriend died two days ago and I'm giving a guy I just met false hopes in nailing me in the bedroom. Jeez Louise, I need therapy.*

There was nobody on the factory floor, apart from herself, and all was silent in the building. The night was still coating the world in its thick shadowy blanket and all the bad guys out there were probably wondering where the hell the Slayers had gotten too.

She had no Rycan to bring her supper in bed and to snuggle up to as they watched a late night movie together. She had no Rycan to make love to her in the early hours of the morning- whispering the words 'I love you' into her ear. And she had no Rycan to kiss tenderly on the lips as the sun rose in the morning, pouring bright rays through the window and onto the bed where they lay in each others arms.

All these thoughts made Kiya's eyes well up and she threw the mug in a rage, where it rolled and clanked against the metal doors at the other end of the factory, splattering lukewarm hot chocolate over the dusty floor.

Nobody came to inspect what had happened. They were all either asleep or preparing to do so. Or at least that's what she assumed, with the exception of Kieran, who was still washing away the nights dirt and sweat in the shower room.

Suddenly, Kiya's stomach rumbled so loudly, she thought the earth would split open and spew little Hell-spawn onto the premises. She needed to eat *really* badly.

Cooking took her mind off things. She fried eggs and bacon, made toast and drank from a large carton of orange juice until there was nothing left. Even when she'd consumed every last crumb of her meal, she felt as if she could eat more. With wandering hands, she browsed through the cupboard, checking tins and reading labels on everything she could find. Eventually she settled for a very *large* bowl of cereals, enjoying the cold and creamy taste of milk in her mouth and the pleasant crunch of the food itself.

It came as a huge surprise when Zeke walked across the room all of a sudden.

"I can't sleep. Tell anyone that asks that I'm out," he said calmly, without looking directly at her. He was pulling a faded denim jacket over his skinny arms and was walking with his shoelaces untied on one boot.

Kiya didn't ask questions. She didn't care where he was going or what he was planning on doing, as long as she wasn't involved, that was fine by her. He could go find a drunk at some bar and rant and rave to him if he really needed someone to whine to, but she hoped he didn't find a woman, because he didn't deserve to get laid with an attitude like that. Not tonight at least.

When he reached the doors, he gave the broken mug a quick glance, then slammed them shut behind him, making the room shake noisily.

I wonder what Kieran will think of this, she thought.

Zeke didn't take Siren's truck because he *really* wanted to get wasted. He wanted to drink all that he could in the remaining hours of the evening, for as long as the pub landlord kept his bar open, which in these troubled times meant an all-night lockdown if he was lucky.

He wasn't one for drink driving, but he sure as hell regretted leaving the factory without a vehicle as he plodded along the road towards civilisation.

The trek into the city took him an hour and a quarter, giving him ample thinking time. He thought about Michelle and how she'd played him for a fool their entire two years of being together. He'd wanted to have children with her and live happily ever after, as one can only hope when two people 'tie the knot.' He'd been rather lucky in life until his wedding day. Since then, it had been all blood and guts; slaying demons and growing wearier by the second. There was no drive in him to settle down like there had been once. All he had was Kieran, his best mate, to confide in and a few bearable Slayers, who were too busy being concerned about their own crappy existence to care about his. Not that he blamed them for it. It wasn't like he wanted to be the centre of the universe.

'The Pixie's Wing's Bar' was the first place Zeke approached, but found it was already closed, with its regulars trapped inside. He tried tapping on the door, but an angry voice told him to "Take off" when the bar-owner couldn't take the noise anymore.

The city lights illuminated each step Zeke took on the dusty sidewalk, feeling the wind pick up all around him as he went. There were a few homeless people in the doorways of silent shops that were weakly pleading for spare change as he past them, but he ignored their cries and kept on walking towards the flashing red lights of 'The Blood Moon Inn.'

He inhaled in expectation, placing a numb hand on the bronze door handle and giving it a push, feeling relief wash over him as the door squeaked open.

Inside there appeared to be a snooker tournament going on in the main area of the floor, housing about ten rowdy men in leathers and an equal amount of hookers, all dressed in skimpy clothes, their tits on display under mesh tops or see-through bras. All of the ladies looked worn around the eyes and not *one* of them seemed to don their natural hair colour; Zeke could see dark roots growing through on the tops of their heads.

As he stood in the door way, admiring the flesh on display before him, he felt a hand touch his shoulder.

"Take your eyes off my women," said a huge, bear-like *beast* of a man, with a bold head, leather jacket and jeans. He had beady, dark eyes and an earring dangling from one lobe, sporting a miniature silver dagger.

"Forgive me," Zeke apologised, backing away.

Sat around the bar were a few lonely souls and a man and woman, with their heads bent low in conversation.

"What'll it be?" asked the barman, who was typically wiping out a glass with a dirty dishcloth.

"Surprise me," Zeke said miserably, slipping onto one of the high stools next to the only female with a dress sense in the joint. She wore tight black jeans, strappy-heals, a Chinese style, silk, blood red top with golden dragons stitched all over it and her blonde hair up in a bun, with chopsticks sticking through it in an X shape.

If she hadn't been talking to another man, Zeke would have tried his luck with her. There were plenty of alleys nearby he could take her too if she was up for some fun…

"…says it'll be ready soon," she was saying, as Zeke focused on her soft, melodic voice. "We're growing in numbers everyday and they'll be plenty of us to over-power *you know who.*"

"I don't give a flying fuck about how many of you there are or what your plan is. I want payment! I'll keep giving him what he needs, but I'm growing impatient-"

"Calm down, Worm," she said, cutting him off. "You'll get it. But these things take time."

"Yeah, and time is blood," the man replied with a sigh.

Zeke's drink came in a frosted glass, cool to the touch and full of bitter tasting heaven. He made a point of leaning forward to pay the barman, only to cut his glare to the right so that he could catch a glimpse of the male who was speaking to the sexy blonde. He was a weedy looking man, with limp, greasy black locks of hair and very oily, pallid skin. His clothes didn't look like they belonged to him either, for his shirt was loose and tatty and the trousers unstylish and baggy.

"Speaking of which…," the lady said wryly, "I'm feeling rather peckish."

"Aren't you *always* hungry, considering the nature of your species?"

Zeke was confused. Did the skinny guy mean women, or something else entirely?

"I'm only here because I'm the strongest of my kind. I drink from the weak and turn those I think 'worthy' into a new recruit. There aren't many others who have the privilege of changing enemies into allies-"

"I think you should quieten down, Annara," the pale bloke whispered. But it was too late. Zeke could just about decipher 'vampire talk' when he heard it, and this chick was definitely a bloodsucker, loose in the city. He couldn't tell if the male was, however. He was pale- yes- as if he could do with some blood to colour his cheeks, but he didn't hold himself like a vampire. He looked weak and washed out, with shifty eyes that darted all around the room in a nervous manner. This guy was human, working alongside the bad guys, which made him just as bad as the un-dead in Zeke's opinion.

Calmly, Zeke downed the last of his drink and watched the blonde leave, wiggling her ass around to catch the eyes of every man looking her way. On passing Zeke's stool, she blew him a kiss, revealing shiny, sharp fangs. Yup, she was definitely one of them.

Shit, Zeke thought, *why did this have to happen to me tonight? Kieran always goes to bar's with nothing to report. This is just my luck!* There was nothing for it. He'd have to find that bitch and stake her before she could do any damage. "Here goes nothing."

Chapter 13

The Feeder and the Slain

The pale man didn't follow the 'Annara' girl he had been speaking too. Instead he drooped his head low with a sigh and sipped at his drink lazily. Zeke watched him for a further few minutes. When the guy lifted his arm up to scratch his flaking, greasy scalp, the sleeve of his baggy shirt fell down, revealing bite marks all over his skin.

A 'Feeder,' Zeke realised- someone who gives vampire's their blood for usually just one of two reasons. Reason one: they worshipped bloodsuckers and hoped that one day they would be turned into one too. And reason two: vampires may find a human valuable in some way and offer him something in return for his services. There was no guessing which reason this guy was giving his blood. Loneliness maybe? It's not every day an ugly thing like that could sit and chat to an absolute *goddess* of a girl, like Annara.

Being relatively sure the guy wouldn't intervene, Zeke feigned a tired stretch and pushed his empty glass forward.

"You leaving already?" the Barman asked, lifting his head and stroking his thick brown moustache with a free hand.

Zeke nodded. "I only came for a quick one. Got work to do-" he lied.

The stool scraped against the dull grey concrete floor noisily, turning the heads of a few hookers. They were probably making sure one of their customers wasn't making a dash for it, because that meant one or more of the girls wouldn't be getting paid. They didn't bat an eyelid when they realised it wasn't one of their bikers, who many were gyrating against already.

The night air hit Zeke in the face like a block of ice. He shivered through and through, wishing he had more fat on his bones, and drew his denim jacket in closer around his neck. All the streetlamps were fizzling on and off due to faulty wiring in the district and the street itself had gained a few stray cats since Zeke had last walked along it.

He didn't know where to start with Annara. She could have taken off in any direction and if he picked the wrong one, many people would die that night. It was a matter of fate. Would he chose the right direction or not? If he did, he might save a few people but, if he didn't...

Zeke deduced that a vampire needed to get back to its home before sun-up; otherwise they'd be toast and the only dark pit that they tended to dwell in was beyond the wasteland, and into the graveyard almost two hours walk away. With that in mind, he headed back the way he had come, in the direction of his own home.

It was just by luck his eyes registered a missing homeless man. The guy who had pleaded for change was absent from his doorway, leaving behind a blanket, rucksack and newspaper. He knew from witnessing something like it before, that the homeless didn't leave their belongings behind, even if they were going for a piss. They'd just unzip and do their business a metre away from where they were housed, regardless of who could see.

The wind blew hard, lifting the newspaper off the ground and scattering its pages across the street as Zeke located the nearest alley. If they weren't both down there, then by God he didn't have a *clue* where else that bitch was feeding.

As he approached, a black cat escaped from the shadows in alarm, almost slipping on a frozen puddle in its haste to leave. There was nothing but the sound of water dripping from a broken pipe onto a large metal dumpster.

"Homeless guy...?" Zeke murmured. "I have some change for you now."

Suddenly, something flew at him, knocking Zeke to the ground. It was the homeless man, stiff and very much dead, with his eyes rolled up in his head and a chunk of skin ripped off his neck, still oozing the last drops of blood Annara hadn't had the time to finish.

She laughed joyfully as Zeke pushed the dead man off him, performing a neat flip to an upright position and pulling a stake from his inside pocket.

"Why are you running?" he yelled breathlessly, as she scampered around him. "I thought vampires loved to take on guys like me. I don't mind having a bash at fighting. Get back here you piece of shit!"

Annara kept running, but turned to hiss like a feline at his remark. She was fast, but not fast enough in those heals. She tried to increase her stride and speed, but the added pressure caused a heal to snap and she hit the ground as a result, tearing the knee of her trousers to reveal pale skin underneath.

Zeke was on her in a second. As she scrambled to her feet, he kicked her hard in the face. The second time he did so, she was ready to catch his foot, twisting it until he lost his balance and hit the ground.

She tried to turn and run again, but Zeke's hands reached out and gripped her ankle just in time, dragging her to the floor with him.

"Get off me!" she bellowed as he climbed on top of her, raising the stake above his head in preparation for the penetration of her heart. She hissed hysterically at the sight of the wooden object and as a desperate reaction, grabbed one of her Chinese chopsticks from her hair, driving it into Zeke's shoulder.

"FUCK!" he yelped, dropping the stake accidentally. He couldn't believe how much pain he was in, especially when he removed the hair accessory from his torn flesh. Blood dribbled down his chest, soaking through his shirt.

Annara wiggled out from underneath him and stood over Zeke, watching the pitiful human clamp a hand over his wound. She'd suffered worse than that and healed in a mere minute- ready to take on the world again. That's why she thought humans were most definitely the weaker species and were not designed to survive this century. Vampires were evolution! They could live forever and heal at an extraordinary rate. They could have sex without getting impregnated and their strength and agility was incredible. She didn't give a fuck about losing her soul the day she was 'turned.' She didn't need it- all those feelings of guilt and sorrow. Admittedly, the sunlight thing was a problem, but if most people conformed to the vampire way of life, it would just be the opposite to the human schedule of working all day and sleeping all night. People would be able to see the earth in its dying days if they never grew old! Now wouldn't that be a sight?

"Annara likes this one," she said, kneeling down in front of Zeke and lifting his chin with one hand. Zeke wondered why she was speaking this way, until he saw the shadow of a skinny, frail looking creature approaching.

"Just eat him and get out of here," the man said angrily.

"My motto is to *always* play with your food. It makes the drinking of blood so much more *satisfying*."

"You never played with me."

Zeke heard Annara growl in the back of her throat. "That's because you disgust me, Worm."

Suddenly, the man came over and slapped Annara in the face. She looked away for a moment, then turned back with a grin. "You should watch yourself, Tristian because the next time I drink from you, I may just finish you off."

The man scowled, looking more worried than he was letting on, then left the pair of them to their business, disappearing into the night.

"Where was I?"

Zeke tried to get up, but was forced down again by Annara's powerful grip as she licked one fang hungrily.

"You're lucky I just ate because I would have drunk from your fucking brain stem by now."

"Lucky me," Zeke wheezed. He looked at the wooden stake and felt his luck leave him as Annara threw it away with her free hand.

"Naughty naughty," she whispered, wagging a finger in his face.

Zeke spat at her and felt the energy he needed to crash his forehead into hers, throwing her to the concrete in pain. He ran for his life, towards the fallen stake, but screamed in agony instead as another of the Chinese-chopsticks drove its way into his lower back, between two ribs.

"You bitch! You fucking bitch!" he cried as she ruthlessly twisted the stick around inside him.

"Ooh you're a tough guy aren't you, thinking you can defeat me?" She pulled the stick out and turned Zeke around to face her, pushing him against the wall of a derelict shop. He spluttered and coughed then screamed again as she pushed the chopstick into his right thigh.

"Now lay down like a good boy and let me tend to your wounds," she whispered menacingly in his ear, allowing Zeke to slide to the floor. She giggled at the fun of it all. With her talons, she ripped the jacket off Zeke's body and found the hole in his shoulder. Her eyes lit up and slowly, she began to lick the wound with her long pink tongue, sucking the blood out like a baby drinking milk from its mother's breast.

"Delicious," she said happily, with red smears all around her mouth. "If I didn't know any better, I'd say you were one of those self-righteous Slayers that always meddle in our glorious uprising!"

Zeke wanted to hit Annara, but couldn't lift his fists. His arms felt like a pile of bricks, heavy and lifeless at his sides. His head was all fuzzy and he could feel an eternal tiredness washing through him. How could he have fallen? How could he have let her win? He realised then that the reason why he'd never fallen before was because he always had Kieran to watch his back. He wasn't cut out to be a *lone* Slayer, just a fucking side-kick.

"Please-" he groaned, feeling blood in the back of his throat.

"Don't beg," Annara scolded him suddenly. "I know some vampires relish in it, but *I don't*! I want to drink from men of honour- unless I'm starving, in which case anything will do. Have some dignity man. Suck it in!" Her eyes flashed silver- the colour all vampires eyes turned when they were hungry or angry.

"You were right by the way." Zeke spoke with great effort. "I am a Vampire Slayer. Not a chosen one, but a man who enjoys seeing your kind explode."

Annara hissed at him, scraping her fangs against his neck, then drew back, smiling broadly. With jagged movements, she bent her head to inhale Zeke's scent.

"I thought I could smell death on you-" she snarled, referring to the previous nights battle in the graveyard. "Do you work alone?"

"The hell I do," Zeke said, trying to lift his arms again. "I have friends and they'll slaughter you when they find out what you've done."

She was listening intently, the dead brain cells in her head fizzing with activity. "There's something I can do about that-" She lifted her own wrist to her mouth and bit down hard, pooling blood from the fang marks she left behind in her pale skin. "I'm going to give you a gift. A gift of eternity, because you have potential in your veins. I can taste it."

"Get away from me, hag!" Zeke shouted, finally managing to move his arm enough to slap her hand away. But she only laughed at his resistance.

"So feisty! I like it," she cackled. "But I'm afraid this isn't something you can object too." Annara gave Zeke a wink, then licked the blood off of her skin. With tiger-like strength she grabbed him by the back of the neck and forced his mouth to hers, entangling him in a kiss that combined their saliva, as well as the vampire blood. Zeke tried to rip his head back. He tried keeping his mouth closed tight, but she wrenched his jaw open with one hand, wiping her bleeding wrist across his lips while whispering excitedly, "Drink up, Slayer. Taste the power. Feel your soul leaving your body..."

Kiya was sleeping peacefully when Kieran's heavy boots, clomping around the factory floor, woke her from her dream about staking twenty oncoming vampires without breaking a sweat, while the other Slayers stood and watched in awe.

"Could you pace a bit more quietly?" she cried, burying her head under Roxy's pink blanket to block out the noise.

"Do you know what time it is?" Kieran asked her, frantically.

"Bed time?" she said, hopefully.

"Jesus, it's midday and Zeke hasn't come home yet."

"So, the guy has issues and wants to rectify them with drink. Let him have his fun-"

"No!" Kieran snapped, then stopped to compose himself, taking deep breaths. "He's never done this before. If he goes out drinking he's back by ten at the latest."

"What are you trying to say exactly?" Kiya pondered, feeling her dreams leaving her and reality biting away in the form of a major headache.

"I'm saying he's gone and got himself hurt."

"Or laid," she offered.

Kieran frowned. "This is Zeke we're talking about. Michelle only stayed with him for as long as she did because she thought he had a promising career- meaning riches and a cosy home life for herself. When she realised he was going no where, she upped and left. No one would willingly flirt with Zeke- not unless I'm there to instigate things."

"That's mightily harsh of you."

"It's the truth!" he retorted loudly.

"What's going on?" At the sound of all the ruckus, Roxy emerged from her bedroom with dark circles under her eyes and messy blonde bed hair. "I heard raised voices."

"Zeke's missing," Kieran explained, worriedly.

"He always comes back," Roxy notified him with a yawn.

"Screw this," he said wistfully. "I'm going out to find him."

As Kieran placed his hand on the handles of the factory doors, they burst open, almost knocking him over.

"Zeke? You're okay!" Roxy grinned in celebration. But her smile soon faded as Zeke hit the floor, grasping at his chest and leg with disturbing cries of anguish. "Shit! What happened?"

Everyone present ran towards the fallen Slayer, including Kiya, and rolled him over to examine his body. He was shaking like a leaf and crying tears of pain.

"He's been stabbed a few times," Roxy reported, leaving to fetch the medical kit from Zeke's bedroom without a moment's hesitation.

"Zeke-Man, what happened to you out there?" Kieran began bombarding him with questions. "When did this happen? How? Who the hell touched you?"

"Attacked..." he explained, barely above a whisper, his eyes fluttering in and out of focus.

Kieran stopped flustering around his friend and tried settling his worse fear. With nervous hands, he checked Zeke's neck for bite marks. *All clear*. It must have been a street beggar or someone getting nasty with him in a bar brawl, because if it were your average vampire, they would have left their mark on his neck. At least, he *hoped* that was the case.

Half an hour later, Roxy had the wounds cleaned and wrapped in bandages, discovering the third stab mark on his back to be particularly messy. Kiya threw up- believing it to be her morning sickness- but claimed it was the sight of the holes in Zeke's skin.

Kieran frowned at her suspiciously. "You've seen a lot worse than this, and yet the sight of small stab wounds has you puking in my kitchen sink. What gives?"

"I guess it's all been building up," she spluttered, blushing in thankfulness as Kieran kindly held her hair back. When her stomach was settled, she moved back to the sofa, where Zeke lay in an unconscious state, sweating profusely. How many more injuries were the Slayers going to suffer over the next few days, because already it was becoming ridiculous.

"Here-" Kieran handed Kiya a glass of water and a small part of her shuddered with gratitude. She got the impression he was making up for the kiss he'd forced on her the night before.

"Do you guys always fall this hard?" she asked, pointing at the blood stains seeping through the white bandages and taking a sip of her drink.

"Things have never been this violent, until now," he said, showing agitation.

"Do you think this is a warning, or was Zeke just in the wrong place at the wrong time?" Roxy chipped in, stroking Zeke's hair.

"I'm hoping the latter. But I can't be sure until he wakes up."

As if Zeke had heard the call, he stirred in his sleep, shaking even more violently than before. Roxy placed a cold flannel on his head and whispered words of comfort. It was strange seeing her do so, because just a few hours before, she had been in the same position, only it had been a lot less nail-biting.

"Zeke-Man, wake up," Kieran said, nudging his friend into life. "Who did this to you?"

Zeke coughed pitifully, opening two squinty eyes with very red coloured whites. "Kieran?" he asked quietly.

"Yeah, its me."

"I'm sorry man," he said, attempting to get up. His face creased up with pain as he shifted, and Kieran pushed him back down, telling him to remain flat on his back. His eyes fluttered again blearily.

"Just give me a name, that's all I need."

"Girl-" Zeke mumbled. "Annara she called herself... stabbed me-"

"That's good. What else can you tell me?" Zeke looked ready to pass out, so Kieran clapped his hands in front of his face. "What else can you remember, Zeke? Stay with me now."

The tension was eating away at both Roxy and Kiya. They were witness to Kieran's desperation and felt strongly for the man who was trying to speak to his best friend, with Zeke's bandaged stab wounds on display and a greatly distressed mind filtering through.

"A man watched... encouraged her... He's a *Feeder*."

"Who's a Feeder?"

"Tristian."

"*Tristian*!" Kiya yelled in surprise, with an anguished glint in her eyes. "Tristian was involved?"

"It may not be a Tristian you know-" Kieran reasoned with her.

"There's only one rat bastard in this area that I know, who'd be around when something like this happens. If there's death and blood involved, he's usually lurking, like the sick *freak* he is. What did he look like?"

But Zeke was out like a light, leaving Kiya's question unanswered. He needed to rest now, and regain his strength. Kiya would have to wait for confirmation when Zeke was ready to speak. What the Slayers didn't know was that the Zeke they knew and cared for was long gone and that in his place was a soulless killer. A vampire- or at least he would be in less than twenty four hours. The clock was ticking.

Chapter 14

An Enemy Inside the Headquarters

Kiya was furious at the news. Furious that no matter where she went or what she did with her life, Tristian was always there to make it awkward somehow. She'd allowed Kieran to explain to her what a 'Feeder' was and found her blood pressure rising even more.

"That shit!" she screamed in a rage. Roxy ran to her, putting a hand on her shoulder to calm her down. "Where does he get off doing sick things like that?"

"We'll get him," Roxy enthused. "Either he wants to be one of them or he's asked for some sort of treasure in return for his services. Chances are we'll catch him when we patrol the graveyard sometime- looking for the one he's working for to get his payment. I'm sure we'll nab him, Kiya."

"No," she said sternly, "I don't want anyone to hurt him."

Kieran raised an eyebrow, "And why the hell not?"

"Because I want to be the one who makes him suffer, you hear me?"

He raised his hands in understanding. "As long as you guys leave the bony neck of that Annara chick to my strangling expertise, then I'm a happy bunny, sweet cheeks."

"Don't call me that," Kiya growled.

"Sure, Princess."

She ignored Kieran's wearying sense of humour and hit the showers to refresh herself. She hoped that by the time she was clean, dressed and covered in a light layer of make-up, Zeke would be coherent and ready to do some explaining. It turned out he was very much dead in posture and mentality, so Kiya could do nothing but sit and think about all the things she was going to do to Tristian when she got her hands on him.

Roxy offered to take her outside for some target practise after a long, slow hour of just sitting there, using trees outside to hang targets from the branches. When Roxy discovered that Zeke had failed to retrieve her favourite bow, she was most upset, but settled for her spare, which was shocking pink in colour. Kiya borrowed Siren's spare set of throwing stars and selected a random gun that almost blew the targets to pieces on impact.

"Careful," Roxy said pensively, admiring the accuracy of her female friend. "These are the only targets we have left until I order some more."

Kiya nodded brusquely and continued to blow holes in the bulls-eye of the furthest target. *Guns are too boring*, she thought vividly. *Just pointing, aiming and clicking the trigger loses its appeal after a while.*

"So what do you think?" came Kieran's cool voice from behind. "Are you going to hang up your blade and take a gun out for a ride next time?"

"I thought you were meant to be keeping an eye on your pal in there?" Kiya asked ineffectually.

"I filled Siren in on the situation now that he's up. He's offered to do it while he makes himself some food."

Kieran had changed clothes since the girls had left the factory for target practise while the rain was holding off. He was now in a dark purple coloured shirt, open at the neck to reveal a necklace made of black and silver beads, and a pair of dark trousers held up by a leather belt, sporting a hefty looking silver buckle. His shoes were shining from a fresh polish- a lot less heavy than his biker boots by the looks of it.

Kiya couldn't help but notice the stubble on his face, growing thick and dark, and the way his hair blew behind him in the wind, revealing neatly trimmed side-burns. He could have been a male model if he wasn't a killing machine by profession.

"Think it'll rain tonight when we head out?" Roxy asked.

Kieran scratched the back of his head. "I'm in two minds about that actually-"

"You mean you don't want us to go, or you're not sure if it'll rain?" she asked curiously.

"I mean I don't want *you* to go," he told her sceptically.

"But I'm okay!" she protested and to prove her point, she let an arrow fly from her bow, where it penetrated the centre of the target she had been aiming for.

"I need you to look after Zeke."

Roxy bit her lip. The real reason she didn't want to get left behind tonight was that she had plans for the following evening- her date with Logan. She'd rather die than miss the opportunity to spend a night out with him and Kieran would freak out if she missed two patrols in succession.

"I'll stay with Zeke," Kiya offered. "I really want to speak with him if he wakes."

Kieran was frowning at the two girls.

"And I wanted to ask you something-," Roxy said hesitantly, letting the bow fall to her hip limply. "I er- kind of have a date tomorrow night with an old friend."

"*What*?" Kieran cried. "You have a *what*?"

"A date," she persisted. "With a friend. I've already told him I'll go-"

"You should consult me before you go making plans, Rox.' You know that."

"So I can go?" she pressed.

When Kieran approved her request, she jumped onto him, squeezing him tightly, and gave him a big kiss on his rough cheek. "Thank you, thank you, thank you!"

"Alright. Alright, calm down," he laughed. "You can come with Siren and me tonight and Kiya can stay here. That way, you're both happy."

Roxy was dancing around in pure exhilaration, humming something to herself as she made her way inside, apparently finished with her archery lesson. Kieran watched her with a smile then turned to Kiya, who was putting Siren's throwing stars back in their bag.

"Is that okay with you?"

"That's fine."

"Good good." He swung his arms back and forth nervously, observing the black clouds in the distance and breathing the fresh air deep into his lungs. He'd needed to come out and feel the cold wind through his fingertips because seeing Zeke in pain was just making him nauseous. He was a smart guy and had a niggling feeling that his friend would not last more than two-maybe three- days. Zeke's blood loss was too high and in Meridion- often referred to as The Dying City- hospitals were so low on supplies that they only assisted people who were likely to pull through. If someone walked in with two arms missing and a chunk bitten out of their torso, they'd advise him to go home and say farewell to any loved ones without batting an eyelid. Cruel world, huh?

"I hope you realise that Zeke getting hurt is not your fault, right?" Kiya said, standing up to face him. His eyes fell to the floor.

"He's been my pal since we were kids, you know? I just feel as if I've let him down somehow."

"He'd never blame this on you and you know it."

Kiya felt a lot of compassion for Kieran as his eyes began to water. This was a man whose hard, rock-like persona was beginning to crumble before a woman he was only just learning to trust. He was expressing weakness. Love. Fear.

"Whatever happens to Zeke is the result of gross unfairness in the everyday lives of human beings."

"Maybe-"

"He was in the wrong place at the wrong time. Shit happens."

Kiya was right. Shit did happen.

She wasn't sure why she did it. Perhaps it was because when Rycan died, she'd needed a hug more than anything and had received zero comfort from people because they were too afraid to approach her. That's why she put her arms around Kieran, drawing him into a hug. He put a hand on her waist and his head on her shoulder and she- quite timidly- caressed his muscular back.

She wasn't sure about Kieran, but she knew *she* felt a lot better after that.

The Slayers left the factory feeling a lot less enthusiastic than usual. Roxy was her usual lively self, but the men were very sullen as they grabbed their weapons and said their farewells to Kiya and a sleeping Zeke.

"If he wakes, give him water straight away," Kieran instructed on passing. "And you might want to keep a weapon handy, in case something potentially life threatening gets in."

Kiya wasn't stupid, but she didn't voice this.

"Don't come back injured this time," she said to them all. Only Roxy smiled.

When the door was closed behind them, silence fell. The air was cool and crisp and the light outside was dwindling. In the kitchen, the tap was dripping lazily into the sink.

Kiya stared at Zeke. Just stared at all the lines and scars on his moist, pale face. His eyes were moving creepily under his eyelids and she noticed one of his fingers twitching.

"Wake up, would you?" she begged, tapping his shoulder. There was no reaction. She thought about doing something very cruel- pressing on one of the wounds to get his attention- but realised how wrong and down right *evil* it would be to do so.

I'll make something to eat while I wait, she thought decidedly, leaving his side for the kitchen.

Zekc's eyes shot open the moment Kiya turned her back on him, yet he remained still, trying not to alert her to his state. He glanced around, expecting to see Kieran and the other losers that followed him around- too far up his own arse to disagree with what he had to say most times. What a pathetic bunch they all were.

He sniffed the air and marvelled at his heightened senses. His hearing was immense and his eye sight sharper than a hawks. *Man, this feels good.* But how could he tell if the transformation was complete? Moving his tongue around, he brushed it against a new set of fangs, still growing in length. His wounds were healed too. No one had noticed because they were concealed under bandages, but he knew, as he ran a hand over the bloodied areas that there was no longer any broken tissue to be found.

After he'd analysed all the changes he had undergone, he realised how hungry he felt. But this wasn't a hunger for some Kentucky Fried Chicken with ketch-up and a large coke. He hungered for blood.

Kiya almost bit her own tongue off when two strong arms grabbed her from behind suddenly, throwing her to the floor. The knife she'd been using to cut her ham sandwich in half clanged to the ground with her, but was kicked out of her reach as Zeke picked her up by her hair. She felt a scream rise in her throat as she saw his eyes change colour to a magnificent silver.

"You're a....you're a-" she stammered, in too much shock to be capable of fighting back.

Zeke wrenched her head closer as she tried to untangle his hand from her hair. Her scalp was burning as he tugged the strands mercilessly, making her eyes water in pain. Instead of answering her, he sniffed her hair and neck. The blood was racing through her body now- he could sense it- and the stench of fear made his body come alive with excitement. Once again, he dipped his head down to inhale Kiya's scent, then stopped dead. *That was odd*, he thought, picking up on something interesting. "You're pregnant?" he said. Kiya's eyes flashed fear at him. "There's another life growing inside of you and you never told anyone."

She shuddered then brought her heal up into Zeke's crotch, feeling his grip loosen on her hair. It gave her the opportunity to twist herself free. With panic guiding her, she found a throwing star and tossed it at him. He only laughed as it embedded itself in his thigh.

"Zeke- I know there's still a part of you in there," she tried, moving around the table as he approached her, exposing his pearl white fangs.

"So what if there is? I'm the upgrade. The new and *improved* Zeke. The Zeke that has a higher calling now."

"I just need you to tell me where I can find Tristian," she said hopefully.

"What makes you think I'm going to help *you*?" he hissed, then slashed a hand toward her, missing her head by an inch. Kiya ran around the table again, keeping plenty of distance between them.

"Tell me where you saw him."

Zeke shook his head. "Sorry, no-can-do."

Kiya gritted her teeth. This guy was really beginning to piss her off. But if she killed him, how would she explain what had happened to Kieran and the other slayers? What would they do if *they* were in this situation? Was there a way to reverse what had happened so that Zeke was just 'Zeke' again?

It was night outside now- another miserable evening with a light rain pitter-pattering on the flat factory rooftop.

"Why don't you just save me the chase and get that tight ass over here so I can bite you already?" he whined, in a very Zeke-like tone of voice.

Kiya braced herself as he jumped onto the table, kicking guns and daggers off in all directions and hitting Kiya in the face with a pistol. She reached up and touched her head. There was blood. Zeke licked his lips.

"Hmmm… can you smell that?" he asked her ominously. "Dinner is served!"

He leapt off the table and ploughed into her, wrapping bony fingers around her neck. The two of them rolled backwards and Kiya had to fight to keep Zeke's mouth from reaching her neck. She placed one hand on his face and the other on his throat and pushed him back with all her might.

"You probably let that vampire do this to you!" she cried breathlessly, putting her knee into his ribs. "Poor, pathetic Zeke just couldn't handle being in Kieran's shadow his whole life so he let some chick bite him. You're a loser! No wonder Michelle left you!"

Zeke hissed in anguish and managed to scrape a fang across Kiya's cheek. Kiya felt the tooth and decided to change tactics by releasing Zeke's neck and punching him in the side of his face several times in quick succession. He snarled and rolled off her, then grabbed her by the neck. Kiya felt her body and legs leave the ground. She was choking to death.

"I may have been those things before, *bitch*, but I'm better now. And when I'm through with you, I'm going to personally fuck Kieran up. You got that?" He touched

Kiya's belly with one hand, sensing the presence of a growing child and then brought it down to the point between her legs. "I could do more than just bite you, you know, but I'm being a gentleman... for a change."

Kiya was struggling to stay conscious. Her eyesight was perforated with black and red spots and her lungs were burning from the strain. Just as she was about to pass out, Zeke dropped her to the floor.

"I won't kill you- *yet*," he said thoughtfully, watching her breathe in heavily. "Because if Kieran comes home and finds bite marks on your neck and me missing, he might assume Annara came back to finish the job. So I need you to tell him what has happened here and that I'll be waiting for him." He paused. "Kieran was right about one thing, Kiya. There is a war coming. And this time, he's going to lose."

Kiya coughed and spluttered as Zeke stepped over her. He didn't bother to turn back as he left the factory. He was too hungry and couldn't wait to see what Meridion had to offer on its menu that night.

Chapter 15

Doors

"I'm beginning to wonder if leaving Kiya with Zeke was a good idea-" Kieran said, breaking the neck of a vampire and staking it through the heart. The explosion of ash hit him in the face, clouding his vision for a brief moment. He even felt some of it go down his throat, which wasn't uncommon, it just made him feel ten times thirstier.

"What's she going to do?" Roxy said, putting an arrow between another vampires eyes as it ran towards her, hissing and snarling. "Kill him?"

Siren sliced a vampire in two, splattering blood all over his fellow Slayers, to which he received unhappy glances from both of them. "Sorry," he shrugged, putting his sword back in its case between his shoulder blades as all the potential threats vanished.

The graveyard was cast in a layer of silvery mist this particular evening and was glistening with wetness as the thin rain floated down and clung to everything in sight. It was the type of weather they all hated- rain that seemed to hit you at all angles no matter how or where you went to try and avoid it. And even though it was light rain, it soaked them through just as much as rain that lashed down on them like arrows. Cold, wet arrows. Kieran shivered.

The Slayers had discovered a nest of vampires in one of the mausoleums this particularly dreary night. As they'd patrolled the area, starting from the centre of the graveyard and working their way north, the rancid smell of a dead pizza delivery boy had tickled their nostrils and they'd found him lying on a stone coffin, surrounded by a pack of hungry teenage bloodsuckers. Now that the vampires were all dead and dusted- for good- Kieran and the group had the gruesome task of taking evidence from the dead, in order to inform any family members and friends he belonged to.

"I hate this part," Roxy moaned, cringing as Kieran slipped a hand into the boy's pocket. There was a wallet inside, with a driving license, pizza delivery I.D, a bank card, some old cinema tickets and a photograph of what appeared to be the boy and his brown haired, bright eyed girlfriend. There was no address to be found.

"We leave him?" Siren asked.

Kieran nodded, "No address means no home to visit. I'll post this to the police station tomorrow with a description of where the body can be found. Let them deal with it."

Roxy was sad. She hated seeing dead bodies- the kind that weren't likely to wake up and bite your neck to shreds at least. She always asked herself: *Could I have prevented this if we'd found the nest sooner?* There was no point in dwelling on it. She'd seen a lot of death now and was beginning to build a wall to harness any emotion she had towards her job.

The Slayers patrolled for a further *three* hours, wandering closer to an area thick with trees. Sometimes they'd find vampires hiding in there, in the shadows, and would chase them out like rats to face their execution. There were no stragglers on their arrival. No 'lone' bloodsuckers whimpering from lack of blood consumption. Only darkness and the sound of their own breathing.

"Do you believe in ghosts?" Roxy asked suddenly, keeping an arrow at the ready. She trod cautiously through the grass, making sure to keep her eyes and ears alert like Kieran had taught her.

"That's an odd question," Kieran said. "Why'd you ask?"

"I was just wondering. Is there a heaven to go to if any of us fall in battle, or will we wander the earth for eternity as nothing more than a faded memory? An ethereal being? Or perhaps a mere shadow?"

"Are you worried you're going to die soon, is that it?"

Roxy shook her head. "We're all going to die eventually, but in what circumstances? It's just- seeing Zeke hurt and all-"

Kieran swallowed hard. "He's fine! Now don't go thinking you're next, darlin' because I need optimists here. You guys are going to be fighting with me for many years to come, okay? So let's forget the whole 'death' thing and focus on patrolling for now."

"Sorry," Roxy apologised quietly. She felt she'd touched one of Kieran's nerves and it always made her feel guilty afterwards. It wasn't often they saw Kieran in a bad mood and never a pleasant thing when he was. He was their stone. Their rock in the middle of all the madness. If he was happy, they were happy. It made life just that little bit easier on them.

"Hey, do you see that?" Kieran said unexpectedly.

They had come across another small opening in the trees, with a mound of earth in the centre. Having an uneven area of ground was far from out of the ordinary in Meridion, but the fact that there were two solid metal doors embedded into the top of it made the Slayers all the more curious.

"Access to the sewers maybe?"

Kieran looked confused. "Hmmm, but if that was the case, why the fancy entrance?"

Siren brushed his hand over the surface of the door. It was cold from all the rain water pummelling it. The Mayor had ordered all underground passageways to be locked up many years ago, in order to limit the entrance-ways vampires and werewolves could use to get into the city, but if this were one of those entranceways, why was it locked from underneath?

"Weird." With a gentle tap, they listened closely to the sound of the metal clanking- echoing down what seemed to be a tunnel from within.

"It's nothing guys," Roxy complained, then raised her voice, "But that isn't-"

A vampire darted out from behind a tree suddenly, dressed in a black trench coat that resembled a cheap, black plastic bag over its body. It's short black hair was slicked down from the rain and its eyes were glowing silver in the night.

Roxy kicked it hard in the chest and followed through with a quick hit to the face, using her right fist. The vampire didn't seem too concerned with her blows though. Instead, he eyed up the doors in the floor, looking at them hopelessly between hits. Kieran noticed its behaviour and joined Roxy, grabbing the vamp' by its neck and throwing it into the doors, where it lay panting.

"You were coming here, weren't you?" Kieran yelled, pointing his shotgun at the creature's heart. The vampire's eyes flickered from left to right in a frenzy. He couldn't get away because Siren and Roxy were on either side, waiting for him to try and escape. "What's wrong? Not in a talking mood?"

The vampire growled in the back of its throat, bearing its fangs to the group.

"Hey- we've seen it all before!" Kieran snapped. "What you need to remember is *we're* the ones pointing weapons at you and *you're* the helpless vampire with nothing but elongated canines right now."

This comment angered the creature and it took a swipe for the gun. Kieran sighed and shot it in both its kneecaps, blasting the bottom part of both legs off and leaving a bloody mess behind.

"Are you going to talk?" The vampire was recoiling in pain, too wrapped up in its agony to care about the sound of Kieran's voice. "I think we should leave him here," Kieran said to the group. "He won't be drinking blood with no legs for quite some time. It'll be a message for anything down there when they find him." He indicated the doors.

"So you think it's a nest?" Roxy asked.

"More than likely. These guys have to go *somewhere* when the sun comes up right?"

"Well then, why can't we just break in and slaughter everything?" Roxy implored.

"We don't know what we're dealing with here. I'm two men short, Rox. We can't take any chances right now."

Kieran bent down and gave the vampire a gentle slap across its cheek to get its attention. "It was nice speaking with you," he said, and then left with his soaking wet Slayers in tow.

The sound of scratching jolted Marko from his sleep. As he opened one droopy eye, he felt a splash of something across his face and assumed it was rain, but as he wiped the liquid from his skin, he found it to be red in colour.

"Blood?" he said to himself, looking up at the doors above. He could just make out something lying across the gap in the centre of the two rectangles of steel that made up their entranceway. Between the gap poured blood. "Now what?" *Was someone feeding up there?*

Marko left his stool and grabbed his keys, climbing the short distance to the padlock that held the doors closed. As he undid the chain, the weight of whatever it was above forced the doors through, knocking him off the ladder, and crashed in a heap on the floor. When he hit the ground, he felt the object bash into him, landing on his chest and legs. "Ouch! What the-?" His words caught in his throat as he noticed the face. "Brother-?"

His identical twin was a wreck, bleeding from the stubs that used to be his legs. There was no silvery lust for blood in his eyes or the usual confident grimace; just quivering lips and a weary expression as he reached out and grasped Marko's hand.

"I scr…screwed up," Alex trembled.

"No. No," Marko assured him, "We'll get you fixed. We're immortal remember? I'll get you through this."

Marko abandoned his duty of watching the doors for intruders and dragged his brother down the corridor to their chambers, leaving a trail of blood behind them. Most of the underground inhabitants were all out hunting for fresh blood or bedding 'Feeders' right then, who'd visited the graveyard offering themselves to the vampire population quite freely. It made Alex's sobs easily unnoticeable in the depths of the vampire refuge.

Alex was looking paler than normal as Marko left him lying in the middle of the floor, which was made up of various pieces of carpet and rug they'd both stolen from skips and dump-sites in the city. Their room was lit with candles that flickered ominously and all around, the stone walls glistened with water that never seemed to evaporate. There were no bed sheets on the mattresses in the corner of the room; vampires didn't feel the cold like humans did, so they felt it wasn't necessary to have such a thing. It would only get covered in blood anyhow and no one would volunteer to wash them clean.

"I'll get you someone to feed on," Marko promised, and left his twin to bleed over their bedroom floor.

As he made his way through the twisting maze of corridors, he thought about the night his twin and he had been 'turned.' They had been leaving a nightclub together with two beautiful women, drunk and ready to drop their knickers at the click of their fingers, when they'd *all* been ambushed by a pack of female vampires. *He* had kept a cool head, standing gallantly in front of his woman in a protective manner, which was the main reason he had been bitten, but not killed. His brother however, had fallen to the floor and begged to be turned quite willingly- revealing to his twin that he had been a 'Feeder' for two years, due to the stress of high school exams and their abusive father.

One of the vampire ladies recognised Alex as the one she fed on most nights and gave him a choice. "You or the girl, *Insect*?" There had been no hesitation. He threw the dumb blonde to her knees and watched as the vampires ripped her to pieces in, drinking her dry and leaving limbs all over the place.

Marko had lost all respect for Alex after that, as he was taken by one of the fanged women. He felt disgust when he saw how Alex smiled as the vampire started to drink from him. But when the pair had lost their souls and been reborn into the society of blood sucking vermin, they'd decided one thing. They'd look out for each other no matter what, and together, bask in the delights of living for eternity at each other's side.

Alex's actions were in the past. Marko liked being a vampire, though he despised not being his own man, for even in this society, he worked under someone else.

"Annara!" Marko cried, banging on her door. He was aware that she'd been out the night before, so he assumed she'd be at home this time, drinking from a Feeder instead. There were too many vampires just to let them all go out hunting at once, so they took shifts, leaving the colony once every two nights. If you were a 'favourite,' the shifts didn't apply. Marko and Alex were not valued members of the vampire society. Annara however, *was*. She was one of the oldest vampires, having been around for hundreds of years and had seen more than Marko could imagine. Even though she had the opportunity to hunt whenever she wanted, she still liked to stay home sometimes and 'play' with whoever she felt was worthy of her company. Tonight was one of those nights.

The door opened a fraction.

"What do *you* want?" she shot at him, through the gap.

"It's Alex. He's badly injured. I need a Feeder."

"Well you can't have mine-"

"*Please*!" he begged.

Annara sighed and opened her door a little more. She had her blonde hair in cute little 'school girl' pigtails, tied with silver ribbons, and was wearing pink hot pants that clung tightly to her perfect ass. Marko gulped as he came face to face with her breasts also, exposed and looking *very* beautiful in the candle light and from her plump lips, a trail of blood trickled.

Marko wanted to lean forward and lick the blood clean, but knew better than to invade Annara's personal space. She'd grown tired of him now and didn't allow him to visit her quarters like she used to.

"Ever since the day I turned you, you've been nothing but a nuisance in my life! I knew I shouldn't have listened to Misty that night we found you and just ripped your fucking head off like I did to your bitch-"

Marko cringed inwardly. He was quite thankful the woman he had been with that night was not a girlfriend-just someone he'd picked up on his regular evenings out. There was no regret over her death really, just disappointment that he hadn't got laid.

"What happened this time, Marko? He got a boo-boo when he went out to play?" she asked in a mocking, motherly tone.

"No. He got his legs torn off."

Her eyes sparked silver for a brief moment.

"He what?"

"He was left on the doors I was guarding. Someone had blasted his legs clean off."

"Who did it?"

"I don't know!" Marko cried feeling impatient. "Just give me a fucking Feeder would you?!"

Annara smiled at the sound of his raised voice. "I like it when you get all nasty. It's been a long time since I've seen you all worked up and sweaty." She brushed a painted pink talon over his lips then sliced his forehead open suddenly, marvelling at the blood that dripped down over his nose and around his eyes like red tears.

Marko was pissed off now. He pushed her out of the way and burst into the room, finding a man lying in her bed.

"Who's this guy?" he asked in bewilderment, as Annara came up behind him. He sniffed the air and realised quite despairingly that the guy lying naked in Annara's bed was another vampire, not a Feeder she could dispose of.

"The name is Zeke," he said with a grin, showing no shame in lying there naked and on display. There were little trickles of blood on his chest from where Annara liked to nip people during sex. Oh how Marko remembered that part…

"He arrived an hour ago. A new recruit for the master," Annara explained pleasantly. "I thought I'd show him how *fun* being a vampire could be." She giggled and pounced playfully onto the bed, kissing Zeke quite passionately and allowing him to peel off her hot pants.

"Hey-" Zeke said, leaving her poised ready to take him inside her. "You're brother was probably killed by a guy called Kieran Nightley. He's a Vampire Slayer who patrols these parts with a small group of losers who think they can make a difference in the world."

Marko had had enough of the spectacle he was witnessing. He left the room feeling quite nauseous and started banging on every door he passed, trying to drive the image of Zeke and Annara out of his thoughts. Eventually, he found a weaker vampire drinking from a teenage girl and dragged her to his quarters, watching miserably as his twin drank from her veins.

After five minutes of ravenous sucking, the teenage girl realised that Alex wasn't easing up like he was meant to, for the vampire code stated that 'Feeders' were not to be killed unless they had performed an act of betrayal against vampire kind.

"Hey, that's enough. I'm feeling kind of woozy here," she complained, trying to rip her wrist free from Alex's mouth. He pinned her down as she shifted position and forced her face to the side so that he could clamp onto her creamy neck with ease.

"What are you doing?!" she screamed in fear. "I don't do necks! My mother will know I came here!"

Alex didn't stop. He failed to abide by the vampire code that night and let the girl wriggle like a fish on a hook, being drained of all energy and life force until she lay dead on his mattress.

Marko watched with pity- pity for his brother, not the little girl with the dying light in her eyes. He knew there was nothing he could do to help him further. As soon as their master caught wind of Alex's disability, he'd rip his heart out without a moments hesitation.

The vampire army had no room for wounded soldiers.

Chapter 16

Broken Hearts

The wide open doors trapped Kiya in a state of paralysis as she sat on the floor, watching the rain drops coating the sand and dead earth outside the factory. Cold air was blowing into the building punitively, not that it made a difference- it always felt cold inside the factory whether the door was open or not.

For a while, Kiya cried softly to herself. She felt like a child with a grazed knee, waiting for her father to come along and kiss it better. Only it wasn't as simple as that, was it? Her entire heart needed a good patching up and her soul was becoming defiant towards her actions. She felt mentally weak and tired, but her body was still alive with the adrenaline she'd felt as Zeke had attacked her.

With him gone, there was no reason for her to stay watch anymore so her Samurai sword found its place on her shoulder again and she quickly left the factory with money tucked in her boot. As long as she returned before Kieran and the Slayers, she'd be home in time to explain what had happened.

Aimlessly Kiya wandered towards the city, roughly heading for where it thrived the most in the evenings, and then found herself changing direction- dragging her numb body to her mother's front door. She owed it to her to prove she was still alive at least.

Kiya sighed as she looked at the crumbling bricks and blue door of her once happy home when she was younger, with its brass knocker in the shape of a fox's head that had always fascinated her so. There was a light coming from within, and on the window she saw a poster stuck to the glass. It had her face on it, and above the photograph was the word 'WANTED' in big bold print.

Wanted? She thought in panic, then read the rest of the text hurriedly. *Wanted for inhuman acts against another Meridion citizen. If you have any information on this woman, please contact 5242-999. Warning: Do not attempt to approach this criminal for your own safety.*

Kiya choked. What was going on? *Inhuman acts*? Then she clicked. Carl must have taken his story to the police after all and now she was wanted for slicing his arm off. After some hyperventilation issues, she calmed herself and thought logically. This guy had nothing on her. Even if someone spotted her out and about, she'd be gone before the police could reach her. But her mother? How could she put a poster up to aid that bastard's case? Did she fear her too? Did she want to see her executed on the Stone Table just like her future son in law?

"Go to hell," she whispered to the voices inside the home. Her mother usually invited her lady friends around for an all night alcohol binge once a week. "You've just lost your daughter for good."

She left feeling incredibly pissed off and completely betrayed. For a while, she paced the front yard struggling to control the thoughts that were rushing at her a mile a minute. She wondered what would have happened if she'd actually entered the house hold, with all her mother's friends inside holding their glasses of wine, and just sat amongst them with an eerie grin on her face. They'd have been petrified, that's for sure, but would her mother actually have the guts to pick up the phone and dial the number on the poster? Did she *really* believe her daughter was a bad person? Maybe she feared Kiya might hurt her, which as tempting as it was in the current circumstances, she'd *never* be able to perform such a vile act; regardless of how her mother felt towards her now.

In a way, Kiya *was* a bad person. She'd cut a man's arm off, which was as stated on the poster 'an inhuman act against another Meridion citizen.' But no one knew about Carl's provocation, because *her* story didn't seem relevant to the people who'd made the poster. Who were the police going to believe- a man bearing his severed arm in his one remaining hand or the girl that carries a Samurai sword around wherever she goes? People didn't realise she wasn't the type to just flip and start cutting people apart, unless she had good reason to. That was serial killer shit! Surely her mother knew better than that?

Kiya tried to forget about it all and left the front garden to visit the place that had started most of her troubles. The Stone Table.

When she arrived, she found she couldn't bring herself to move any closer than where she was- standing on the opposite side of the street. The vertical stones were all slick with rain water and the centre stone, lying flat in the grass, was being used as a seat for two unfamiliar people.

Kiya didn't want to alert the couple to her presence. She watched them sitting there with their backs to her, leaning in close to talk. The male was sitting very rigidly, with his back as straight as an arrow, but his head tilted down. The girl was turned slightly towards him, dressed in a tight-fitting denim jacket. Her hair was the same shade as the inky black sky, tied back in a pony tail.

Why have you come here? A voice in Kiya's head asked suddenly. Her face was blank as she stared at the stones, completely dumbfounded. *You have no reason to see this place again.*

A cinema screen featuring the execution exploded into life at the back of her mind. She saw Rycan's face, wet with sweat and yet his eyes full of serenity and love for her. She'd wanted to break the neck of the executioner. She'd wanted to hit all the spectators. All the anger she felt towards society had reached its maximum when Rycan had died. She hated them all, with their gormless faces and their coffees in hand, watching the event as if it were nothing more than a fascinating spectacle at a museum.

"I don't know why I came," she whispered to herself, in the comfort of the darkest shadows the street had to offer. It almost seemed predatory, lingering in the dark as the couple in front of her conversed, unaware of her presence.

You need to leave now. It is not safe for you here.

"Safe?" the word lingered in the air. She didn't think she'd ever feel safe again.

Go home.

Kiya tore her eyes away from the Stone Table and ran through the streets, her coat billowing out behind her in the rain as she jumped over huge puddles that were glistening in the dips of the uneven concrete. The rain lashed against her face- no longer the fine, floating texture it had been earlier that evening- blurring her vision slightly, but feeling refreshing against her skin. If she stopped running now, her muscles would cool and she'd probably freeze to death. So she ran home at a steady pace-stopping for nothing. When her throat became dry, she opened it to the skies and allowed the rain to soothe it. When her legs began to ache, she continued to push harder, until she was back inside the Slayer Headquarters- the only safe place she had now.

She had no more than five minutes to grab a towel before Roxy, Siren and Kieran arrived home, looking just as drenched as she was.

"Everything okay?" she asked, forgetting her immediate predicament of explaining Zeke's whereabouts.

Kieran didn't answer. His eyes were wider than a vampire's on a hunt and were focused on the empty sofa behind her. His hair was in thick tangles, dripping all over his broad chest and shoulders, but he didn't even think about grabbing anything to dry himself off like the other Slayers were currently doing.

Roxy threw a towel at him out of kindness, but he failed to catch it in his daze. When she saw his reaction, she looked at the sofa and paused also.

Siren was in the kitchen and hadn't noticed anyone was missing at all.

"Where-?"

Kiya raised her hands and approached him cautiously. This was not going to be fun. "I'm sorry Kieran-," she began.

"Where is he?"

She didn't know how to tell him what had happened. There was no easy way. "He's not here."

"I can fucking see that!" he shouted, going red in the face.

Roxy came to Kiya's aid. "Calm down, Kieran! Let the girl talk."

She swallowed. "He attacked me, Kier.' He's not... He's not human anymore."

Kieran was in shock, so Roxy said the words for him. "He's a vampire, isn't he?"

Kiya nodded slowly. "He's gone to them now, I think. It was about two, maybe three hours ago. I assume he needs to feed..."

Kieran looked away, putting a hand to his face, then turned back sharply. "Did you try and slay him?"

She remained silent. The attack had been pretty crazy. All she had thought about doing was getting away from Zeke, not fighting back.

"If he's a vampire, why didn't *he* kill *you*?" he pressed.

She had an answer for that one at least. "He wanted me alive so I could explain to you what had happened. I think he was trying to prevent you from sending out a rescue party. He doesn't need rescuing." She paused. "He needs slaying."

Kieran turned on the spot, moving towards the doors, then faced the way he'd been previously. He was agitated and full of adrenaline. He wanted to punch something but held back.

"Zeke has fallen into shadow?" Siren queried, from the sidelines. He had a banana in one hand, ready to peel.

Kieran couldn't stand being in the room anymore. He snatched the towel off the floor and stormed off to his room, leaving the Slayers to gawk at him in bewilderment and pity.

"Poor Kieran," Roxy said softly, when he was out of earshot.

"I had a premonition that this day would come," Siren muttered, quite disturbingly. He kept a straight face, peeling his banana slowly. "Zeke has become a creature of the night and Kieran will have to face him someday."

"Who wins?" Roxy asked, testing Siren's prediction.

"That has not yet been decided by the Fates."

Fates? Kiya thought. *There are no characters who weave events to their liking like these 'Fates' he speaks of. Those were fairytales you told kids to put them to sleep on stormy nights. Events happen because of the choices humans make and the paths we follow. If Kieran decides to leave the city, for example, he'd never have to face Zeke, which would blow Siren's 'Fates' theory out of the water, right? It's all foolish talk.*

"Are you a Warlock, Siren?" Roxy was glaring at him as if she'd never seen the guy before. There had to be something to clarify his weirdness.

"I am an orphan and have no clue as to who my real parents are, so perhaps I have inherited some magical qualities from them, who knows? But in all truth, I don't feel like anything special. Not like our *Healer* here-" he pointed to Kiya.

"I'm not special," she said modestly.

He shrugged. "That's your opinion," and with that, Siren put the half peeled banana in his pocket; folded his towel in his arms and left the girls to find a place on the sofa, still dripping wet and shivering.

Kiya dried her hair carefully, making the strands frizzy and wavy as she grinded the towel between her palms. Roxy was patting her face and neck dry, deep in thought.

"Will he be okay do you think?" Kiya asked suddenly.

Roxy knew to whom she was referring. "Well, you have to admit, it's one heck of a blow. Zeke was his best mate since high school."

Kiya's head sunk low. "I wish I hadn't been the one to tell him."

"You're probably the best person *to* have!" Roxy enthused.

"Why's that?"

Roxy smiled warmly. "Isn't it obvious? He *really* likes you, Kiya."

Her heart warmed at the words, which surprised Kiya greatly. She shouldn't be feeling like this. *She shouldn't!* But right then, she wanted to go after Kieran and give him a massive hug. All she wanted to do was make him feel better. But why was this happening now, so soon after Rycan's death?

"He kissed me the other day."

The atmosphere became static with Roxy's excitement. "He what!?"

"Shhh!" Kiya warned, "Lower your voice."

"Sorry."

"I was winding him up and he kind of grabbed me and...you know."

Roxy sighed. "Well then my suspicions were correct. I could tell he had the hots for you the day he found you lying on his sofa!" She giggled. "He wanted to be the first to approach you, even though Siren was the one who noticed you first. When he walked over, he just stared at you for about five minutes, leaving us all standing there like lemons. I think it was love at first sight."

"Love?" Kiya scoffed.

Roxy nodded, "Perhaps."

There was silence for a moment as Kiya reflected on Roxy's words. She didn't think Kieran 'loved' her. That was absurd! He could be so infuriating at times, with his '*Princess*' this, and '*Darlin*' that. All the smooth talk he spouted and the hints of wanting her seemed like a bit of fun in the work place, that's all. And what of her own situation? Losing Rycan was enough to keep any guy away from her for a while, surely?

Her thoughts became less negative as she drifted back to the kiss. It had been over with too quickly in her opinion.

What? Her mind snapped. *Too quickly? Listen to yourself! You're acting like you wanted more!*

"I have an idea," Roxy said. "Why don't you take some tea in to Kieran now?"

"What? I'm not going to become his bitch now that Zeke is out of the picture."

"No," Roxy corrected her. "I don't mean it like that. I think it'll break the ice a bit. Don't leave him in there to stew. Go talk to him."

"Why don't you do it?"

"Because I'm not the girl that makes his blood race-in a good way."

Kiya looked at the kitchen and sighed. "How does he take it?" she asked.

Chapter 17

The Positive Side of Death

]Marko received a rather loud knock on his door at around two o'clock in the morning, just as he was tending to his half-asleep brother. Alex cowered at the sound.

He'd been trying to sew Alex's legs up, but had failed miserably, for there was not enough skin to drag over the stumps, and was now attempting to use the flames from one of the torches hung on the walls, to burn the wounds shut.

Marko's first thought as he heard the knocks was that someone had discovered he was not stationed by the entranceway into the graveyard, like the rota said he should be at that present moment. If it was who he thought it was, they'd be most angry with him right now and would probably throw him to the Master for punishing, depending what mood he/she was in.

Before Marko could even move to the door himself, it came flying open.

"Oh... it's you two," he said, relieved and disappointed at the same time.

Zeke and Annara were very much *drunk*. It was one of the side effects of drinking the blood of a fellow vampire- it worked the same way as alcohol did on a human. Annara and Zeke must have drank a lot from each other, for they were falling all over the place and laughing like hyenas. The difference between a drunk vampire and a drunk human was, vampires sobered up a lot faster, so it wouldn't take long before they were both their usual evil selves.

"Whoa," Annara said, looking at Alex's legs. "They sure cut him up good." A loud girly giggle exploded from her mouth, which tore through Marko's nerves and made him want to slap her hard in the face to shut her up.

"Would you leave me in peace, *please?*" Marko pleaded, preparing himself to burn Alex's other leg after the success of the first.

Annara was too enthralled to leave now and as both Zeke and herself watched the revolting process of melting Alex's flesh. To try and stifle the flow of blood from his missing limb, she gripped Zeke's arm tightly. Alex let out a scream that ripped through the night and left him panting on the floor like a wild dog after it had run long and hard with its pack. Even vampires could suffer pain, though they were already dead.

Marko knelt beside his brother, holding the flaming torch behind him, and stroked Alex's hair lovingly. "It is done, brother."

Alex managed a small smile in return, before his eyes rolled back in his head and he passed out on the mattress. His legs were black and crispy on the ends, but at least there was no more blood drenching the bed.

"Uh-oh!" Annara exclaimed, "Someone's been a naughty boy!" She was kicking the dead girl on the floor with a metal healed boot. Marko's eyes flashed silver. He hadn't expected Annara to show up and now she'd report the matter to their Master! After all, she was his right hand *vampire*.

"He had to," Marko mumbled simply, referring to his brother.

Zeke didn't care much for the sight of the dead girl. He had been satisfied sexually and now he needed to get outside and drink something before he starved to death. When he'd left the factory earlier that evening, he'd smelt out the underground cave of bloodsuckers like a wolf to a rabbit and had found his girl- Annara- lying in bed, waiting for him. Sure, they'd fucked like champions, but now he wanted her to take him out for dinner.

"Not to be rude or anything," he said, trying to keep his cool, "But I'm hungry and I want to eat something before the sun comes up. Time is ticking children."

Annara let go of Zeke's arm and approached Marko, who was still holding the torch in one quivering hand. He looked at her, then to the girl, and as a jerk reaction, set fire to the dead body. Maybe he'd be in less trouble if it was Annara's word against his. He'd just have to dispose of the bones before anyone could find them.

Annara was sobering up now, for she was capable of walking straight again. She made a point of waltzing around the room in her shiny boots, stabbing the metal heal down into the earth and leaving dips in the ground- avoiding all the rugs on purpose. She was still in her hot pants but was also dressed in a white shirt, which she'd twisted in a knot at the front to reveal cleavage and a smooth flat belly. Through the white shirt, Marko could just make out her nipples. Annara was never one to cover up.

"I thought we'd swing by and ask if you wanted to come out and play, seeing as you haven't seen the moonlight in quite sometime," she suggested, putting hands on Marko's shoulders and massaging him gently.

Zeke felt a pang of anger course through him as Annara touched the other vampire. His eyes were flashing silver and his face with burning red. He didn't know vampires could feel jealously, but right then, he wanted to rip Marko's head off. He wasn't even good looking! Hell, you wouldn't even think he was a vampire if it weren't for the tell-tale sign of fangs. Marko gave off a 'university dweeb' vibe- one of the slightly attractive guys that manages to pull once every three months at a student bar, but decides to settle down with one special lady eventually; reading her fucking poetry about how much he loves her. *Give me a break*, he thought.

Zeke grabbed Annara's wrist suddenly and she looked at him with puppy dog eyes. He kept a stern expression, but felt it ease as she raised his hand with her own and licked his knuckles with her long pink tongue, tasting the salty sweat on his skin.

"Are you coming or not, Pencil Neck?" he taunted. He wanted Marko to fear him and say no to Annara's request, but unfortunately, Zeke's new 'hard man' persona failed to intimidate him.

"Let me put this fire out and I'll be with you."

Annara clapped her hands together joyfully like a child who'd just been told she was going to Disney Land. She could sense Zeke was pissed off by it, but didn't want him to get the impression *he* was the one that made the rules in the underground now, just because he was a Slayer turned rogue. *She* had the authority in this place and answered only to the Master, who was teaching them all how to work together and grow in numbers so that they could one day- *soon*- take Meridion for their own.

"We'll wait by the entranceway that leads directly into the city," she informed Marko, and grabbed Zeke's shirt collar, leading him out into the hallway. He didn't resist at first, but then whirled her around on the spot and started kissing her ravenously.

Annara was always ready for moments like this and between kisses, felt his average sized bulge with her skilled hands.

Being a vampire rocks, Zeke thought. *This girl wants it every five fucking minutes. I'm in Heaven!*

As she released him from his trousers, Zeke pushed her against the wall and pulled her hot pants down, pushing himself inside the warm, wet haven between her legs. He hadn't expected the sex to be so damn good- because of the rather significant detail of them being very much dead- but all his senses were heightened and even the orgasms made every inch of him throb with the utmost pleasure that not even God could have perfected for a human's love-making.

Zeke thrust harder into her, kissed her creamy neck and then bit her shoulder as he felt the pleasure building. Blood was trickling into his mouth as he sucked at her skin and the sound of her growls and cries of pleasure made him pound her even harder. Soon, she was so overcome with the sensation of their act that Annara almost bit a chunk out of Zeke as she came loudly.

Zeke just smiled, gave her a moment to relax from the thrill of it all and then thrust into her again as fast as he could, pulling out for a moment so that he could turn her around and take her from behind. He marvelled as she bent over with her hands spread against the wall, allowing Zeke to get a good view of her perfect ass.

He finished with a growl that made his eyes flash silver and his fangs grow in length, caressing her ass as he felt the release gradually dying away, and as he pulled out, he thought about how much he loved being the man who got to fuck such a beautiful creature. Kieran had been wrong-the vampire way of life was the *ultimate* adrenaline rush.

"Thanks for the quickie, gorgeous," he whispered in her ear, as she straightened her arched back. Her long legs looked incredible in those heals of hers and Zeke loved how she stood shamelessly on display in the middle of the vampire underground.

Annara was grinning from ear to ear. "No problem, Sweetheart."

The pair of them were getting dressed just as Marko entered the hallway and locked his bedroom door behind him with a silver key. "Since you two have finally stopped fucking for five minutes, I propose we grab someone to eat before the sun turns us all into extra crispy vampire corpses, okay?"

"Jealous that I'm fucking your girl, Marko?" Zeke said, feeling a rush of confidence since he assumed the little prick had heard them having sex right outside his bedroom door.

"The ship that Annara and I were once on sailed a *long, long* time ago. So if you think you can annoy me with your moaning and groaning as you play with and pleasure my ex, you're very much wrong. Besides... Annara *always* comes back and visits me every once in a while and we fuck just as much as the next vampire," he said lightly and with an air of defiance. "So don't go thinking you're anything special."

Zeke was furious as Marko brushed against his shoulder. He looked to Annara and urged her to explain herself with his glare, but all he received from her was a shrug and a wink.

"You actually sleep with that guy?" Zeke asked stiffly.

"He could say the same about you," was her reply.

Annara saw Zeke's jaw tic and she passed him without a word, feeling as if she had gained her power back over her men; for they were *her* men. *Everyone wants Annara*, she thought pompously. *And Annara wants everyone else.*

Zeke found that vampires moved faster than your average human being. A distance that would take humans an hour to reach on foot took a vampire half of that. Also, vampires didn't feel the strain on their legs like others would have, which made it less of a chore to get places without the aid of a vehicle.

Annara strutted through the underground, turning the heads of vampires with her amazingly toned and perfectly sculpted ass, in those little pink hot pants that Zeke had the honour of walking behind most of the way. It wasn't until they arrived at the city entranceway she'd spoken of- guarded by four very large, muscular men- that his attention was stolen away.

They were huge. Two were black, the others white, and all were showing muscles that would make *The Terminator* shy away. Each of them were wearing chains around their neck-which was attached to the wall behind them, and as Zeke approached, he noticed they didn't bear the scent of vampires but of...

"Werewolves," Annara explained. "Useless for the purposes of our vampire army, for obvious reasons- one being they aren't vampires- but *perfect* when you need muscle in this place. We chain them up so they can't run rampant through the underground until *we* say they can. This world belongs to vampires- not dogs." Her words seemed to touch the nerve of one of the dark skinned men and his lip curled up angrily. He clicked his knuckles as he rolled his fingers into fists of steel, then loosened them as Annara approached. With a wave of her hand, the men began to move in collaboration.

Above the werewolves were large slats of wood, held in place by the earth and rock the underground had been carved out of, and in the centre of these slats was cut out a hole. The four men stood in a circle under this hole, facing away from each other and each of them reached up in unison to touch the dark shadow that covered the entrance. With the pulsating of muscles and the shaking of arms and legs, they worked together to lift whatever was obstructing the vampire's way out.

"That's fine," Annara told the men, as a gap was opened above, just about big enough for the three of them to climb through one after the other.

"Allow me," Zeke offered, lacing his fingers together and allowing Annara to put a dirt covered boot into his palm, so that he could lift her up and out. She obliged him, and with admirable swiftness, left Zeke and Marko starring up at the half-moon from below.

"After you," Zeke said cordially to Marko, then pushed passed him anyway, jumping from one wall, to the next- gaining height each time- and eventually grabbing a hold of one of the wooden slats. Annara reached down and helped him out of the ground, bringing him to his feet with ease and helping him brush the mud off his shirt.

Marko wasn't in the mood for showing off. Instead, he politely asked a werewolf to give him a lift up, and was practically thrown through the hole and onto the grass before the other vampires.

"Why don't those guys fight back?" Zeke asked in bewilderment, watching the werewolves peeking up at the moon with wide baleful eyes. They'd had the perfect chance to rip Marko to shreds, but had passed on the opportunity in order to help him out of a hole!

"Werewolves can be strange creatures." Annara began. "Some like to roam the woods and hunt wild deer their whole lives and *some* like to be chained up like the dogs they are, working for human hearts, which they get on the full moon. We section off part of the underground and drop off a couple of humans to run around through the maze of corridors- screaming and begging for mercy- so that the werewolves can chase them and... *you know.* It's their payment, you see. They work for us and we reward them at the end of it."

It made sense, though he hadn't been aware of this as a Slayer. If Kieran had known this was going on underground, they would have torn the place apart *years* ago to put a stop to it.

Now the vampires were all out in the open, Zeke couldn't believe his eyes as he realised where it was they were standing.

"We're inside The Stone Circle-?" he cried in awe. Surrounding him were the vertical stones that made up Meridion's most famous landmark and on the floor- not in its natural position- was the Stone Table itself; a place of sacrifice and much blood shed between humans. "This is crazy!" He watched in astonishment as the werewolves inside the hole, reached up and slid the Stone

Table back over the top of the entranceway, hiding everything from human sight. "You guys have been gaining access to the city under the Stone Table this *whole* time?"

Annara licked her right fang hungrily before answering. "That passageway is new. It's for the purposes of our war yet to come and it isn't used very often, accept by me and whomever I deem worthy. If we used it all the time, humans would notice us and report it to that jerk-off Mayor they have running the show in this shithole. When our army is fully recruited and trained, we're all gonna come out through the Stone Table, split up and coat this city in human blood."

"That's if all goes to plan," Marko piped up. He'd been watching Zeke and Annara in silence for quite sometime now, looking rather bored.

"It *will* go to plan!" Annara barked.

"If the Master quits being in that weird mood of his lately. Why can't he just fuck like normal vampires? I get the impression he's pining after some chick? It's really starting to piss me off. He's going to lose focus!"

"Shut up, Marko. Stop being so fucking pessimistic."

"Someone has to give you a reality check, *Annara*," he retorted.

She growled at Marko, low in the back of her throat and stormed off, with Zeke in tow. They were in the heart of the city and somewhere, there was a tasty morsel on their way home to a family who would never get to say what they really wanted to their loved one, when they later discovered they'd been killed by a vampire.

Zeke inhaled deeply. Two streets over there was an alley cat feasting on a rat. He sniffed again. To the south, a couple of hundred yards away, there was a teenage girl crying as she ran through the streets.

"Dinner is served."

Zeke followed the perfumed scent of the girl as he moved through the darkness, sensing that he was close. As he rounded a corner onto Rees Street, he caught a glimpse of her, keeping to the lamplight on the sidewalk.

She was about fourteen, wearing a baby blue jacket with white fur around the hood and a pair of tight denim jeans. Zeke could smell the salty tears on her cheeks and found himself licking his lips instinctively.

The sound of a mobile going off caused him to withdraw for a fraction of a moment, but as a stroke of luck, the girl dropped it in her haste to answer, and the small contraption broke to pieces on the floor.

"Are you okay?" he asked suddenly, pushing through the darkness and appearing before the terrified teenager.

She was too stunned to reply.

Zeke was struggling to conceal his fangs as he spoke. He wanted to make the kill clean- no screaming, no running- he was too damn hungry to have to play with his food first.

"Let me help you." He bent down with a naturally friendly air about him, giving the girl a false sense of security and all she could manage to stammer was a quiet "Thank you."

Her hair was brown and smelt of lemons. It made Zeke's nostrils tingle and his heart speed up. As he reached for the back of the broken mobile, the girl did the same and to her surprise, both hands clashed in her moment of frenzied gathering.

Zeke took his chance. He grabbed the girl's hand tight and twisted her arm back behind her until he heard the bone snap. The noise made his eyes flash silver and his teeth elongate. Her screaming was stifled under his palm, but it gave him a rush just to feel it vibrating against his skin. Finally, he was about to taste the sweetest beverage he'd ever come across- young, virgin blood.

As he drank the delicious liquid, a thought crossed his mind.

"Thanks for dinner love," he whispered coolly in the girl's ear, just before she died in his arms. "Now, I need to send a message to a friend."

Chapter 18

The Unthinkable

The atmosphere in Kieran's room was prickly and tense as Kiya entered after a few loud knocks on his chipped, uneven wooden door. The room was very thin in width, but long in length, and if Kiya held her arms out straight from her sides, she was able to touch both walls with ease. The floor was the same unclean texture as the main factory floor, with its dusty, hard surface, but Kieran had attempted to put a rug down next to his bed, to provide some sort of comfort to his feet. There were no pictures or posters on the walls and no books, DVD's or CD's anywhere to be found, like normal people would have owned. The room was simply made up of a bed, with black quilt covers; a desk, close to the door; a small window on the far wall, that was made of mottled glass so no one could see in, and a shiny black lamp with its shade missing.

Kieran was lying on his side, on top of his bed covers, staring at the wall opposite him. On the other side of the wall, Siren was probably lying in his bed also, waiting to fall asleep as the recent events rolled over in his head. They had both lost a close friend tonight, but Siren found it harder to express his misery. Usually, when something got him down, he'd just go to his room and reflect on it- praying to God in hope of finding some peace.

Kieran didn't stir as Kiya entered- at least, not until she walked over and perched on the end of his bed, with her ass a mere inch from his toes. It was then that he rolled onto his back and propped his head up to look at her, by folding his arms behind his head.

"Hey," he said penitently. "Sorry for shouting at you earlier-"

Kiya had held off seeing Kieran for at least two hours before making his cup of tea and bringing it to him. As time had moved past during those two hours, she hadn't been able to bear waiting any longer and had left Roxy to watch late night television alone.

"I brought you tea," she said with a smile, placing it on his desk next to the shade-less lamp, which was attracting a small grey moth to its bright glow. She despised moths and hoped to God it wouldn't start fluttering near her face because she'd end up screeching like a girl- even though she had every right to.

"Thanks," he grinned, but it faded quickly. After a pause, he looked Kiya square in the eye and asked, "Did Zeke hurt you?"

Kiya's thoughts drifted back to Zeke's hands around her neck. She thought of how she'd felt the life being choked out of her, to its very brink, then being dropped to the floor where she'd watched him spout out his threats and then run away.

"A little," she said plaintively. "But the physical hurt is nothing compared to what *you* must be going through."

Kieran wasn't blinking and Kiya had the feeling he was seeing images of his best mate in his head. All the good memories he had weren't likely to increase in magnitude now that Zeke was on the other side. Only bad would follow this terrible twist in his life.

"Is there anything I can do?"

Kieran didn't answer her question. He was staring at her now, watching the way she dipped her head down as she spoke rather nervously and how the light glinted off her bottom lip, making it shine enticingly. Her slightly damp, long brown hair kept tumbling forward and she had to reach up and tuck it back behind her ears every so often, giving him a better view of the right side of her pale face.

"Why are you so nervous?" he asked unexpectedly.

"I'm not!" she argued, turning to face him directly.

"Do I make you feel that way, because I don't mean to-" he sat up and brought his legs into a cross legged position, making sure he didn't touch her as he did so. With his face so close now, Kiya turned away again and focused on the wall in front of her. She couldn't allow herself to fall into his soulful gaze- could she?

"You don't make me nervous. That's absurd! You're my boss, right? We're just two people working together, who happen to live under the same roof."

"Instead of work colleagues, why don't you try *friends*?" he suggested.

Kiya thought about his words. Friends were the type of people she gossiped to on the phone; went shopping with at weekends, or went out for a drink with on Friday nights. Roxy was becoming a friend- though nothing like the ones she used to have. Roxy was female and had to face the same dangers as she did, which made it inevitable that they'd grow fond of each other. Everyone needed someone they could relate to and trust with secrets.

But Kieran was a guy! She'd had male friends in high school and as much as they would kid themselves they were just looking out for her, they all tried to put a hand down her panties at some point, saying "But I thought you liked me?!" before storming off, never talking to her again because they didn't feel they were good enough to be in her company anymore. No one likes being rejected.

"Okay," she said, trying to make it sound convincing.

Five minutes past, in which Kiya wished there had been something in the room she could point at and ask Kieran about to arouse conversation. As it was, there was nothing in the room of interest, accept for Kieran himself. She couldn't exactly say: "*Nice moth you've got there Kieran! Where'd you get it? What's its name? Has it been in your bedroom for long?*"

Kiya could feel his eyes on her in the dead silence and it made her want to leave the room immediately, because the more he stared at her, the more she wanted to stare back.

"Could you pass me the cup?" he asked, just as she was about to get up and go.

She passed it over obediently and shivered as his rough fingers brushed her own. "Cold?"

She looked at him in confusion. "Oh, no! No... I'm fine," she cried eventually.

He smiled, took a sip of the tea she'd made him and placed it on the floor next to one of the steel bed-legs. As he swallowed the lukewarm mouthful down, he noticed a cut on Kiya's forehead- the result of Zeke's fang scraping against her- and he reached out automatically to inspect it further. When she flinched in response, he apologised and dropped his hand quickly. "You have a cut- right here." He indicated the position of the cut on his own head, for her to have some direction.

Kiya touched herself and felt blood flaking off between her fingertips. "It's nothing," she said, then stood up sharply. "Look I'm going to leave you sleep, okay? You're probably tired after slaying and all that- so I won't intrude any longer."

Kieran looked disappointed, then sighed. "It's just as well I suppose," he said casually. "You're driving me wild, sitting on my bed and not allowing me to touch you."

Kiya's eyes widened. She paused for a long, breath-taking moment and then, the unthinkable happened.

She swooped down on him and kissed his lips; putting her hands on his biceps for support. He responded instantly, lifting a palm up to cup her face- savouring the electrifying kisses and each stroke of her tongue against his.

They remained locked like this for what seemed like an eternity.

Kiya dragged her hands over Kieran's broad shoulders- brushing nails across his back and then up through his long brown hair. Daringly, she shifted her body over him, spreading her legs so that she was sat on top.

Kieran was trying to resist undoing Kiya's clothes. Her scratch-resistant top she'd purchased from 'Bianca's' was looking far too tight on her soft, slim body and he had to close his eyes to stop himself from thinking about lifting it up over her head, to reveal the rest of her naked, creamy coloured flesh.

As Kiya whipped her head back for a moment, to remove the hair from her face, Kieran suffered from even more dirty ideas of just flipping her over right there and then and pulling her trousers off- running a hand over her long legs. It was making him ache for her until the point of pain and all he could think about was how satisfying it would be to slip inside that w…

"Wait," Kiya said, putting a hand on his.

Without realising it, Kieran had had his hand on Kiya's trouser zip and was in the process of pulling it down. *That's what you get for thinking with your dick,* he thought matter-of-factly. He hadn't even known he was going in for the kill until her voice had broken the spell.

Kiya was breathing heavily, sat on top of him, looking more beautiful than ever with her rapidly rising and falling chest and bright red cheeks from all the kissing they'd embarked on. She was looking down at Kieran's half unbuttoned shirt now, focusing on anything other than his handsome face.

"Don't tell me," he said slowly. "You can't do this?"

She nodded and Kieran felt his spirits sinking. He knew it was all too good to be true. "This could have been the start of something special," he added.

Kiya raised her eyes to his again. "It will be," she said, though unconvincingly. "I thought I was… I just needed…" She stopped stumbling over her words and took a deep breath. "Can I sleep in here tonight?"

It wasn't what he'd hoped she'd say, he had to admit. "Sure. I'll take the sofa."

"No-" she stopped him. "Stay. Please?"

He understood. It wasn't sex she was after. It was comfort! She was feeling lonely and needed someone to take her mind off the bigger picture. But he wasn't the type to tell a lady to fuck off because they were sad. If it was comfort she wanted, he'd be a gentleman and give her every ounce of comfort and love he had.

"Sure." Silently, he got off the bed, pulled back the covers as far as they'd go with her still sitting on it and motioned for her to get underneath. She smiled- though looking as if she was about to burst into tears- and crawled underneath, still fully clothed.

Kieran stood over her for a moment and allowed her to get comfortable. The bed wasn't a double, but it was slightly bigger than a single. As long as they stayed close, there would be plenty of room for the both of them.

Quietly, he unbuttoned the rest of his shirt, dropped it on the rug and slipped in next to her. He wasn't sure if she wanted his physical contact anymore, until she turned around to face him and put an arm across his chest, encouraging him to touch her. It made him warm inside as she did so and without fear, he placed an arm around her, drawing her in closer until her head was resting on him.

He listened intently to the sound of her breathing as it slowed to a steady, rhythmical pace that indicated she was asleep. Five minutes later, he fell asleep too.

He'd never felt so comfortable with a woman he'd *almost* had sex with in his whole life.

Kiya woke when the first rays of sunlight had penetrated the dimpled glass window, splashing a warm glow across her tired eyes. She opened one with great effort and examined her situation that morning.

Kieran was lying on his side with his face partly buried in her long brown hair and with his arm draped over her hip. His face was soft and emotionless as he slept on, unaware of her conscious state, and there was a very light layer of natural oil coating his skin.

Kiya marvelled at his slightly parted lips and thought about planting a kiss on them.

If you do this Kiya, there's no going back, she thought. *You have no right to get attached to this guy if you're only going to pull out when you've had a change of heart. You can't screw with his emotions.*

Her conscience was right. She had woken up beside Kieran like a lover would. If she kissed him and he woke to her touch, he'd think she was falling in love with him or something. Maybe it was better if she just left now and explained later that she had been in a weird place in her mind and that she'd just needed someone that night for reasons she hardly knew herself.

Rycan was obviously a part of her misery in all this. She felt as if she was replacing him too soon. But love is love right? It's unconditional and unexplainable. It can hit you at the most inconvenient times and go against everything you think is right.

Do I love Kieran?, she asked herself with guilt laced through every word. If Rycan could hear her thoughts, he'd lose all respect for her. *No*, she thought. *He wouldn't because he'd want me to be happy.*

It was all too much. She was getting a headache now and wanted to switch off again until she was completely refreshed and re-energised.

Whatever I feel for Kieran can wait.

The second time Kiya awoke, Kieran was wide awake and watching her.

"Morning," he said tenderly, weaving a hand through her hair.

She smiled in response and wiped the hair back from

her eyes. She could only imagine how terrible she must have looked and tried to keep her face out of view by sitting up so that he could only see the arch of her back and the tangled mess of her brown locks.

"Did you sleep well?" he asked, keeping his tone friendly and cool.

"Yes. Thank you," she assured him.

Kiya felt like she was caught in a web. A web that had a spider she actually *wanted* to be captured by. But her mind was still hazy on whether or not she was doing the right thing.

"I'm going to shower," she told him monotonously. As she moved, Kieran made a sighing noise behind her that he couldn't control. He didn't sound pleased and it made her feel terrible.

"We'll talk later okay?" she promised him.

Just as she was about to exit the room, the door burst open and Roxy came bounding in. She didn't look surprised to see Kiya there. She was too panicked to care.

"Kieran- there's something you need to see."

Kieran kicked into gear the second she'd finished her sentence and ran from the room, following in Roxy's footsteps. She was leading him outside, where the rain had eased off, but had left the ground full of deep shimmering puddles. Face down in one of them was the body of a teenage girl. Her hair was dirty from the dead earth, blood and rainwater congealing together and her clothes were torn to tatters. Kieran carefully rolled the body over and found bite marks in her neck.

Vampires.

"That's not all," Roxy informed them shakily. The group followed her finger and found themselves staring at graffiti messily scrawled all over the front of the factory doors. The words were made up of a mixture of dirt and blood, reading: *Slayers Beware. We know where you live now. You WILL fall.*

Kieran scratched his head and looked at both Kiya and Roxy in turn. There was only one person who could have informed the vampire population where their headquarters were situated.

"Zeke," he mumbled, looking at the teenage girl with sadness in his eyes. She looked no older than fourteen. *How could someone be so sick*? he thought miserably.

"What are we going to do now?" Kiya asked, as Siren joined them.

The four Slayers stared glumly at the graffiti for a while. Siren didn't need to be filled in. The sight of the dead girl and the words on the wall was explanation enough. They were all in *very* big trouble.

"I've been dealing with vampires for years," Kieran breathed in an even tone. "Zeke is no different from the last. We're better equipped than they are and have never lost a battle before- although there have been casualties, I'll admit, and some pretty close calls. Don't sweat it guys. This is nothing to worry about."

"So it's business as usual?" Siren asked with a determined air.

Kieran nodded.

"What about the girl?" Roxy pointed out. The attention of the group returned to the poor dead female still lying in the puddle, with her face slightly bloated and her eyes full of an eerily frozen fear from last night's blood bath.

"Fetch me a blanket. I'll take her down to the station. While I'm at it I'll inform them of the pizza delivery boy in the graveyard too."

"The police don't mind you waltzing into the station with news and evidence of dead bodies do they?" Kiya queried sceptically. The police force in Meridion were a joke. She was surprised they didn't cuff Kieran and throw him in to the lions den for bringing news of so much death and claiming 'the vampires did it.'

"I have a friend in the station. She's a woman I used to be close to, who became a high ranking police officer after high school. She takes her job pretty damn seriously, unlike the rest of the pigs they have working at that station. Emilia handles the vampire cases in Meridion you see- and I help her out."

Kiya felt a pang of jealously. She was almost tempted to ask if she could join Kieran, just to get a good look at this 'Emilia' woman he spoke of. She was probably beautiful. She hated the idea of there being a spark between them that could be rekindled. It was such a cliché! Things like that happened all the time- on the television.

"Let's get her inside," Kieran instructed, picking the body up with ease. The dirty puddle water dripped over his rippling abs, that were exposed to the afternoon sunshine. In his haste to see what Roxy had to show him, he'd failed to put his shirt back on.

It pained him to hold the teenage girl. She was so young and innocent looking. How could he have let Zeke do this to her? He should have patrolled longer the night before. They should have burst through those mysterious metal doors in the graveyard, regardless of their small number, and just blasted hell out of whatever was down there.

There was one thing he was sure of now. He would stake Zeke the first chance he got, without any hesitation. That bastard didn't deserve to walk the earth.

Chapter 19

The Master

Annara found Zeke's creativity at the old factory to be quite a turn on, as he bravely covered the walls in blood, knowing full well that the Slayers could come out and blow his head off at any given moment. She was nervous by it all, but just as equally enthralled, making sure to watch from a fair distance, with Marko at her side, so that if worse came to worse, they could both leg it out of there before either of them got hurt.

"You find this funny?" Marko asked incredulously, waving a hand at Zeke's silhouette, as he smeared his bloodied hands over the metal doors of the factory. "It's imbecilic!"

"When the fuck did you get so whiny?" Annara spat at him, her arms crossed over her impressive breasts.

Marko raised an eyebrow. "When my brother came back to me with no legs."

Annara's wide eyes changed to slits. "It should be *you* wiping the blood of a virgin girl over those walls- not 'Zekey Boy' over there! Those Slayers have done more damage to *you* than they have to him. Grow a spine, Mark'! *Jeez*," she argued, hoping she was planting ideas in Marko's head, to perform some daring acts like her new vampire friend. He didn't take the bait though. He was too damn comfortable standing alone beside her in the desert wasteland, than to go picking fights with demon slaughterers.

"The *old* Marko always used to try his hardest to impress me," Annara implored, sounding emotionally hurt. She pouted like a child, but it didn't hold for long.

"The old Marko used to think immortality meant what it said on the tin, too. But that isn't really true, is it?" He was getting completely fed up with Zeke's games now. He just wanted to leave and get back home to Alex. Time was against them. If they didn't leave soon, the moon that shone down on them would soon be replaced by a blazing fireball that would cook the flesh off their bones and leave nothing but a small pile of ash in their places.

"Fuck this. I'm out of here. That little prick at the toll booth won't let us out now and we've got less than an hour to reach the Stone Table-"

"Sean will let us through if I tell him too."

"So it's *Sean* now? Don't tell me you've slept with *him* too? And since when did he let *vampires* through?" Marko asked sceptically.

"He doesn't. He lets *Annara* through because she once showed him what a *real* woman looks like naked and he never hesitates to grant me access to the graveyard when the sun is coming up after that *very* special night."

"If that's the case, why didn't we just go through the toll earlier this evening?"

"Because if those Slayers catch us waltzing through the gates at dusk, they'd nail us, *idiot*."

As Annara finished arguing with Marko, Zeke appeared before them, looking sweaty and incredibly demonic, with his blood-stained clothes and dripping red fangs. There were smears of dirt across his cheeks, as well as a mixture of earth and blood up to his elbows.

"Enjoying your first night as a vampire?" Annara asked him with a devilish grin on her lips. She already knew what his answer would be.

"Hell yeah! I just painted me a picture using a fourteen year old girl's blood! It doesn't get more wild than that."

"Sorry to interrupt your enthusiasm for art, *Van Gogh*, but we need to get out of here. NOW."

"Chill out," Zeke snapped. "We're leaving, just as soon as I scratch that bastard's bike."

The three vampires left the wasteland on foot, running across the dusty earth like a pride of lions. Zeke felt an incredible sense of freedom that he'd never had at the factory and Annara felt like the ruler of the roost, with her two men at her side. Marko wasn't enjoying the wind on his face as much as the others, due to the agonising fact that the sky was losing its inky darkness and becoming very pink on the horizon.

At the toll booth, half an hour later, Annara pounded on the glass and threw Sean out of his sleepy state. He had his head resting on his control panel and had been catching some z's- something his father would have been furious about if he ever found out- but who could blame him for falling asleep? He just wasn't cut out for the night shifts!

"Open the gate!" Annara screeched at him, clicking her long talons against the glass. "And make it snappy, kid."

Sean managed a curt, open mouthed nod and allowed the three vampires access to the graveyard without hesitation. He'd rather they go home than hang around him, but felt a wave of guilt slap him as Kieran's friendly, trusting face flickered into his minds eye. “I hate vampires,” he grumbled to himself.

Marko was terrified as the sun’s rays first began to coat the land. The graveyard was suddenly becoming luminous and he could already feel his skin tingling from the heat.

“I can’t believe you talked me into to coming out here!” he cried in fear as a small cloud of steam began to emit from his shoulders and hands. He wasn’t proud to admit it, but he was on the verge of tears.

“It’s not much further,” Annara informed him, although she knew she didn’t have to tell them both this, for they could tell for themselves how close the metal doors were.

Five minutes before they reached the forest that concealed their entranceway, the sun finally lifted high enough to give the vampire’s something to *really* worry about.

Annara screeched in pain as her right arm- exposed to the sunlight- burst into bright orange and yellow flames, and she started to flail her arm around in panic. Zeke did an honourable thing and ran to her flaming side, using his body mass to try and shield Annara’s right side from further burning. It was awkward, but effective as they ran side by side.

Marko was yelping and groaning as one side of his face began to blacken. It hurt so badly, he almost stopped in his tracks to grab at his skin, howling like a wolf to the moon. If it weren’t for Zeke giving him a good shove in the back, he would have been left standing there to face the dawn.

The shadows of the forestry acted as a bucket of water would, slapping them face-on and dousing out the flames. Zeke's body had only partially begun to simmer-showing signs of grey smoke pouring from his skin- for his body was still being conformed to the vampire gene that Annara had planted inside him. He wasn't all *vampire* yet, as much as he felt and looked it.

"The sun can still cut through these trees. We need to get inside," Marko panted, hunched over and looking as if he were about to vomit. He was suffering from burn wounds all over his cheeks and forehead and it made Zeke cringe at the thought of damaging his own profile. His face wasn't exactly attractive, so the last thing he wanted was burns thrown into the mix.

Annara took the lead again, slamming her fist into the metal doors of their vampire haven as hard as she could.

"Open up! Open up damn it!" she screamed, denting one of the doors with the force of her iron fists.

Silence followed as she listened in wait.

"Who the fuck is on duty down there?" she asked curiously.

There was a pause, broken by a very nervous Marko.

"Uh... that would be me."

Annara looked at the locked doors and then back at Marko. "We're locked out because *you* didn't find someone to take your place?" she asked as calmly as her voice would allow, advancing on Marko slowly. He took a step back and found himself against the large trunk of a tree.

"M...My br...brother was hurt. I h...had to help him. You must understand-"

Just when it looked as if Annara would cut Marko some slack, she swung her clenched fist at his nose and broke it instantly. It knocked him back on his feet, where he lay on the ground spluttering and moaning as his own blood poured into his mouth thickly. Even vampire blood that belonged to *yourself* could make you feel drunk and he was already feeling drowsy from the amount that had slid down the back of his throat.

Annara stood over Marko for a while, but wasn't looking directly at him. She was examining the canopy overhead and thinking about their impending doom. The leaves above were not very thick and would definitely allow the sunlight to penetrate when it reached a higher point in the sky.

"Well, so much for seeing Meridion fall, huh?" Zeke mumbled light heartedly.

"You can shut up!" Annara shouted, rounding on him with a flash of silver as she pinned her eyes on him. "Marko was right. We never should have let you start fooling around at that Slayer's house."

"Wait a minute!" Zeke yelled angrily, "Think logically here before you start attacking me with your bullshit blaming technique. Even if we'd been back here ten minutes earlier- even an *hour* earlier- Dickweed here would still be on the wrong side of the fucking doors, wouldn't he?"

Zeke was right. Marko was the one to blame. No, the *Slayers* were the ones to blame. If they hadn't have cut Alex's legs off, Marko would still be on duty and they would never have been locked out, like they were now.

Annara gave the door a few more pounds then slumped next to it. A spot of sunlight was resting on her thigh, but she was too infuriated with the unbearably *dumb* male species to move as it prickled her skin, giving off the rancid smell of burning flesh.

As if God was cutting them all some slack, Annara almost knelt down and prayed to Him in thanks as a clanking noise sounded from within the underground.

"Open up!" she shouted desperately through the tiny gap in the doors. "We're locked out."

With a great sigh of relief, the doors opened inwards to reveal a most unexpected sight. There was a man clinging to the ladder, observing the three vampires with a critical eye. A man that Zeke had never been introduced to.

"Sir-" Annara murmured, jumping up and standing up straight to express her respect and will to serve.

Zeke raised an eyebrow as he witnessed Annara's behaviour. "Who the hell is this dude?"

The young, handsome vampire answered him smoothly. "I'm the leader of the vampire army, of course. And *you* are one of my new recruits. Some have even come to call me their 'Master' as time has progressed and I'm just too proud to correct them."

"Sorry Mr Pompous, but I bow to no one-"

Annara hissed quietly at the sound of Zeke's words. He obviously didn't understand greatness when he was in its presence.

Suddenly, the man who'd appeared inside the entranceway was upon Zeke in a flash, gripping his throat tightly. Zeke felt the man's fingernails biting into his skin and couldn't help but notice his eyes flashed red, instead of the usual vampiric silver.

"Annara turned you into one of us for the purposes of my army and I will have it no other way, you hear me? I know your type. You reek of human cowardice and now that you've been given the gift of immortality you think you're suddenly an assertive, untouchable, fantastic and fearsome fucking stud who can do whatever the hell he wants. Am I right?"

Zeke made an odd noise in his throat. It wasn't that he needed to breathe- for he was dead and required no oxygen- but he couldn't come up with any snappy retorts because his words were no longer coherent. If he'd had the guts, and the opportunity, he would have told this 'Master' guy to bite him.

"I'll rip your heart out if you so much as step out of line, *boy*. Now tell me, where have you three been that has you in this current state, *huh?* If it weren't for the fact I was looking for Annara, you would have been left out here to burn!"

"I was taking Zeke on his first hunt," Annara explained in an even tone of voice. She knew there wouldn't be a problem with showing a new recruit the vampire way of life. It was like an initiation into the group. Most 'newbie's' went through it.

"I see," the Vampire Leader replied crisply. "And where did you all go?"

"He found a girl to eat, in the heart of the city, and we later went to the Slayer's Headquarters-"

The Master's eyes flashed blood red again. "You stay away from there!"

Annara was taken aback by his sudden burst of outrage.

"You are not to go there!" he continued to bark at them, "*No one* is to go there- not even ex Vampire Slayers-" this was aimed at Zeke. "I have set plans in motion and you're all dumb enough to fuck it up for me! There's no need to be interfering with Slayers until I say the time is right. Got that?"

"Yes sir," Annara said. She was looking shamefaced, as if the last thing she ever wanted to do was disappoint the man that stood before them all.

It was only when Marko whispered a "Yes sir," also, that the Master turned on him at last.

"Tell me, Marko- why are you out here, when you should have been on door duty from dusk till dawn?"

Zeke could see the rising panic on Marko's face. He was struggling to control a stutter and was looking around wildly for help from Annara, who had turned away from him to examine her talons.

"I...I..."

"Perhaps it has something to do with your brother, who is lying uselessly on his bed right now as a big pile of ash because I had no choice but to stake him through his worthless heart."

Marko visibly gulped. He couldn't fathom the fact that he'd just lost his brother, for good this time. There would be no more hunting together. No more blood baths. They'd never own an apartment together with their own human slave, like they'd always dreamt of having when they'd heard the vampire underground was going to war.

"You two are a joke and you're putting a black mark on all vampire kind."

The Master was leaning in closely to the quivering Marko now. His body rippled with muscles in his tight black, sleeveless shirt and Annara felt her eyes flash silver in excitement as she watched him flick a tongue over Marko's neck.

"I'm usually a very merciful bad guy," he said primly. "But the truth is Marko, the time has almost come to take over Meridion and I can't have vampires locking my leading lady outside to burn in the sunlight-,"

Annara grinned happily. The Vampire Leader needed her and it made her feel wickedly important. *It's good to be me*, she thought and almost let out a cry of joy as the Master bit Marko's throat, followed by a series of vigorous and violent slashes with his finger nails, pulling Marko's body to pieces as if he were a rag doll.

"That's why you bow to me," he spat blood at Zeke, who was standing with an astonished expression, frozen on his pale face. The Master was quite blatantly in a dangerous mood. "Now the pair of you get inside. If I'd wanted a tan in this sunlight, I'd have stayed a human."

Zeke approached the door and realised there was no going back now. He'd left Kieran and the comfortable world of slaying to become someone who worked for an even scarier person. In appearance, The Master looked like he'd never even reached adulthood, although his muscles and penetrating glare suggested he was capable of looking after himself in the big wide world. Marko's now non-existent body was evidence of that.

"After you," he said with a growl in his throat.

Zeke looked wistfully at the hatch and jumped through, without using the ladder. When he landed, he felt the vibrations from the impact running up his legs, but bit back the urge to grimace in pain. The Master did the same, only he made it look effortless, and Annara used the ladder, wiggling her ass as she went- like she always did when the opportunity arose.

"Shall we?" the Master said, indicating the corridor.

Zeke followed with Annara at his side and felt all his confidence leaving him. One wrong move now and he'd be toast.

Chapter 20

The Games We Play

"That bastard scratched his name into my bike!"

Kieran could be heard screaming as Kiya walked towards him. She had to stop suddenly, because a wave of sickness threatened to hit, and before Kieran noticed her strange behaviour, she ran around to the other side of the factory and vomited onto the dusty floor in private, putting a hand on the brick wall for support. As she wiped her mouth clean, she prayed Kieran hadn't heard her gagging and tried to keep a straight face as she returned to the parking area, under the damp, dead trees. On the body of the bike, scratched into the black paintwork, was Zeke's name glinting silver in the sunlight.

"What a complete asshole!" Kieran cried, fumingly. "Now I'm gonna have to scratch *my* name somewhere on *him*."

Kiya was aware that Kieran was fighting a bad mood. He kept eyeing his bike dejectedly and then twisting away from it to stop himself from kicking the damn thing over in a rage. He loved his bike too much for words and it had been with him since he'd left high school- a gift to himself for making it out alive! It had never needed any service on its engine or frame, and had never gained a single nick in its paintwork- until now.

"You could always get a new one."

Kieran sighed. "It wouldn't be the same."

He eventually realised that dwelling on the damage to his vehicle was quite pathetic and instead tried to change the subject to a greater issue- one that was a lot more grim. "I've rolled the girl up in a blanket and put her in the back of the truck, because there's no room in the front to just drive around with a dead body. I've also put a rain cover over the back to conceal her. I wanted to ask you-"

Kiya crossed her arms over her chest. "If I'd come?"

He nodded and gave a weak smile. "For the company?"

It made Kiya smile back, although dealing with dead bodies was not the time to be showing any signs of happiness. "I could do with getting out of here for a bit."

With the girl in the back of the truck and the pizza delivery boy's wallet in Kieran's coat pocket, the two of them slid into the front seats and took off down the road, leaving tire marks in the muddy, wet ground as they went.

The sun was bright this particular day, when it wasn't behind grey clouds, and it reminded Kiya of the expression 'calm before the storm.' Meridion usually had its days of peaceful skies and tranquil winds and then, when you least expected it, lightning came crashing down all around you and thunder shook the world out of its stupor. At least for now there wasn't any bad weather to add to the already gloomy atmosphere.

"I'm glad we're alone," Kieran said suddenly, keeping his eyes fixed on the road, but wanting to look at Kiya more than anything. He was keeping a straight face, but found it hard to keep his voice even.

"Didn't you get enough *alone* time with me last night?" Kiya joked, but bit her lip as she finished speaking- realising it sounded harsher than she'd intended.

"I just want you to know that... that I *do* care about you, Kiya, *a lot*, despite what you may think." He paused. "These past few days have been...well, *strange*, I have to admit. I've never fallen so hard and fast for a girl before, like I have with you-"

"Kieran-" Kiya tried interrupting.

"No. Just let me finish. I've been rehearsing this in my head all morning as you slept, so just let me say my piece."

She closed her mouth and leant back in her seat, trying to look less rigid than she actually felt. Her face was heating up and her hands were becoming clammy. She felt like a school girl again, and tried telling herself she was an adult now. These things happen. Deal with it.

"I um...I don't know if you feel the same way about me, and it doesn't really matter right now, because things are getting dangerous, as you fully well know. I just want you to know that I'm going to be there for you, even if it kills me. Literally. I don't want anything to happen to you, because... I care about you too damn much."

Kiya believed him. His hard man exterior was a mask for the sensitive, kind individual underneath and she believed every word he said about her. He wasn't going to say all those things just to bed her. Her heart told her he was being genuine and it was now urging her to be genuine back. It was the least she could do.

But she didn't. She remained in stunned silence for the entire journey to the police station. And as they pulled up, she realised the big, unbelievable mistake she'd just made.

"Kieran?"

"Yup," he said quietly.

"Did I mention I'm wanted by the police for inhuman acts against another Meridion citizen?"

He frowned. "Are you being serious?"

"I'm afraid so. I found posters at my mother's house last night."

Kieran took his eyes off the road to glower at her. "What happened exactly?"

"Nothing, I just went to see my mum and saw a poster-"

"No," Kieran cut in. "What did you do to get in this situation?"

Kiya bowed her head. "You know the night I broke into the factory?"

Kieran made a grunt of acknowledgement.

"I was running away from something I did." She paused. "A guy attacked me, with intentions of rape and I kind of sliced his arm off for doing so."

"Damn!" Kieran cried, "I dread to think what you would have done to *my* dick if I'd tried putting it in you last night-"

"Hey, this is serious!" she slapped Kieran's arm and he grinned. "Less of the *dick* talk, okay?"

"Don't worry about it, Princess...," (Kiya rolled her eyes at the pet-name) "You can sit in the truck with your head down and I'll go inside and speak to Emilia. When she comes out for the body, I'll tell her you're Roxy in one of your wigs. As long as you don't make eye contact, she'll believe me."

"I hope so."

The police station was a few streets over from the Stone Table and it had a car park full of beaten up, old police cars, with their bumpers falling off and cracked windows disconcertingly on display. There were no officers outside the dull, red brick building and no sign of life behind the glass double doors. *Must be on a mission to find a doughnut stall*, Kiya thought stereotypically.

She hated this place. It had been the same building she had been taken to when she was interrogated about Rycan's whereabouts on the night he'd found the Mayor's daughter dead with *his* sword sticking through her fatally. The memories hurt and she tried her best to do what Kieran had advised- keeping her head down and her eyes away from the dreaded place.

As Kieran slipped out of the car, he returned to Kiya's window and leant in to talk with her before departing. "You know, you could just sit down with Emilia and tell her what happened that night. Do the statement thingy and I'll back you up all the way. She can bring the guy in who tried raping you and you won't have a black mark over your name any more."

"What if they don't believe me? I'm sorry Kieran, but I can't risk being executed on the Stone Table right now. I've got too much to live for."

Kieran thought she was referring to *him* for a fleeting moment, but his excitement died as she continued with, "I haven't even found Tristian yet and I *will* get my revenge, no matter how long it takes. *No one* will take that from me."

"Okay, crazy lady," Kieran said, in a light hearted manner. It wasn't his nicest pet name for her, she had to admit. "I'm just going to leave you stew for a bit, okay? And make sure you don't go letting out any of that anger on *me*. I told you I liked you. I'm not out to hurt you-"

"Yeah, yeah," Kiya grinned, shoving him in the chest to move him away from the window. "Just get in there and do what you came here for."

"Hmmm. You know, I might just ask Emilia out on a date while I'm at it... since you're not interested-" he said teasingly.

"Would you really want to risk pissing me off right now, after you've just heard what I'm wanted by the police for?" Kiya replied threateningly- though in a friendly manner.

Kieran swooped through the car window, leaning in close to her again. "So dating other women would piss you off, huh? Does that mean you're actually thinking about being my girlfriend, or am I *way* off the mark here?"

Kiya was smiling uncontrollably now, feeling her cheeks reddening. She hadn't grinned this much from a conversation with a guy since she'd first met Rycan. It felt good and she wasn't ashamed to think it.

"Get out of here, Kieran. You're blocking out the sun and it's not like we get much of it in this city."

"You can come with us, if you want," Kieran continued, good-humouredly and moved back out of the window slightly. "We can all go out for dinner- I'm thinking oysters and wine- then hit some clubs. We can finish the evening off by checking into a hotel- all three of us- and spend the night getting frisky."

Kiya was biting back laughter now, but she didn't want to break her feigned expression of annoyance with the man who was making cocky threats of sleeping with another woman, just because *she* wasn't ready.

She crossed her arms haughtily and wiggled a finger for him to come back to her window for a third time.

"Am I being punished?" he asked, wincing. "I can take your blow. Strike me down. Don't leave me in suspense woman!"

Kiya looked intently at Kieran's face and felt all guilt leaving her. He had his eyes closed and was trying to prevent a smile from curling his lips up. Oh how he made her heart pump a mile a minute! She took one long look at his face- that handsome, soul shaking face- and kissed him.

He didn't open his eyes for the duration of his punishment- if you could call it that. Instead, he focused on the rhythm of her tongue flicking against his and how she filled his heart with warmth and joy. He was quite relieved when she pulled away though, because he had felt the stirrings of a hard-on that would have been mightily tough to conceal in his jeans.

"Well. I think I'm gonna try pissing you off more often if that's what I get for being such a bad boy."

Kiya pointed a finger at him. "Don't think you know how to work me just yet, Mr Nightly, because I may change tactics."

Kieran winked. "I guess I'll have to be careful around you then."

In the space of time it took Kieran to walk across the car park, Kiya couldn't drag her eyes off him. She could still taste him in her mouth and felt the need for more. It was all so wrong, but felt *so-o* right.

The front desk was empty. There was no steaming mug of tea waiting for its owner to return to it and no computer whirring with information on its screen.

Kieran was used to the creepy feeling that all the officers in the building were dead. He'd walked into the police station so many times over the years that he was beginning to wonder if he could be classed as a 'cop' now too.

The waiting area was pretty crummy for a police station. It had torn green chairs, with their inner stuffing on display, and posters that dated back to before he was even born! The tile floor was old and covered in muddy boot prints and in one corner of the room, on a graffiti covered table, was a wilted pot plant, that was shedding its leaves from lack of water.

"Yo, anyone here?" he tried, crying out through cupped hands. There were two blue doors on either side of the secretary's desk, both of them requiring a code to unlock for admittance.

Suddenly, Kieran had a brain wave and daringly climbed up onto the desk. There was a contraption he'd seen an officer use before; when a certain button was pushed, you could speak into a microphone that reverberated your message all around the building.

He cleared his throat and lifted the microphone to his lips. "This is an announcement for all officers who are still capable of walking without a waddle... please come to the front desk. You're extra large order of sugar coated, sprinkle covered doughnuts has arrived. Thank you."

There was a small clicking sound as the connection was broken and Kieran slipped smugly back behind the desk to wait. It didn't take long for someone to appear.

"What do you think you're playing at?" came a strangled cry as an obese officer ploughed through the door on Kieran's right. "I should arrest you for touching our equipment without authorisation!"

"Will you chop my head off for it? Or just my hand?" Kieran quipped.

"Hey... shut up wise ass, or maybe I'll cut something else off you probably wouldn't want to lose."

"Ooh officer, you're making me blush."

The officer looked directly at him and scowled. He was trying to fold his podgy arms over his visible 'man-boobs,' but settled for leaving them resting on his extra large belt- for it was less of an effort this way.

"So what do you want Mr. Underwear Model?"

"What I always want. To talk to Emilia, of course."

"A smart guy would have used the microphone to ask for *her*, not just for any old officer." The guy smiled cruelly.

"Yeah, but I was just checking if the lard arses on the force were actually doing what they're paid to-"

The officer made a guttural noise and reached to his belt, grabbing his shiny black baton and taking a swipe at Kieran's head. Kieran ducked and twirled away elegantly, just as the right door opened again.

"Stand down!" came the commanding tone of a woman, who did not sound impressed by what she had just walked upon. "I saw you both on surveillance and knew this conversation would probably end in a fight if I didn't intervene soon."

"If you'd let me finish, it would have ended with my foot up his arse and my baton down his fucking throat," the police officer said through wheezing noises. Somehow, the beautiful female officer and Kieran both doubted that.

Kieran put an arm around the officer's wide, moist back and whispered in his ear, "Chest pains are your heart's way of saying, phone 999. And I don't mean the police station, in case you're too dumb enough to work that one out."

The officer shook Kieran's arm off and skulked off in red hot fury, loosening the tie around his extra large neck and slamming the blue door on the left.

"You always have to make an entrance," Emilia said, trying to hold back a smile. She didn't approve of Kieran's behaviour, but it made a nice change in the usually grim atmosphere that the station delivered each long and tiring day. "You have something for me?"

"Unfortunately, yes."

"Let's step outside," she suggested.

Kieran paused- his eyes widening. *Lets just hope Kiya has her head down,* he thought as he followed Emilia's slim, well toned body out of the dreary station.

She was definitely a fine looking lady, with her splendid hips and small round ass. Her brown hair, which was naturally wavy, was tied in a tight ponytail and her eyes were hazel in colour. The blush on her face exaggerated high, prominent cheek bones and her lips shone with a fantastic fullness. Kieran had known the taste of those lips years ago, but wouldn't dream of re-living it now. He just couldn't love her anymore. Not like he thought he did in high school, before they went their separate ways.

When she stopped on a lower step than he, Kieran got a face-full of Emilia's large breasts. In his opinion, they didn't look right with such a skinny waist, but he wasn't about to tell her she needed a breast reduction. She'd probably kick him in the balls if she heard words like that coming out of his mouth.

"Here-" he said simply, handing over the wallet in his jacket, then explained in as much detail as possible where she could find the body of the boy and what the cause of death had been.

"That's about the seventh killing by vampires we've had this week alone," she sighed solemnly, "And that's only the ones we know about."

Kieran saw Emilia's eyes go vacant for a moment, then he spoke in a soft voice of the girl in the back of the truck.

"About fourteen you say?" her thinly plucked eyebrows rose. "Ah, fuck. We had a mother on the phone last night, and first thing this morning, telling us her fourteen year old daughter hadn't come home. I didn't want to tell her she was probably dead, as you can imagine, so I gave the poor thing some hope and promised I'd find her girl. I was hoping against hope she'd just stayed at a friend's house, but no one I managed to contact had seen her after she left a house party pretty late."

"I'm sorry to have to bring you the bad news," Kieran apologised, scratching the back of his head and staring at the truck. "The body is in a bit of a state to be honest. Roxy found her this morning outside the factory. The vampires… they kind of know where our headquarters are now and wanted to leave a message."

Emilia looked bewildered. "How and why?"

"Zeke. He's one of them and I think he's going to try and take us all on, single handed."

Her face melted sympathetically at the news that Zeke was no longer on their side. "I'm so sorry Kier-" Kindly, she reached out and put her arms around Kieran's broad shoulders, squeezing him comfortingly, trying to cure some of her own pain in finding out the girl she'd spent all night searching for was dead. "I'll be honest with you, Kieran. I'm getting tired of fighting the good fight, and I'm only thirty one! Do you think there might be a city somewhere that isn't over-run with vampires, werewolves, murderers etc that we can both retire to?"

"I wouldn't go, even if there was such a place."

Emilia smiled. "Me neither."

There was silence between the two of them for a while, before it was suggested Kieran bring the girl in, so that they could phone the mother and have her identify the body as her daughters- an extremely gruelling and heart wrenching task. After that, there was nothing left to do but say goodbye.

"Sorry the visit was so short."

"That's okay," Emilia said, giving an encouraging smile. "We should go out sometime, perhaps? Have a drink or two?"

Kieran felt like laughing at the irony of it all- thinking back to winding Kiya up in the car about asking Emilia out on a date. "I don't think that's a good idea."

"Why? Your new girlfriend in the car won't like it?"

Kieran stared at her in shock, but hid it quickly. "That's Roxy-"

"Don't make me out to be an idiot, Kieran," she shot back. "I know that isn't Roxy. I'm a police officer. I'm not blind. She had her head suspiciously down most of the time we were outside but eventually, she couldn't resist a peek at the woman who was hugging her man."

He looked down at his shoes speechlessly.

"I'll overlook the fact she's wanted by police, because I assume that's the reason you told her to lie low right?"

"I never could keep anything from you," Kieran grinned reminiscently.

"And you never will," she replied coolly. "Now get out of my police station. I have a mother to phone who's worried sick and a new surge in vampire activity to prepare for."

With that, Kieran left.

Chapter 21

Fairytale Romance

Roxy chewed her lip excessively as she rifled through her wardrobe, throwing potential outfits onto her unmade bed and grumbling to herself as she went. Getting ready for a night out was meant to be fun, but she was *so* racked with indecision, it was beginning to make her brain hurt.

The main cause for her lack of enjoyment in the matter was the fact she didn't know where Logan was planning on taking her. Okay, so she *assumed* it was going to be out for dinner somewhere, but what if she dressed completely wrong for the occasion? She wanted to look seductive, but not too slutty. She wanted to appear glamorous, but not *too* over the top and in your face.

She didn't even want to *think* about shoes and make-up just yet, for it would only throw her into a fit of agitation that she didn't think she'd be capable of controlling right then.

After narrowing it down to five ensembles, she began trying them on in turn, using the full length mirror she'd made Kieran attach to the back of her door a few months ago. She wished Kiya was there to give an opinion, and to help her zip up, tie up and whatever else needed to be done to keep the clothes on her curves. It always helped having someone to confide in and ask for honesty- something she'd never had with her upper-class, snobbish, emotionally dead mother all those years ago.

Just as Roxy was taking her bra off to try on a black and red corset, her bedroom door unexpectedly swung open, paralysing her with complete alarm.

"Oh, shit," came Kieran's genuinely surprised, husky voice as he closed the door again snappishly.

"Don't you know how to knock? How many times do I have to *stress* this to you? Stay out of my room, unless it's a life threatening situation!"

"I'm *real* sorry, Darlin,"' Kieran apologised heartily. "I was just letting you know that Kiya and I are back from the police station and that everything has been dealt with."

Roxy frowned at the shadow he was casting in the slightly ajar doorway but knew he wouldn't be sly enough to try and sneak a glimpse at her breasts. He appeared to be making progress with Kiya now, as she'd discovered that very morning when walking in on the pair of them. "Fine. I'll speak with you in a minute."

Kieran paused for a minute and then spoke through the gap once more. "I think you should go with the violet dress. It complements your shape and captures peoples eyes- the way the material floats about your legs. Plus, it's not often we 'Slayers' get to see our Roxy in something normal girls wear."

"What's so good about being normal?" she asked, without expecting an answer. "And besides. How do you know what I look like in that dress? I haven't even tried it on yet."

Kieran laughed nervously. "I kind of walked in on you when you were twirling around in the bathroom, trying on your stuff a few months back and like I just said, it captures people's eyes, the way it floats about your legs."

Roxy's face turned a distinct shade of white. She hadn't noticed the door to the bathroom opening when she'd tried having a 'girly' moment of putting on pretty clothes and strutting up and down in her heels. She'd felt depressed that particular afternoon, wondering if she'd ever find another man, and had wanted to remind herself she was a good looking gal- not just a killing machine.

"Thanks Kieran," she smiled, putting the corset down and watching the door close behind her. *I guess I don't need a woman's help after all,* she thought. *And if I find these clothes were inappropriate tonight, I'll just kick his ass tomorrow.*

When Roxy entered the factory floor, the only person present was Kieran, who was laying on the sofa with his feet up, staring up at one of the broken windows as the sunlight wavered outside.

Her feet made shuffling noises in the sparkly high heels she had donned, but she managed to compose herself enough to look elegant in her gown after a few baby steps.

Kieran's face brightened as soon as he laid eyes on her.

"There's my girl," he smiled, standing up to pull her into a hug. Roxy blushed at his touch, feeling her breasts being pressed against his broad, muscular chest. "You look beautiful."

"Thank you."

She straightened the material with flattened palms and sat down with Kieran, feeling greatly out of place. He was in his usual shirt and trousers and she looked like she was about to get into a limo with the Mayor and go to the last remaining theatre in the world, somewhere near the Niya Sanctuary, West of Meridion- a place where people had developed their own religion *against* God, which had been an unusually peaceful movement.

"I feel uncomfortable," she muttered truthfully. "How can I fight in this thing if something comes up?"

"Just don't. Run away. Phone me. Phone Emilia. Pretend you didn't see it. It's your choice, just don't go thinking you *have* to save the world on your night off okay?"

Roxy sighed. She wasn't sure if she wanted to do this anymore. She was too nervous! Maybe she should cancel and let her love for Logan just die. *But he's the one*! her mind protested, *Your soul mate*!

"So," Kieran said in a conversational tone of voice. "Who is this guy that has my Roxy all head over heals?"

"A friend from school. You're not the only one who has them-" This comment was reference to his ex-lover in the police force.

"When will he get here?"

"He's not. I've booked a taxi to come and pick me up. We're meeting at the Stone Table."

"Why'd you pick such a miserable place to meet? It gives most people the creeps. The Sun Tower would have been better. Nice view and all that jazz..."

"It was his choice. Besides, the weather is shitty and I don't really want to be on top of a building in this wind and rain."

Kieran nodded. "Makes sense."

Roxy couldn't stop twiddling her fingers, making them sweaty and moist as she stared up at the clock on one of the far walls in the kitchen area. Another fifteen minutes and she'd be swept away to her Prince Charming, dressed like one of those Disney princesses' and feeling very un-Slayer-like for a change.

"Where's Kiya?" she asked suddenly, to take her mind off the wait.

Kieran had been biting a fingernail in the silence and couldn't be bothered to separate his mouth from his finger as he said, "Shower."

"Are you two an item now?"

He stopped chomping now and looked gravely at Roxy. "It's hard to say."

Roxy wasn't sure whether she had the right to pry further, but she had nothing better to do and felt she knew Kieran enough to have him open his heart just a little bit to her. "Is she giving you the cold shoulder?"

He sighed. "Not exactly-"

"But are you at least sure she's interested?" she pressed.

"Yes... *No*... Yes," he cried in quick succession.

"Well, which is it?"

"Hmm. Fifty percent yes, fifty percent no," he said, feeling kind of ridiculous. This was crazy! Since when did he chase after women? *They* chased after him! Maybe he should have just asked Emilia out and fucked her for old times sake. Become the man he once was. Relentless, sexy, a fantastic lover and a million times more 'man' than he was being now.

"How can she be sure of her feelings for you if you aren't even sure about your feelings for her?" Roxy enquired.

"What the hell is that supposed to mean?" Kieran asked abruptly, allowing his confusion to simmer on the border of anger.

"Well," Roxy said calmly, "If you don't know how each other is really feeling, then you'll always be in denial. *She* will always be in denial. I bet she's beating herself up for kissing you!-"

"Hey, wait a second, Baby doll." Kieran cut in, "She ain't beating herself up over me. *No way*."

"How can you be sure? She lost the man she loved, right? She probably feels she's not capable of loving another man again after what happened to him, unless *you* make her feel loved back and that it's okay to share these feelings. Let her know it's the right thing. Tell her you need her! Tell her… you *love* her."

Kieran sat there in silence for a moment, brooding over her words.

"What makes you think I love her?"

Roxy shrugged. "I don't think. I don't know what goes on in that head of yours. But you need to figure out whether that's truly how you feel about her before *she* can do the same."

Kieran grunted in acknowledgement of her words, just as the sound of a horn beeped outside the factory doors. "Sounds like your ride is here," he said monotonously.

Roxy put a hand on Kieran's, gave it a squeeze and left in a flurry of silken violet material, clasping a small black handbag in her left hand. Before leaving the building, she turned back around and blew a kiss in Kieran's direction.

"I love you, Kieran," she said with a smile so warm it made his heart beat harder.

"Just not in the 'marry me' and 'have my children' way right?" he laughed.

She gave him a nod and left him to his thoughts, feeling uplifted as she slipped into the back of the old, lime green taxi cab.

"To the Stone Table," she instructed and the factory became nothing but a spec on the horizon.

Roxy could not control the shivers that ran up and down her spine as the taxi cab pulled up slowly beside the deserted Stone Table.

She was there at last. There was no going back now.

The journey had been pretty dreary. The man driving didn't speak much English and instead of keeping his eyes on the road, he kept looking in his rear view mirror and trying to catch a glimpse at Roxy's cleavage. At one point, he even muttered "*such nice tits*" in his broken accent. The pig.

Roxy wished she'd taken Siren's truck, but knew she wouldn't have been able to because the Slayers needed their vehicles for the night's hunt- a hunt she was excluded from for once.

The Stone Table itself was cast in shadow and as she squinted to focus on it, she could have sworn she saw it move an inch. But with the windows so grimy and the earth covered in a light mist outside, she came to the conclusion it was just her eyes playing tricks on her.

"This right? Yes? This right?" the man asked, turning his head around from the front seat to gawk at the teenage girl in his cab, sat with her hands neatly folded in her lap. One wrong move, and Roxy would snap his neck.

"This is fine. I just want to wait for a moment until my friend-" As she was about to say the word 'arrives' a shadow fell across the car window, closest to her, and the door swung open creakily.

She felt her heart jump into her throat, but sunk back down into the seat again as Logan reached a long arm into the cab, offering her a hand. He was smiling down at her, looking over the moon with happiness at the sight of her and as he assisted her in leaving the cab, he took a step back to admire her true beauty.

"You never cease to amaze me, Sonja."

Roxy was too overwhelmed with joy to scold him for using her real name. Instead, she twirled around for him like a toy ballerina in a music box and asked if he liked her dress.

"Word's can't describe how delicious you look," Logan grinned.

The taxi-cab driver poked his head out of the window as Roxy was showing Logan her gown and let out a high pitched whistle of approval.

"Hey," Logan snapped, throwing a few pound notes at him. "Clear off."

The man exclaimed something nasty in his own language and sped off in a cloud of smoke, losing a few notes out of his open window that Logan had no desire to retrieve. He watched the cab disappear into the night, made sure they were alone at last and bent his arm for Roxy to link hers through.

"Shall we?"

She nodded and he began to lead the way.

Roxy felt as if she were walking on air as they went. She was with her Logan and it felt so good! He was dressed in a black suit with a navy blue velvet shirt, unbuttoned at the top to reveal the creamy flesh of his hairless chest. His blonde hair was blowing back from his smooth shaven face as they walked in the chill, light wind and his movements were all of confidence, including his stride.

"You look very handsome," Roxy said, just as her left heel became wedged between two paving slabs and she stumbled onto the concrete, cutting her knee open. "Shit. Shit!"

Logan fell to the floor beside her and lifted her dress to reveal the wound, trying to convince her not to be embarrassed by what had happened by showing his utter concern for her well being. "Did you twist your ankle?"

Roxy moved the hand from her reddening face. "No. No, it's just a cut. It's nothing really."

He nodded and pulled a tissue from his suit pocket, dabbing at the blood on her knee. "This is a bad time for cutting yourself,"

Roxy smiled nervously. "And why's that?"

"Because there are a lot of vampires in these parts, or so I've heard."

Roxy raised her eyebrows. She hadn't thought of that. The last thing she wanted was to slay a blood sucker in front of him. He'd think she was a freak! Didn't men dislike women who were stronger than them?

"Let's get you to the nearest restaurant," Logan suggested sweetly, and with a sudden swoop he lifted her up into his arms and carried her like a husband carries his bride to their wedding bed.

"You're strong, for a pet shop worker."

Logan laughed. "I don't work there anymore."

She frowned in confusion. "Were you fired?"

He shook his head, showing no strain as he carried her through the dark streets. "I quit. I only worked in that Mall in hope of finding *you* remember… and now, I have you. I don't need to spend dawn until dusk hiding away in that place, regardless of how attached to the puppies I get."

This made Roxy smile. "You were really waiting for me?"

"For as long as it took."

Her face softened as she gazed deep into his eyes. "That's so sweet."

Suddenly, Logan stopped. He spent a moment washing his gaze over the pale beauty in his arms and then kissed her, revelling in the warmth of her mouth and her tongue brushing against his. She tasted like strawberries.

"Fuck this," he remarked restlessly as they parted. "Let's just head straight to the hotel. What do you say?"

"Can we order room service if I get hungry?" she asked lightly, trying not to show the slight disappointment she felt in not getting the chance to sit down and share an extravagant meal with him.

"Certainly," he promised.

"Then let's go."

Chapter 22

Intimacy at Dusk

Getting a room was not a problem. The hotels in Meridion didn't house many visitors, because no one wanted to spend the night in the city, if they could help it. So there were very few staff on call at the Hotel Sunset and very few things to offer customers for a comfortable and enjoyable stay. Basically, you got your bed and your shower and if you were lucky, a television- that's if it hadn't been stolen.

The man behind the desk was trying to look important as Logan carried Roxy through the foyer, but the fact his moustache was a fake, as well as his French accent, totally ruined the illusion.

"I want the best room you have."

"Certainly, Sir," the man drawled politely, eyeing up Logan's wallet full of notes.

How in God's name did a pet shop worker make so much money? Roxy thought. But then again, there was nothing stopping Logan from saving up a few quid in the period of time they were separated. He was an honest, hardworking guy and his cash was bound to be his own, *right*?

"Where iz your luggage?" the fake French bloke queried, keeping his lips tight and his hands behind his back.

"We have none," Logan informed him. "We only plan to stay for the evening."

The man's face creased up in confusion for a moment, then melted back to its wooden, uncaring expression. "Zis way then." Before leaving, he snatched up a key from the many rows behind him and swivelled expertly on the balls of his feet.

He led them both through the 'Hotel Sunset' as if he didn't want them to notice how crummy the place was. Logan was struggling to keep up the pace and had to drop Roxy eventually so that they could follow behind the man in an equally hurried fashion. The corridors were extremely depressing. The red and gold striped wallpaper was ripped in places and even falling clean off the walls at parts! The scarlet carpet was dirty with muddy footprints and the portraits and paintings, hung in various places, had cobwebs and chewing gum stuck all over them.

Roxy cringed. This was as good as it got in Meridion.

"We 'ave one room for special visitors. Room one o' one. Here iz your key. Enjoy your stay at 'otel Sunset."

"We will," Logan said mischievously, looking seductively over at Roxy as he turned the key in the lock.

They ignored the fake French guy as he exited their company and instead, pushed their way into the room, in a hurry to find the bed. Roxy was giggling ecstatically and Logan was already freeing his upper body from his suit jacket, throwing it onto the dirty floor.

The room itself was a whole lot more preserved than the rest of the hotel. It's wallpaper was intact and its paintings relatively clean behind glass that hadn't cracked or broken off completely. On the wall, protruding from a rack, was a black television with a homemade aerial designed out of a metal coat hanger and next to *that* hung a clock with working hands!

"Not too shabby," Roxy admired, with her hands planted on her hips. She checked the view from the window- nothing special - and then flung herself on to the bed with its red silk bed sheets rippling all around her.

Logan was standing at the foot of the bed, gazing at his girl and smiling broadly.

"It's just like Prom night," he said reminiscently.

"Accept we've both had sex a lot more since then and know what we're doing this time."

Logan's face dropped for a moment.

"You *have* had sex with other women, surely?" she asked, feeling positive the answer would be 'yes.'

"I couldn't," he said quietly. "None of the women I became close to were anything like you Sonja, in so many ways. It felt like I was cheating on you every time I was about to sleep with one of them, so I never went all the way."

Roxy looked at him with pity. She'd had such a power over this man that he couldn't even have mindless sex with anyone over the time they'd been apart! How sad and frustrating it must have been for him!

"If that's the case," she said sweetly, creeping over to him on her knees, "Let's make this night unforgettable."

"Indeed," he growled, watching her every move with excitement growing in his eyes.

Roxy slowly unbuttoned his shirt for him, feeling her blood pumping faster as she revealed the perfect, muscular body underneath, with its rock hard abs and pecs. He had definitely changed since their first naked encounter, for back then, he was only in the process of making his body look like a God's. Now, the process was complete and it made her faint with desire at the sight of it.

"How come you're so yummy?" she asked playfully, kissing his chest and rising to meet his lips.

"How come you're such a tease?" he avoided her question as she stroked his erection through his trousers.

Roxy licked her lips, keeping her wide and beautiful eyes on him as she unzipped his trousers. As she did so, Logan used his fingertips to pull the thin straps of her dress from her shoulders, revealing bare breasts underneath that he just couldn't wait to taste.

The violet material of her dress pooled around Roxy's thighs and feet as she wriggled around on the bed, slipping free of the gown to provide Logan with better access to her body.

"I love the way your body looks," he told her.

He lightly caressed her nipples with his thumbs as she kissed him passionately, then he left her lips to taste them in turn. She was so perfect and her skin so soft! He had to fight the urge to bite down on her.

She was the envy of all the women who he'd denied his love to. And believe me, there were a lot. He'd tried to forget about her and move on, but something always forced his mind back to her. He wouldn't feel complete until he had all of her. Forever.

Roxy sighed with pleasure and pulled Logan closer to her, so that she could feel his erection in the palm of her right hand. It's warmth and length startled her- for she had almost forgotten what it was like to be this intimate with the guy of her dreams. She felt as if she were discovering him for the first time again.

"I'm not sure how long I can wait for you to open your legs to me, Sonja," Logan whispered in her ear, sending shivers down her neck and across her face.

She smiled and fell back on the bed, resting her head between the silk covered pillows and revealing her most private part to Logan- throwing her thong to the floor.

A growl escaped his throat- animalistic and full of wild intent.

"I'm all yours," she said, stroking a toe over Logan's chest.

He pounced instantly, burying his face in the crook of her neck and licking her warm, soft skin with his tongue; kissing and sucking at her flesh. She was too perfect to mark, so he avoided leaving any love-bites- although the temptation was there and hard to fight- and instead, focused on her lips as he prepared to spear inside her.

"Tell me you love me," Logan said, in a rather demanding tone of voice.

Roxy shivered. She wanted him to fill her up. She wanted to be riding him now and not lying there like a virgin in wait of the highly anticipated first thrust.

"Tell me, Sonja. I need to know-"

"I do," Roxy said truthfully, putting a hand to his face. "I do love you. I love you so much, Logan."

His smile widened and he thrust into her at last, slow at first to come to terms with the marvellous sensation then faster to see the satisfying look of pure pleasure on Roxy's beautiful face. Her nails scraped across his back as he hit the very back of her, time and time again.

She was incredibly moist with need for him. Each stroke had her screaming in ecstasy, crying his name and trying to kiss him between moans.

"Oh...God...," she breathed, feeling the pleasure building, but before she could climax, Logan pulled himself free from inside her.

"Turn over," he instructed.

She did so without question and felt him enter her from behind. The pleasure was immense. She could feel him gripping her ass as he thrust deeply, making her head explode with stars. When at last she climaxed, she crashed to the bed, feeling dizzy beyond belief and completely spent.

"That was..." Words couldn't describe it.

"I'm glad you enjoyed it as much as I did," he grinned, "But I'm afraid, we're not finished yet."

With strong arms, Logan scooped Roxy up until they were laid sideways on the bed, her body curled against his, and again he entered her.

She lovingly kissed the arm that was wrapped around he, and cried out as Logan picked up the pace. Again she climaxed- although it was not as powerful as the first time- and was aware that Logan was finishing inside her by the look on his handsome face, all screwed up with the force of his orgasm.

"Woah," he sighed afterwards, pressing her against his chest in a tight hug. "That was definitely worth waiting for."

Roxy snuggled in closer, feeling content in his arms.

"I love you," he said softly in her ear, then pulled away from her.

She sat up automatically as he slid off the bed, feeling anxious as he walked across the room. Was that it? Was he going to leave her now he'd been laid? But why? How could he? He loved her! At least, he *said* he loved her. This couldn't be happening!

Fear took over as she watched him bend down to pick up his suit jacket, giving her the perfect view of his firm ass. It was incredible how scared she felt right then and she knew it must have been because she genuinely loved the guy.

And now, he was going to walk out on her, just like he'd done before. They'd be parted again, maybe for longer this time, and she'd go out of her mind wondering when he'd show up in her life.

"You're going aren't you?" she asked nervously, trying to hide how petrified she was. It hurt her, having to talk to the back of his head as he fumbled with the jacket.

"No," he said eventually, then turned to face her. His face was slightly red in the cheeks.

Roxy sighed inwardly then felt her nerves spasm again as he approached her once more.

There was silence as he stared at her- still physically exposed on the bed sheets.

"Sonja," he spoke clearly, but with a hint of a waver, "Will you marry me?"

Time stopped.

The sweat on Roxy's forehead went cold and her skin went pale for a moment, before her heart regulated itself at last and her lungs started working again to assist in her breathing.

"I want you to do me the honour of being my wife," Logan said, extending his hand to give her a good view of the diamond engagement ring he had in an open, blue velvet box.

With shaking fingers, she reached out and stroked the small band of white gold, looking into Logan's eyes.

Her instincts said 'no,' but her heart screamed 'Yes! Yes! Yes!" And one piece of advice Kieran had once given her was to always follow her heart. Sometimes instincts are there to prevent you from making mistakes, but your heart always knows best where to find happiness. And right now, Roxy's heart was beating soulfully for Logan.

He scratched the back of his head. "Say something, Son.' Your silence could kill a guy-"

She shook her head from its daze and jumped up, wrapping her arms around Logan's neck.

"Yes," she whispered in his ear. "Yes, a thousand times over."

"I was hoping you'd say that," Logan said, with joy sparking across his face, and with the strength he had left in him, he picked Roxy up off the bed and spun her around, feeling the happiest he'd ever felt.

"Here-" he said, as she landed on her feet beside him. Roxy held her finger out as he slid the ring on and couldn't contain her beaming smile. "I'd do anything for you. I hope you know that."

Roxy nodded. "I know."

"And," Logan continued, "I'd like to think you'd do anything for me because that's what people who truly love each other do."

"Of course," she said, though she wanted to add the words, 'within reason.'

"Good," he said happily. That was all he needed to hear.

Roxy slept all through the remaining hours of the night and was distraught to find Logan missing as she woke the next morning, still naked under the bed sheets.

To make sure she hadn't been dreaming, she checked the engagement ring on her finger and smiled, even through the panic that was rising inside her.

The sunlight outside was bright and eventually, she noticed a sheet of paper lying at the end of her bed, next to some money.

It was a letter from Logan.

My dear Sonja,

I wish you had been awake for me to say these words instead of writing them, but you looked so beautiful as you slept, I didn't have the heart to stir you.

I meant what I said last night. I love you, more than you could imagine and I'm absolutely thrilled you feel the same way. Nothing will separate us now. Nothing. And I can't wait to be your husband, for as long as we both shall live.

I'm sorry I didn't say goodbye but I promise I will see you again- before you know it- and when I do, I'll explain everything. Don't worry about me- like I know you will anyway. I'm stronger than you may think.

Wait for me, my beautiful Sonja. We'll be together soon.

All my undying love,

x Logan x

P.s. The money is further payment for the hotel room. I hadn't anticipated the room would be in use all evening- though don't think I'm annoyed by it! I'd buy you the hotel itself if I had the money! Enjoy your morning and make the most of the room service. I love you. L xxx

Roxy was completely baffled as she let the paper float onto her lap.

She didn't want to feel sad about it, but the tears came anyway.

Before then, she had felt a great hunger to the point of almost gnawing on the pillow, but now she felt like she was going to throw up the emptiness that was in the pit of her stomach.

What could she do now but wait? And what could be so important that Logan had to leave her lying naked and alone in a hotel bed?

"Kieran-" she trembled into the phone, after deciding she couldn't bear to linger in the room much longer. "Would you come and pick me up from the Hotel Sunset?"

She could hear Kieran shifting his mobile so that he could make out her words better. They were muffled and broken from all the sobbing.

"Sure, honey," he said, trying not to sound as tired as he felt. "I'll be straight over. You hang tight."

As the phone went dead, Roxy dropped it back onto the bedside table and wept into her hands. She'd been thankful he hadn't asked questions, but Kieran was more of a do-er than a thinker. If he thought she was in some sort of trouble, he'd move Heaven and Earth to find her and it made her feel greatly indebted to his kindness.

"How could you do this to me Logan?" she breathed, steaming up the window with her breath as she scanned the streets below. They were all relatively empty and the roads made even the *graveyard* look lively. The world was washed with a miserable grey colour, because of the black clouds looming overhead and further out, past the buildings and the South Meridion Bridge, lightening was streaking across the sky.

"He'd better have a damn good reason for doing this to me," she cried, as she caught a look at her face in the mirror by the dressing table. Her usually perfect complexion was blotchy, with big black circles around her stinging red eyes.

You're being silly, her mind reasoned. *He probably got called away on an emergency. After all, you didn't speak about family much, so for all you know, he could be close to his father again. He could be in hospital at some ones bedside!*

But wouldn't he have said if someone had been hurt? The letter didn't sound particularly urgent, just apologetic for having to leave her.

All the time she was showering and getting dressed into her violet gown again, she thought about what could have happened, until a knock at the door saved her from her tormented thinking.

"Who is it?" she asked cautiously, keeping her hand on the metal chain.

"Johnny Depp," came the response, "I believe you ordered a strip-o-gram?"

Roxy laughed and granted Kieran access to the room.

"Hey Darlin," he said warmly, leaning against the doorframe. "You all right?"

It was a bit of a dumb question; if she had been okay, she wouldn't have needed to phone him.

Solemnly, she shook her head, right before her body collapsed and her mind went blank of all thoughts and feelings.

Chapter 23

Pre-War Words

...she'll be fine...passed out because she didn't eat more than likely... be okay,"

Roxy became conscious three hours later, and could hear the sound of Kiya's voice explaining her condition to the other Slayers on the factory premises, in a very disjointed way.

She just about managed to part her dry lips and murmur something, but couldn't string any words together just yet. The Slayers responded instantly.

"...awake..." came Siren's voice.

"Are you okay, honey?" This was Kiya. She was stroking Roxy's hair back from her sweating forehead and stared at her with a concerned look in her eyes.

"What the hell happened to me?" Roxy asked, lifting a hand to her face. It was pounding with pain and making her eyes ultra sensitive to the spotlights dotted around the factory ceiling.

"You collapsed when Kieran went to fetch you from the hotel," Kiya informed her softly. "He had to carry you out of the building while the manager had his back turned because he didn't want anyone to be suspicious. Luckily he bought Siren's truck because he wouldn't have been able to ride with you on his bike. We think you fainted because you didn't eat or..."

"...or that that '*friend*' you slept with last night had his fun and drugged you to make a clean exit," Kieran butted in, standing nearby with his arms folded across his chest.

His words were the blow she needed to wake her from her fuzzy state.

"Logan didn't drug me! There's no way he could have, unless he put something on his tongue or lips- which I sincerely doubt- so don't go giving me that 'angry father' glare, Kie'. And besides, he left a note apologising for leaving so soon. What kind of a guy drugs a woman, leaves a goodbye note and promises they'll come and find you again, huh?" she said, in Logan's defence. At the mention of the letter, she felt suddenly disappointed that it was still on the bedspread at the hotel and not in her possession for her to re-read.

"He left a note you say?" Kieran repeated incredulously. "Well that's convenient! And he promises to strike again too? Jesus Roxy, where do you find these guys?"

"Fuck you, Kieran!" Roxy bellowed, getting to her feet. "He didn't drug me. I didn't eat a thing all day yesterday because I was so nervous about meeting him and I slept through breakfast too. That was probably why I collapsed. End of story."

Siren was watching in silence and put a hand on Roxy's chest to push her back down onto the sofa. She allowed him to do so without argument, letting her legs go limp again but keeping her face directed towards the biker.

"Guys, do we really need to be yelling at each other right now?" Kiya exclaimed, waving her hands in the air like a bird taking flight. "For crying out loud!"

Kieran made a face like a scolded child and left to grab an apple from a bowl on the kitchen countertop, which he munched from the other side of the factory floor. It took him a while, and a lot of apple swallowing, to finally apologise for his unnecessary comments.

"That's okay. I'm a big girl now. I don't need someone telling me my boyfriend is an asshole. I can figure that out for myself." Roxy said, more calmly than before.

Kiya brushed her long brown hair behind her ears and approached Kieran as Siren bent down low to speak consolingly to Roxy. From what she could hear, he was offering to fry the young lady a hearty English breakfast, complete with her favourite- fried mushrooms.

"I don't like the sound of this guy," Kieran said in undertones as Kiya stood before him; her thumbs in her jeans pockets and her plain red t-shirt giving him a pleasing view of her flat, toned stomach.

"I've seen him before. He looked quite nice. The guy was tending to puppies in a shop window at the West Meridion Mall and when I burst in on them both in the pet shop, he looked like he couldn't bear to let her go."

"Puppies?" he scoffed, rolling his eyes. "Everyone knows a guy does that when he wants to bag a chick."

"So *you* go out and handle dogs when you're on the pull as well, do you?" Kiya grinned. His stubborn scowl broke as his lips curled into a smile.

"Not exactly," he admitted. "But I see your point. Perhaps I've misunderstood this *Logan* fellow."

"Perhaps," Kiya agreed with a nod.

"...but my instincts say otherwise," he added ominously.

Zeke tried to look relaxed and un-intimidated as the Master called everyone into ranks so that he could see his army at its best; skulking up and down the lines to drive his face into others and referring back to Annara who was talking animatedly from where Zeke stood, towards the back.

The other vampires looked tense. Some clicked their knuckles and clenched their fists in anticipation of something big happening and others were keeping their eyes steadily to the front- their fangs peeking out from their top lip menacingly.

Zeke's fangs had grown to their full length now and there was no way to conceal them like he'd been able to during the first few hours of his change. They made him feel like a wolf, or a lion even, and as he licked them in an amused manner, he pricked his soft pink tongue-bleeding ever so slightly.

From the front of the cave, where they were now situated, the Master's head turned sharply towards Zeke. Annara's too. It made a shiver run through him and he looked to the guy on his right, wondering if it could be him the Master was showing interest in.

Zeke was wrong of course. The Master, instead of taking the long way around, walked through the centre of the great mass of killer vampires and pushed anyone still in his way until they hit the far walls on either side of the room.

"You-" he said, pointing a finger at Zeke's pale face.

Zeke focused on the Master's mouth because his flaming red eyes frightened him. The mouth was normal, like a humans, with no hint of now having or *ever* having fangs. If it weren't for the fact he'd seen the guys eyes turn blood red in anger, he would have thought this guy was an impostor among stronger beings!

"Where's your teeth?" Zeke asked, finding an ounce of his bravado.

The Master smiled a cold, bitter smile and then shot his arm out at break-neck speed, gripping Zeke by the throat.

"Dude, I was only asking!" Zeke cried in strangled moans. "Lay off me would you! You need me in this war!"

The Master was about to break Zeke's neck when his sense of reasoning overwhelmed his death-strike mode and instead, he lowered the gangly ex vampire Slayer to the moist cave floor. Zeke was right. He needed him in all this. He would be the perfect match for the main Vampire Slayer- the guy who had put the team together in the first place- Kieran, and if he wanted to keep Kieran from getting to him, Zeke, as well as the rest of his army, was the sacrifice he needed so that he might succeed in what he was hours away from attempting. If his people survived, great! There'd be vampires to celebrate with and drink blood with till the end of their days.

"I have something for you to do tonight, the second the sun falls below the ground."

Zeke nodded in understanding. If it meant leaving the underground, he was more than willing to do whatever the Master asked of him. "Annara is going with you. She'll tell you what to do."

Zeke made to move, but the Master grabbed him by the front of his still bloodied shirt. "This is the most important part of my plan," he implored, with a quiver in his voice. "Don't let me down."

"I won't," Zeke assured him, feeling slightly curious as to why he had been chosen. Was he one of the favourites now, even though the Master seemed to enjoy hurting him a lot?

When The Master let go of Zeke's shirt, he felt his body shaking from the fear of failure. It was not acceptable! He could not bear it if someone messed up his final move on the chess board.

The army was growing restless now. They had been standing for near to an hour whilst the Master dealt with individuals and they were beginning to wonder if they could slip away without him noticing. However, three hundred vampires slipping out the back door was bound to be noticed by someone! Therefore, no one dared to make the first move.

"My brothers and sisters," the Master bellowed from the back of the room, leaving Zeke to his thoughts. His voice echoed off the rocky crevices and hit the vampire army like a ton of bricks as they snapped back to attention, reforming their ranks. "It is time!"

An excited gush of noise came from the army as they turned to the vampire next to them, expressing their utmost happiness that the wait was finally over.

"Tomorrow night, you will be led into the heart of Meridion to take what you have rightly desired for many years!"

A cheer burst from the crowd, dislodging mud and small stones from the roof of the dirty cave they were all huddled in, and many slapped their partners on the back in exaltation. The Master had to raise his voice even more now to be heard.

"I know you will do me proud. Once Meridion is ours, we will branch out and take many more cities, but for now... I want each of you to dance in the blood of the innocent and remember that it is *I* that gave this to you.

I! None of you would have thought to work as one if it weren't for me. You were like drowned sewer rats, hiding away and hoping to snare a human once every ten to twenty years. So my brothers and sisters, you now have the opportunity to make up for those torturous days and nights you've spent, weak from hunger. And those of you who are new to my army should think themselves lucky that they have joined us in time for the most memorable battle in vampire history!"

Annara moved to her Master's side, for the entire time he'd been speaking, he was moving towards the front again, where the ground was slightly higher. From there, he could see the faces of every vampire in the room.

They were stronger now, stronger than what they had been when he'd first encouraged them to move into his underground lair. The lair itself had been an old mine, buried under Meridion years before the city was even crafted, and now providing the perfect cover for the vampires from daylight. They had made it their own, giving it torch light and places to make rest. A rise in the amount of Feeders had also been the result of having somewhere for them to hide away- replacing their inner pain with the physical, as the vampires willingly drained them.

There had been enough blood for everyone.

"Tomorrow we will have victory as long as you fight together as one. Fear nothing and no one! I believe we can do this and you should too. So go now, my worthy army, and enjoy your last day as exiled demons in the bed of your makers!"

The army cheered again and some of the vampires even began kissing the first member of the opposite sex they could stick their extra large finger nails in. It became an army of sexually hungry maniacs within seconds, all groping at thighs and tugging at clothes.

"Disgusting," The Master pronounced to Annara, who had been smiling at the crowd of potential porn stars. Most of them were leaving the cave now, with two, maybe three lays in tow. They were all semi-naked, or completely undressed, and running around like girls and boys in the Playboy mansion, which was now, believe it or not, a home for a thriving feminist group.

"They're just enjoying themselves," Annara explained reproachfully, feeling a rising need to do something sexually pleasing herself. She looked at the Master, with his blonde hair and toned body in full view, and felt the time was right to say her piece.

Oh how she'd waited for this moment.

"You know," she began, "I've known you for as long as we've been creating this great movement of yours," Annara whispered, moving around the Master's back to speak directly into his ear. "And I've never seen you take a vampire into your bed."

The Master's jaw ticced. He could feel the hairs on his body stand on end as she moved around him like a serpent temptress, all slippery and full of masterful, gentle strokes in all his sensitive places.

"I do have sex, if that's what you're asking," he intoned, keeping his dignity intact.

"I think you're lying," she said, aware of the fact that Zeke was pushing his way through the crowd to reach her. "I know you go out at night sometimes and I know you've spent most of your time searching for something, but I've never seen or heard you with another woman."

The Master turned around and grabbed Annara by the shoulders, shaking her.

"Have you been following me, Annara?"

She shrugged nonchalantly. "Perhaps."

The Master's eyes were red now. "And why is that?"

"I needed to know that I could trust you enough to lead us to victory, not to our deaths. I needed to know you were the man for the job, *Sir*." Annara was certainly finding her voice now. "The only reason why these vampires listened to you wasn't because you made them fear you, it was because *I* made them fear you! I told them stories. I made them think you were better than them. I made them *want* to work for you, even though you had been 'turned' more recently than most and have much less experience."

"Why didn't you just start this yourself? You're my second in command, Annara. What was stopping you from taking over?"

She was looking paralysed in thought and when she spoke, her voice was barely audible.

"Because...," she said, her eyes watering. "Until I met you, I didn't think it was possible for vampires to love-"

The Master took a step back from the young woman before him and stared at her with a look of surprise. She was not his leading lady anymore, with all the enthusiasm of a ten year old on a children's sports day. She was a creature overwhelmed by a human emotion and needing to know if there was anyway she could satisfy the way she felt.

"I thought...," she bravely spoke up, "I thought perhaps, you might love me too?"

The Master did love, yes, but not this bleached blonde, cocky man eater.

If he told her he didn't love her, she might rebel. She might ruin everything when he was so close to getting what he wanted. What could he say to keep her on his side? What could he do to persuade her she was doing the right thing?

If he filled her with lies, he would have to kill her later when the job was done. Yes. That's what he'd do. She was expendable once she'd delivered the goods and losing Annara was no skin off his back.

As much as it sickened him to do so, he forced his mouth to loosen into a smile- one which he hoped looked believably loving- and gestured for her to move into his open arms.

Annara blinked and came towards him, nestling her head against his chest.

"I do love you," the Master lied, stroking her hair and feeling no compassion for the girl what so ever. His skin crawled at the thought of her touching him, especially because he was aware of the fact she'd bedded everything in the underground that made eyes at her.

"I love you too, Logan."

The Master- Logan's- face creased up at the use of his human name, but he hid his contempt just in time as she looked up and moved to meet his lips. He kissed her back, feeling no tingling sensations of like or love for the girl, and prayed she wouldn't try feeling for an erection, because there was only *one* girl he was capable of getting it up for and she most *definitely* wasn't her.

"My special girl...," he cooed in her ear as she returned to snuggling into his chest. "Will you lead my army for me?"

"Will you make me your queen?" she asked boldly.

Logan's face twitched slightly, but she didn't catch it.

"Certainly. I was going to ask you as soon as you returned from the carnage above ground. I couldn't dream of asking any other."

She laughed and kissed him again.

"Go with Zeke now, and do what I have asked of you."

Annara looked disappointed. All the other vampires were spending the day having wild pre-war sex and *she* was stuck with lanky legs Zeke, on a mission that she didn't really understand the purpose of.

"But why do we-?"

"Uh-uh!" Logan said, pressing a finger to her plump lips. "No more questions. Just do it and I promise, I will lay with you the morning after we take Meridion, for that is when I most desire celebrating with the woman I love."

Annara's excitement seeped through her stone cold veins once more and she skipped like a school girl towards a very disgruntled looking Zeke. She didn't much care for Zeke's feelings anymore. In fact, she hated him being near her. She was to be queen! She didn't need him looking her up and down like she was a piece of meat- *his* meat.

"This is what we have to do, *Dog*-" she growled, switching to animalistic, warrior woman mode.

"Woah-!" Zeke said, moving away from her. "What did you just call me?"

"A dog. Why?"

"You think you can just treat me that way and expect me to do yours and *his* bidding? Well you're wrong. I'm out of here."

Annara slashed her nails across Zeke's throat, cutting it a millimetre deep- not enough to cause any real damage, and he stopped in his tracks immediately. "If you want to keep your ugly head you'll do what he says. Turn away from me again and I'll see to it you suffer an execution worthy of a cow in a meat factory."

"I hate you, *bitch*," he hissed, rubbing his stinging skin. There was very little blood pouring from the wound, for it was pretty much all dried up inside of him now. He needed to drink from a human to keep his body feeling fresh and alive or else he'd resemble a corpse.

"I hate you too," she replied with equal emphasis. "Now listen to me… if we fail, the Master says this war is as good as over, so don't go fucking this up…"

Chapter 24

Grounded

Roxy lay on the sofa, sedately nibbling on a mushroom and feeling a lot stronger now that she had eaten something. She had regained clarity in her head and found her usual perkiness restoring itself, after she'd pushed Logan's disappearance to the very back of her darkest thoughts.

What more could she do besides wait for him?

If she thought about it too much, she'd go insane. The best way to tackle her situation was to forget she was awaiting his arrival, or a message even, altogether. That way, she'd find peace and maybe be rid of any memory of him completely. She could be strong. She could be brave. She could manage being alone, just like she used to.

Siren had kept to his word and had made her a big plate of fatty fried foods, which she now devoured in front of her friends without a display of manners. Each bite made her taste buds quiver and her stomach pleaded for more as she made her way through the variety of cooked niceties. It had been a long time since she'd eaten this much food, that was for sure, and the fried bread perched on the edge of the feast made her feel as if she were sinning as she took a large bite out of it, dripping with oil in her mouth.

Kieran was playfully distraught about Siren using pretty much all the ingredients they had for Roxy's sake; finding his pack of bacon and the last few slices of bread missing from the stash he'd hidden for his lunch (you couldn't hide anything from Siren.) He'd wanted a bacon sandwich and complained light heartedly that the least Roxy could do was offer him a rasher of that juicy pig he'd had his heart set on.

"Sorry Kieran," she said, more lively than she'd been previously, "It's just too good to share!" And with that, she munched up the remaining piece, leaving nothing but a small splash of grease in its place.

"You're looking better already," Siren commented, taking her empty plate from her at last and handing her a banana to nibble on, as well as a glass of water to wash everything down with.

"I feel ready to face the night ahead," she chirped, licking her lips clean comically.

"If you think I'm taking you out slaying tonight, you have another thing coming," Kieran said suddenly, planting himself in front of her and preparing himself for any back chat. Surprisingly, it never came.

"You're the boss," she shrugged, biting the head off the fruit she'd taken her time to peal. "I don't mind kicking back and watching whatever re-runs they have on television. Ooh... I think there showing a *Buffy* marathon tonight actually!"

"It's nice to see you're so enthusiastic about staying behind, but I was thinking more along the lines of you getting some sleep, not watching Sarah Michelle Gellar kissing handsome vampires."

"Which one, Spike or Angel?" she asked with a broad, mischievous grin. "Because I'd do them both, but personally, I favour the dark haired David Borea-"

"Roxy, this is serious!" Kieran raised his voice, which shocked both Kiya and the youngest Slayer, who was laying like a queen on his sofa. The banana dropped to her hip as Kieran's brow creased into a deep frown. "I need you to regain your strength because we're coming to the final showdown here! I can feel it. *You* need to be ready." Roxy looked taken aback by this. Was she not ready enough by Kieran's standards? "Do I really have to remind you how serious this is? You're fucking nineteen years old! I was mad thinking I could make you one of us! Look at you... you've barely seen daylight because you sleep through most of it and the night only brings evil. To be honest, I wish I'd never brought you here, into this environment-"

The atmosphere was raging with tenseness. Kiya was biting her lip as Kieran spoke, sending mental cries to him along the lines of, "Quit while you're ahead!" and "Shut the fuck up you big idiot, you're crushing the poor girl's spirit!" Unfortunately, Kieran wasn't a mind reader, and instead, he made Roxy feel more and more like a twelve year old, being grounded by her Daddy. He was making her feel like she had never been good enough for his team and that *really* hurt her inside.

Kieran scratched the back of his head. "Wait... I'm not saying this right." He sighed, feeling angry with himself. He was digging himself a hole and was about to be buried in it.

"No Kieran. I'm reading you loud and clear." Roxy got up from the sofa, letting the tears stream from her eyes. "I'll leave tomorrow..."

"Wait!" Kieran said, "Let me make you understand." He reached out and grabbed her left arm, just as she was turning to storm off, and he pulled her back to face him. As she stared into his eyes, he lifted his hands and brushed the long blonde strands of hair back behind her ears, cupping her pretty, innocent face in his rough palms.

"What I mean is...I regret making you a Slayer because I feel as if I've stolen your chance to have a better life." This was sounding better at least. "You've been hurt so many times lately and I feel as if it's my fault. If I hadn't brought you here, you could be living in a better place right now, training to be a fucking primary school teacher, or a lawyer!"

Roxy blinked and fat tears dripped from her eyes into Kieran's hands on either side of her flushed cheeks. "What fun would that be?" she said, smiling at him but not feeling happy in any way.

"Some people think so," Kieran muttered. "But that's not the point. I want you to be safe, Rox.' You're like a daughter to me and daughters shouldn't be thrown into dangerous situations."

Roxy breathed in sharply. "You're only saying these things because since you've gotten to know me, you're afraid you've made a mistake. Not only am I suffering, *you're* suffering. You don't want the people you love and care about to fall. You've lost Zeke... *it wasn't your fault.* And if you were to lose me, that wouldn't be your fault either. You asked me to be a Slayer because you thought I was capable. I am. I've *proved* that on countless occasions so don't tell me you have regrets. I don't want to hear them! You should be proud of me for what I've done so far."

"I am proud." he assured her passionately.

"Then back off and let me do my thing."

She pulled her head from his grip and stepped away three paces. Kieran was looking bemused and worried at the same time.

"I chose to fight. You aren't making me. I'd slay alone if you fired me, because slaying is all I know now. At least with you I have friends to back me up."

"It's just sometimes I feel as if this job is smothering you."

"It is...sort of," she was almost at her bedroom door now. "But I wouldn't want it any other way." Finally, she was turning the door knob and was half way into her bedroom when she turned back and spoke one last time. "I'll stay here tonight and rest, but tomorrow, I'll be joining you on patrol. Forget I ever mentioned leaving, okay? I want to be with you till the end."

"Sure thing, Darlin."'

As Roxy disappeared from sight, Kieran slumped onto the sofa, keeping his eyes averted from Kiya and Siren whilst he mentally kicked himself for being such a jerk. "While I'm crushing people today I may as well finish with telling you..." he pointed at Siren "...that your blocks are too slow, and that *you...*" he indicated Kiya "... have a sloppy sword hand."

Siren put his hands together in a prayer position and responded monotonously with, "You are very much wrong, Kieran. I block slow because it allows my wrists time to relax before I reach for a weapon."

"That's the stupidest thing I've ever heard!" Kieran laughed, slapping his hand against his thigh.

Siren grinned. "I know. I thought I might have been able to fool you, since you never really question my methods. I admit, I have no excuse for my lame blocks. Thank you for pointing out my faults."

"No problem, Jackie Chan."

Siren moved away then, and practised some 'blocks' in the far corner of the room, testing his true ability and making sure he put all his strength into deflecting the imaginary blows his mind was concocting. Truth be told, he didn't often *need* to block in battle because he usually managed to take out an enemy before they had the chance to strike. He was too fast for them. Though apparently, his blocks weren't. But it wouldn't take much for him to rectify this little fault in his combat skills.

"My sword hand isn't sloppy, by the way," Kiya said grumpily. "I have fantastic skill with a blade. After all...I was taught by the best."

"Rycan?" Kieran queried.

The name Rycan coming from his lips made Kiya withdraw inwardly. It was just too weird. She never wanted to hear that name being mentioned by Kieran *ever*, for it only reminded her of how her feelings for him seemed to be cruel against her dead lover.

"No," she said quietly. "My sensei. He trained us both."

Kieran let out a large sigh.

"What was that for?" Kiya asked, watching the muscles in Kieran's face tensing, then releasing repeatedly.

"Nothing. I..." He stopped. "It's nothing."

"Well it's obviously *something*," Kiya observed.

He bowed his head low and spoke in hushed tones. "I just don't want to do this job anymore. I can't stand it. It's not as fun as it used to be and I find myself hating this place more and more each day."

Kiya waited a moment, then placed a hand on Kieran's back, caressing him gently. "No one is forcing you to do this," she pointed out.

"True," he agreed. "I just wish there was more to my life than fighting vampires and sleeping in this dump."

"You'll find it," she encouraged. "You'll definitely find it."

"I'd like to think," he said timidly, taking her hand in his, "That I already have."

Kiya blushed and could say nothing as he lifted her hand to his lips, kissing it gently. From behind them, the pair could hear Siren leaving the factory floor and entering his bedroom to give them some privacy.

Kiya then had a sudden attack of the purest guilt she'd ever felt. She was pregnant and Kieran still didn't know! The longer she left it, the more distrustful she became to him. He'd think she was a bitch if she waited too long to tell him. What the hell was she playing at?

But right now, I need him, she thought as she smiled back at him, *if this fight is as big as he says it is, I need to know he'll be there for me. That won't happen if he hates me for not telling him sooner.*

"Kieran... I-"

No, her mind interrupted. *Forget it.*

"What is it?"

"I was wondering if you'd help me with some sword fighting techniques," she said hurriedly, before her lips could announce she was 'with child' and ruin everything she had with this man.

"Certainly."

Kiya expressed an awkward smile as she passed over her Samurai sword, which was always close at hand. She hoped he hadn't noticed her tone had been serious before, then had switched to something less dramatic in order to cover up what she was about to say. Kieran, being Kieran, wasn't aware she'd been about to share a huge secret though.

"Nice to hear you call me something other than 'Princess' or 'Doll' or 'Babe' or whatever the hell shit it is you come out with, anymore."

"Hmmm, you're right Sweet Cheeks," he said sarcastically.

"How predictable," she mumbled, and the pair moved to find places in the most open part of the factory, displaying their best moves to one another with the use of Kiya's sword and helping to perfect what Kieran had described as 'sloppy.'

With the sunset being little more than an hour away, Kieran briefed the gang- just Kiya and Siren now- on what was to happen, and gave Roxy a stern warning to remain locked inside the building while they were away on patrol.

"Don't let anyone in, you hear me? I have the key for when we return, so don't worry about staying awake to grant us entry. In fact... I forbid you to go anywhere near the door completely!"

"What if there's a fire?"

"Then for your own safety, I advise you to get the heck out of here. Not that there's much to burn besides my smelly sofa, the beds and your mountains of clothing."

"I have to have a lot of clothes! And is it a crime to look good?"

"If it was, they'd have locked me up and thrown away the key long ago," Kieran replied arrogantly and the ladies in the room smirked at the comment. Siren rolled his eyes. He'd been with Kieran a long time now, and was pretty sure he'd heard him say something along those lines on countless other occasions.

"Okay. Siren, it's just you in the truck-"

Kiya put her hands on her hips. "How am I gonna get there?" she demanded, knowing full well what the answer would be. "Fly?"

"By holding me tight, Babe, on the back of my bike." He winked at her wickedly.

"Can't I just ride with him?" she pointed at a silently watching Siren. "My hair goes all bushy when I ride on the back of your bike."

"That," Kieran said smoothly, "Is why I gave you a helmet, but you refuse to wear it."

Kiya scowled at him and poked her tongue out. She's rather be seen dead than in that dorky looking thing. Okay, maybe not dead. Comatosed perhaps?

"Let's hit the road."

"Wait...," Roxy said, lifting her pink slippered feet up onto the arm of the sofa and resting her bowl of popcorn on her flat stomach. "You never told me if you slayed any bloodsuckers last night."

Kieran shook his head. "Zippo."

"Nothing?" she exclaimed in awe. "Where are these guys hiding? We can't have gotten them all," she was about to mention Zeke still being at large, but thought it best to let that one lie.

"We have a pretty good idea where they're at," he said, envisioning the double metal doors they were all too afraid to open. Not yet at least.

"I hope things stay quiet, for your sakes," she said, then turned to the television. Sarah Michelle Gellar was on the screen, round-house kicking a vampire to the head whilst Willow and Xander stood on the side lines nervously, waiting to get a punch in. It always made Roxy hyperactive and eager to slay when she saw the legendary 'Chosen One' fighting on screen. Watching her was better than being high on drugs! And it often made her wonder where the 'Chosen One' of today was, because they sure could do with her help when times got rough.

"Keep a gun handy," Kieran suggested, passing her Zeke's pistol; fully loaded for her convenience. He held it for a second longer than necessary as she took it from him, and looked away as she placed it next to her half empty bowl of the toffee coated, cinema related snack.

"Look… I'm okay. Just let me go with you! Then you can keep an eye on me like I know you really want to."

"And watch you get hurt?" Kieran asked tersely. "No way. You're staying put just for tonight, so you can get your strength up."

"It's up!" she promised enthusiastically, almost knocking her popcorn everywhere.

"I'll say when its up."

"Fine. Get out of here. You're ruining my favourite show."

"Enjoy watching that vampire-kissing loser," he said, with a wave of his hand.

"Hey!" she protested, but he was already bounding across the room for his shotgun and trusty stake and was in no mood to continue their little argument. "Just because she's cooler than you," she mumbled, turning the volume up with a control she'd found earlier that afternoon, down the side of one of the sofa cushions.

"See you," Kiya said, leaving the factory with Siren at her heals.

"Bye guys," she called, then to Kieran on passing, she said her farewell in a long, drawn out tone of voice. "*Bye Kieran.*"

"Get some sleep," he nagged her fondly.

"Yeah, yeah."

As Kieran left, she heard the sound of his key in the lock. They'd yet to replace the padlock and chain Kiya had broken on her arrival, and now had to rely on the simple key hole that the old factory owner had used years ago, before Roxy was even born.

The silence in the building was a rarity as she settled down in front of the flickering screen, and it didn't dawn on her how lonely she felt until the adverts came on half way through the programme.

"This sucks," she groaned and leant her head back on the pillow she'd brought from her bedroom, thinking about vampires and then dreaming of Logan...

Chapter 25

Stolen Away

The moon was fat when Annara surfaced with Zeke at her side, slamming the double metal doors shut behind her furiously and making her partner jump in fright as a result.

"Easy, love," he complained, waiting for the ringing to stop in his eardrums. "You almost gave me a heart attack." Even if that were the case, which was literally impossible for a vampire, there was no way Zeke would die from it. It would just be a minor discomfort for a moment and then he'd be on his way again, which is why Annara brushed his comment aside dismissively.

"So what's with the gun?" Zeke asked as Annara slipped it into the tight material of her outfit, so that it rested near enough on her ass. It was cold, but soon warmed to the mild- almost non existent- heat of her dead skin.

"It's just in case we have some difficulty."

"Aye... I can't imagine this will be a walk in the park. But is killing really the way to go about things?"

Annara scowled at him for his stupidity and dismissed the chance to bless Zeke with an explanation of her true intentions. The gun shot darts full of a sleeping potion concocted by an ex scientist vampire that had found his way underground like the rest of the Meridion vampire population. She knew they'd need it and had requested a loaded gun before leaving, though slyly turned down the offer of a second for her partner in crime, hoping Zeke might get badly injured on the mission, which would help to ease some of her pain. Pain from the thought of waiting for the Master to take her into his bed and make love to her.

The graveyard, with its moving silver mist and miserable, cracked headstones was silent as they past over the resting places of the dead. This kind of 'dead' hadn't had the same opportunity like vampires had- instead, they were forced to remain in the dirt, decaying and alone whilst their spirits ended up God knows where.

"Can we grab something to eat while we're out?"

"No." Annara said harshly. "No kills tonight. Not now. There will be a batch of Feeders coming in this evening that we're planning on chaining up for future feeding, so you can drink from one of those when we get back."

"Why are you guys chaining them up? I thought the rules were that they had to be kept relatively safe to ensure their loyalty."

"The Master wants us to keep some live stock when we bring in the rest of the harvest to devour, so that there will be something left to eat when the great war is over."

"This war is beginning to sound pretty shitty if you ask me," Zeke mumbled.

"What?" Annara rounded on Zeke in a flurry of talons. Her iris's were a wolves' shade of silver. "This plan is one of absolution. It is a turning point for vampire kind and *you*, Little Man, *sneer* at it? Who are you to question the Master's brilliance?"

Zeke waved her comment aside with his hand. "You're just saying that because you see stars in your damn eyes whenever you look at that kid- with his stupid big speeches and empty threats."

"*Empty*?" Annara cried incredulously. "I wouldn't be so sure about that! And for your information, I believed in Logan *before* I fell in love with him."

Zeke made a hissing noise and then laughed. "I never thought I'd hear you say something like that."

"What?" she snapped, tiring of his whiny little voice and aggravating comments.

"Love. You said you loved him. *You*. The biggest whore in the underground, although to give you some credit, I haven't been a vampire for-"

Before Zeke could finish, Annara punched him in the mouth, knocking him to the floor in complete shock. As he spat out a tooth, she stood before him and kicked him in the side of the head, bringing the stars from the sky into his very mind.

"I regret having sex with you. Did you know that?" she told him with acid dripping from every word. "How come everyone I sleep with becomes a clingy, whiny asshole?"

Zeke was silent. He was lying in the grass, dead centre on someone's grave, rubbing his face and wincing as the aftershock sent rippling spasms of pain through his skull. If he wasn't so afraid Annara would finish him off, he would have given her a taste of his *own* fist.

"Once tonight is over, I want you to stay the hell away from me."

"Consider it done," Zeke promised, wanting nothing more to do with the bitch. He scowled loathingly at her as she walked off; ass cheeks rolling expertly- for she knew full well he was watching- and decided he'd stay away for sure, especially if he valued his afterlife.

"Oh and Zeke- you were a lousy fuck, just for the record," she lied vehemently. She wanted to damage his ego as well as his face and judging by his hurt expression, it had worked.

I wish I could hold your body to the sunlight and watch your eyes sizzle in your sockets, whilst the stolen blood in your veins dries up and your skin disintegrates to ash. But luckily for you, bitch, *I'm not a day-walker anymore*, Zeke thought, his eyes narrowed to slits.

"Get up," Annara shouted, a few yards ahead of him. A gravestone that had shifted in the moist dirt became target for her foot as she passed it, kicking it out of the mud completely until it lay disrespectfully on its back, away from its dead owner. There was a brief tingling of pain in her toes after the impact, but she ignored it and swaggered on through the darkness regardless.

At the gates, Annara pressed the button that linked through to the toll booth. It was a system designed for Meridion to decide whether they should grant access to a traveller, or more importantly, a vampire. As well as the two way radio device, there was a small camera, high out of reach, with a little blinking red light. She stared up at the camera with a snarl, and hissed into the small silver box.

"That you Sean?"

There came a clicking sound and the distinct whimper from a teenage boy.

"I...I've been given strict orders, Annara, *not* to grant access to *anyone* tonight who isn't already a Meridion citizen. Father says-"

"I don't give two fucks what your father has to say on the matter *Sean*. I've got business to attend to and you're slowing me down."

"Annara-" he grumbled. "Kieran will be here any moment. You should turn back... for your own safety. *Please*."

"Let me in!" Annara screeched, slamming her fists into the metal. The power behind each blow made the solid steel gates cave ever so slightly under the pressure.

She stopped the banging before she chipped a nail.

"Can't we just-" Zeke started, but was rudely interrupted with a "Zip it, moron," from his ex vampire lover.

"Look Sean. I don't know if you're aware of this but, we vampires have an entrance into the city that no one else knows about. I can go the long way around, do what I was sent to do and then find the time to return here and rip your head off. So what do you say? Are you going to let a poor vampire into your crummy city, or am I going to have to kill you?"

There was a click as the intercom switched off manually and the doors began to open.

"Your powers of persuasion are admirable," Zeke muttered, putting his hands in his jeans pockets and following solemnly behind her. Threaten anyone with their lives and they'll usually cave.

On passing, Annara pretended to be keeping her eyes on the road, before turning to face the booth suddenly, punching her fist through the glass and shattering it all around herself and a petrified Sean. He cowered behind his swivel chair as she reached in, grabbing his hair and lifting him half onto the window ledge so that she could speak with him face to face.

"Don't ever tell me 'no' again," she growled, her eyes silver and wild. "You're on your last warning now, *boy*." The frightened young man closed his eyes as she raked her talons though his hair and gave him a gentle slap on one cheek. There was nothing more to say. He wouldn't deny her requests again if he was smart.

The Slayers were going to arrive any moment, so Zeke led Annara to one side of the deserted road where there was a relatively thick and bushy hedge for them to crouch behind. When the truck and motorbike could be heard in the distance, the pair began to fidget in anticipation of their arrival.

"The target is called Roxy," Annara said, repeating what the Master had told them. "Were you two close?"

Zeke gave a curt nod. "*Ish*. We stayed up and watched television a few nights. I looked out for her when we were out hunting...but it was all a show," Zeke explained as his true feelings poured out. "I was hoping she'd get close to me and we'd end up having a good fuck, but she didn't swing that way. I had more chance of bedding Siren-"

"And who is she?"

"It's a he. And *he* is the one you need to watch. There's ancient Chinese warrior blood in him, or something like that because he fights like a beast!"

"Well, *we* are beasts," Annara pointed out, "so we're evenly matched."

"Yeah, I suppose." Zeke's voice trailed off, for the motorbike was pulling up beside the tollbooth now.

He could make out Kiya on the back, with her arms around Kieran's waist and her Samurai sword protruding from its carrier. In the truck, Siren appeared to be by himself, nodding along to music.

"She's not with them."

"Then it is just what the Master expected would happen-" Annara began.

"-she's home. Alone," Zeke finished.

"Perfect."

Roxy woke, thinking the bitter cold of the factory was playing havoc on her exposed skin, but seconds later, she located the source of her arousal to be caused by a disturbance outside.

She lay paralysed for a moment, curling her fingers around the gun on her lap, and praying it was nothing but a stray cat, who'd come too far out from the city in hope of catching mice and rats.

The moonlight was strong outside and she knew Kieran and the gang would be getting into their routine patrol by now, so who was outside the factory?

Buffy was still flickering away on the television screen, and at some point during her nap, she'd managed to hit the mute button on the remote control, to be rid of the sound of punches, kicks and Slayer taunting.

Roxy moved now, taking her feet off the arm of the chair and sitting up straight.

Why are you afraid? Her mind interrogated her, *You're a Slayer damn it*!

Another scratching noise made her lift her arm suddenly, pointing the gun in random directions- preparing to nail anything that came at her.

She breathed heavily now. Her arms and hands shook and it became a chore to keep her spine straight.

There was a loud clicking and scraping noise outside, which sent shivers through her soul and as the doors to the factory opened, she almost squeezed the trigger of her gun before she even saw who it was.

Zeke had spent five minutes convincing Annara that she was *far* from capable of kicking in the doors to the factory, after she'd studied them closely. There was no chain around the handles like there used to be, so the only thing stopping them from getting inside was the simple lock and key mechanism, which didn't pose a problem whatsoever.

With a smug expression, Zeke pulled a key from his jeans pocket and waved it in front of Annara's eyes.

"I was a Slayer remember?" he explained to her curious face. "It wasn't like I was planning on sending this back to Kieran in the post after my withdrawal from the team."

He cunningly put the key in the lock and turned it.

Now he could smell fear. Roxy's fear. She was awake and inside the building.

"She knows we're out here," Zeke whispered in a tone that only a vampire or a dog could pick up. Annara nodded in understanding, then pushed through the double doors, aiming her dart gun as she stormed in.

Roxy let out a cry as Annara shot first, aiming the gun at the teenage girl's chest, but she missed as the Slayer dove behind the sofa.

"Roxy baby, it's me Zeke!"

Roxy was catching her breath as she hid behind the back of the sofa like a frightened six year old, trying to keep her gun from shaking violently. She hadn't noticed Zeke walking in, for she'd been too busy avoiding the gun that some bleached blonde skinny bitch had aimed her way.

"Zeke?" she called, keeping her voice steady now. "Kieran isn't here so-"

"I'm not after Kieran," he said matter-of-factly, then swooped his head around the side of the sofa to make Roxy jump a mile. "I'm after you."

She pulled on the trigger and shot at Zeke's face, but before the bullet could meet its target, Zeke was on the ceiling, hissing like a feral cat.

The vampires were too quick for her. She couldn't nail Zeke with a bullet and had almost forgotten about Annara until she crept up behind her, silent as the grave, and tapped her on the back. She felt her long blonde hair being gripped by strong hands and was dragged across the floor by the vampire lady, who's gun was still pointing at her.

Roxy struggled and even managed to shoot Annara this time, right in her chest, but missed the heart.

"AHH!" Annara screamed shrilly, releasing the girl's hair instantly and clutching the gun-shot wound as blood dribbled out from her torn flesh. "If that leaves a scar, so help me God-" she said savagely, watching as the wound healed over in a matter of seconds. There was nothing left to show she'd ever been shot at close range.

This vampire was definitely stronger than anything Roxy had fought before. Only old ones, who'd been around and seen a lot had the ability to heal that fast.

"Now hold still-" Annara commanded, whilst Roxy flipped up expertly back onto her feet. She tried to make a move to the kitchen counter, but was obstructed by Zeke as he fell from above, landing on his feet in front of her. He wrenched her arms around her back painfully, knocked the gun from her hand to the ground and held her in place whilst Annara advanced.

"Get off me!" she cried desperately, wriggling in Zeke's masterful hold. He wasn't going to let this girl go. Not if he could help it.

"I wonder why the Master wants this chick so badly?" Annara asked ponderously, stroking the gun's point across Roxy's cheek.

No one knew the answer to that but him.

"Dinner?" Zeke suggested.

"Maybe," she said dismissively.

"Please Zeke… don't do this!" Roxy pleaded.

"Too late," he hissed as Annara shot a dart into the girl's shoulder, making her crumple in Zeke's arms moments later. He dropped her to the floor like a sack of potatoes and stared at her.

"That was easy," he commented casually.

Annara's nose creased up at his words as she passed him, heading for the kitchen. She returned with a pair of scissors.

"What are they for?"

She said nothing in response. Bending down to the sleeping human, she stroked the extremely lengthy blonde hair and then began hacking at it with the scissors, her eyes silver with glee. It made her feel exhilarated, destroying something that the girl had taken so long to grow, and as the chunks fell away, she felt that little bit more triumphant.

Being bad was good.

"Grab her and let's get out of here before those Slayers get back and find us."

"Wait…wait!" Zeke exclaimed unexpectedly. He crouched down, putting his knees on either side of Roxy's hips and kissed her roughly. Even more sickeningly, he began to grope at her breasts. "That's for all the nights you held back from me," he said to the unresponsive body.

"Come on!" Annara demanded, pushing him off the girl.

Zeke was smiling merrily as he lifted Roxy up into his arms and left the factory, remembering seconds later to grab his key from the lock.

Chapter 26

Everything Here Dies

Sean had been extremely on-edge when Kieran had pulled up beside the toll booth that evening. His face was of a paler shade than usual and very moist with sweat. He'd held his head low on Kieran's arrival, so that his hair shielded most of the tell-tale signs that he was troubled. But on questioning the lad, Kieran discovered that Sean had been feeling particularly miserable that evening because he'd ended things with his girlfriend, before the Slayer's arrival, and she had *not* taken it too well. The window, Kieran had first noticed- for when he'd reached up to tap it, his hand had gone right through- was smashed till nothing remained, except little pieces on the tarmac that resembled icy hail stones, and according to Sean, his girlfriend had thrown the chair at it after he'd sat her down to tell her the bad news.

Eventually, the Slayers left the boy to sulk. One thing Kieran didn't have time for was advising a teenage boy on how to handle some chick. An aggressive chick too, by the sounds of things.

Other than that, the night was showing to be uneventful. No vampires. No Feeders making their way through the graveyard. No night visitors, to lonely graves. Just three Slayers, all geared up with nothing to kill.

"Give it another hour or two. We don't want them to start thinking we're giving up early every night, because they'll start using it to their advantage," Kieran suggested, glancing up at the full moon and wondering if there might be a werewolf on the premises, to give him something to get his blood boiling. It was beginning to get ridiculous now- they were going days without seeing anything they could stake.

"I for one am glad there is nothing to kill," Siren commented mildly as they strolled between weathered gravestones. "Fighting breaks the relaxing calm of night, and as you know, I prefer the silence more than slicing vampires in half."

"Then why aren't you a preacher, or a fucking mime artist if you like your silence so damn much?" Kieran asked.

"Because we work with what we're given. And I was given the ability to aim true and master martial arts. Mimes don't use props and I prefer to carry a blade." He swished his Samurai sword through the air with that comment, stirring up the air around them.

"What did you do, before you joined us?" Kieran asked Kiya suddenly.

Kiya jerked from her thoughts, that were seemingly vaster than the star blotted sky, feeling unprepared for any type of interaction with her friends. She'd been watching the darkness so intently, that her eyes had started to sting, and it took her a second or two to construct a sentence. "I...I was a teacher. A nursery school teacher, up until... you know."

"Do you miss them?" Kieran asked quietly, his eyes piercing into hers as he walked on autopilot..

"Who?"

"The kids of course."

Her expression went blank as she thought of the children she'd taught. They'd given her enough paintings and uncoordinated sketches to wallpaper her entire house! She'd never had the heart to throw any of them away either and instead piled them up in her basement, tied neatly together with red string. Seeing the kids faces when they presented her with something artistic- always beaming with pride and cheeks all rosy- made it hard to be rid of anything they gave her. She felt the children should be encouraged in these artistic matters because the world was changing for the worse, and before long, books, paintings, music and everything else that required some form of 'talent' would soon disappear. All that would matter to people would be finding something to fill their bellies with each night.

"I do, yes. But teaching was never really what I wanted to do," she lied through her teeth, so that the other Slayers didn't think she had a soft spot after all. *Who'd ever heard of a nursery school teacher leaving her day job to kill things?*

"Then what did you want to be?"

Now she was really lost for words.

"Nothing... I wanted to do nothing."

"Well, nothing doesn't pay the bills," Kieran pointed out quite obviously, smirking to himself, then letting it fade when he realised he wasn't being funny at all.

Suddenly, a stirring from inside a small bush nearby startled the team and Kiya put a hand to her sword as a bird fluttered out from the undergrowth in a flurry of wings and loud chirps. It's frenzied attempt to fly and its unexpected brush with human life caused it to blindly plough into a gravestone, where it keeled over and lay stunned on its back.

Kiya moved to the bird and scooped it up into her hands, watching its little chest rising and falling rapidly. It's beak was hanging open wide from the shock- it's tongue moving back and forward with each breath- and its eyes seemed panic stricken with the fear of her touch. Eventually, the small, soft brown feathered animal died, closing its eyes and shuddering with fright one last time.

"Why does everything in this city die?" Kiya asked aloud, surprised at the sound of her own voice in the dead of night. Kieran put a hand on her shoulder.

"It was a baby. Most baby birds die here. That's why there's never any life to speak of, besides us and the vampires. Their little minds can't take the darkness and the scary things that come out at night and they just die, like this." He brushed a finger across the brown feathers of the bird's unmoving chest and then took the creature from Kiya's palm, laying it down beside the bush it had run from, for the sake of the mother bird who might be searching for its young.

It's just a baby, Kiya's mind gabbled. *A baby. A baby. A baby.*

"I don't feel too well," she groaned pitifully, lifting a hand to her head to feel the heat from her brow blazing like a fire. Her stomach was also stirring unpleasantly.

"Do you think you can hold on till we finish patrolling?"

She wanted to say no, but knew she had no choice but to follow Kieran around the graveyard until he said they'd been there enough. Besides, she couldn't take

Kieran's bike and if she drove the truck back, Siren would have to do the whole 'wrapping his arms around Kieran's waist on the journey back' thing, which wasn't the most comfortable way of travelling for two *macho* men.

Her nod was enough to convince him she could manage, but inside, she prayed nothing required contact with her blade that evening.

Fortunately for her, nothing came and they returned to their vehicles, an hour and half before dawn. They waved Sean goodbye as the sky showed signs of a rising sun, giving the world a slightly orange tint to it, and rode home to find a most worrying sight.

"Who unlocked the factory doors?" Kieran queried, barely audibly, for his surprise had left him frozen on the spot and his lips barely capable of moving. Kiya jumped off the back of his bike to stand in awe beside him and Siren was already off at a run, entering the factory with his sword drawn- poised for a fight.

It looked as if more nightmares were about to begin.

Chapter 27

The Breaking Down of Minds

"I don't fucking believe it!"

Kieran stormed out of Roxy's bedroom, almost knocking the door off its hinges and lifted the latch up to enter the underground showers, bounding down the steps with heavy footfalls and then running back up them, equally as fast, expressing more anger and turmoil on his handsome face after failing to find what he was looking for.

"The gun is still here and there are bullets missing-" Siren addressed Kieran calmly but could not hide the air of anxiety about him. It was plain to see he feared for Roxy also. Kieran snatched the pistol from Siren's hands and checked to clarify his findings. He was right of course. Roxy had used the gun on someone. Or had someone used the gun on Roxy?

"This can't be happening!" Kieran bellowed heatedly, wanting to smash his fist through something to stifle his inner pain for a moment or two.

Kiya was glaring at the television, flickering with faces of morning television presenters, smiling cheerfully as they went through the days newspapers, as if the society couldn't read the fucking headlines themselves!

With nimble fingers, she switched it off and made a point of moving to touch Kieran soothingly on the wrist. He let out a loud sigh as she did so, twisting his hand around her fingers and clutching them tightly. "Do you think this has something to do with that boy she met the other night?"

There was silence.

"We can't just go accusing-"

"I know that!" he snapped, unfairly. "But right now, I need to visualise whose neck I'm going to snap for doing this."

"She may have left the place willingly," Kiya suggested, looking to Siren for his opinion on the matter.

"But why use the gun?" he pointed out. "And what of the door? There's no forced entry anywhere in the building. Someone was either invited in, or had a key already-"

"Zeke?" Kieran's eyes flashed brightly. "You think Zeke could have done this?"

Kiya didn't hear what the men were saying anymore. Her thoughts were captured by something lying on the floor, near the kitchen counter, amongst the dust. It was light in colour. A small mound of something fair, catching the sun ever so slightly. As she moved away from Kieran, she realised what it was she had found. Hair. Roxy's hair.

The men had stopped talking amongst themselves now and were watching silently as Kiya extended a handful of the long blonde strands towards them both, allowing clumps to slip through her fingertips and float to the floor like leaves on an autumn wind.

"Oh, *shit*. Shit! Shit! Shit!" Kieran cried, throwing Zeke's old gun across the room to hear it clattering against the wall loudly. "I'm going back to the graveyard."

"Wait!" Kiya called after him. "What's the use in going there? Sean would have told you if she'd gone that way, surely?"

"I'm beginning to wonder if that kid knows more than he's letting on. Smashed glass and a face that looks as if it saw the dead rise to try and kill him? He must have seen something! He *must* be lying to me!"

"Be reasonable, Kieran. He's just a kid. What are you going to do, beat it out of him? And besides, he probably knows nothing. There are *other* places we should check first. Roxy's parent's house. The West Meridion Mall, where she first met this *Logan* guy. You could speak with Emilia and find out if she's heard anything-"

Siren interrupted Kiya's flow with, "Maybe you two should get a few hours sleep first. I will drive around the city myself and search for her."

"How can I sleep knowing Roxy could be hurt?" Kieran spat in contempt.

"For once, I am taking command here," Siren said assertively, which was quite out of place for the Chinese man. "You are full of rage and fatigue right now and you will help no one in this state. Go to your room and get some sleep."

"Don't tell me what to do. I'm your fucking superior!"

"And Roxy is my friend just as much as yours," Siren retorted, putting his Samurai sword away in its protective sheath. "Stay here. I will return before midday. Then you can go and do whatever *you* think is best."

Kieran threw his hands up in the air. "Whatever, Dude. Just hurry up and get your ass back here."

Siren bowed and turned to leave, exiting at the pace of a brisk jog.

It took Kieran a while to make a move himself, reaching into his jacket pocket and clumsily punching in Emilia's number, whilst caressing his left temple with a free hand. She was quick to answer his call, but could shed no light on the situation.

"I'll keep an eye out for her and alert the rest of the force on the matter."

"Something tells me she won't be hiding in a doughnut shop, Em'," he said, followed by a weak laugh.

"Ha ha, Mr Stereotype," she replied. "If you think you can do this job any better, why don't you join us? Whip the boys into shape?"

"I've told you before, I don't like the uniform."

Emilia chuckled. "Not black enough for you?"

He smiled, though she couldn't tell. "Just keep in touch."

"Will do."

"Oh and Emilia-"

"Yup?"

"Be careful tonight."

"Why? What's happening tonight that's any different to usual?"

"I'm going into the lion's den to chase out any rats I can find and I *think* these guys have been waiting for such an event, so they're probably more prepared than I dare imagine. I need you and your guys ready in case they breach the walls and get into the city. It could be a blood bath. But then again, I may be wrong."

"Thanks for the warning. And all the other warnings you've given over the years."

"Well, I never was a flower's giving kind of guy-"

"Don't remind me."

Before Kieran could protest, the line went dead. He snapped the mobile phone shut and shifted his face to view Kiya, who was standing fixedly to his left, twining her hands together in angst.

"I need sleep," Kieran admitted, defeated.

Kiya nodded understandingly. "Me too."

He starred at her for a while, trying to find the words to use that would encourage her to join him in his bedroom, but he couldn't bring himself to say them. Instead, he entered his room alone, dismally aware of the fact Kiya was entering Roxy's room, for it was now vacant, much to his distress.

In the heart of the graveyard, Kiya was alone and face to face with two *very* pissed off looking vampires. One male, the other female; they circled her cautiously, keeping their eyes on her sword whilst licking their fangs hungrily.

The female was unusually chunky for a vampire, but fast none the less, changing direction quicker than Kiya could predict. The male was of an average build and had floppy black hair, long in the front so that it covered one of his two silver eyes, and spiked up jaggedly at the back to reveal a tribal tattoo at the base of his neck.

"Stay the fuck away!" Kiya warned fiercely, trying to keep the blade pointing at both their hearts by manoeuvring it back and forward through the air sharply.

She was losing her nerve. Each swish of the blade was becoming more and more sloppy and her vision was unexplainably blurring. Reaching up, she wiped her brow with the sleeve of her jacket and in the instant she took her eyes off the circling un-dead, one of them dashed forward- the male- and landed a blow to the side of her face, knocking her deftly to the floor.

Her skull exploded. She was only vaguely aware of her surroundings, and sensed shadows before her eyes just as she felt the cruel and excruciatingly painful impact of a foot to her lower stomach, repeatedly.

"No! Stop!" she mouthed in agony, then croaked out more cries for mercy. "Stop! Please! I'm... I'm...." She couldn't say 'pregnant.' They'd find it even more enjoyable, knowing they were destroying a mother-to-be's hopes and dreams. Two kills for the price of one. It would be like having Christmas early to them.

Finally, the blows stopped, though the pain lingered, rippling through her exhausted body and making her convulse. She felt a spasm inside of her and the foul metallic taste of blood rose in the back of her throat, sloshing thickly over her tongue and dribbling out from between her cracked, dry lips.

The vampires were no where to be seen now as she dragged herself over to her sword, which had fallen in the grass. The stars became the eyes of many more vampires as she collapsed and lay with the cool breeze prickling at her face, eyes drooping and tears spilling from them. There was no hope now. Her baby was probably dead. Just like the baby bird had died in her hands...

Everything dies here.

Just as she was about to slip into a darker night, in the folds of her tormented mind, a hand brushed her cheek and a face appeared above her. At first she thought it was Kieran, but then it became more apparent that the man was in fact her beloved Rycan.

"You...you...?" Words evaded her. He was caressing the back of her head silently, with no emotion on his perfect, sweet face, besides the slight glint of tears in his eyes.

"Shhh," he whispered softly, as the breeze ruffled his dark hair.

Kiya managed to lift a hand to the lining of his jaw, feeling the familiar roughness of his stubble. She didn't know how he was there with her, but he was, and she felt safe again.

"I think... I think I've lost our baby," she sobbed, heart broken, trying her hardest to block out the shuddering aches and pains below.

"Let me make sure-" he offered kindly, although Kiya was baffled as to how he could find out such a thing.

That was when she felt the coldness of a blade twisting in her gut and the breath escaping her throat faster than she'd ever imagined possible.

"I'd rather our child die than to see it be raised by some other man," Rycan spat icily, pulling the small blade out by its slick, bloodied handle only to drive it back into Kiya's soft flesh for a second time.

As she lay there dying, she looked up into the eyes of her lover and coughed up more blood, until there was far too much for her to manage breathing anymore. The last thing she saw before she died was Rycan's face changing into someone entirely different. His hair grew longer, greasier and blacker. His face looked thinner and whiter than milk. His smile was created with smaller lips, thin and devoid of any red/pink colouring.

"Kiss me Kiya," Tristian asked of her. "Kiss me like you mean it and the pain will go away."

Death became a mercy as he leant in to touch her lips with his own.

"Kiya! What's wrong? Wake up! Wake up, damn it!"

Kiya was in such a state, that she almost punched a concerned looking Kieran in the face as she was torn from her nightmare, hair all matted and her face dripping with sweat. Her clothes clung to her wetly, suffocating her, and she felt her breathing becoming more and more difficult. In an outburst of tears, she ripped the clothes from her body, throwing her top to the ground and clawing at her bra, breaking the clasp after a minute or so of struggling.

Kieran tried to hold her flailing arms as she scraped her hair back from her sticky face, but was knocked aside as she turned her back on him, pealing her trousers off, but leaving the black thong in place. Her flaming hot skin instantly cooled to a more bearable temperature as she stood there shaking, and she rubbed her belly, still astoundingly upset- in fear of the worst.

"Kiya…?" Kieran said, in a panic stricken tone. "What's wrong? Speak to me. I can't help you unless you tell me what's wrong."

She turned back to him then, observing how his brow was full of deep worry lines and how his eyes looked desperate to know what had brought about such strange behaviour.

The fear inside of her began to ebb, and she managed to lift her arms up and around Kieran's neck, holding him close and pressing the rest of her body against the warmness of his muscular torso.

He didn't know what to think, but he knew she needed his love right then and so he put a hand on the back of her head, and the other between her shoulder blades, hugging her protectively.

"It was just a dream," she whispered to him, her words scratchy due to a parched throat and mouth.

"Must have been one hell of a dream, Darlin,"' he said, stroking her hair lightly. "But whatever happened, just remember it isn't real."

Kieran's words calmed a part of her soul that was so greatly on edge, it had its toes dangling in the fires of her own hell.

"It isn't?" she asked dumbly.

"Of course it isn't. Everything is going to be fine. I'm here for you."

He was about to tell her he loved her, but bit his tongue before unleashing the truth. Maybe this wasn't the time or the place?

"I want a shower."

"Sure. Go. I'll be waiting up here if you need me."

"Stay with me-" she pleaded, gripping him tighter than she had been.

He furrowed his brow. If the situation wasn't so tense and erratic, he would have found this quite a turn on. "Fine. Come on then. Let's get you cleaned up."

They left Roxy's bedroom holding hands, both battling with thoughts and unanswered questions that neither could voice. But one thing they were both pretty sure of was that they needed each other.

They really *needed each other*.

Chapter 28

A Touch So Comforting

The warm water pummelled her skin, washing away most of Kiya's discomfort as she stood under the water, resting her head against Kieran's dripping wet chest. She had been so shaken up, that she hadn't cared about standing naked under the showerhead with an equally unclothed Kieran. He however, had been restless and unsure of what she would deem suitable in this situation, and had hovered on the outskirts of the shower room for a while, until she had lifted her hand towards him, coaxing him under the water with her.

Kiya had slipped out of her thong tiredly, no longer bothered by Kieran's eyes on the part of her she'd taken such care in hiding. He'd looked away out of respect, but couldn't help gazing up and down her body as she put her hand on the waist band of his underwear silently, tugging on it until it fell to the floor beside her own.

Placing her head against his chest was all the encouragement he needed to stand over her protectively, caressing her slick arms and shoulders with his large palms, then lifting her chin up to face him.

The water was cascading over her hair, making it stick together in one long silky mass down her back, glistening enchantingly, and her eyelashes were shimmering with droplets. Her lips looked invitingly wet as Kieran observed their pink colouring, plump and perfect, soft and delicious.

Biting his own, he resisted the urge to kiss her right then. It wouldn't have felt right, taking advantage of her vulnerable state. Instead, he picked up a flannel, which was resting on a small shelf beside the water valve and lathered it up with soap.

Kiya allowed him to rub the flannel across her back, gently stroking it across her skin, leaving behind foam in its wake. Already she was feeling better.

With a small smile, she reached out for the other flannel folded neatly on the shelf and began the same process as Kieran had, brushing it over his rippling muscles and touching each one with inquisitive fingertips.

Eventually, the pair returned the flannels to their shelf and shampooed their hair without each others help, running fingers over their aching scalps and feeling the niggling pains ease away ever so slightly.

When they were done, Kieran was almost disappointed as Kiya switched the shower off and walked across the tile floor towards the towels, her ass on display as she made her way to the other side of the room.

They had not spoken throughout the entire experience.

Kieran watched her dry herself for a while, standing naked before her and forgetting about the creeping chill spreading across his body now that he was out of the warmth of the water. Kiya was absorbed now in patting her skin dry, touching the towel to the back of her neck, brushing it across her breasts and down over her long legs. He couldn't help but feel aroused by it all.

"Someone's happy to see me," she said, indicating his erection.

"You're just so beautiful," Kieran said covetously, walking towards her.

As he leaned towards her, Kiya parted her lips, believing he was about to kiss her until she embarrassingly realised he was reaching for his towel. Turning a vibrant shade of red, she looked away and wrapped her own towel around her head, keeping her hair from wetting her skin again.

"I'm going upstairs to grab some clothes," she informed him, picking up her bundle of damp clothes from the tiles and making her way to the door. "It was nice-" she stopped. "It was nice," she repeated lamely.

She left before she felt the urge to run back and kiss the guy who was standing in wait so hopefully, completely naked and in need of her. She thought she'd gotten away with it, until he called her back to throw a towel her way.

"You might want to cover up before you go upstairs. Siren could be back-"

"Of course," she nodded, slipping the towel around her body and tucking it in just under one of her armpits to hold it firmly in place. The cotton felt smooth and comfortable to the touch, now that her flesh was dry.

Kieran wanted to pull her into a kiss, but as his mind had decided previously, now wasn't the time.

"I'll follow you up."

The atmosphere was a little awkward above the basement as Kiya slipped into her leathers, held in place with a belt designed to look as if there were silver bullets all around the length of it and put on a simple black top with long sleeves and a v-neck.

"Is he here?"

Kiya shook her head as he approached, dressed in black jeans and a dark red shirt, opened at the top, as usual, to reveal his impressive chest. As he eyed his surroundings, he brushed his long hair with a black comb. Kiya smiled at this, and did the same with her own hairbrush, ripping away at the long locks of her dark brown hair.

"There's no sign of him yet, but give it till twelve. I'm sure he won't keep us waiting."

The clock read 'eleven forty five.' Siren was probably making his way back now.

"Do you think he'll have her and this whole ordeal will be over?"

"I hope so, Kieran."

The two Slayers eventually ended up on the old sofa, waiting patiently for Siren's arrival. Kieran was sitting up straight with his back to a dusty cushion and Kiya had her head resting on his left thigh, feeling tingles running through her as he brushed his fingers through her damp hair. They were silent and nervous. The odds of Siren finding Roxy somewhere in the city on his first round of looking seemed extremely slim.

"No luck I'm afraid,"

Kieran had been dozing when the Chinese man had entered their domain, looking worn out and sounding gloomy. His thick black eyebrows were low on his face, overshadowing twinkling eyes and his blue t-shirt had large sweat patches under the armpits. "I drove through every possible street and checked every back alley. She's not lying in ditch somewhere- that I can assure you."

"Emilia knows nothing either," Kiya piped up, "At least now we're all eighty percent sure she's still alive."

Kieran was silent. No one could be eighty percent sure of anything.

"Let's go," he instructed, lifting her head off his lap and standing up.

"Where?"

"To her parent's house. They've been looking for her since she left home. Perhaps they've finally brought her in-"

"But what about the Mall? It closes at two thirty on a Sunday. She may be there right now, in that pet shop or Bianca's place."

"Then we spilt up."

Kiya nodded, feeling her heart sink a little at the prospect of searching for Roxy without being at Kieran's side. She wanted his company. She needed to feel protected. She needed someone to take her mind off the baby inside of her, hopefully still alive and growing.

"I am tired. I will sleep and be ready for you at dusk." There was a pause. "Do we still fight at dusk, without Roxy?"

"It is for Roxy that we go and fight-" Kieran said.

Siren bowed in his usual way, placed his Samurai sword on the kitchen countertop, grabbed a carton of orange juice from the fridge, poured a generous amount into a large, clean glass then retired to his small bedroom at the back of the factory.

Kiya tapped her foot gingerly on the floor.

"We still fight?" she asked again.

Kieran nodded. "Of course. If we don't find Roxy today, we sure as hell will tonight, even if I have to cut the throats of everything that crosses my path."

Kieran's words scared Kiya. There was a hunger in his eyes familiar to a vampires. *Bloodlust*. He wanted to see someone suffer for taking Roxy from his team. Just like he wanted to make someone suffer for the loss of his best mate, Zeke.

"She could be... one of them," she pressed on him, stirring more anger in his soul. Kieran grunted, but said nothing to this remark. Instead, he made his way to the weapon's table, with long brisk strides, grabbed a small silver dagger with an ivory hilt and a handgun, tucking them both into compartments in his jeans. Kiya quietly made her way to Roxy's room, selected a blonde wig from the bottom of her wardrobe then returned to Kieran, with her samurai sword already on her back.

"I take the truck?" she asked, her blonde wig moving unnaturally as she moved her head. It was already beginning to itch her and she'd only been wearing it for five minutes.

"No. You ride with me."

"But I thought we were splitting up-"

"I'll drop you off," Kieran explained firmly. "Whilst you check out the Mall I'll give her parents a visit. They live just a few blocks over. Then I'll meet you back outside."

"Are you sure you don't want me to go with you?" Kiya tried, hoping he'd say yes.

"There's no time, Darlin."'

"Okay." Her head sunk at the sound of his words, but she snapped out of her personal misery to focus on the matter at hand. A girl's life could be in jeopardy. They needed to find her before something bad happened.

Kieran left in a swirl of dust, set on auto pilot as he mounted his bike and kicked it into gear. Kiya felt a stirring of sickness in the pit of her stomach, but managed to suppress it. She'd missed breakfast again and now, she was about to miss lunch. She had to stop doing this!

"Thank you, for this morning," she mumbled shyly, gripping tightly onto Kieran as they left the factory behind. He slowed the bike down to hear her better.

"No problem," he said, pleasantly. Then added, "but if there's something you need to tell me Kiya, I think you should just come out and say it."

What's that supposed to mean? her mind reeled. *He knows you're holding something back from him!*

"I don't know what you're talking about," she said simply, biting her lip behind his back.

"We showered together, Honey. That must have meant something to you, *surely*?"

"I...I needed a friend."

"Friends don't wash each other's naked bodies, unless it's some sort of porn video with clean freaks as the stars."

Kiya smiled a little, but her fears returned and the smile faded to worry lines.

"Don't read into it too much, Kier.' My heart can't deal with it at the moment."

"Right, right." he said, hiding his disappointment. *Face it man, she's playing you. Playing you for a big, fat fool.*

As Kieran twisted the throttle, revving the bike's engine, he banished thoughts of Kiya to the back of his mind. *Not now. Not now.*

Love can wait.

Chapter 29

Separate Ways

Time was against them now. Roxy was out there somewhere and the sun waited for no man. At dusk, they needed to be ready to make their move into the underground, hoping that the element of surprise would play to their advantage.

Kieran was concerned about taking Kiya on the mission. She'd been with them for less than a week and already she was losing it! He wanted to suggest seeing a doctor, but had the feeling she'd refuse point blank. All he could do, for now, was keep a close eye on her and make sure they both came out of this alive.

His feelings for Kiya were stronger than ever, brimming over into the more pressing matters life was dealing, and he was losing his focus because of it. If he could just say a heart-felt "I love you," he knew his feelings would simmer down- but this was not the time nor the place.

It was hard allowing her off the back of his bike; feeling the grip of her arms loosening around his waist as she swung her long, *damn fine* looking legs from over the seat onto the pavement. His operation- his *team*- was at its frailest, and seeing Kiya preparing to part made him pray that it wouldn't be for the last time.

Kiya stood there for a while, her blonde wig rippling in the wind and her long black coat flapping about her slim, sexy figure. She had creases in her brow- concern? worry?- he didn't know, but he got the impression she didn't want to leave him.

The crowd outside the West Meridion Mall was its usual vast self. Teenage kids, chilling out before the school week began all over again, moved around in packs, slapping each other on the backs and laughing noisily. The girl-groups were all yapping away, either heading into the building with excitement written on their shiny, Barbie-doll faces or leaving, with an assortment of brightly coloured bags filled with cosmetics and clothes.

One group noticed Kieran perched expertly on the leather seat of his motorbike and purposely cruised towards him in their ridiculously high heels, giggling and whispering to each other. They were all slim, with perky breasts and glossy hair, dressed in tight fitting jeans and turtle necks, or long sleeved tops and big, stylish scarves. They were the rich kids of Meridion- without a doubt. One member of the group even had the guts to approach Kieran, ignoring Kiya standing silently before him, her sword on display for all to see.

"Neat bike," she trilled, flicking long blonde curls behind her ears. "Can I take a ride with you?"

Kieran's face flushed red and he looked nervously up at Kiya, who was glaring daggers at the teenager.

"Sorry Sweetheart-" he said coolly, "I'm taken."

The girl made a cute face at him, pouting her glossy lips and cocking her head to the side. "Come on! Just one trip around the block?" she whined playfully. "I've always wanted to ride something so dangerous looking,"

Her eyes darted to his crotch and she smiled innocently at him.

"Didn't you hear him?" Kiya snapped, stepping in front of the girl. "He said he was taken-"

The girl took a step back in surprise, taking the whole of Kiya in. She wasn't dressed like the other girls, visiting the Mall to pick up sexy lingerie. And her sword meant she wasn't there to let people push her around either.

The group of girls behind their ringleader all scowled at Kiya, standing in the leader's view of Kieran and threw brash comments her way.

"Why don't you go home and play with your dollies?" Kiya suggested frostily.

"Whatever, *bitch*," the teen retorted, then plucking up some courage, she approached Kieran and handed him a little pink card with a number written on neatly in silver pen. "Call me when you're single."

"Get out of here!" Kiya barked, urging the girl to leave at a faster pace. She was even more furious when she saw the other girls praising the leader as if she'd done something incredibly cool, staring a warrior woman in the face and offering her man a younger model *right* in front of her.

"I bet you enjoyed that?" she turned to Kieran. The shade of red had faded from his cheeks now.

"What can I say? I've still got it."

"You'll have nothing in a minute if you don't zip it. Now kiss me whilst that bitch is still looking then drive off. We don't have time for this."

"Yes Ma'am."

Kieran kissed Kiya passionately, stroking his tongue against hers and savouring the feel of her lips against his.

But when they parted, there was no smile on her face. It had purely been revenge on the teenage girls.

"I'll see you in about an hour and half."

"Good luck."

Kieran smiled faintly and sped off, startling most of the crowd with the revving of his engine. The party of teenage girls had thankfully moved on.

As Kiya entered the Mall, one of the fairy enchantments left its pillar, and the cover of the ivy, to perch on her shoulder, letting out a squeal of protest as she waved her fingers through the image, shattering the tiny beads of light that gave the creature life until there was nothing left of it.

All the other fairies glowered at her as she strolled past, poking their tongues out and making noises of dislike. But Kiya was on auto pilot. She didn't care for fairy spells. She cared about finding Roxy, and with the crowds so thick, she wasn't sure she'd have much luck.

Firstly, she took an elevator to the level housing the pet shop and made her way over, praying that Logan would still be tending to puppies, or goldfish, or whatever the hell it was he did for a living.

The door made an almighty crashing sound when she entered, alarming a small cluster of people at the front desk. There was a little girl with short platinum blonde hair, half tied up with a red ribbon, and a boy, with similar features, clutching a small white cat to his little chest. Next to the children stood their mother, hair reaching down past her shoulders, blonde with a hint of grey, and staring fearfully at Kiya, whose blade peeked over one shoulder.

"Come on now Laurie, Michael. Let's pay the nice man and get home to Daddy."

The children cheered. The boy- Michael - pressed the squirming snowy white kitten closer to the print of his 'Goonies' t-shirt. The little girl, in a red dress and white tights, petted the kitten joyously on the top of its furry head, making it 'mew' cutely at them.

Michael noticed Kiya standing in the doorway and left the family without a word, watched by a frightened looking Laurie. The child's approach paralysed Kiya, but she managed to put on a friendly face as he stared up at her.

"My Mummy bought me a kitten for my birthday!" he proclaimed, holding the kitten out for Kiya to acknowledge. She knelt down before the boy, becoming level with his big blue eyes.

"That was nice of her," she said, trying not to sound awkward. "What are you going to call him?"

"I don't know," Michael screwed his face up in thought. "He looks like snow doesn't he!"

Kiya smiled at the child as he stroked a small hand over the creature's back. She was mesmerised by him, so adorable... so innocent... He was silly for speaking to a stranger like this, but she couldn't help but feel thankful towards him for doing so. It created happy images in her mind of having her own child.

"I think your Mummy wants to leave now," Kiya told the boy, noticing the mother turning in horror to find her son standing with a woman bearing a sword. She was completely aghast, and snatched the hand of her daughter up hurriedly, making her way over to Michael with anger in her eyes.

"Come away from her Michael," she scolded him, taking his free hand whilst the other gripped the kitten.

It mewed again as the boy was jolted and dragged out of the pet shop.

Silence ensued.

Kiya moved to the counter now, where the fat man was lifting a mug of tea to his lips and turning the page of a newspaper. There were crumbs down his front and a pungent smell of b.o. wafting from his sweaty armpits.

"It's half price on kitty litter today and seventy five percent off that damn monkey that no one wants to give a home," he informed her cheerlessly, without looking up.

"Where's Logan?" Kiya asked, straight to the point.

"Who?"

"Logan… the young man who was working for you. Blonde hair. Handsome. Took a girl into the back room with him a few days back-" she hissed indignantly.

"Never heard of him."

Kiya's face twitched in anger and she reached out for the guy's mug, tipping the contents all over his fat front. Luckily for him, it was only lukewarm. The only damage done was an extra stain on his extra large t-shirt.

"Hey… you dumb bitch! Who do you think you are coming in here and doing that in *my* pet shop? Get the fuck out before I call security!"

Kiya unsheathed her blade and pointed it at the man, who put his hands up in the air automatically. "My friend is missing. She has a lot of people who love and miss her and I know Logan has something to do with her disappearance. Now tell me where he is or I cut one of your *big* ears off."

The man swallowed. "He…he quit, a d…day or so ago."

"Be specific!" Kiya demanded, placing the cold steel against the man's earlobe.

"I...I don't know. I didn't pay much attention. He was here one day and the next he never showed up. Never let me down before then, he didn't. Used to be here before the sun came up and left when the sun went down-"

Kiya listened and watched intently. The man's brow was slick with sweat, but he had become confident enough to let his hands droop, even with a sword pressing against the side of his chubby face. "Where can I find him now?"

"How am I supposed to know? Didn'cha hear me, woman? He left without a word. He could be anywhere. He could even be dead for all I know."

"What about employee records? You must have taken an address?"

"The guy wasn't employed by me. He says he wanted to work here on a six month work experience thingy. Didn't ask for money at all, because he said his lifestyle didn't require cash, or something like that. But I still slipped him a few pound notes on days we were blessed with customers." A bead of sweat rolled down the man's face and splattered onto the sharpest point of Kiya's blade, running a slimy track down the length of it. Kiya gritted her teeth at the sight and recoiled, dropping the blade to her hip.

"You better not be lying to me-" she warned, with a dangerous look in her eye.

"Do I look like the type of guy who would risk getting killed for some guy I hardly know? Come on, lady! That's as much info' as I can give ya. Now buy something, or get the fuck out of my shop."

Kiya put her sword away and glanced at the monkey rattling its cage wildly. The poor beast was flashing its little, sharp teeth at her in an expression of pain and discomfort and jiggling up and down on its hindquarters; tail wrapped around the door to its small enclosure. She felt a pang of pity, but let it douse out as the creature began to screech unbearably.

"That monkey is better off dead than hanging there like that-"

"Don't I know it!" the pet shop owner scoffed, returning to his paper. "But I ain't no murderer."

There was no need to hang around any longer. Her next stop was Bianca's.

Kieran parked his bike and glared up remorsefully at Roxy's parent's mansion. He hated it all coming to this-asking *them* for help and information, of all people! The slimy bastards.

The pastel pink windowsills; cream walls; extravagant rose bushes; lush green grass and dancing sprinkler devices, gave off an elegance that no one in Meridion could afford to even look at, let alone purchase for themselves. These people were rich alright. The last of the rich families to still live in the city, besides the Mayor and his associates.

As expected of the rich, the house was surrounded by tall, neatly trimmed hedges and sporting an iron gate, double the height of Kieran, bearing not a single scratch in its black paintwork.

Roxy's parents wouldn't let Kieran in even if he asked nicely, so he skipped the formalities and went straight into 'disrespectful visitor' mode, shimmying up the metal bars and swinging over the top onto the gravel driveway below.

He was sure Roxy's parents had already been alerted to his presence by now.

"Excuse me, Sir," came a deep, assertive voice from a tall dark skinned man approaching Kieran at a rapid pace. His hair was long and black, tied back in a pony-tail and he was dressed in a navy blue security outfit- walkie talkie at his belt. "Turn around and get off this property *immediately*."

Kieran strolled past the man- unabashed - waltzing straight up to the front door of the jaw dropping building without batting an eyelid.

The dark skinned man caught up with him and placed a firm hand on Kieran's shoulder. "I don't think you heard me," he said forcefully, "Leave now."

Kieran shook his mane of hair behind his head and turned to the man before him, observing his thick black eyebrows, unsmiling large lips and penetrating dark eyes. "I'm sorry man, I didn't hear you," he replied, making a move as if to leave, then giving the security guard a swift uppercut to the nose- hard enough to stun the guy, but not enough to kill him like some blows had been known to. Blood splashed down the man's face within seconds and he reached for a gun inside its holster as an afterthought to the pain.

But Kieran was too quick. He had the gun before the man's fingers could grasp it and pointed it at the centre of his forehead. "Make this easy for me because I'm done with playing the nice guy," Kieran said as calmly as he could. "Open this door and let me in. I wish to speak with the lady and gentleman owners of this household-"

"They're out," the man replied.

"You're lying. It's a Sunday and these lazy, rich assholes have nowhere to go in this shitty world except to sit in their lounge and sip tea from their bone china."

The man was noticeably chewing the skin that lined the inside of his mouth now, keeping his eyes fixed on the gun.

"Open the damn door, or I'll kick at it all day and night until there's a big enough hole for me to squeeze my body through if I have to."

A loud exhalation rushed from the guy's lungs as he reached for some keys in his pockets and gave Kieran the access he needed. Surprisingly, he was met by Roxy's parents the second he set foot on the eggshell coloured tiles, standing in a hallway bigger than most of the homes in Meridion.

The security guard made his way over to his employers and stood protectively in front of them, giving Kieran only a partial view of both male and female behind him. Kieran lowered the gun, but kept his finger on the trigger, and nodded a hello to his audience.

Roxy's father made a 'tutting' noise, glancing briskly to his wife. She had her lips pursed, dressed in a crimson dress and supporting a glass of red wine in her aged palm.

"This is the man who stole our little girl away," Roxy's father announced.

"I don't need telling twice, Dear," his wife replied wistfully. Her words were crisp and sharp.

"You can leave us, Merek."

The man- Merek- threw an unsure glance at his boss, then made his way into an adjoining room, no doubt listening in on the conversation from the sidelines.

"I came because Roxy is missing-,"

"Lost her did you?" the woman asked primly.

Kieran's jaw ticced. "Try using 'kidnapped' in your sentences."

Another tutt. This one less audible.

"She was taken from our headquarters- her hair chopped off and left lying all over the floor."

Roxy's mother managed a quick glance at her husband, expecting some sort of reaction to this rumour of foul play.

"Sonja is safe, I can assure you," he informed the intruder.

"Then she's here?" Kieran exclaimed, stepping forward in his haste to know everything. The man, with his greying hair and snappy dark coloured suit, advanced on him, unafraid by the biker and his handgun.

"She is no longer your concern."

Kieran's calm snapped. He grabbed the front of the man's suit jacket and shook him vigorously. "Of course it's my fucking concern. She always will be my concern, you asshole."

"I suppose you *love* her?" he questioned Kieran in an sarcastic tone of voice, putting thick, purple veined hands over his attacker's and prying them off his suit before it wrinkled.

"Not in the way you may think, but she's still important to me. Now tell me everything you know."

"Or what?" the woman asked, taking a sip of her wine delicately. "We've been searching for our daughter for quite sometime now."

"Why do you want to keep her here so badly?"

Roxy's mother lifted a finely plucked, dark eyebrow. "Who said anything about *us* wanting her?"

The silence in the room expanded whilst Kieran looked at both of Roxy's obnoxious relations, standing there with carefully rehearsed poise and refinement. Each of them had a daunting smirk.

"She's here?" Kieran muttered, hopelessly.

"I'm afraid not," replied the father.

"We don't want a daughter who has been tainted by riff raff like yourself. She's nothing but a *whore* and if she ever sets foot in my house, I'll set the dogs on her. Tell her that from me, if you ever find her of course."

Kieran was fit to explode. He didn't understand what he was hearing. Roxy was so sure her parents had been looking for her, but quite blatantly, they were disgusted with their own flesh and blood. So why the search? Why the flyers and calls to Emilia?

"You're working with someone aren't you-?" he said slowly, thinking how it made sense now. "You were looking for Roxy on behalf of someone else."

"Sonja *is* wanted by another, but I'll be damned if I tell you who," the mother barked.

"Logan, right? This Logan guy I keep hearing about has been looking for her and using *you* to do the dirty work, or at least some of it?"

"Leave now." Roxy's father stepped closer, placing a hand on Kieran's chest to nudge him back. "And *never* utter that name in this house again."

"You fear him?" Kieran realised. "He's a bad person isn't he? Tell me what he's doing with Roxy?"

"The police were notified the second you climbed over my gate. Leave now, or spend a hefty sentence in jail."

He wasn't going to get anymore out of them. Roxy's mother was already turning away from the conversation in a swirl of satin cloth, striding expertly in high heels across her polished, tile floor.

Kieran nodded and left. Feeling the draft as the front door slammed shut behind him.

At least I have a name, he thought. *That narrows things down a little...*

Chapter 30

Cat and Mouse

Kiya touched her wrist to her forehead, trying to wipe the dull ache from her head and feeling the heat rising exhaustingly inside her. Dizziness was threatening to consume her, so she put her hand at the base of her neck and massaged gently, easing some of the tension with her prying fingertips.

Shoppers were moving swiftly now, aware of the pressing 'closing hour' and trying to hit a few more shops before their time ran out. It was thinking of this that made Kiya realise she should be doing the same, only for a different reason than to find a cracking bargain.

As she cast her eyes over her surroundings, they came to rest on someone sitting at the café- where she had first got to know Roxy. It was weird... that day seemed so distant now.

Kiya didn't want to blink. If she blinked, the person she was staring so intently at might vanish and her chances of reaching them would disappear to. So slowly, she put one foot in front of the other, moving soundlessly across the shiny Mall floor; her fingers itching for the hilt of her blade.

The person in question was alone, sat hunched over a coffee mug, their hair almost falling inside it. They were dressed in dark clothing. A long black jacket. Black jeans. All set against white skin and making the person look as if they were a corpse trying to pass for someone 'breathing.'

Kiya stopped.

Her eyes were stinging from lack of moisture, but she continued to force them open.

But she had been spotted. Her cover was blown.

Tristian put a hand on the table to support himself and rose from his seat outside the cafe, wondering when he should make a run for it.

He hadn't known it was Kiya at first. The prospect of a pretty blonde thing moving towards him had been too much of a farfetched idea and it had taken him a long time to recognise her features, deciphering that the lady under all that blonde hair was in fact his new-found enemy. His beautiful Kiya, looking deadly, showing disturbing signs of wanting to rip his heart out.

Tristian gulped, caught in her gaze like a deer before car headlights. She made a move forward again, apprehensively, and his feet kick-started into motion at last, carrying him away from the warrior-woman, whose blade was now drawn.

He threw his metal legged chair to the ground, and a few more after that on exiting the café seating area in an attempt to slow her down, bashing a shoulder into an elderly man who was poised to sip his beverage and knocking it all over the poor guy. Outcries ripped out from many of the shoppers as he rammed into many more carelessly, detaching shopping bags from people's fingertips and unsteadying bystanders.

Kiya was on the rampage also. She too cared little for the innocent people of Meridion, who were seeking comfort in their Sunday afternoon shopping trips. Anyone standing in her way felt the front of her palm pushing them aside brutally and she soon lost count of how many she was bound to leave a bruise on.

It became a game of 'cat and mouse' among a million dogs, who could turn on them both at any moment and throw them down if they so wished.

Tristian's black hair flew about his scalp wildly, giving her a target to follow with her sharp eyes. He was fast, but not quite as fast as her, and as she reached out a hand to grab a hold of his greasy locks, she managed a jagged tug, only to have the hair come away in her hands grotesquely.

He was falling apart. Was it stress or something else? But she didn't wish to care about his reasons for bad health. Instead, she threw herself back into the chase.

Tristian reached the elevator a few yards ahead of her and waved at Kiya triumphantly as the doors closed. He was safe, for the moment, the slippery little worm.

Kiya cursed at his luck and pushed the button rapidly, disturbing bystanders as they stood aghast at her uncivilised behaviour.

"Excuse me!" came an outraged cry, "You almost had my eye out with that thing!"

She rounded on a male shopper, bearing similar features to the Kentucky Fried Chicken guy- white hair and beard, black framed spectacles, and clutching a cane for support. "Then I must have missed my mark," she told him darkly .

The man muttered a "Well I never-" to the audience around him, and cried out again as she shoved through the crowd once more, making her way over to the balcony edge. People watched her in anger as she glanced over the side.

A tall, leafy tree grew from a large marble container, filled with soil and surrounded by benches. It was decorated with the familiar fairy enchantments, giving it the impression of a shimmering, sparkling Christmas tree.

Kiya made a very quick calculation on the distance from the balcony railing to the tree's safest looking branch and to the crowds amazement, she threw herself over the edge, grabbing a hold of the branch at the last second with one hand- her sword clattering to the floor below.

Shoppers were yelling now, pointing up at her in awe as she flipped herself over onto another branch and caught sight of Tristian moving through the crowd, in less of a hurry than previously.

He already thinks he's won, her mind roared in anger.

She saw her chance, and took it.

Leaping like a feline in its prime, she landed on Tristian's back and slammed his face into the floor, hurting her knee on the ground, but managing to cushion most of her fall with her enemy's body.

Sure, she had no sword, but she still had her hands; she flipped him over, preparing to strangle him- just until he passed out, so that she could drag him off somewhere and finish the job properly.

"I've waited for this chance, *Tristian,* and you actually thought you could get away from me!?"

Kiya's eyes were flashing feelings of incredulousness as a teenage boy, beneath her, twisted and turned in fear of his attacker. The boy's skin was not the same greasy texture as Tristian's, and his lips were much fuller, although his build and hairstyle were practically identical.

"My name's *Arran*! *Jeez*, what do you think you're doing lady? I think you've broken my back. *Ouch*… oh shit. My mum is going to flip out if I have to miss a few more days of high school for this-"

Kiya was on her knees, staring at the boy stupidly, wishing his face would change into the man's she had been pursuing. And as she sat there, in shock and disappointment, she was unprepared for the sudden pounding of pain against her back.

Tristian had used Kiya's spine as a foothold to plant his heavy boot onto, leaping over her head and running onward and out of the doors, into the rare winter sunshine.

Kiya stared on in dismay. How could she have failed? How was it possible that justice would allow him to slip from her grasp?

"For fuck sake!" she yelled, putting her hands over her face. Her chest felt as if it would explode from all the strain her body had just undergone.

"Can I go?" Arran asked her, lying stiffly on the ground.

"Get out of here kid-" she mumbled in a defeated tone.

The mouse had certainly outsmarted the cat this time around.

Chapter 31

Witch In The Mall

People were edgy as Kiya stood up. Her exhaustion was evident by the way her body drooped downward slightly, but it wouldn't take her long to catch her breath and be on her way again. She was a lot fitter than most the slobs in Meridion after all.

There was no one willing to approach her after such a shocking display thankfully, though they all remained in their little huddles, giving her perplexed glares and boisterously discussing how she had dived from the balcony, and from there, jumped onto an unsuspecting victim, slamming his face quite disturbingly into the floor. The boy in question had hobbled off to the 'Medi-Centre' situated at the back of the Mall's first floor.

Kiya wanted to lash out at the lot of them. She had made a spectacle of herself, foolishly so, and the last thing she needed was Meridion talking about her-spreading her tale like one of Jesus' miracles.

Kieran is going to kick my ass if he catches wind of this, her mind cringed unhelpfully. The thought of him picking up a newspaper and reading about her swinging from trees like a chimp in the Mall wouldn't bode well for their secret identities as Slayers. What if people tried investigating into her life further?

As she bent down to pick up her fallen sword, a blinding flash hit her in the eyes. A man, with an expensive looking camera, was trying to take some close-up shots without Kiya's permission, following her annoyingly as she walked.

"Back off," she warned him, pushing him aside. The camera jostled in his hands but he managed to keep a tight hold of it before it crashed to the floor. He appeared unfazed by her anger towards him and continued to snap away, causing more raucous discussion among the shoppers.

When the elevator doors closed behind her, Kiya sighed heavily in relief and slouched against the back wall, closing her eyes and blocking out the tedious background music. It was becoming obvious that she needed a *long* vacation, but she knew that the only way she'd ever *truly* be relaxed again was if she were dead and buried. One small blessing was the fact that her new 'snap-happy' fan had not followed her into the elevator with his shiny toy.

There was a little over half an hour left now of store opening time, and only one place left that Kiya could think to look.

Bianca was standing at the door of her shop to greet her, as if she had known Kiya was on her way. She smiled broadly, placed a hand on the warrior's back and escorted her inside the store.

Kiya was too miserable to object to the woman's touch. She admired the older lady's attire- long black skirt, sparkly black sandals, an emerald green blouse and sequined black shawl resting over her shoulders. Around her neck hung a pair of spectacles, which were bobbing up and down against her body as she walked.

"Tell me, lovely, what's the problem? I heard a bit of a ruckus on the bottom floor. That wasn't you by any chance?"

Kiya felt as if she were being interrogated by a head teacher as they came to a stop. She tiredly leant against the shop's front counter and pretended to be interested in a pamphlet about a 'Bianca Store Card' before speaking.

"I need your help," she said, avoiding Bianca's first question.

"So do many, but I'm just an old soul now, providing beautiful clothing for strong women like yourself."

Bianca was always smiling Kiya realised. She bore such a trusting face that it was hard to feel angry in her presence. Bianca was comfortable, standing before her, as if the sword and troublesome lines in her pretty face didn't scare her one little bit.

"You're aura is dark. Tell me, why are you so angry? Do you ever feel peace anymore?"

Kiya made a noise of scepticism in her throat. "You read auras?"

"Yes. Just like you are a Healer, my friend."

Kiya snapped to attention. "Who told you that?"

Bianca laughed and raised her hands to the young woman's surprised expression. "Relax. Relax, Dear. Not only can I read auras, I can detect any special talents people may have inherited from the old days, when magic was ripe in Meridion and schools actually *taught* kids how to cast spells!"

Kiya thought about her teaching programme at the Nursery School, where she had worked most of her life. The closest her young students had ever come to learning about 'magic' was when she'd read them all an afternoon story, to calm them after an exciting lunch hour in the playground. None of them were remotely aware that magic had once existed. Instead, they believed it was something invented by J.K.Rowling- featured in the colourful Harry Potter books that their older brothers and sisters all had lined up along their shelves.

"That's quite a talent you have," Kiya admitted, forcing herself to relax more.

"Well it's one of many, honey. Didn't Roxy mention to you that I'm a witch?"

Kiya's mind jolted at both the use of Roxy's name and the word 'witch.' Witches in Meridion didn't usually admit to their magical roots in front of people, so openly. She tried to hide her insecurity in the presence of the old woman by continuing the conversation as pleasantly as possible.

"You still practise magic?"

"Do you still heal?"

Kiya was becoming aggravated. Why was she always turning things back around so that the focus was on her?

"We can't deny our abilities. We should be proud of them. You would make an excellent doctor or a medical surgeon if you fully embraced your gift."

"I'm not that good," Kiya informed her. "My power... it's a little weak. My mother didn't approve of it, but my grandmother tried encouraging it secretly."

"Oh, I see. But that's to be expected. The older generation prefer to keep the old ways alive if they feel it will be of some use to their families in the future. I suppose your mother refused to be tutored by your grandmother and so your granny tried to salvage your ability before it died out?"

"Something like that."

Bianca looked lost in her own world for a moment. Her shop was emptying now and she was feeling the silence seeping in through the open doors. This was how she liked it most. No rushing. No messing up of her clothes on their racks. Just calm. But calm didn't bring in the money, which she knew all too well.

Kiya was hesitant to speak. Something about Bianca and her wisdom frightened her. What if she could read minds? What if she knew she was pregnant? Maybe she could tell her if her baby was going to be okay…?

"I assume you came here to ask something of me?"

Her heart jumped in surprise, knocking her from her thoughts.

"Yes… yes, I did." Kiya leant forward and whispered in Bianca's ear. "Roxy has gone missing."

A cry escaped Bianca's throat and Kiya came to the conclusion that she wasn't a mind reader after all, for if she had been, she would have known this already.

"*Missing*?"

"We left her at our headquarters and returned to find nothing but her hair all over the floor."

"Was there blood?"

Kiya's jaw ticced. "Why do you ask?"

"Because if there was blood, then you can be sure she is dead."

Kiya was shocked by this analysis. "Excuse me?"

"Well, Roxy is a warrior, yes? And her body is missing you say? If she had fought for her life, there's bound to be blood somewhere, whether it be hers or the attackers. She's too quick to have someone just walk up and drug her. She has probably been kidnapped and will either be put to some use by her kidnapper or killed at another location."

"I didn't see any blood. Just hair."

"Well, my dear. I *can't* tell you if she's dead or alive. What I *can* do is locate her body for you."

"You can do that?"

"As long as I have something that belongs to Roxy, then yes."

Kiya glanced around helplessly for a moment, then ripped the blonde wig off her head. "Will this do?"

Bianca smiled and took the mound of blonde hair from Kiya's eager hands.

"Perfect, my dear. This will do nicely."

Bianca closed the store ten minutes early, apologising heartily to her female customers and offering them a ten percent discount when they came to the counter to pay. As soon as the store was clear, she locked the front door and dimmed the lights, signalling for Kiya to follow her through to the back room.

In an adjoining room, Kiya came upon a whole array of outfits in preparation for selling. There were items on 'upper body' mannequins, bearing materials held in place with pins and there was also clothes wrapped in plastic, piled on top *and* under workbenches.

"Do you make all these yourself?"

Bianca laughed. "Oh gosh no. I design most of them and send my drawings to another company. Then, when I receive the clothes, I sometimes change the design a little, until I deem it fit to go out on the racks with the rest of my products."

Kiya brushed her hand across a large white sewing machine as she followed Bianca further into the back of the office. Here, there were less clothes on the small desk or scattered on the floor in piles. It was more of a storage room for coat hangers.

"Take a seat."

Kiya was directed to a chair with a velvet pink cushion and she perched on the edge, trying not to knock any of the coat hangers over.

"Can I get you anything? Tea? Coffee? Martini?"

"Um… I kind of have to meet someone in about ten to fifteen minutes so I'd appreciate it if we could do the spell pronto."

Bianca shrugged. "I believe there's always time for tea, but if you say otherwise, my dear, then we best push on. Pass me that pot plant over there,"

Kiya glanced around and found an aloe vera plant growing in a little brown pot beside her chair. Its green arms stuck out in all directions, but a few, Kiya noticed, had been broken off.

"Thanks." From a desk drawer, Bianca pulled out a rolled up piece of paper, which she spread across the length of her table, and held down at its curled corners with four white candles, lighting each in quick succession. The paper was a large map of Meridion.

"Have you done this before?"

"Oh yes. Many a time. I like to keep track of my friends, but more importantly, my enemies." Bianca was busying herself now with a small brown bowl. She ripped part of her aloe vera plant and squeezed its thick gooey contents into the base of the bowl, then added other ingredients from small, plastic, sealed packets that she brought out from another drawer in her desk. Kiya recognised dried rose petals, bay leaves, slices of garlic and something that looked like a severed crows foot being added to the mixture. Last of all, she cut off part of the blonde wig with a pair of scissors and added it to the bowl with haste.

"Does it take long to work?"

Bianca was humming to herself as she stirred the ingredients around with a spoon. When she was satisfied it was mixed, she smeared it all over the map messily.

Suddenly, the map came alive. Each line and name-place glowed brightly with a pure white light, illuminating Kiya's intrigued face.

"So?" she pressed, trying to find any sign of Roxy being mentioned on the map.

Bianca sighed.

"It didn't work did it?"

"Of course it worked," she assured her boastfully. "This can only mean two things. Either Roxy is somewhere 'off the map,' meaning another country. Or, she is underground."

"What if she's dead?"

"Then the map would still show where you can find the body."

There was silence for a while as Kiya reflected on this information. She watched the candles flickering and the ingredients shimmering, just as Bianca gave a swish of her hand, making both map and mess disappear.

If Kiya had something of Logan's, she could have done a location spell on him also, but as it was...

"Thank you for your help." She stood to leave.

Bianca reached out a wrinkled hand and placed it on Kiya's wrist. "You will tell me when you find her, won't you?"

She nodded in reply.

"Thank you, dearest. I can't be losing my best customer now, can I?"

Kiya didn't feel like matching Bianca's smile and instead, left the room.

Out front, the store doors were still unlocked, though a warning alarm was bleating loudly to encourage people to pick up the pace. There were only a handful of shoppers left and they were all making their way to the main exit, where a bald security guard stood in wait with a big bunch of keys. Some shoppers stood by the doors for a moment, zipping jackets up to their chins and pulling them in tighter around the neck, for it had begun raining heavily outside. No one noticed Kiya leaving- the daredevil pregnant woman who swung from the tree- minus her blonde wig.

Seeing Kieran on his motorbike was a breath of fresh air, although she knew full well from the results of Bianca's location spell that he would not have Roxy with him. He was looking dishevelled and very wet, but forced a weak smile on his handsome face as she approached.

"She's not on the map," Kiya explained, causing Kieran to break into a stupefied expression.

"Excuse me?"

"I hooked up with a witch. She cast a location spell and the results say Roxy's either underground or outside the city."

"Well, I know which I'm betting on," Kieran muttered deep in thought.

"How were things at her parent's house?"

Kieran let out a loud breath of air. "Let's just say they aren't as interested in finding Roxy as we are."

Kiya frowned. "What's that supposed to mean?"

"It means, they wouldn't shed too many tears if they heard their daughter was dead right now."

"Jeez… that's fucked up." Kiya immediately thought of her own mother and father. Maybe they felt the same way about her now?

The rain was coming down so hard that it made visibility next to zero, and Kieran's boot almost slipped as he kick started the bike. His hair was tangled across his face and his eyes were forced to narrow to slits against the wind, but still he pushed on, eager to feel his shotgun in his hands and for the night to fall around them.

He would take Kiya and Siren into the mouth of Hell with him if it meant getting Roxy back and finding Zeke for that final showdown.

Chapter 32

Love and Freedom

They went unnoticed as they had passed the Slayers distantly on their way back to the underground, dragging Roxy along in the dark, and Annara and Zeke managed to complete their mission without any big hiccups.

Sean had bravely left the confines of his toll booth to cry out in vain at what he was now seeing, but after a bit of persuasion, he allowed them to take the innocent Slayer girl into the graveyard.

"Are you going to hurt her? She was your friend Zeke-"

"Hey, stay the fuck out of my business!" Zeke snarled at the boy, "And open that fucking gate."

Suddenly, Annara dropped Roxy's legs and ran over to Sean, hissing like a wild cat, giving him a perfect view of her extra long fangs and the push he needed to grant them access to the South Meridion Bridge.

The sky was becoming heavy with rain clouds as they finally made it to the hatch and Annara could tell, by the position of the moon and the colour of the sky, that there was still enough time to join the pre-war celebration and maybe even pick up a bite to eat.

"Keep an eye out for werewolves," she said, watching Zeke giving Roxy a 'fireman's lift' in order to carry her down the ladder. "They won't attack a vampire when they're playing their hunting games down there, but they might try and rip the girl from your arms if they can smell fresh meat-"

"Right," Zeke grumbled, almost dropping Roxy from his grasp. When the ladder ended and the floor met his feet, he breathed a sigh of relief. "So now what?"

"We leave her with Shannon and go report to the Master."

"Shannon?"

Annara smiled, "Didn't you know the Master had a younger sister?"

Zeke imagined a female version of the Master and cringed. He hoped the 'attitude problem' didn't run in the family. "Cute," he whispered to himself sarcastically. "Brother and sister playing dead. Their parents must be so proud."

The underground was thriving with life. Werewolves couldn't hunt as they usually did on full moon days because the corridors and bedrooms were all teeming with vampires dancing and kissing each other. Most had given up the chance to morph into their wolf-states and were instead standing tall, looking like any other man who spends too much time working out at the gym, but licking their 'paws' every now and again in a most un-human fashion.

It was hard manoeuvring the drugged Slayer through the crowds. Vampires could smell the human blood, and in their excitement, reached out to stroke the girl's hair and body ponderously. One vampire even tried to slip in a nibble on Roxy's ankle, but Annara smashed a quick kick into the creature's jaw, sending it scampering away.

Zeke was smiling for the first time in ages. There were just so many beautiful vampire women, dressed in skimpy clothes and rubbing their bodies against each other seductively. Their eyes were full of lust and intensity, wiggling fingers at him to coax him away from his job and giving him sly winks of encouragement. One girl even had the balls to squeeze his ass on passing.

"Hey Zeke, would you *focus* please?" Annara snapped from the front.

Zeke cast his eyes downward in shame, then lifted them again to meet the eyes of a lady in emerald green, see-through material. She had a toned stomach and jet black hair rippling down her curved back as she danced with a veil floating about her mouth. Everything about her movements and visage reminded Zeke of a gypsy enchantress, swirling around and casting her dark spells on him until he wanted nothing more than to kiss her.

Finally, he let go of Roxy's arms, dropping her precious head on the dirt floor, and ran to the woman, sweeping her off her feet and kissing her with the veil between their lips. He knew that the pain to the back of his head was only to be expected as Annara came up from behind him, giving her knuckles something solid to come in contact with.

"Leave Zeke alone *Leona*. Go find someone else to fuck-"

The gypsy vampire girl scowled at Annara and waved goodbye to Zeke, throwing herself into the crowd once more and dancing her way over to another vampire, with gelled black hair and a set of rippling stomach muscles on display. It was as if her encounter with the ex-Slayer had never existed and Zeke sighed solemnly, turning to reach for Roxy once more.

But Roxy's body wasn't there.

Annara gave him a panic stricken look, then snarled at him- pushing vampires out of the way. She found the girl being dragged into a room by two teenage vampire boys, looking joyous at the sight of their beautiful find.

"She's mine, dude. I get first bite!"

"Hey, you promised we hunt together for eternity and that we share everything we kill," the other complained, blowing his dark dyed-blue hair out of his eyes.

Without a word, Annara kicked one of the lads in the side of his face and gave the other a swift punch in the throat, knocking them away from the sleeping Slayer with ease.

"This is the Master's meal," she said waspishly. "Not *yours*. Now run along and play."

The boy who had taken a foot to the face replied with, "She was just lying there. How were we to know she was yours?"

Annara pushed the boy aside and picked Roxy back up by her thin legs, nodding to Zeke to grab the arms and move more swiftly.

When they reached Shannon's headquarters, they almost collapsed exhaustedly onto her bed, dropping Roxy onto the bed covers. If it weren't for the fact that Shannon was lying naked in a bed with two men, she would have welcomed the company...

"Excuse me!" she cried, still keeping a hand on top of one of the male vampire's heads as he disappeared under the covers. The other was paying attention to her breasts whilst touching his erection. "Tell my brother I don't need to have meals sent to me! I'm perfectly capable of hunting myself."

"This girl isn't for you, Shannon. We were told to bring her here to you before reporting to... thc Master." Annara had almost called him Logan, but didn't want to give Shannon the satisfaction of knowing she- Annara- was also of great importance to her brother now. Not yet at least.

Shannon's hair was dyed a horrid pale pink colour and reminded Annara of candy floss spilling from her scalp unattractively. She had younger skin than most vampires, for she had been 'turned' at the age of nineteen, and little watery eyes, which she used to get whatever she wanted from the male vampire population. Her breasts were a lot smaller than Annara's, she noticed amusingly, and her body looked too skinny to be sexy, but being a direct relation to the Master gave her *some* power over vampires and she was always capable of bedding most things without any trouble what-so-ever.

"Put her on the floor. I haven't finished with Spiros and Damien yet."

The man above the covers smiled handsomely and gave her a kiss on the side of the face before she leant down to put him inside her mouth. It made Annara glower harder at the teenage girl, watching in disgust as the girl gave a sloppy blow-job to the man who was now growling in ecstasy.

"The girl stays here. No harm can be done to her... *apparently*. So that means no snacking. He wants this one alive and untouched. We'll return later after we've been further instructed."

Shannon resurfaced quickly. "Fine, fine. Get out of my room. Stop ruining my evening."

"*Slut*," Annara muttered uncaringly, as she left the room, knowing full well that *she* behaved in a similar manner ninety five percent of the time.

"Let's find Lo... the Master and hurry this charade up. I want to find a man to play with before tomorrow night."

"I'm sure that won't be hard," Zeke replied, thinking dreamily of Leona in her beautiful green attire, dancing like an angel- revealing her private area to him. "We still have tonight and the rest of the daytime tomorrow to have our fun."

"Well, you obviously aren't aware of how *many* men I had in mind," Annara said, leading the way to Logan's headquarters.

Logan was sat on his throne caressing his temples, slouched down as far as his ass would allow before it could tumble off the edge, and listening to the distant rumbling of music and screams in his underground lair.

He hated it.

Living in caverns carved out of rock and dirt made him feel as radiant as a sewer rat. He deserved better than this. He wanted a house of his own and a bride in his bed. He wanted to touch Roxy's long silken hair as she slept beside him through the day, followed by the sharing of a human for breakfast, as the sun slips below the horizon.

The wait for an ideal way of living was killing him. And he couldn't help but be pessimistic about Annara's promise to deliver.

She hasn't failed me before, his mind reminded him. *But I seriously regret sending that Zeke to assist her.*

He left his chair; a chair made by one of his supporters who had been a carpenter in his human life, and had insisted on crafting him a throne. Looking at the gift made him queasy, but he accepted it with heartiest thanking, trying not to discourage the pawns in his war for freedom. And for love.

Leaving the 'throne room,' he cut across the hall to his headquarters. It was the most lavish of all the bedrooms in the underworld, with paintings hanging from the filth encrusted walls and purple drapes hanging from a four-poster bed. There was even a chaise longue, which Annara used to lay on during their private meetings.

"It won't be long now," Logan promised the Priest, who was tied up with rope and kneeling in the corner of the room beside a bedside table. The sweat dripping from the Holy man's face was immense. His eyes were wide with fear and his dog-collar covered with flecks of blood after the struggle it had taken to drag him from his little church near the centre of the city. Logan had had to kill a young women, who had been witness to his arrival in the early hours of the evening, using her as an example to what he would do if the Priest didn't cooperate.

On the bed lay a leather bound Bible.

The Priest mumbled incoherently and cringed as Logan placed a hand on the top of his thinning grey hair. "I'm sorry to have taken you so far from home, Father Casey, but you're a vital part in all this-" he took his hand away and sat down beside the bound and frightened man, giving him full view of the blood that still coated his hands, from a previous meal.

"You wait until you see her. She's a beauty, like no other. A pure hearted gem with a passion for slaying my kind, and yet, I love her all the more for doing so." He laughed a little. "I bet you think I'm crazy?"

The man refused to reply through the rag tied around his mouth.

"Well... love can make you do crazy things."

He reached out now, causing the Priest to lower his head in fear and with his bloodied hands, he loosened the rag until the Priest's mouth was free from obstruction.

"That's better." Logan smiled, feigning a friendly tone of voice.

"I won't do what you've asked of me!" the man said gruffly.

"You saw what I did to that poor member of your congregation, Father. Don't make me do it to the rest of them. How would you live with yourself?"

Father Casey thought back to the moment Logan had wrenched the lady from her pew, where she had been praying silently, throwing her to the floor before him. When he had refused to do what it was Logan had asked, the vampire punched and tore his way through the woman's chest, presenting her heart to the Holy Man and tossing it at him as if it were nothing more than a cricket ball.

"This is *wrong*..." Father Casey groaned in despair. "Wrong! Wrong! Wrong!"

"Father!" Logan cried melodramatically, "I thought you were supposed to *encourage* marriage between couples?"

The Priest was breathing heavily, hunched over on his knees like a man waiting to be shot or beheaded. He didn't want to speak further with the vampire. There was little more he could say or do without suffering for it.

A knock at the door startled both men, human and vampire alike, and Logan patted the poor Priest on the back. "Don't worry. I'll get it." But his amusement died when he assumed it would only be an army recruit looking for some words of wisdom, or a female looking to get laid by the Master of the underground.

"What is it?" he muttered monotonously.

Seeing Annara made him happy for the first time since they'd begun working together and he had to admit, Zeke's face was also a welcoming sight.

"She's here?" he asked fervently.

Both of his vampire minions nodded.

"She's at Shannon's, like you instructed."

Logan brushed his hand through his blonde hair, leaving red flakes of blood behind. He was finding it hard to contain his excitement. "She sleeps?"

"Like a log-" Zeke piped up.

"Perfect." He left the pair standing outside his door in confusion for a moment, while he grabbed something from a clothes rack in his room. On a hanger, vibrantly sparkling, was Roxy's green velvet prom dress; the same one she had worn on the night they had first shared in the ultimate act of love. She had looked like a princess that night, and now, he was about to make her his queen.

"Have Shannon put this dress on her."

"I'll do it-" Zeke offered.

Logan's eyes flashed red. "*You* are no longer needed. Now fuck off."

Zeke didn't need telling twice.

Annara was stroking the material of the dress suspiciously and wondering, why the Master would want to dress a Slayer up prettily if he was only going to eat her?

It didn't make sense and she wasn't about to let him see Roxy in something so fine.

"What's this all about?" she asked, stepping through the door uninvited. Logan stood his ground, feeling the closeness of Annara's body as she pressed herself against him ever so slightly. His lip curled in discontent.

"Do as I ask-"

The sound of the priest stirring inside the room increased Annara's curiosity and she pushed her way into the bedroom further, staring in awe at the man on the floor.

"I thought you only drank from women?"

Logan shrugged. "I had a change of appetite I guess."

She sniffed the air for any sign of a female being in his bed and found no traces of there ever having been a human or vampire between his quilt covers that evening. This information satisfied her; she felt the need to lie on his bed sheets seductively, licking her lips till they glistened.

"Why don't you forget about the Slayer and eat me instead?"

Logan's mind reeled. He should have known Annara would do everything in her power to get him into bed.

"Baby," he said serenely. "You're spoiling my surprise for you."

Annara twisted her body around until she was on her stomach, glancing up at Logan with interest. "You have a surprise? Tell me!"

He shook his head. "But then it wouldn't be a surprise."

"But I want to know!" she whined.

He sighed. "Fine." There was a short pause. "I brought a Priest to marry the two of us- and the girl is our substitute for a wedding cake. Wedding cakes have to look decorative and *tasty*, Honey, hence the pretty dress."

Annara squealed suddenly just as the Priest said, "I thought you were marrying-" but received an evil glare from Logan for speaking out of line.

"What about *my* dress?"

Logan's mind whirled rapidly. "After you have Shannon dress the 'cake,' you can go find one for yourself. Surely one of the vampires in this God forsaken hell hole has a pretty dress for my darling Annara to slip into?"

If Annara had a heart, it would have been beating a mile a minute. She couldn't believe what she was hearing. *Marriage between vampires is absurd!* she thought, *but the Master obviously wants us to keep some of the human traditions alive. And people will recognise me as a queen at last if we wed! I'll be the sexiest queen ever in the history of the world and all shall remember me for my beauty.*

"When do we wed, my King?"

"After the war."

"But why not before?" she complained. "We have the Priest *and* the 'cake'."

"Yes, but we have no guests. Plus, I wish to start my new life with you *above* the ground, in a celebration of love and freedom."

"Well, if that's what you want-"

Logan grinned a false smile of adoration towards the idiotic vampire.

"It's what I've *always* wanted. Now go and do as I've asked of you."

When he eventually got rid of the bleached blonde pain in his ass, he rounded on Father Casey with a threatening glint in his eye.

"The wedding goes on as planned. Tomorrow night."

"You wish to wed the vampire?"

Logan hissed. "Don't be so fucking *stupid*. Annara doesn't really want me. She wants power. Now, I suggest you get some sleep, Father. You've an important ceremony to conduct for me and I won't have *anything* screw this up!"

Chapter 33

Old Friend. Old Flame.

Spiros' tongue flicking against her was *sensational* as Shannon's eyes rolled back in ecstasy, savouring the rippling pleasures and groaning loudly. The Greek lad was by *far* her favourite play mate and he *never* ceased to impress her with his sexual talents. She knew she had done the right thing by 'turning' him on the eve she had set out from Karanthian to Meridion with her brother. And like a lost dog, he had followed her scent and found her again- a pale damsel standing in the moonlight that overcast the graveyard whilst she chewed on the neck of an elderly woman, who had recently buried her husband.

"Does this please you, my Princess?" he asked her, lifting his head out from under the bedcovers. His dark lashes fluttered as he blinked against the brightness of the candles around her bedroom and threw a quick glance at Damien, the vampire of a similar age to himself, who was behind Shannon now, giving her slim shoulders a massage.

Spiros never liked threesomes, but it was the only way he could ever be in Shannon's company. Rarely did she take less than two vampires into her bed; she was just greedy that way, being the sister of their Master- the leader of a new and great revolution. She wanted to be known for her audacity in the bedroom, and the men she sired on her late night hunts were always the type you'd expect to see in porn movies. Conveniently, they all had impressive packages too.

"You're doing just fine handsome," she smiled broadly at him, twiddling a strand of pink hair around her finger. Spiros dove under the sheets once more.

"I grow weary of this," Damien announced idly, feeling an ache in his palms from all the massaging he was giving. "May I enter you now?"

Shannon's smile faded and her head snapped sharply towards the high school hunk she had chosen to join her this particular night. "*Excuse me*?" she cried. "You get to *fuck* when I say so and now you've gone and lost that chance *buddy*!" She added to this statement a swift slap to the boy's face, leaving bleeding scratches behind from her manicured and black painted talons. Damien's jaw ticced but he kept his lips sealed.

"Get out from under there Spiros!" she growled suddenly, feeling her temper expanding. "I can't concentrate."

Spiros shot Damien a look of hatred as he rose to join them on the surface, keeping one hand planted on Shannon's cold thigh. Desperately he hoped she would grant him access to the haven between her legs, but his chances were looking slim, thanks to the impatient fool sat behind his Princess' back.

"Leave me." she said neutrally.

"But-" Spiros began, but stopped as she put a finger to his lips.

"You may stay."

A grin exploded across his face.

Damien wasted no time in jumping off the bed and fell when his foot struck an object on the bedroom floor. As he landed, his stomach came to rest against the torso of a female. He grumbled hungrily at the very sight of her.

"Is this chick meant to be doing that?" he asked, observing the way her eyes were fluttering open, then closing again. Her lips were parting and shutting rhythmically also.

"Beats me-" Shannon mumbled from the bed, feeding her hand through the strands of dark hair on Spiros' head. If he could purr like a cat, he'd be doing so with each blessed touch of her hand.

Damien was mesmerised by the girl on the floor, lying stiffly, with her hair all sprawled out around her pretty face. He noticed it was cut unevenly, but it didn't alter her beauty in any way. Lying on top of her like this made him hard suddenly and he felt compelled to kiss her.

"Damien, why are you still here?" Shannon shouted furiously.

He moved his face away from the sleeping girl and instead of kissing her, left moodily, with a juicy Feeder girl and a quick lay in mind.

With Damien gone at last, Shannon cast her eye to the floor beside her bed, giving the girl a once over. Immediately, she recognised the face and the familiar shape of her body.

"Sonja?" pushing Spiros away harshly, she twisted her body around until her toes were dangling over the edge of her king sized bed, watching as the girl's face flickered with the faintest signs of life. The fact that Roxy was drugged was a hindrance. Shannon wanted nothing more than to show her old high school pal her new set of fangs and the men she was bedding. Always being the underdog had made her bitter during her last few months in high school.

"So this is why Logan wanted to return to Meridion so badly?" she mused, ignoring Spiros as he re-started the massaging process that Damien had begun, easing the tight knots around her neck and back. "I did wonder why he wanted to be here so desperately. And even on arrival, he was always skulking off, working like a commoner in the safety of that Mall, claiming he was picking out victims for us to tail in the evenings when it was time to hunt."

"She is a friend?" Spiros queried.

Shannon was quick to reply with "Once upon a time, yes."

"Did she betray you, my Princess?"

"In a sense," Shannon replied. "She stopped caring about my feelings and ignored all my problems because she was becoming more and more obsessed with my brother. She was blatantly choosing him over me- her best friend- for a shag on prom night and the delusion that he loved her."

"If our great leader came here to bless this girl with eternal life, then perhaps they are in love?"

Shannon jumped off of her bed. "Gosh! How could I be so fucking stupid?!" she exclaimed, stomping around her room and waving her arms about in a frenzied way. "Of course he'd come for her! I never even saw him sleep with anyone, and there were so many girls throwing themselves at him, dead *and* alive! I thought he was just a chicken shit- not wanting to disappointment anyone as he rose to greatness in the underworld- but now I understand his intent. He was saving himself for her-" she gestured quickly at her old friend.

Spiros felt out of place as he crossed his legs and watched the woman he adored pace about, making noises of discontent and frustration every time she looked at the human.

"I bet he put her in here just to wind me up!" she spat derisively. "Well, he won't be so fucking smug when he finds I've drained his bitch dry of her blood!" Defiantly, she knelt down beside Roxy and gave her aroma a good, long sniff. Her neck smelled faintly of a strong perfume, applied maybe a day or two ago and still lingering on her soft, warm skin. Shannon's eyes flashed red- as opposed to the usual vampiric silver. This ability was the result of an experiment she had discovered via an intrusion into an old vampire's dwelling, when she and her brother had almost been caught out in the light of dawn. This peculiarly talented vampire had created a dye that could be injected into the iris' of a vampire in order to alter the colour of their silvery rage to whatever shade they desired. The man had claimed it was new and that no one other than himself had used the 'eye-dye,' so Logan had agreed to pay with human sacrifices to have the dye inserted into himself and his sis,' believing it would pass them off convincingly as something greater than any other vampire they met. The injection had hurt unspeakably, but it had worked, just as Logan had hoped.

"My gut tells me you should leave the girl alone," Spiros suggested, before allowing Shannon to take the bite she so desired. "It might enrage him."

"And since when do I listen to your gut?"

It was at this point that there came a rap at the door. Shannon placed a hand on either side of Roxy's face and grazed a fang across her cheek, pricking her flesh and leaving little speckles of crimson blood behind.

"Shouldn't you get that?" Spiros pointed out. "It could be important."

Shannon hissed in annoyance and ran to the door knob, throwing it open with a growl and a flash of her bright red eyes. Annara walked straight past her, curiously holding a gown in her arms.

"Ooh!" Shannon beamed, her eyes returning to their natural colour, "Is that pretty thing for me?" She followed Annara into the bedroom, trying to stroke the material in the vampire's arms. Annara wrenched the dress away as she did so.

"This is for the girl," she reported in a business like manner. "Dress her for the Master."

Shannon pouted. "He isn't *my* Master. Why should I help him dress up an old flame?"

Annara stopped dead in her tracks. "What did you just say?" Her eyes were wide and sparkling.

Shannon kicked Roxy in the side, as if testing how solid her ribs were. "She's one of my brother's old girlfriends. Well, the *only* girl he ever slept with when he was human anyway-"

Annara lifted a hand up to stop the girl. "An old lover?"

A thousand thoughts were crashing around in her skull. Shannon became background noise to her fears as she glanced down at the twitching Slayer. *He couldn't be in love with her, surely*? It went against everything vampires were, loving a Slayer, who would kill everyone in their underground homes if she was handed a stake and a fifty/fifty chance of survival.

Shannon was aware of Annara's distance and took the dress off her without a struggle, holding it against her body and twirling around for an excited Spiros, who was cooing and clapping his hands merrily. As she moved to the mirror in her bedroom and gave her reflection some consideration (the idea that vampires had no reflection was nothing more than a myth, their bodies still being a physical mass.) and realised that the dress was also an item that sparked up bad memories.

"No way!" she groaned in shock.

Annara snapped out of her thoughts after coming to the conclusion that Logan's ex girlfriend was nothing more than a *huge* sacrifice, to prove how much he loved her on the day of their wedding.

"What is it?"

"This dress! It's her old prom gown. The one she wore to the dance when my brother asked her if she'd be his partner for the evening."

"Give me that!" She snatched the dress from Shannon's hands resentfully. "This dress means nothing. He probably had it brought here because he knew it was the only thing he could get that would fit her."

Shannon scowled. "Whatever you say."

"Now put this thing on her and wipe that blood off her cheek. If the Master sees you've damaged her, he'll rip your throat out."

"Not if I rip his out first," she grumbled, bending over Roxy and brushing a finger over the tiny bite marks she'd caused, licking the blood off and relishing in its sweetness. When she lifted her head up, Annara had already gone.

Chapter 34

"I Love You"

Siren had prepared spaghetti bolognaise, served up on three separate plates and still piping hot, when Kieran trudged into the factory, soaking wet and shivering. Kiya followed in his wake, tossing the soggy blonde wig onto the floor, wearied, and giving Siren a solemn look of failure as she stood with her back against the disheartening view of heavily falling raindrops.

"Don't despair," Siren reprimanded softly. "We've done all that we can, for now."

"Yeah- I'm sure making a delicious bolognaise is going to bring Roxy back," Kieran snapped sarcastically.

"Hey!" Kiya shouted, alarming both men. "There's no need to talk to him like that!"

Kieran sighed. "Yeah, I know."

"You can be such an asshole sometimes."

Her words cut into him deeply and he felt the need to retire to his bedroom because of it. If it weren't for Kiya looking so exhausted and miserable, he would have left to brood all by himself, but as it was, he found she was a good enough reason to stay.

The sunlight was refracting brightly of the rain drenching Kiya's body, giving her a shining, shimmering physical state, an almost ethereal appearance. The curve of her waist and hips looked exaggerated as her silhouette shook from the cold and there seemed to be no defining lines around her face and hair. All Kieran could see was the outline of a beautiful woman and her sword peeking over one shoulder.

"I think we should all sit down and eat. Build up our strength and what not..."

"An excellent idea," Siren boasted, ignoring any insults Kieran had thrown his way just moments before. He slid two full plates towards his friends eagerly and handed over two sets of chop sticks.

"Um... could I trouble you for a knife and fork?" Kiya asked, holding the chopsticks uncertainly and hoping she hadn't offended the Chinese Slayer. He nodded with a smile and gave her the desired implements she required.

Having no stools around the counter made it awkward to eat. Kiya became self conscious of the tomato sauces staining the skin surrounding her lips and was right in doing so, for Kieran paused in mid bite to wipe an orange mark from her skin. He smiled. She blushed.

Kieran was trying not to think about how cold he was, soaked through to the skin, because he wanted to convince himself he was completely happy at that point, standing around the kitchen counter with what was left of his vampire slaying team. He kept thinking about how things had gone so tragically wrong over the past few days and couldn't help thinking it was something he had done. Now all he wanted to do was make things right. He'd lost Zeke, but there was still a chance he could bring Roxy back.

"That was amazing," he insisted, after swallowing the last of the minced beef and long spaghetti strands.

Kiya was only half way through her mound before giving up on it, claiming she was full to the brim.

"Lovely, Siren. Thank you." Carefully, she placed her knife and fork on the plate and pushed it forwards. "I hope you don't mind-" she said, turning to Kieran. "But I think I'm going to lie down."

"Dusk is a few hours away. Don't you need to gear up and stretch? Maybe go through some moves before we head out?"

"I will... later," she promised. There was no need to discuss anything further and so she left the men to talk whilst thinking about wrapping a duvet cover around her soaking wet body.

In Roxy's bedroom, she lay still for a while, thinking of her old, serene lifestyle and how much it had changed. Eventually, she came to the conclusion that she must have done something terrible in a past life, and now, she was paying for it.

This is your destiny, her mind said emphatically. *A destiny in blood. You were born to fight this fight. And you were destined to fall in love again...*

Kiya was sure now that it wasn't her mind speaking, but a little voice in her head that was rebelling against her rationality. She didn't want her head over-flowing with such ideas. Falling in love again? She just wanted to curl up in a ball and sleep. She wanted the knowledge of a possible upcoming war to dissipate into the dark unknown so that she could pretend for a few hours that she was at home, in her own bed, waiting for Rycan to finish work and join her.

A smile crossed her lips as she slipped into this false reality she was forcing upon herself, but the vividness of it all began to decrease with time and Rycan's face was fading from her memories. It was no longer her dead lover but someone else...

"No..." she whispered sleepily, a tear escaping from her right eye.

And instead of Rycan, she saw only Kieran.

"I don't want to be alone," she sobbed, partially trapped in a shallow sleep, but aware of her thoughts being voiced.

She woke to the touch of a hand against her face.

"You aren't alone." Kieran was smiling nervously down at Kiya as he brushed his hand over the tear track left on her skin. "I'll always be here for you, if you want me to be."

Kiya shifted under the covers and sat up, lifting her aching arms up and around Kieran's neck.

"I'm sorry I treat you so badly at times-" she said penitently.

"Don't worry about it, Angel. I'm used to chicks giving me a hard time."

"I never really intended to... I just... There's just so much anger inside of me."

"Don't sweat it."

Together, they rocked back and forward comfortingly in silence, until Kieran broke free from her grasp and presented her with a black velvet box- larger than a container for a ring, but blatantly from a jewellery store.

"What's this?" she asked, becoming slightly sheepish.

Kieran's lips creased upwards warmly as he lifted the lid, revealing a beautiful, three inch long, white gold cross on a slender chain. It had a small diamond in its centre, where the lines crossed, and on the back was her name, neatly engraved.

"I managed to slip in some shopping just before the

Mall closed. Roxy's parents weren't the warmest of people, and they had me out of their home earlier than I'd anticipated. So I used my time wisely and bought you a gift to show you how much I... care." He almost said 'love you.' *Bad Kieran. Bad.*

Kiya touched the cross with her fingertips and then lifted her hair up suddenly, revealing the back of her neck. Kieran registered her prompting and placed the chain around her neck, right before he planted a kiss on the curve between her neck and shoulders.

Kiya shivered pleasantly.

"I'm sorry-" he apologised

"Don't-" she said.

"I should leave you sleep."

"But I'm already awake now."

He lingered on the edge of her bed, wondering what she was implying. She still looked damp from the rain and her clothes were all wrinkled, although he noticed she wasn't wearing anything other than a thong on her bottom half, as the bed covers moved from across her lap.

Kiya felt the breath leave her chest as she gave Kieran a fond stroke across his brow with her thumb. He was so handsome and *so* adorable. He was kind and giving. He was brave and strong. The list went on and on and in a blur of these unvoiced, descriptive words, she leant forward and kissed him affectionately.

But he pulled away.

"How many times are we going to do this and then part feeling guilty about what we've done?"

"You're right," Kiya admitted.

"I can't help the way I feel about you, and yet with every kiss I feel as if I'm taking advantage-"

"You aren't," she said simply. "I'm the one who keeps

taking advantage of you." She paused. "But not any more."

Kieran stared into her eyes, hoping to find more in them than just mystery.

"I'm ready to give myself to you."

He sighed, but not in relief. "It shouldn't be about *giving*-"

"Then what?"

He swallowed and scratched the back of his neck. Dipping his head down, he brought it back up again with the following words on his lips:

"It should be about *love*, Kiya."

There was a pause.

"Do you love me?" Her voice was wavering and breaking slightly.

He nodded. "Yes. I do. I... I love you. From the moment I saw you, something exploded inside my chest and I knew you were the missing part in this life I lead. Every look you've ever given me has shaken my soul to its core and each moment I share with you has me aching for more. To touch you... to breath your scent, it's driving me crazy just thinking about it. I never believed in God until I found you because for once, I felt sure he had placed an angel in my company. And I find myself itching for excuses to get you on the back of my bike, just to feel your body pressed against me..."

Kiya was in a state of shock. She hadn't expected something so poetic from the biker and her heart was pumping harder and faster with every word he declared. His eyes were intense with longing and love and although the truth scared her a little, she felt as if she had always wanted this moment to come.

"Kiss me."

Kieran placed a hand on her cheek and pulled her in closer to his lips, tasting her mouth and feeling a completeness that he had failed to achieve previously, for their kisses had never been shrouded with the knowledge of his love for her before now.

She put a hand on one broad shoulder and allowed the other to trail over Kieran's muscles, still slick with a mixture of rain water and sweat. His eyes were penetrating hers, willing her to touch more of him. And she did, without any reluctance.

Rycan is dead, she thought ruefully. *Because of this, I've been denying myself this great man.*

Her thoughts paused as Kieran nibbled at her skin.

How long does God ask a woman to wait before it is acceptable to take another man into her bed? A month? A year? Never perhaps?

"Kieran-" she whispered, her voice racked with the sound of her pleasure.

Who cares if Kieran came along a few days after Rycan's death and stirred up all the butterflies in my stomach?

"I just wanted to-" She moaned softly as he slid his hands beneath her thong.

The heart wants what it wants, no matter how wrong it seems.

"I-" She met his lips as he encouraged her to lay on her back, sliding her thong down her legs with ease. They kissed again and again.

It isn't wrong to care for someone as much as I care for this man.

Kieran regarded Kiya's half naked body with an overwhelming sense of desire pulling at his heart strings. As he shed his clothes, Kiya wriggled out of her own, until the only thing left was the necklace he'd bought her, dangling elegantly from her neck.

I need him to touch me.

She parted her legs and breathed in deeply as he leant gently against her, throwing the duvet off the bed, and with a brush of his hand through her hair, he entered her at last, feeling some of the aching in his heart ease.

I love him.

"I love you, Kieran."

He lifted his head to get a better view of her.

"You don't have to lie to make me feel better about what we're doing. You're just saying th-"

Hurriedly she placed a finger against his lips.

"I'm sure."

He broke into his biggest smile yet, revealing dimples on either side of his mouth and began to move inside her, thrusting at a medium pace to allow her to adjust to the sensation of him.

Kiya admired the way he was taking his time, believing that he genuinely wanted to love and care for her. It wasn't just about a quick lay and she got the sense that he was revelling in every second they spent together. Her body was shuddering with the pleasure of the sexual activity and her brow was beginning to perspire. Every moment she spent joined with Kieran, she felt her spirit relaxing and her passion increasing.

"Will you still love me tomorrow?" she asked suddenly as he pulled away from her mouth.

He grinned. "Tomorrow and the next day. And the day after that-"

"And if I die, what will you do-?"

Kieran stopped moving. "Don't say that," he told her firmly. "You're not going to die."

"I'm just speaking from a realistic angle here, Kieran. There may not even be a tomorrow for us. And if you survive this big fight, you're going to go through hell afterwards. I know you will. I've been there myself-"

"What are you getting at Kiya? Can't we just enjoy what we have now?"

"I just want you to know...," she said, "...that I would have stayed with you, till the end."

Kieran pulled out of her, having lost his sex drive completely. He was angry that their intimacy was short lived, but he knew Kiya was only trying to outline her feelings, before it was too late.

"You're scaring me with all this."

She sat up with him, draping her legs over his thigh and resting her head against his shoulder. At last she was at peace with her feelings for him, but she was beginning to wonder if she should have held off until *after* the upcoming war was over. And maybe... if they made it out alive...she could tell Kieran she was pregnant and that...and that *he* was the father a couple of weeks further down the line. It wouldn't be so cruel. They could stop slaying and move into a house together and raise the child she had growing inside her as one big happy family.

"We'll get through this," she said determinedly, taking a hold of his hand.

"I'm glad you think so," Kieran replied.

He stole a look at her naked body and smiled, feeling a stirring below that suggested he could now finish what he'd started. Kiya lay down once more and gripped his neck, pulling him in roughly for an explosive kiss.

"Now," she said, with a wicked smile, "I want you to show me what you're made of."

Chapter 35

Make Death My Reward

The sun was up. Logan could tell, by the increase in temperature underground, that the fatal kiss of the sun's rays were struggling to evaporate the rain from a heavy down pour in the early hours of the morning.

His Priest was asleep now, having been scared out of his wits to the point of passing out during Logan's feeding- a pretty female, who had been out taking a jog, hair tied back from her heart shaped face and body firm and toned, no longer capable of running ever again. *She had been real tasty.* The Priest had gagged at the sight of the blood and sunk into unconsciousness, giving Logan's ears a rest from all his complaining- at last!

Now, it was time to get his beauty sleep. All that delicious blood had made him sleepy and his bed had been faintly calling his name, whilst he paced about the room, thinking about going to see his beloved 'Sonja.' But he couldn't yet. He just couldn't.

Vampires didn't need to sleep as long as humans. Three hours- five if they were feeling particularly exhausted- was sufficient, and Logan needed the rest more than he'd realised. Darkness consumed his shell of a body as soon as his eyes closed.

Tristian bent over double, breathing in quick painful rasps as he used a lamppost for support, ignoring the strange looks he was receiving from a mother and daughter leaving a house hand in hand. When they asked politely if he was feeling alright, Tristian tried to growl at them, like he'd seen the vampires do to their victims, or to people that made them angry in general, but he only managed an odd coughing sound that made him look mad, not *mean*. The mother dragged her daughter away without another word.

He had been shaken to the core by his encounter with Kiya at the West Meridion Mall and had fled to the only place he knew he would be safe- if his aching limbs ever got him there. He couldn't help but fear that Kiya was still in pursuit of him, but he was seventy percent sure that she'd stayed in the Mall once he'd escaped.

His business at the Mall had been a lot more complicated than Sunday shopping. He had been trying to pin point something succulent and juicy for the Master of the underground to feast on, by way of further earning his reward, and had been caught off guard by the ravishing, yet dangerous Kiya. What a close call that had been once she'd spotted him! If the elevator hadn't been conveniently open, he may have suffered from a Samurai sword in the back- *not* something many people could survive in this day and age.

The Master's so-called 'war' was happening that very evening. He was aware of this. And now was the time for him to receive his gift, whether he had a human offering or not- before Kiya could make mince meat out of him. Besides, he'd presented the Master with enough meals these past few months to earn him immortality. But of course, it wasn't just eternal life he desired. There was something more human than that.

Kiya's love.

"I will have you," he said, envisioning Kiya and her long, dark brown hair, holding his hand; touching his face; peeling off his trousers.

When he reached the Stone Table with a parched throat, he tried to shift the rock himself, scraping his palms against the rough surface and feeling a dull ache build at the base of his spine. There was no way he could move it alone.

"Psst," he whispered, after checking the perimeter for bystanders. "Hey open up! It's Tristian- the guy who brings you lamb chops, *remember*?"

There was a long, drawn out silence, in which nothing happened besides the rise and fall of Tristian's chest. Then to his relief, the rock moved just enough to allow him access to the underworld. It was a bit of a tight squeeze, but he got through in the end, dropping down into the centre of a werewolf pack that was thankfully in its human form.

"Hi," he said, waving to them nervously. "I'm just...just passing through if you don't mind."

One of the men, with a closely shaven scalp, large flaring nostrils and muscles that would make the Terminator shy away, moved his arm suddenly, only to brush a dried, dislodged root off Tristian's shoulder. Tristian cowered under the man's touch, smiling edgily and trying to move away without provoking any trouble.

"Nice Doggy," he uttered under his breath, when he was sure the beasts chains wouldn't extend far enough for them to grab him and rip his fragile body to shreds.

The vampire population was quiet as he passed through the weaving passageways, carved out of the mud and rock, suggesting that they were all taking their naps before the war. There were a few stragglers mind you, leaning against walls, smoking joints and feeling far too drowsy to want to reach out and grab the scrawny human that was passing by.

"Hey...Hey Tristian!" one of them called out in a mellow tone. He was an American boy, wearing nothing but trousers and a beige cowboy hat, which was hiding the boy's eyes under the shadow of its rim. "You grown a dick yet?"

The boy sitting next to the American started chuckling in approval, passing a half made cigarette over and offering a small brown chunk of cannabis resin to add to the tobacco.

Tristian ignored the taunts. He was aware of the fact Logan and Annara had made him a laughing stock among the vampires. Always grovelling. Always bringing peace offerings. He fucking worshipped the ground they walked on and people laughed at him for it! He was a human, trying his best to survive in a world that was about to be threatened by creatures of the night. For days now, he had changed from apartment to apartment- preying on single women who lived alone- and occupying their homes for a day or two before moving on, in case the police ever caught up with him.

Logan's bedroom door was unguarded. This wasn't usually the case, but it appeared he had sent his muscular soldiers away to enjoy their last moments before the war. With a sweat drenched countenance, Tristian pounded on the door and waited like an obedient dog.

There was no answer for a long while, but after a second round of abrupt hits, the door swung open brashly.

Logan's hostile eyes were aglow with red colouring and his expression oozed with hate for the greasy little man at his door, but Tristian refused to turn his back now. He had nowhere else to go.

"M...Master. I...I must speak with you-"

"I have no time for this you slimy little prick. I told you before: NEVER wake me during nap time. It makes me cranky. Believe me, you won't like me when I'm cranky." His eyes were bulging from their sockets, blood red and frightening in the light of the torch-lit corridor.

"B...But I need you to turn me now, before it's too late."

"Why would I do that *worm*?"

"I can help you, when the vampires take over the city." Tristian tried his hardest to hide his uncertainty. There were a few whimpers here and there that he could not prevent, but Logan appeared to be listening, which was a good sign.

"What exactly can *you* do? You're not even half the man one of my soldiers is. In fact, I'm not even sure you are a man."

Tristian bit back a fiery retort. He had a good mind to drop his trousers and prove he had a penis but didn't want the Master to rip it off in a rage. "One of the Slayers. The...The girl I've requested you leave to me... I can draw her away from you. You may find it hard to fight more than one Slayer at a time if it comes to it. I can make sure they don't get the opportunity to surround you. She craves for *my* blood, Master. All sense of reason will elude her when she sees me after I murdered her lover."

"I have Zeke to distract the Slayers. Especially the one who leads them."

"But what of the girl? She is stronger than you think."

Logan lifted his chin and with enthusiasm laced in his words he said. "I can take her."

Tristian scowled. "How can you be so sure? Do you really want to risk it now that your dreams are but a hand-span away?"

"You doubt me?" Logan advanced on the small, pale faced humanoid until he was pressed against the wall with nowhere else to run.

"No... I d...don't. I just wouldn't want your time with the woman you love to go interrupted. I love this Slayer, but she *hates* me. If I could just overpower her and turn her into one of us-"

"You were *never* one of us," Logan pointed out, his fangs elongating as proof that they were on totally different levels.

"Look-" Tristian said, raising his voice in aggravation. "You promised me immortality and I'm asking for it now so that it may benefit the both of us. Please Master! Grant me my wish and you shall never hear from me again."

Logan stroked his chin thoughtfully, eyeing up the mere weed of a man. It was true- Tristian would be of more use to him as a vampire, though it pained him to think it. And he could relate to the guy in some way. He loved a woman- a Vampire Slayer- and would go to great lengths to have her.

Without warning, Logan stretched his mouth open wide and bit a chunk out of Tristian's shoulder, spraying warm blood all over both their faces and up against the wall. Logan was impressed that the human didn't scream. Instead, he closed his eyes and grunted in discontent, biting his lip until his teeth left behind little indents in his white skin.

Now, Logan had to provide the human with some of his own blood. With a hiss of pain, he made an incision across his left palm, until it dripped with red fluid. He then held it forth.

Tristian's eyes were wide with longing. "Thank you! Thank you so much!"

The sucking noises coming from between his thin, bloodless lips made Logan want to vomit, and when he was sure Tristian had tasted enough of his blood, he pulled his hand away sharply, thrusting the man onto the floor with unfathomable speed.

"Ask me for anything again and I slit your throat."

Tristian nodded in understanding, watching in a mind numbing state of euphoria as Logan slammed his bedroom door shut.

Just a few hours now. Just a few more hours and I'll be a vampire, he thought. But his estimate for the change was very wrong.

Already, his soul was beginning to fade and in its place, there was only rage and obsession. An obsession in the name of love.

The grip of death on Tristian's body consumed him faster than most, for there was so little of him to corrupt with the vampire gene that was now circulating his body.

Some human's didn't take to the 'turn' as well as others. Within ten minutes of being bitten and left outside Logan's bedroom door, Tristian became feverish.

His eyes flashed the unnatural silver of a vampire, with a stab of pain through his skull each time and his vision blurred as if he had tears brimming over.

The blood in his veins had turned to ice, making his muscles seize up in agony and his furrowed brow sweated profusely, running tracks of salty bodily fluids past his pulsating temples and down his pale cheeks.

The heart in his chest took its final pump and then ceased to move.

The breath in Tristian's lungs was expelled one last time.

But his brain remained functional.

A new set of razor sharp fangs glinted from his open mouth, but Tristian was unaware of this. The pain from the transformation had dashed his mind into oblivion and on the dirt floor he lay, unconscious to the world.

Chapter 36

Sleeping Beauty

Shannon touched the blonde strands of jaggedly cut hair and smiled at Annara's attempt to destroy the teenage girl's image. One thing Shannon knew about Roxy was that she would *never* cut her hair higher than the base of her spine, therefore, the new unruly hairstyle *had* to be the result of a jealous vampire. There was *no way* Roxy would chop it off, and in such a messy way at that!

When Roxy moaned in her poison induced sleep, Shannon's body jolted. If she'd had a working heart, she was sure it would have stopped all over again for she hadn't expected a reaction to her talons feeding their way through the girl's hair. The sound of Roxy's awareness to her touch gave her a fright.

Spiros had helped carry Roxy to the bed before being dismissed from Shannon's room, leaving her with the daunting task of stripping her ex best friend of her clothes- this being a job she *really* didn't want to be a part of. It had been a struggle, dragging limp arms and legs out of holes and trying to shimmy the dress over Roxy's thighs, up past the stomach and finally, high enough to conceal her breasts. Then, with a rough 'yank' she flipped her over onto her front and zipped the gown up, carelessly catching her hair in it.

"What does Logan see in you?" she asked the sleeping female, whose face was pressed into the bed covers unflatteringly. "You look like your average 'dumb blonde.' No one likes a dumb blonde, accept school boys whose minds are possessed with the idea that the only thing in life that matters is fucking any chick the second they hit puberty."

She looked at her nails and scowled at the blood trapped under them, growing darker in colour with age. Somehow, blood always managed to get into the hardest of places, no matter how careful she was when biting into an innocent human's neck.

For a while, she thought about other ways she could subtly defile the Slayer's exterior, so that her brother didn't point the finger at her. She thought about filing random nails down so that they were all uneven. She considered pulling one of the girl's front teeth out so that there was an unattractive gap in her pearly whites. She sniggered at the idea of piercing the girl's nose and lip with a dirty needle, knowing full-well it would get infected and become a hideous mark on Roxy's pretty face.

"Oh Sonja. You're so lucky you hold my brother's interest because I would have hunted you down and slaughtered you and your friends the second we returned to this city."

"Kiya?... Is... that... you?"

Shannon let out a girlish scream of fear as Roxy lifted her head groggily, scanning the room for signs of her Slayer companions. She wasn't sure what to do. There was a lamp, for decoration (there was no electricity underground) that she almost smashed across the girl's head as a jerk reaction, but she lifted her hands up in self control and backed away from the bed. There was no use giving the girl a concussion when her brother would be by to claim her at some point.

"Hey sweet heart. How are you feeling?" she asked, biting back the bitterness she felt for the girl.

Roxy tried turning her body but fell suddenly, back into her original position. She tried again and found the second attempt had more of a result.

"Kiya?"

Shannon sighed haughtily. "I don't know who you're talking about." With shrewdness creeping into her voice, she changed her posture to portray how annoyed she was feeling with the situation. One leg stuck out jaggedly whilst she leant most of her weight on the other. Her arms were crossed over her chest and she couldn't stop biting the skin that lined the inside of her mouth- a nasty habit she'd developed during boring high school lessons.

The temperature in the room suddenly dropped a few degrees.

"You're safe. That's all you need to know."

Roxy lifted a hand to her head. It was pounding like a drum and all her body parts trembled as they tried kick starting into life.

As she glanced around the unfamiliar room, her mind became more distressed with every passing moment. She could remember being at home in the factory, then being ambushed by Zeke and some woman with bright blonde hair, almost white. And now, as she touched her own hair, her heart wrenched with sorrow and she cried rivers of tears.

"My... my hair! How could you? How could you do this to me?"

It felt light on her head and uneven in style. She'd never cut the length, other than paying for a minute trim of the dead hairs, since the day she was born. Nineteen years of growing and it had all been chopped off in her sleep.

Shannon drew nearer.

"You're... you're not the girl who took me-" Roxy realised in confusion, observing the girl's pink candy floss coloured hair.

"Of course not," Shannon remarked. "I've got better things to do than go kidnapping Vampire Slayers. Believe me!"

Roxy squinted, trying to match internal memories to the pink haired teen before her. It didn't help that her vision was ever so slightly impaired still, but she managed to note the appearance of the girl and sunk back onto the bed in shock.

"Shannon?"

The girl nodded gracefully, giving her a low curtsy.

"You... How can this...? What are you doing here? I thought you went to Karanthian with your brother before finishing the exams at high school. You told me you were never coming back."

"I did. Plans changed."

"Is Logan here? I need to speak with him! Where are we?"

"Slow down-"

"And how did you know I was a Slayer? Did someone put an advertisement in the paper or something because-?"

Shannon's eyes flashed red, far from her control at this point. "You're giving me a headache! Just shut up, bitch."

Roxy sat in stunned silence. She glanced around the room and noticed the door was slightly ajar. When her strength returned, she could easily make a run for it and find her friends again.

"You're a vampire?" she said, in a quiet voice. She didn't want to believe it. Even though their friendship had ended badly, she'd never wanted her friend to die and be reborn into darkness. No one deserved that fate.

"Ding! Ding! Ding!" Shannon mocked. "You're right!"

"And does Logan know?"

"Honey, of course he does."

That's odd, Roxy thought. *I'm sure Logan would have mentioned this very important fact. Unless he was trying to protect his sister from being killed by a Slayer?*

"Now tell me what the fuck is going on."

"I'd love to, but I'm only under orders to change your attire, not give you the tour."

Now Roxy was aware of her outfit- totally different to what she'd been clothed in before she was drugged. Her old prom dress conjured images of her first night in bed with Logan and she knew instantly that he must have had something to do with this.

"I need to speak with him-"

"Well you can't."

Roxy made for the door. Shannon reached it before her and kicked her old friend in the stomach, knocking her back across the room, where she fell in a heap of green velvet.

"You can't leave. The others won't understand your importance and they'll kill you."

"What are you *talking* about?" Roxy groaned in frustration. Her head was hurting again and she'd bent her wrist in an awkward position as she'd hit the floor, leaving it throbbing in pain.

"We're underground."

Roxy had gathered that. The walls of dirt surrounding her told no lies.

"Why did they bring me here?"

"I told you, I'm not at liberty to say."

"Have you hurt Logan?"

Shannon grinned wickedly. It hadn't been *her* who had bitten Logan. Try reversing it! He was 'turned' in Karanthian and had completed his change into an immortal creature next door, in the bedroom opposite her own. When she'd heard him mumbling fitfully, she'd gone to investigate and had left the room with a chunk missing from her throat. The bite hadn't been enough to kill her and as she suffered the agony of the wound, Logan had approached her, offering her a blood dripping gash in his arm- asking her to drink and join him before it was too late. There had been no going back after that. She couldn't tell her parents that Logan was un-dead and she didn't want to go to the hospital and explain that her brother had bitten her. So she became a vampire with him, and together, they ate their father in a fit of blood lust, sparing his hysterical wife, for she had been a lot nicer to the pair of them during childhood than anyone else ever had.

"Logan is fine."

"Tell my what you want with me."

"I don't want anything to do with you, Sonja."

"Then where can I find Logan? You took him from m didn't you? That night we went to a hotel! I woke up e was gone! That was *your* doing! You've always ealous cow. You just can't accept the fact he'd rather spend time with *me* than his childish, kid sister. And why do you think that is Shannon?"

"Because you're a little whore who'll part your legs for him!"

Roxy laughed in a humourless manner. "In a way, you're right. *I* can sleep with him, but *you're* a blood relation, therefore, you can never be as close to Logan as I am."

"You're a sick bitch."

"And you're about to feel my fist in your face."

Roxy lunged for a clump of Shannon's pink hair and ripped her head back, giving her a rapid round of solid punches to her little nose, splattering blood all over her pale dead face. The vampire girl retaliated by biting down on Roxy's wrist as she caught it in mid-hit, but the Slayer twisted away before she could wrench a chunk of flesh from her body.

"Do we really have to fight?" Shannon asked, sounding as if she had better things to do.

Roxy was standing in a fighter's position, fists clenched and held before her, legs slightly parted. She rocked back and forward on her feet, eager and tense at the same time.

"I know you've always hated me since the day Logan asked me to the prom."

"That wasn't fair of him!" Shannon screamed unexpectedly. "He knew how much the prom meant to the both of us. He could have just left us both to enjoy *our* prom the following year, but he had to split us up and offer to take you out on the evening of our silly teenage dreams!"

"Listen to yourself, you're pathetic!" Roxy retorted. "A night out with a bunch of school kids was *far* from my high school dream."

Shannon's brow was creased with anger lines. "Don't pretend like it didn't matter! You left me to go dancing with the older students and didn't think about how I would feel!"

"It's just a silly prom. You're being *so* unreasonable."

"All you had to do was persuade someone to take me and I would have given them anything!"

"Is this really what this is all about? A dance you weren't invited to?"

Shannon stamped her foot. "Yes it is! Is that so hard to believe?"

"If you'd stayed to finish the school year, we could have gone then, but you left out of the blue."

"Because you changed and my feelings for people altered. I've changed too and you're about to see how much-"

Her fangs extended to their full, most terrifying length and her eyes flashed the colour of blood as she threw herself in Roxy's direction, fighting on an overloaded emotional system. She knew she shouldn't be touching the Slayer, but her heart screamed otherwise.

"I hate you Sonja!" she screeched with unimaginable gusto, slashing her nails across Roxy's sweat beaded cheek and separating the skin into a yawning wound that spilled fresh blood. Shannon's nose instantly picked up the scent of it, and the animal beneath her breast- that had replaced her dying soul- urged her to lap up the life fluid.

Roxy had fallen to the floor again as she felt the searing pain in her face- having nothing to use as a weapon and now with the disadvantage of being lower than her my.

can't believe how much you hurt me," Shannon eething with pent up agitation. She was holding her arms at her side, twiddling her fingers in jagged motions, as if physically holding back the need to stick her nails into the sides of Roxy's soft, creamy neck. "I'll be damned if I ever see you as our Queen."

Roxy's mind registered the words, drawing nothing but nonsense from them, and took her chance to trip Shannon when her bare feet were in range of her own powerful legs. She was on her back before she could yelp and became pinned down by Roxy's freakishly strong body.

"When did you get so damn good at fighting anyway?"

"I had parents who never really gave me the time of day and a big old basement with gym equipment and punch bags. You do the math."

Shannon snarled. "You never showed me the basement-"

"You never asked."

There was nothing in the room that could complete the act of slaying a vampire. No chair to break the leg off of. No pencils to poke through Shannon's chest, just enough to stab the heart. In one corner, there was a wardrobe- not exactly convenient, unless by some minuscule chance, when kicking the doors through, it splintered perfectly into the shape of a stake. *Not likely.*

"Can't finish me off can you?" Shannon laughed, wriggling her torso about like a fish on a hook. She managed to get an arm lose and took another swipe at Roxy's face, which Roxy dodged milliseconds before impact. And the hits kept coming. Shannon was in 'kill an old friend' mode. She wasn't about to calm down and shake Roxy's hand at the end of their tussle.

Roxy had no choice but to jump off the flailing beast and head for the bedroom door. As she reached the handle, she felt talons grip her hair and slam her face into the wood.

The adrenaline coursing through her body prolonged the impact of pain long enough for her to perform a round house kick to Shannon's skull and an elbow to the girl's temple- possibly 'killing' blows if she had been a human opponent. But it only made the vampire girl more angry.

There had to be a weapon. Anything.

She used the lamp and cracked it on Shannon's scalp, but it only threw her off Roxy's scent for a second.

As she wrenched open the wardrobe doors on the other side of the room, she found a whole mess of belongings piled up on the top shelf, and some rather vulgar outfits on hangers.

With a throbbing brain and stinging injuries, Roxy reached up for a comb, perched on the edge of the top shelf. It was designed to have a pointed handle, which hairstylists used to part strands of hair quicker and more neatly than if they were using their fingers. Gripping the end that had teeth, she swung around and stabbed the long pointed handle into Shannon's chest- three times, in quick succession.

"Fuck!" Shannon shouted in a mangled cry of pain. Her fragile body had been marked with holes leaking blood and her cute baby blue nightdress was becoming stained, the longer it took her vampire healing ability to work its magic.

Vhilst standing there in awe of the comb protruding her chest, Roxy dashed around the side of the and made for the exit. Her heart was beating a mile a minute and her chest felt as if it would explode from the panic boiling within, but at last, she was outside the room and fell into the arms of-

"Logan!"

"Sonja-" his voice was serene and soft like silk as he came face to face with his bride, even though it was before schedule.

"I woke up and your sister... she was there! And we fought. She tried to kill me. I wanted to get out and find you. I needed to know you were okay..." Roxy touched Logan's cool face to prove to herself he was still alive and unharmed. "Did they hurt you?"

Logan smiled in bewilderment. "Who?" He was feeling fit to explode at the sight of Roxy's bleeding exterior and ruffled dress, but for now, he would play the part in a cool headed manner, then deal with his sister later.

"The vampires!" she gushed, glancing over her shoulder in fear. "They're going to kill us. I think they're going to perform some sort of ritual and your sister must be the leader, because she put this dress on me...the one I wore on the night we-"

"Made love?"

Roxy blushed at his words, thinking he would leave her sentence unfinished. But it struck her then that her fears were not duplicated in him.

"Why aren't you afraid? We need to get out of here!"

Logan placed a hand on Roxy's head, trying his hardest to suppress an almighty flash of red from his irises at the sight of her befouled, once beautiful hair. It had been like a shimmering, golden waterfall down her back before now, capturing his gaze on many occasions. It had been his way of identifying her in a crowd when they were in high school together. Now, she looked like a penniless student, kicked out of home and getting their hair cut at a hairdresser's college for free.

"Look into my eyes Sonja."

Her panic stricken expression gave in to the sound of his gentle tone and she tried relaxing in his gaze. Tears sprung to her eyes as she thought about their predicament.

"I don't want them to hurt you," she said aggrievedly.

"Shhh. We'll get through this," he assured her. "Everything is okay. I'll make sure no one lays a finger on you."

Roxy didn't know why Logan was so relaxed in such a chilling environment, where death could be around every corner, but she relished his confidence and rested her head against his chest, gripping his black shirt with a blood splattered hand. All the pain was ebbing away as she allowed his touch to consume her mind and all the noises of the underground ceased to exist.

"It's going to be okay," Logan whispered, lifting a syringe from his pocket, full of the sleeping drug his people had developed.

She didn't see it coming. She didn't even feel it penetrate her neck. But she felt the darkness filling her head and fell- a dead weight- captured in Logan's arms before her face hit the dirt.

I had been right in thinking these heartless creatures would fail to care for my girl, Logan thought, stroking Roxy's hair and gritting his teeth in rage at the sight of it. Her bleeding cheek smeared blood over his hand, which he stared at in wide eyed wonderment. The colour was so vibrant against his pale skin. Slowly, he lifted it to his li‑ ‑nd stretched his tongue towards it, withdrawing at ‑ second.

‑ouldn't want to spoil your dinner, he thought.

Chapter 37

Kill or Be Killed

With a sudden splash of water to the face, the Priest woke with a disgruntled choking sound, feeling a wash of depression cloud him as he realised where he was. The flames of candles bore no sympathy for him and the shadows on the walls conjured images of demons watching from all four corners of the room.

Logan was unsmilingly staring into the old man's eyes.

"I want you to do something for me."

The Priest sighed. "Now what?"

"My girlfriend...Sonja. She must stay here while I send the troops out into the city. Already, she has been attacked since she was brought here." It felt degrading, asking a human, who had chosen the path of righteousness, to help him, but desperate times called for desperate measures. "Watch over her and I give you my word, you will leave this place alive."

"And be the only human left to walk the city, whilst your minions shed blood all over God's great earth? Death seems like a mercy, boy."

Logan's eyes grew wider. "Please, Father. Protect her. She is human, like you. When the ceremony is complete, you can leave the city and head for the mountains. It'll be long before our kind reaches higher ground and you will be safe there, until the end of your days."

The Priest sat in silence. He took one look at the teenage girl lying with her eyes tightly shut, on Logan's magnificent bed sheets and gave a curt nod of acceptance to the task.

Logan cut the man's bonds and lifted him to his feet.

"You'll need this, in case someone tries to put up a fight." He held a wooden stake out- something he had fashioned from a broken pool cue in the game room a vampire had insisted they have, to pass the eternity of time.

"How do I-"

"It's easy," Logan informed him, without any shame. "Aim for the heart."

"But what if her human friends come for her-"

"Then they'll leave a bloody corpse, won't they?" he grunted.

The Priest looked dumbstruck. "You're asking me to murder a-"

"A life for a life, Father. You either kill or be killed. Make your choice."

Turning his back on the old man bearing a weapon was not the brightest thing Logan had ever done, but he was confident in believing the Priest would refrain from trying to stake him. If he wanted to continue breathing the God given oxygen, he wouldn't even think about it. And Logan was right. He left his bedroom without receiving any gaping wounds whatsoever, only a slight feeling of reassurance that Roxy would still be waiting for him when he got back.

Shannon was in floods of tears when he found her in her bedroom, shaking and shivering in her blue nightgown and smearing mascara all around her blotchy face. Fear of her brother had made her this way. When he had lost his soul, he had become a very unforgiving creature and she knew he'd be furious with her.

He didn't knock. He didn't ask for admittance.

He entered like a cold shadow, eyes red and teeth clenched, gliding over to her bed whilst she sat in a pool of her own blood, for her chest wounds had yet to heal and the comb was still wedged between two of her ribs.

There was no comfort about him. He felt betrayed.

Shannon lifted her tear streaked face when she couldn't bear the silence any longer and sniffed pitifully, trying to encourage some empathy from her sibling.

"She stabbed me. And she broke my nose."

That was of course obvious. Logan hadn't thought she'd put the comb into her own flesh; that would be absurd.

"Was the dress hard to get on her, or did you manage without any trouble?" he asked demurely.

"It was easy enough," she spoke quietly. Her eyes were brimming with fear.

"So if it was *easy*, sis, why did you feel it was appropriate to slice her face open and give her a new hair cut? *Hmm?*"

"The hair wasn't my fault!" Shannon bellowed in her own defence, springing up from the bed to face her brother more directly. "Annara brought her to me already spoiled. I swear to you, brother. And the cut on Sonja's face was the only way I could get her to back away from me before she finished me off. You know Slayers- they're resourceful. She probably would have dusted me eventually, if I hadn't have fought back."

Logan moved his hand, which startled his sister to the point of taking two steps back in fright, but he simply gripped the teeth of the comb and yanked it free from his sisters body. She made a guttural noise of protest, but sighed when the comb was out.

"Better?"

She nodded. "Thanks."

He began to pace the room now. "Do you know why I have brought Sonja here?"

"To bring back old, painful memories?" she asked sarcastically, feeling more relaxed in her brother's presence now. How could she think he would harm her? Her own brother!

"I smell the envy cascading from your body." His nose wrinkled in disgust.

"Well yeah-" Shannon replied impishly.

"I was hoping that one day, you might put the past behind you."

"Jeez! Give me a break would you? If I'd known you were coming here for her in the first place, I would have told you to fuck right off! I hate her! And I hate *you* for thinking the sun shines out of her ass!"

Logan's facial muscles rippled with tautness.

"She will be Queen."

"I want to be Queen! Why should I be second best to her? I won't be, damn it!"

"Say that you will follow her ruling, as well as mine, faithfully and without any of this jealously your essence reeks of."

"No way! I'd rather listen to that dumb bitch Annara than a Slayer."

"Say it, Shannon!" Logan screamed. "Say you'll play nicely."

"Fuuuck yoooou," she said, extending the pronunciation of each word and adding to the effect of her curse by extending her middle finger towards him.

In the blink of an eye, Logan swooped upon Shannon's hand and bit her finger clean off, leaving a bloody stump in its wake that spurted blood out in an amusingly unpredictable fashion.

Shannon was caught in the headlights of her own disbelief, standing with her mouth wide open; the whites of her eyes became more vivid than the irises.

As a mark of further disrespect towards his sister, Logan spat the finger at her head and watched as it bounced off her broken, bloody nose.

"You bastard," she mouthed. "You *bastard*!"

Like a five year old, whose Barbie doll had been taken from her by an older child in the park, Shannon bawled her eyes out at the sight of her finger lying on the floor.

Logan's face twitched at the sound of her wailing and he automatically gripped her throat to stifle the noise, like he did with all his subjects if he happened to dislike what was spewing from their mouths.

"You can be Sonja's maid. I'll see to it that you're chained up in the kitchen of our magnificent home and we will drain blood from human's all night. You will get *none* for yourself-"

Shannon's eyes filled with tears. "I won't." She croaked out.

At the sound of her refusal, Logan threw her to the floor. She tried crawling away from him and came to halt when the side of her bed pressed against her back. Beneath the bed, she spread her fingertips and found something that made the terror in her dead heart decrease slightly.

"I won't bow to you, brother of mine. I know the real you," she said boldly, keeping her hand out of Logan's sight. He was standing over her with his arms folded across his chest. "I know all this bravado it fake. Anyone can kill one of their own kind and have the rest of us cower in fear. You're not worthy of my loyalty, because brother's are meant to put family first and you never have."

"I could have killed you the day I turned."

Shannon shrugged. "So what do you want from me? A cookie? You killed me and made me a vampire. Or, you could have killed me and put me in the ground for good, like we did to Dad. So big wows!"

"I thought you liked being immortal."

"Sure. It has its perks. Up until your head grew bigger and you started this little revolution that I never wanted to be a part of."

"Then why are you still here?" he asked.

"Because I love you, the way a sister should-"

Logan rolled his eyes. "Give me a break."

"-And it's because I love you, that I have to do this."

From beneath the bed, she dragged out her old hockey stick, jumped to her feet and snapped it over her thigh, until jagged splinters of wood protruded from its ends. She almost got a clean shot to Logan's chest, lunging forward with the sharpest of the two halves, but her brother managed to shift his body speedily away from the path of death and wrenched the stick out of her pincer like grip.

He was behind her before she could breathe the word "Please-"

"So you want to kill me do you?!" Logan said crisply and with a note of hysteria rising within him.

"It's like you always told me," she said, accepting her fate now. "Kill or be killed, right?"

Logan laughed. "At least *something* I said got through that thick, ugly skull of yours." He was not at all offended by her attempt on his life.

Shannon no longer struggled against her brother's cold, crocodile-bite like grip and instead, she closed her eyes, thinking about her life, her triumphs, her regrets and how much she had wanted Logan to say he needed her. Just once. So that she could feel loved.

"Family stick together-," she rasped. "Family stick together."

There was silence as Logan pressed the broken hockey stick against the thin material of her nightgown.

"In Hell... maybe we will."

He left the room feeling no sadness for what he had just done- even as he wiped the ash off his clothes and hands.

Chapter 38

The Sledgehammer

As much as they'd wanted to, Kiya and Keiran had very little time to lay sedately beside each other, still moist with sweat and feeling satisfied- legs weaved together affectionately. Kiya wasn't content unless she was touching as much of Kieran as she possibly could. Kieran felt the same way about her.

"We should get a move on," he said, stroking the side of Kiya's face. It was extremely warm to the touch and the thought crossed his mind that the next time he came to touch her, it may not be hot with life anymore... He shuddered. How he despised his mind sometimes.

"I know," she replied, trailing a finger up and down the length of Kieran's arm, focusing on one of the more prominent veins. "But I won't lie to you- I'd much rather stay like this for what's left of the day."

Kieran sighed. "I wish we could."

After a further five minutes of silence, the pair accepted the fact that they couldn't lay in bed any longer and both left in pursuit of a quick shower.

Siren was performing tai chi as they shuffled down into the basement and Kieran could have sworn he'd thrown a wink his way, on passing.

The shower felt good, as always.

"You stick close to me tonight," Kieran said as he scrubbed his muscles down with soap.

Kiya smiled. "If it makes you feel better."

He nodded and turned the shower off, allowing the last of the water to cascade over his back.

"I'll see you upstairs."

There was no room for mistakes tonight, so to avoid obstructing her vision, Kiya put her hair up in a high, elegant ponytail and decided, as she glanced at her make-up bag between two of the sinks, that she would apply a little mascara and blush before heading up. As she pencilled some eye-liner on, the expression 'leaving a beautiful corpse' sprung to mind and she screwed her face up at the thought of her head being so full of inappropriate phrases on such an important night.

I'm not going to die, she sang to the sound of each heart beat. *I'm not going to die.*

"I must be going insane," she uttered, whilst giving her face one last check in the mirror. It was pale and the bags under her eyes had been troublesome to cover.

Above the basement, Kieran and Siren were rifling through their pile of weaponry, slipping as many silver and wooden stakes into their belts as they possibly could. Kieran was bare-chested, but not for long. He pulled three navy blue and black vests off the floor, from beside his feet, as Kiya approached and dumped them on the table with a grin.

"Courtesy of Emilia. Bullet-proof and very effective. She gave them to me for just such an occasion-"

Kiya took one of the vests and turned it around in her hands. It felt lighter than she'd imagined and the material was rough to the touch. Over her little black strap top she'd slipped on after she'd showered, she began tightening the vest around her body. Kieran came to her aid instantly, assisting in fastening the straps into place.

"I know this is the wrong time to say this," Kieran whispered in her ear, "But you look hot in this police gear."

Kiya patted his arm playfully and turned to help him attach his own vest to his body.

"So do you," she whispered back, when the last strap was fastened in place.

Siren was smiling at the pair of them as they kissed briefly and pretended to be interested in one of his throwing stars when Kieran glanced his way. He admitted it was nice seeing his boss so happy, but he was beginning to wonder if their decision to become intimate was a bit ill-timed. Kieran was not one for controlling his emotions in the battlefield. But it was some people's opinion that uncontrollable emotions were what gave a man the ability to slay his demons successfully. Well, one could only hope that was the case tonight.

"We go in together. No splitting up. There's no telling how many bloodsuckers are down there. Every room has to be checked. If we can pick off a vamp' that's alone, we can interrogate him as to where Roxy is being held. You hear me? Stealth is necessary. Accuracy is more important than making good time. If we have to stay down there for three days straight, we will. Got that?"

Kiya and Siren nodded in turn.

"Just watch your backs. It's like dropping bunny rabbits into a pit of half starved vipers."

"Great," Kiya mumbled sarcastically, "Now I can't wait to get started."

As she had grown accustomed to doing now, Kiya kitted up. She concealed a silver stake under her trouser leg, two wooden stakes strapped around both wrists and hidden under the sleeves of her leather jacket and finally, she placed her Samurai sword on her back.

"Are you sure you don't want this?" Kieran proffered a gun her way. "It's loaded with silver bullets."

"It's okay. If I hide too many weapons on my body I don't think I'll be able to move as fluidly in a fight."

Kieran had his shotgun and stakes at his disposal, but to the Slayer's confusion, he dragged a sledgehammer over from where it had been propped up against the wall in wait.

"Ready?" he asked the bemused pair.

"Planning on making mince meat out of vampire faces are we?" Kiya indicated the heavy tool in his hand. It's solid metal head was leaning against the side of his right biker boot.

"Oh, this thing?" he said casually. "It's to get through those metal doors of course."

The Slayers nodded in understanding.

"And maybe to cause some damage to a few skulls while I'm at it."

As the group headed for the door, Siren said with a smile, "I hope you are referring to vampires and not the two of us."

Chapter 39

Taking What's Ours

"I'm a vampire." Logan said, observing the way her eyes twinkled with love for him. "And vampires need blood." She was listening to him intently- hanging on his every word as is if he were God made flesh, blessing her with his physical state, face to face. As he lifted his hand to her cheek, she practically purred. "That is why we are going to build a thriving community together, in which no one ever goes hungry. Just you and me. Getting whatever we want, when we want it. And that, my sweet, beautiful girl, is why we are proving ourselves a superior species to humans. Because we are able to join as one and share what God has provided us with- not like those lowly dogs up there, who flit away their lives on pointless things. We focus on what's necessary."

"I'll certainly look forward to sharing a glass of blood with you when we have the humans under our control."

"Indeed. Now let's go and speak with our great army one last time."

Logan presented his arm to Annara, who grinned broadly, slipping her hand through and groping the muscle of his upper arm. She was dressed in a tight black strap top and green hot pants, with knee high, metal capped, black boots and her hair was scraped back with copious amounts of gel, to keep it out of her eyes when she was ripping people's spines out. Her style was simple, yet effective and the rest of the female vampire community would have done well to mirror her attire.

As the pair made their way through the labyrinth of corridors to the cave, where their army was gathered, Annara became increasingly concerned over the small matter of Logan's outfit. It was tedious, she knew, but it was a concern none the less.

"Honey," she said as tactfully as she could. "Don't you think you should change before we head above ground? I don't think that suit is appropriate for…er… killing in. I hear there could be police with riot gear and guns, which could mean getting our hands dirty and that suit looks too fine on you to go ruining right now."

Logan glanced down at his snappy suit and smiled inwardly. *Dumb bitch*, he mused inside his head. *If only she knew.*

"I'm not going."

Annara stopped walking, causing her grip on Logan's arm to pull him sharply to a stand still. "*Excuse me*?"

He smiled his most dazzling smile. "I'm not going."

She choked on her words. "But…but *why*? You said we were doing this thing together! I had to kill my closest female vampire companion for these boots and I picked this outfit out just for you, so you could see how hot I look when my t-shirt is clinging to me, drenched in blood!"

Not all *vampires find wet t-shirts a turn on*, he thought derisively. *When would Annara grow up? Hadn't the centuries knocked any sense into her?*

"I'm sure you'll look beautiful sweetheart, but I'm afraid I can't go. And besides, they'll be plenty of other opportunities for me to see you in *and* out of that outfit, I'm sure."

"But I don't understand."

That's because the few brain cells you had when you were living, died the day you were bitten and now your skull is an empty shell you ugly cow.

"There's no use in the both of us going up there. I'm pretty sure the Slayers will be mooching around for our 'wedding cake' later and I want to be here to give our guests a most gracious welcome."

"I can't believe you don't want to fight by my side! Like the King and Queen should do. It'll set a good example to the rest of them if they see us. We'll earn the utmost respect!"

Logan could tell time was pressing on and that any longer and they would lose their army's motivation. The last thing he wanted was to walk into the cave and find them all fucking each other grossly and unashamedly, like they had done in the past, during training. *Damn vampires and their overactive sex drives.*

"Look, we don't have time for this."

He moved away from her, but felt a pull on his arm as she dragged him back. The fury inside of him exploded at that point and he slapped her hard across the face for her foolish behaviour. As she cowered and forced a hand to her stinging cheek, Logan's eyes returned to their natural colour and he extended a hand to her as an apology.

"I'm sorry."

She remained silent and still.

"I'm just nervous about tonight."

It was understandable. “That’s okay,” she replied quietly, taking his hand.

“Don’t worry about me,” he said pleasantly. “I’ll be down here waiting for you. No Slayer will ruin our chances of being together, I promise you.”

Annara reached her hands up and around his neck and planted a kiss on his lips. With a wink she said, “I’ll bring you back something tasty.”

He slapped her hard on the ass. “That’s my girl.”

An almighty roar of appreciation met their ears as they entered the cave at last, and on the highest vantage point, Zeke stood, dressed in an unbuttoned, navy blue, shirt and black jeans, held in place with a black leather belt. He was awaiting his orders from the Master, for they were of a different nature to the rest of Logan’s people.

The sea of heads writhed, bouncing and bobbing almost obscenely as arms flew up into the air and cheers echoed off the walls, unhinging clods of mud from the ceiling that fell like dark rain. Feet stamped the ground and the werewolves among the crowd howled at the roof.

They were eager to leave and taste human blood.

Logan felt his lust for the hunt stir inside his breast as he stared down at his people, and he almost wished he didn’t have prior engagements so that he could join them. But seeing Annara standing on a rock to give herself more height, made him all the more anxious to get rid of her.

“This is it!” he yelled.

The voices of his people dimmed.

“Your time has arrived.”

Vampires licked their fangs. Werewolves licked their lips. Both species couldn’t stand still in their excitement.

"I think," Logan said, "You all know what to do."

There came a sudden rush for the exit.

Vampire pushed vampire. Werewolf nipped hungrily at werewolf. They stampeded through the underground to the awaiting opening beneath the Stone Table, ready to spew from the ground like a wave of lava from a volcano, only with jagged teeth. The smaller, weaker vampires were crushed under the feet of the strong, but all of them managed to get out of the cave eventually.

Still standing in the centre of the cave however, was a man. He had the faint outline of a six pack on his thin, pale white stomach and slightly more impressive arms than what he once had.

Logan waggled a finger to the man and he obeyed.

"What's *he* doing here?" Annara looked disdainfully on.

"Tristian is one of the family now."

Annara threw her hands up in the air, "I thought you were joking about making him a vampire. I mean, look at the state of this guy!"

Logan liked that Tristian annoyed his partner. It made him a valuable asset to the team, just to see her squirm before him.

"He will entertain the female Slayer that he has told me about."

Zeke stepped forward. "You mean Kiya?" he asked. "No offence, Little Guy," he said, turning to the silently approaching Tristian. "But she would kill you in a heart beat. I mean, I *hate* the bitch, but there's no denying she's a hell of a good fighter-"

"Maybe that's because I killed her boyfriend," Tristian informed Zeke, failing to hide his pride as a grin burst across his thin lips. "I killed the Mayor's daughter and Kiya's man took the blame. He's buried in the ground without a head because of me."

Zeke's expression of disgust turned to one of joy as he high-fived the skinny vamp.' "Nice work, Little Man! Ten out of ten for grossness."

"Enough." Logan snapped suddenly. "You can swap stories of deceit and unfair-play when you're on duty. Just leave me, the pair of you. Zeke- Tristian requests that you leave Kiya to him. Is that understood?"

"Perfectly."

"So get the fuck out of here."

Zeke nodded to Tristian and together they made for the exit that Logan and Annara had entered through.

"Are you ready to join the mayhem above?"

Annara was jostled from her thoughts. It seemed odd to her that Logan would need two bodyguards when he had given her the impression *he* was going to take on the Slayers alone.

"Sure," she said, in a relatively small voice.

"Don't let me down."

"I won't."

She sprung off the small platform and ran across the room with fluid strides in her stolen boots, until Logan called her name.

"Annara!"

She stopped.

"Why don't you spend ten minutes shopping for that wedding dress of yours whilst you're up there?"

She smiled and left without a word- a blood red, tight fitting gown in mind, with sequin straps and a long trailing tail that had delicate roses fashioned to it. Oh how she would be the envy of all!

Logan was relieved to see the back of Annara as she finally disappeared and seeing no reason to stand about any longer, he went in pursuit of the wedding ceremony that was about to begin in his throne room, where his bride to be was lying on the alter in wait, still slumbering soundly, and having no idea what was about to happen.

He didn't know if he was going to be able to convince her to marry him when she discovered he was dead. And would she accept the 'turn' like he had dreamed she would someday?

His nerves were being obliterated.

There was only one way to find out if Roxy loved him as much as he loved her…

Chapter 40

New Territory

Kiya was astounded.

She'd never seen a guy so involved in completely *destroying* something man-made, like Kieran was with those metal double-doors leading to what they believed to be the vampire haven, containing their comrade.

Sweat dripped off him as he swung the sledgehammer time and time again, buckling the metal until it resembled a scrunched up crisp packet, revealing only darkness beneath the cracks.

"Almost there," he divulged, wiping his brow with the sleeve of his long black coat. It wasn't something Kiya was used to seeing him wear, but she felt a pleasant tingle at the sight of him. He looked good. He *always* looked good.

As the wind picked up, she shuddered, drawing her coat tighter around her in hope of savouring the body heat that was escaping. Everything that wasn't covered in her bullet-proof vest was feeling Jack Frost's bite, and it didn't bode well for her if a vampire came looking for a fight. Her muscles were far from warm enough.

Finally, the doors crumpled inwards, breaking whatever was keeping them locked, and a ladder became visible to them in the moonlight.

"Well, whoever's down here would have certainly heard us coming," Siren pointed out, itching one of his ears with his finger.

"So why isn't there a welcome party?" Kieran asked no one in particular. He had almost expected a swarm of blood suckers to jump out of the hole and try kicking his ass right there and then, but the sweet sound of silence was all that came out of the ground as they stood in bewilderment, fully armed and dangerous.

"Is this a good thing?" Kiya questioned the group. Part of her was relieved there had been nothing to slay.

"For all we know, they could have packed up and left."

Kieran refused to believe Siren's suggestion. With a grunt in response, he threw the sledgehammer into the hole, watching the thick darkness swallow it, and after hearing no response to its impact on the floor below, he climbed down the ladder into unknown territory.

"Be careful," Kiya muttered pointlessly, then felt her cheeks warming in embarrassment. Kieran didn't need telling twice that they were on dangerous grounds.

He stopped on the fifth metal-rung. "Stay alert. They may be watching us."

They both nodded at their brave leader and followed in his wake, Kiya first, Siren second.

The silence unnerved them all.

Underground, there was a wooden chair parked to the right of the ladder. Kiya couldn't imagine a vampire sitting on such a thing in a civilised manner, but there it was, reminding her that they were still partially human.

"This place reeks of death," Siren said, just as the putrid aroma hit Kiya in the nose. It was enough to make you want to bend over and vomit a week's worth of good food, but she managed to fight the urge by focusing on the flickering flames of a torch protruding from a wall in the distance.

"There has to be someone down here that we can get answers from," she whispered. "They wouldn't leave this place completely unguarded surely?"

"What do vampires have that is of any value, other than the lives of humans? And even if there were humans down here, vampires wouldn't care too much about watching over them because they'd just relish the idea of going hunting again for more." Siren was speaking more to Kiya than he was to his male friend. He felt as if she still needed tutoring on the subject of vampires, their feeding patterns and behaviour.

Kieran was holding the sledgehammer tightly in both hands, making his leather, metal studded gloves creak. He was watching the flames of the torch dancing and felt his heart leap as a silhouette came into view.

The silhouette became a girl. She was scrawny and her face was covered in a mixture of dirt and make-up. The Slayer's judged her to be seventeen and the expression on her face was of pure fright as she bumped into Kieran, stumbling to the floor from the blow and dragging her body away from the reach of his legs.

He knelt beside her. She trembled in his shadow-sitting in stunned silence.

"What's going on here?" he asked firmly. There was no time to play the 'nice stranger.'

The girl winced, clutching a bleeding arm in pain. It had been damaged before she had walked into the man that knelt before her. "Excuse me?" she said, giving Kiya and Siren nervous glances. She found it daunting, keeping her eyes on Kieran.

"What are you doing down here?" he re-worded his question.

She was looking at them each in turn, obviously fighting inside her head for a valid explanation. Kiya noticed how her long brown hair was unkempt and greasy and her body was caked in enough mud to fill a medium sized plant pot. This girl had been down here for days.

"Are you one of them?"

The girl shook her head vigorously at this accusation. "No. No. I'm... I'm just an art student!" she insisted.

"Then what are you doing here, dressed like that? Are you trying to get yourself killed?" Kieran was referring to the leather miniskirt and see-through lace t-shirt revealing small breasts. She looked like a hooker. Common trash. Not a seventeen year old girl with a passion for painting.

"They like me to wear this sort of thing."

It was obvious now they were dealing with a Feeder.

"When are you girls going to realise that these vampires *aren't* your fucking friends? You may be doing them a favour by letting them take your blood once in a while but they can turn on you at any moment when they get bored of drinking from the same person. Do you really want to die?"

The girl was shaking, her eyes wide and full of tears just waiting to spill.

"No," she said. "No I don't."

"Then why do you come here?"

"To hide," she said, "My step father... he beats me sometimes."

Kieran's tense and unfeeling emotion melted. He extended a palm and lifted the girl to her feet. She was frail and afraid, but he got a sense of relief from her, as if she'd been hoping all along that a knight in shining bullet-proof armour, and a long black coat, would come and save her one day.

"Do you know this place well?"

The girl nodded. "Quite well. Yes."

"Have you seen a teenage girl being brought down here recently? Nineteen years old? Tall with natural blonde hair? Very slim?"

"Sorry," she said, showing her regret in not being able to help him. "There are a lot of girls that come and go down here. I wouldn't know who you're talking about."

Kieran blinked and tried forcing his body to stay relaxed.

"Did you guys come here to fight the Master's army, because I think they left already." She was twiddling her thumbs nervously.

"Say what?" Kieran cocked his head to the side. He wasn't sure if he was hearing right.

The girl checked that there was no one standing in the corridor behind her before she continued. "I must have been drugged or something. They do that sometimes if I tell them I'm going home early. Last night, I heard one of them talking about a war. There was this big celebration when I got here, the wildest I've ever seen. I don't remember falling asleep, but when I woke just half an hour ago, I couldn't find anyone. Not even the werewolves that guard most of the passageways-"

There was silence as the wheels in each Slayer's head processed the information.

"Can I go now? My mum is probably worried sick."

"Not to give you false hope little girl, but your mum is probably dead."

She looked surprised by Kieran's outburst.

"Why are you saying that?" she pleaded. "What's happened?"

"If you knew there was a war, why didn't you tell someone? Do you think those vampires are going to spare your mother just because her daughter is a Feeder?"

"They said I could mark my front door with a cross if I wanted to protect my mum. so I nailed a crucifix to the door a few weeks ago. I know they won't touch her! And as for telling someone about this war, I only knew about it last night. Even if I had known, I wouldn't have said anything, because then people would know I come here. My mum thinks I've been staying at my father's house. She can't know about this place. She'd make me move to Karanthian or one of those small mountain villages that don't even have electricity."

Same old story, Kieran thought bitterly. *Girl has crappy home life. She seeks company in the worst place possible. Roxy was the same, only she didn't allow herself to become a slave to the un-dead.*

"Is there anyone down here that you are aware of? Anyone at all?"

The girl shrugged. "I haven't checked every room, but on my way over, it was pretty much deserted."

"And this 'Master' guy- do you know where he sleeps?"

"No," she replied. "But I can show you where his throne room is. That's where he gives orders and comes up with ideas that he shares with that vampire- Anita I think she's called."

"Take us there."

The girl gave Kieran a small smile, feeling confidence brewing inside of her. Boldly, she took hold of Kieran's hand and began leading him through the labyrinth, but just as they turned the first corner, his mobile phone sounded in his pocket, making the girl jump.

"It's okay," he said, putting a hand up to calm her. The name on the screen read: 'Emilia Mob.' "Hello?"

"Fuck-"

He had to admit, it was one of the strangest responses to a hello he'd ever had.

"Kieran?"

"Yeah," he said, looking into Kiya's concerned eyes. Siren folded his arms over his chest.

Emilia sounded distressed and he switched to loudspeaker so that everyone could hear what was being said.

"Kieran, they're here. More than I can count," she shouted down the phone between ragged breaths. "They've built this tunnel under the Stone Table. God knows how long it's been there! We've surrounded them, but it's hard trying to hold them back. It's hard hitting them directly in the heart when there are so many and some have already gotten into the city. I really need your help. This is your field of expertise right?"

"Shit," he cursed. "Emz, I don't think I can get-"

"I'll go." Siren offered, cutting him off.

"What?" Emilia yelled, "I can't hear you properly. You're breaking up."

"Tell her I'm on my way, but it could be well over an hour before I reach her."

Kieran repeated the information to the female police officer.

"Fine. Just... just hurry!" she said, hanging up the phone.

Kiya looked solemnly at Siren. He was doing a noble thing, but it hurt her to see him offer his assistance elsewhere. The reality of it was, there was a big fight going down. People were going to die.

"Will you be okay?" Siren asked his friends.

Kieran gave him a weak smile. "We'll be fine, mate. But it's you I'm concerned about."

He smiled back and stepped forward, unexpectedly grabbing Kieran in an awkward hug. It was brief, but heartfelt and Kiya was next to feel his touch.

"You'll find her," he said encouragingly. "I'm sure we'll all be back at the factory by sun-up, talking about how crazy our nights have been."

Kiya laughed sheepishly. "You bet."

With a bow in his usual Chinese fashion, he left, scurrying up the ladder and disappearing into the night.

"I guess it's just me and you." Kieran's voice echoed down the corridor as he spoke, and once again, he let the seventeen year old Feeder take him by the hand- the one that wasn't still dragging the sledgehammer.

Chapter 41

It Begins

It was chaos, but it was *good*.

Annara instructed her minions to climb up in groups of twenty at a time, giving them each a letter of the alphabet to go by- so as not to cause a major blockage- as they all eagerly tried scrambling out at the same time. It seemed like a dumb idea, but it worked.

Her army had been obediently waiting for their Second in Command during her conversation with Logan, under the mouth of the Stone Table, and as she swaggered over in her outrageously inappropriate outfit (who said you couldn't go to war and look hot?), they each parted to make a wide path for her.

The first few waves of vampires deployed were granted access into the city without any hiccups. The streets were pretty bare at this hour, but they whooped and hooted like maniacs, rousing human suspicion. The second a face appeared in a window, one of the excitable un-dead creatures would kick their door through and chase them through the house, leaving bloody corpses all over the carpets.

"I think I might bag me the Mayor," one of them said conversationally to another, before biting into the neck of a squirming ten year old girl with a teddy bear in one hand, covering her cream nightdress in blood. He had dragged her out of her bedroom and thrown her onto the street, demonstrating to a female companion how easy it was to reach in and take what was rightfully there's. "It'd be a challenge, you know? I like challenges. Getting into his mansion and killing all those puny security guards would give me the ultimate rush! But then again, I like it when little girls in their bed-wear scream at the sight of me kicking open their bedrooms doors," he chuckled heartily. "Man, that *never* loses its appeal."

"I heard a vampire had to be invited into a house before they could enter-" the skinny vampire chick said, stroking a hand through the little girl's hair whilst her partner chewed away at her fragile skin. The child made gulping noises that could make a blind man weep; you didn't need to see the horror of it to know she was in complete agony.

"You've been watching too much '*Buffy*,"' he spat, covering the woman's face in globules of blood and flesh, which she licked away seductively. "Like I said. You want something, you go get it. There are no barriers here. No spells that can contain us. *Nothing* can stop you and I." He paused in thought. "But don't ever quote me on that, Sweetheart."

Most of the humans were cowering behind locked doors now, praying they would survive the night once word had gotten out about the invasion. They sat with dressing-gowns wrapped tightly around them, clutching children and muttering pleas for protection to their almighty God.

House wives grabbed their meat cleavers and kitchen knives. Children grabbed onto their mother's legs, or took the hands of their siblings, burying their faces into each other as the night filled with the screams of the dying.

However, there were a brave few that took up weapons and went out onto the streets, driven by their own fear. Men, who felt they had a duty to protect all that they owned and loved grabbed their knives, swords or guns and took off into the chilling winds, running towards the sound of the injured and frightened. But the vampires were far too quick for them. Nonchalantly, they'd finish their meals and turn to face their opponents with an air of fearlessness, giving the humans a taste of their combat skills before breaking their necks. Husbands. Fathers. They were perishing faster than the Grim Reaper could count.

There were a handful of humans who actually managed to maim the vampires a little. Knives struck chests. Swords cut through abdomens and arms. Guns blew holes in pretty much everything. But these human's were not trained to strike the correct places and all of them failed to destroy the beasts that were ripping beating hearts out of crying children and women.

The people of Meridion were being exterminated.

Twenty minutes into the fray, sirens sounded in the city, giving vampires cause to glance up from their meals and scowl.

"Pigs!" one snarled to another scathingly, licking blood from its chin.

"I'm so afraid!" the other mocked, licking the neck of a middle aged, single mother and pulling her underwear down in preparation for an act of sin that didn't involve killing her. The woman was retching in fear, carelessly coating her own chin in warm bile.

And so they came.

Emilia was first to slam her car door shut, dressed in her uniform, complete with navy blue bullet-proof vest and helmet, carrying bottles of holy water and liquefied silver to squirt in the eyes of her enemy onlookers, and had access to enough silver bullets to put a stop to vampire life as they knew it.

"Okay boys," she yelled. "Heads and hearts. We don't want to give these assholes a chance to even blink before they're kissing Satan's big red ass."

The police moved in formation, watching each others backs as they created a large circle around the stones.

A vampire, by the name of Kalissco, saw the officers moving in and crept up behind one, dragging them back into the shadows. But as the officer kicked and writhed, another spotted the movement and followed the vampire into the darkness, putting bullets in it's head and heart until it wriggled in a burst of flame- a vampire no more.

"You okay?" the officer asked, lifting Emilia to her feet.

"No time-," she said, flustered, feeling slightly embarrassed about being the first to almost get bitten. She brushed her uniform down with a shaking hand, reclaiming her gun from the pavement where it had fallen. "But thanks."

The officer nodded and joined the rest of them, followed by a crestfallen Emilia, who was already doubting her chances of survival.

"Stay on track," she whispered in the confines of her stifling helmet. "You can't let them kill you yet. This city needs you damn it."

The vampires that were already deep into the city were of no concern to the police officers now. If Emilia sent any of her men into the city to target the early arrivals, she may lose her advantage over the main battle ground, where most of the animals were pushing up and out of the floor like shy rabbits from a dirt tunnel.

Deep beneath the massacre, Annara was becoming impatient with her soldiers.

"Why aren't you fuckers getting up there?" she screeched, punching a burly guy in his big arm. "Go and fight, you cowards!"

The vampires lining the walls of the winding corridors in their hundreds were all muttering about waiting for the police to give up, but Annara wasn't having any of it.

"The next group- E- get up there. And group F, you follow them without breaking the chain. There's safety in numbers. You can force your way into the city, no problemo. So don't give me those frightened, piss poor, girly looks. I swear, it's like commanding an army of five year old chicken-shits!"

Werewolves growled as their arms bulged in protest, lifting the nervous vampires into the air two at a time and rapidly throwing them into the heart of fight, where the sound of guns exploding met their ears immediately.

Bullets struck arms and legs, but only a few found the hearts of the un-dead, causing explosions of flame and the scattering of ash into the wind. It discouraged many of the vampires to see their numbers dwindling in each wave, but there was still hope when a few made it behind enemy lines.

Officers were being taken down, slowly but surely. The vampires were pouncing on them, cracking helmets open like eggs and biting at necks as if they hadn't eaten since the day they were turned. Blood ran through the gutters in rivers and screams practically overpowered the sounds of guns going off.

Emilia was panicking now. All her years as an officer and she'd never lost a single man. Now, she had led them to slaughter. If there were to be any survivors, they would never forgive her.

With fumbling fingers, she reached for her mobile and called the only man she had ever relied on. Just as he answered, a vampire tackled the officer to her right, slashing its claws at the armoured man's head.

"Fuck!" she screamed, smashing a bottle of holy water over the creatures skull and watching as it melted the flesh from its hollow bones. The officer was fine, but dazed and he thanked her graciously.

The numbers of vampires were decreasing at last, but for how long? There could be any number of hell-beasts beneath the city just waiting to rear their ugly heads. The most she could do was keep fighting until the sun came up, when her enemies would have to seek shelter from its deadly rays.

To her relief, Siren had offered to join her, but a part of her hope sunk when Kieran showed no interest in assisting her also.

I hope I live through this so I can tell him he's a jerk-off, she thought, laughing pitifully to herself. She didn't really hate him of course. She just felt an overwhelming sense of disappointment that he couldn't give up the search for a girl that was more than likely dead. Didn't she- Emilia- mean anything to him?

"You're a big girl," she told herself, once the phone was back in her pocket. "Big girls don't cry over long-ago ex-boyfriends."

"Retreat!" shouted an officer, as three times as many vampires came out from beneath the Stone Table. The word spread through the night as if it were God speaking from the heavens, granting them a small blessing to leave the grounds, where so much death was occurring.

"No! No!" she yelled assertively. "Officers stay! We can win this! We just have to keep fighting side by side."

"Retreat!"

"For fuck sake. We can win this!"

Who was she kidding?

Chapter 42

Alone in the Battlefield

"We're gonna win this whether you like it or not," Annara screeched fiercely at her remaining soldiers. "This is *our* night. *Our* war. Don't fuck it up!"

"But the cops... there are too many!" a bold vampire said, stepping forward from the queues of concerned looking un-dead. "Perhaps we should retreat, or go and get some weapons of our own?"

Annara's temper sky rocketed. "We out number those pig-humans ten-to-one you idiots, and we're more advanced than they *ever* will be!" she hissed, driving her nails into the vampire's wrist and watching the blood well up. She had needed to hurt someone for quite sometime now, because it always eased the niggling tensions inside of her. Her battle jitters were only to be expected, especially with Logan picking a fine time to stay home-bound. She would rather slaughter their men and women herself than see them squirm out of taking Meridion for their future empire. Correction. *Her* future empire. "We don't need to fight guns with guns. What kind of a war would that be? There's no way we can lose with our phenomenal strength, unless they bulldoze us all down with machines and blow up the underworld, and believe me when I say that's *not* going to happen."

The vampire bit his lip as she twisted her nails around in his flesh, watching the pain in his eyes as they flashed silver at her- a warning to stop what she was doing. He didn't try to harm her in return however. He just tried to take it like a man, before returning to his restless and anxious comrades, who patted his back in sincerity.

That's better, Annara thought, dripping the vampire's blood into her mouth and feeling an addictive wave of dizziness washing over her momentarily. Shivers ran through her neck and shoulders as the scarlet liquid plastered the inside of her throat.

"I'm going up with the next group," she informed them all calmly, as if volunteering herself would boost their confidence somehow. Many of the vampires looked sceptical and unaffected by her words and it angered her to the point of gripping a female vampire by the throat and snapping her neck. It didn't kill her, but it would take a hell of a long time for her to recover. With a smile, Annara extracted the bracelet from the girl's limp wrist- a cluster of shiny black stones on an elastic- and admired it without any remorse. It found a new home on her paper white skin.

"I'm losing my patience with you all." She spoke in a way that gave no hint as to her true mood. "I think I'll just go fetch the *Master* and let *him* choose which of you dies first." Their were nervous murmurs. "Because you have two choices. Number one; you stay here and get your immortality obliterated by myself or the Master in a very stomach churning way, *or*, number two; you can go up their, dodge your way past a couple of bullets and have a blood bath in the homes of the weak." She paused for her words to sink in. "So what do you say?"

They glanced at each other miserably, then shimmied over to the werewolves in defeat, allowing them to boost them up- keeping the flow consistent.

Annara smiled. She'd had a feeling that a couple of threats would bring them around to her way of thinking.

As sexy as she could manage, she forced her long legs to glide in the direction of the werewolf with the most sex-appeal (not that any of them were particularly unattractive) and gave his muscles a tender stroke. Under her touch, the wolf man quivered, but he kept his expression wooden.

"Give me a lift up and I'll fetch you a Scooby-snack when I return," she promised sweetly, brushing her hand over the stubble on his hard set jaw. There was a flicker of a smile from the great brute and politely, he took her hands in his, bending his leg to provide a step to which she placed one heavy, dirt encrusted boot. From his leg, she brought her other foot up onto his shoulder, finally using her muscular arms to drag herself out of the hole and into the night.

Fifteen, she counted. Fifteen police officers left in good shape, pumping bullets into the confines of the Stone Circle and breaking chips off of rock when they missed their fleshy targets.

As she knelt beside the Stone Table, ducking when an officer in range tried to blow a hole in her face, she felt an unbelievably unpleasant tug on her hope and a staggering sense of regret- realising that even though she'd trained for months to be a part of the vampire revolution, all she really wanted now was to be close to Logan. It broke her heart that he wasn't leading their army with her.

I don't need human slaves to enjoy myself, she thought. *And I don't need a crappy city to call my land either. All I want- all I* need - *is my Logan and a few vampire minions to make me happy.*

The smouldering ash of a disintegrating vampire hit her sensitive eyes, making her curse loudly as she scraped at her face to stop it from stinging, and as she glanced around at her enemies in pain, she caught sight of an officer stopping to reload their gun.

She saw her chance to break through.

An easy kill.

Her eyes flashed silver and her fangs grew to their full length as she ran directly towards a briefly distracted Emilia.

Chapter 43

The Wait

Zeke's eyes travelled over the pale, sickly coloured skin of his new sallow faced partner-in-crime and couldn't help but grimace. He could hardly believe that such a weedy, pathetic looking specimen was the man who had destroyed Kiya's wonderful life- driving her from her home and career, and also, he'd brutally murdered a shit load of young women just to keep a roof over his head as he circled the city, throwing enemies off his tail. Biting down on his knuckles, Zeke stifled a laugh of pure delight.

"What are you smirking about?" Tristian asked sourly, taking his eyes off his arms. He had been flexing them to observe the way his muscles bulged ever so slightly- a new perk thanks to the vampire gene!

"You, man. You're just so wimpy looking and yet you've done more damage to society than any one else, dead or alive."

Tristian frowned at the use of the word wimpy, but felt a sense of pride at Zeke's apparent appreciation towards him. No one had ever really shown an interest in his fight for the right to be a vampire. All that death involved...

"You...you find it impressive?"

Zeke slouched. He was leant against a dirt wall, twiddling a matchstick in his fingers that he'd found lying on the ground. Tristian was parked opposite him. "It's certainly one for the history books," he assured him, keeping his eyes on the red head of the match as it revolved in his hands.

"No one has ever really said anything about my…my work, in such a light before."

The novelty of the match had worn off at last, and Zeke discarded it, tucking his knees up to his chest instead. All this waiting for Kieran to arrive was making him frustrated. He had wanted to sniff him out, but the Master had demanded they stay in one place, in case they missed him somehow.

"So how many girls did you kill all together?"

Tristian's eyes became vacant in thought. "Ten-maybe fifteen. I don't know. I didn't exactly put notches on my bed post, if you catch my drift."

"How'd you do it?"

Tristian faltered. "…Excuse me?"

"How'd you kill them?" he persisted.

Tristian's mind drifted back to the evenings he'd suffered uncontrollable blood lust. Seeing Kiya waiting on the roof of the Sun-Tower for Rycan had made him so furious that he had killed the Mayor's daughter with the sword he'd stolen from their house a few nights before. And after that kill, he'd wanted more. He'd used knives most of the time, cutting off fingers and toes then licking the wounds as the blood gushed out. He'd tried touching the girl's in places they *should* have enjoyed, but their fear and loathing of him made them scream in protest until he'd had to slit their throats or stab them in the lungs. But there was one girl he had grown quite attached to. Not

Kiya. Just a random young woman with hair as soft as silk and eyes the nicest shade of blue. She'd been so afraid that she had promised to let him play his games with her, just as long as he let her go free afterwards. Of course, there was no chance Tristian would let her escape only to gabble to the police, but at first, he'd let her think she had a chance, stroking her kindly and twisting his hands through the bristly hairs between her legs. For a while, he'd kidded himself that she was enjoying it all. There was no flicker of disgust as he'd entered her and she kept up a persistent flow of sighs that gave him the impression it was satisfying her as much as him. Until she asked his name.

"Why'd you ask?" he'd said to her, pulling free from the warmth of her sweet feminine opening.

"I want to know the name of the man who raped me," she spat bravely, her face glistening with sweat and her eyes wide with rage.

Perhaps she had thought he was less of a threat than he'd first appeared- that all he'd wanted was a quick fuck, not a corpse on his hands.

"That's none of your business, bitch," he'd growled, then bit into her neck like he'd seen the vampires do on countless occasions, tasting her blood in the back of his throat and ripping her flesh off in chunks. As she lay there, still alive but in a state of shock, he'd watched her bleed to death for well over an hour, parting only briefly to make a coffee in her pastel pink kitchen.

"Tell me," Zeke said.

"Why do you want to know?"

He shrugged. "I'm bored I guess. Thought it would give me some inspiration or something."

Tristian managed a weak smile. "A magician never reveals his tricks."

There was silence for a while.

Both men were beginning to wonder if Kieran and his crew of super-heroes would ever show up.

In Tristian's hands was a dart gun. He had no desire to kill Kiya *yet*. All he wanted was a few hours alone with her.

"Do you think the war is going well?" Zeke asked.

"I couldn't give two shits," Tristian replied, louder than he'd intended.

"I thought you liked the whole blood and guts thing?"

He shuddered. They'd been together for less than an hour and Zeke was already acting like he knew him- like a friend. Tristian didn't want friends. He wanted women. Even though Annara had mistreated him, he'd wished she'd been sat in the corridor with him instead of an ex-Slayer.

"I'm warning you now. Stay away from Kiya," he said fervently. His brow was beaded with sweat. His eyes were narrow slits.

"I said I would didn't I? Jeez, get a grip."

"I love her," he cried, almost hysterically.

"I get it-"

"I won't have you touch her."

Tristian clambered to his feet.

"What's gotten in to you, you fucking freak? I won't go near your girl! Just sit down and shut up."

"How come you all think you can tell me what to do?" he asked indignantly. "I'm better than you."

A loud sigh of mockery escaped Zeke's lips. "Whatever."

Tristian stepped forward and punched Zeke in the face.

"Jesus! Talk about a basket case! You really are fucked up in the head aren't you? You become a vampire and you think you're some sort of God, is that it?"

He punched Zeke again and in response to the blow, he knocked Tristian flying backwards into the wall by plunging a foot into his gut.

"Keep your hands off of me."

Tristian's rage was ebbing as he fell to the ground. His eyes returned to their natural colour.

"I'm sorry," he apologised. "I think... I think I'm still getting used to the 'turn."'

"No shit," Zeke mumbled, scratching the back of his neck.

"I just... I just want her so badly and it's eating me up inside."

"Women can make you do some crazy things."

"I hate her," he remarked pensively. "And I love her at the same time."

"I feel the same way," said a new and unexpected voice. "Accept, the latter is a far cry from anything I'd ever say and actually mean about *you*, Tristian."

"Kiya!" he yelled, jumping up and fumbling with his gun.

"I've missed you," she said, grabbing her sword.

Chapter 44

Confession

Logan placed Roxy down gently against the smooth white cloth that had been spread neatly over the altar, and made sure her head was in a relatively comfortable position, beside the large crucifix he had acquired merely for decoration in the current circumstances. Her dress dangled over the edges, looking like shimmering pools of paint, just before spilling onto the floor and her tatty hair stuck out at all angles like a jagged halo around her head.

"Do you have your book?"

The Priest stepped out from behind the shadows of the throne, looking tired and defeated with a Bible clutched against his dirty black robes. "It's a bit blood stained from my unclean hands, but yes, I have it."

Logan ignored the 'blood' comment and stroked Roxy's face.

"Is she alive?" Father Casey queried, standing beside the vampire.

"Of course she is." At Logan's words, Roxy stirred awake and even his dead heart managed to summersault beneath his chest.

"Leave us, Father," he instructed hurriedly. "I wish to talk to her alone. I'll fetch you when you are needed."

Father Casey nodded wearily and left, dragging his feet in an irritating fashion.

"Logan...?" Her voice was dry and croaky. She sat up and placed a hand on her aching head. This was becoming a habit. "I don't remember... how I got here."

Logan sighed mildly and sat on the edge of the altar. "Sonja. Are you feeling okay?"

"No," she managed to rasp. "I feel as if someone's taken a sledgehammer to my head."

Logan continued to rub the palm of his hand in circular motions over the area of her smooth back that was exposed in the Prom dress.

"Sonja... I haven't been particularly honest with you of late."

Roxy's head pounded time and time again, but his words were enough to penetrate the distracting agonies within her. "What are you talking about?"

"I've been lying to you." His voice remained cool and collected, soft like silk. It was a relaxation technique vampires sometimes used on their victims. As long as Roxy kept her eyes on him and listened to the tone of his voice, she'd remain trapped in his glare, unable to do anything besides breathe in and out steadily. "I told you I've been searching for you, but to what extent, I never divulged."

Roxy blinked uncertainly. Her lips were tightly sealed, but tears threatened to pour the more she heard from him. She felt awful and to top it all off, she was lying on a table in a weird cave with her boyfriend spouting some sort of confession.

"I came back here to find you...to Meridion. *This* you know. But I had others working at my side, for a sum of money I was quite reluctant to part with."

"What are you *talking* about? What do you mean you paid someone to work with you?"

Logan exhaled loudly (even though there was no necessity for a vampire to breathe, he had trained himself to imitate the process in order to fool people at the West Meridion Mall Pet Shop that he was a living, breathing young man.)

"I spoke with your parents. They agreed to help me find you, but it was never because *they* wanted you back.'

"You mean, all this time I thought they were looking for me, it was only because you had paid them to?" Her head felt as if there were a tribe of men inside using her brain matter as a drum.

"They loved the idea of turning your bedroom into a gym more than the prospect of getting their little girl back and I had to beg them to help me find you once they'd informed me of your disappearance."

Her lips were trembling now. She had always known her parents were not completely in love with her, but she had hoped they'd cared a *little*. The truth was harsh.

"Why are you telling me this?" she asked despondently. "You didn't have to mention all this. A simple 'your parents helped' would have got the message across."

Logan placed a hand over his heart. He regretted crushing her spirit, but felt it was necessary. "I want you to know everything, because I believe we can't move forward until I tell you these things."

"I get it okay! You basically put a bounty on my head in hope that my parents would bring me home safely. Oh, and they don't love me. End of story." She was hurting so badly. Her tired muscles were tingling with the emotion exploding from her heart and head. Once again she felt like that lost and lonely girl she'd been the first day she'd packed her bags and left her comfortable 'rich-girl' lifestyle for a rebellious, dangerous one.

"I also have a confession to make, but first I need to reiterate just how much I love you and that I hope you'll see past my…sins."

Her heart was beating like a bull's in a pit full of matadors waving red flags. If it pumped any faster, it would explode.

"You're scaring me."

"I don't mean to."

"I want to go home-" she whispered.

"Do you really?" His eyes burrowed into hers with their cosmic power to soothe her. All the tension left her body at once and she didn't suspect it was him having this affect over her. "I *do* love you, and more than anything in the world, I want us to be wed." He continued, placing his hand over hers and squeezing it comfortingly. "Will you marry me?"

Roxy tried shaking the grogginess from her cobwebby mind. "Logan-"

"Say yes."

"I will, but-"

"But nothing. You either love me or you don't."

"You know I do."

"Then this makes everything else I'm about to tell you a little easier on me."

Roxy brought her knees up closer to her chest and tried to shift her ass on the uncomfortably hard surface of the altar. It had grown numb and sore from sitting there all this time. "Instead of harping on about marriage and sin, why don't you try telling me why we're in a cave?"

Logan lifted a hand to stop her, as if her questions were unimportant.

"Not yet."

"So we're *not* trapped-"

"Not exactly."

She jumped off the altar suddenly and made for what looked like a door cut out of the rocks and mud. Logan was at her side before she could blink, grabbing her by the arm and snapping her back to a stand still.

"I haven't finished-"

"Then let's get out of here and talk when we're in a safer environment. It smells like dead people down here."

"I *can't* leave. Not yet. Just hear me out."

"Logan. I want to get out of this place *now*!"

She wrenched her arm loose and made for the door again with meaningful strides. Once more he grabbed her arm and pulled her to his chest.

"Stop it!" she yelled, slapping him on the shoulder. "I want to go! Why are you acting so weird?"

As she struggled he tightened his grip. He tried forcing the animal inside of him to remain in the shadows, but her cries of contempt made his heart bleed and his eyes flash a dazzling blood red.

She froze.

His eyes flickered back to normal.

"You-"

He allowed her to take a step back.

"Sonja. I don't want to hurt you," he said as soothingly as possible. "I just want you to understand."

"You-" she put both hands on either side of her head and turned in a full circle before whipping her head back around to face him. Her eyes were screaming with her astonishment at what she had seen.

"Let's talk about this." He moved his hand to touch her and she dodged out of his way as if he had a contagious disease.

"I...I remember being in Shannon's room now," she said, almost incoherently in her rising hysteria. "I...I thought that had been a nightmare or something. Just a hallucination I'd conjured unknowingly. You...her...the- the pair of you- you're...,"

"I'm not here to eat you if that's what you're thinking."

She deflected his outstretched hand once more, knocking it aside with her wrist as if the very idea of his body touching hers revolted her.

"How long have you been this way?"

Logan's head was cast downwards now and he put his hands in his suit pockets in defeat. "Before I came to Meridion looking for you."

Roxy glanced at the door and judged how long it would take for her to reach it. "And what does a *vampire* want with an old girlfriend?"

He stood still as she made her way around the room, inevitably reaching the altar where she clutched the crucifix to her chest for protection. If he tried harming her, she could crack that baby over his head and make her escape.

Logan's eyes were full of sorrow as she approached him, holding the cross so tightly that her knuckles were white. He felt as if he'd lost everything.

"You are free to go," he mumbled morosely. "There is a Priest outside the door. Ask him to take you to the surface. I won't keep you here against your will."

Roxy watched in surprise as he turned his back on her, keeping his head low.

"I haven't finished with you yet," she informed him abrasively.

"Not going to be satisfied until I'm dust, is that it?" he replied dejectedly.

She ignored his words. "You died."

There was a pause, in which he was unsure whether he should respond.

"You died and came here for me."

"What are you getting at?"

Her tone was softening. "I just never realised that a creature with the nature to destroy everything could be so... gentle."

Logan turned, hope flickering throughout him.

"But you don't seem to realise," she continued, becoming angry again, "That I *kill* things like you."

She had expected her words to shock him, but his face remained wooden. Did he think she was lying?

"I'm a Slayer, Logan. A *Vampire* Slayer and part of a team that is probably out looking for me right now!"

"I know what you are," he said coolly. "I had a private investigator hunt you down when your parents were proving useless. He followed you when you were shopping one Saturday and informed me you were staying at a burnt out old factory in the wastelands. That's how I knew I'd find you in the Mall if I hung around a few months. All I had to do was sit and wait until you worked up an appetite for new clothes-"

Roxy lowered the crucifix. "So you knew all about my job and you didn't say?"

"I'm telling you now aren't I?"

"Why didn't you tell me you were a vampire?"

He laughed. "And have you stake me on sight? Don't be absurd! I wanted you here, in my home so that we could talk without you bounding away to that Kieran-"

"*This* is your home?" she asked incredulously.

"A small portion of it, yes. This is my throne room."

Roxy laughed sceptically. "What are you, some sort of King?"

"Yes," he said simply.

She didn't believe him. "Don't you need people who follow you to be a Lord, or King, or whatever?"

"I have. Hundreds of them. They're out doing my bidding as we speak."

She felt dizzy for a moment. The crucifix fell from her hand and she almost sunk to the floor, if it weren't for Logan's quick reaction. He lifted her off her feet and lay her across the altar once more. To his surprise, she began to weep.

"What's wrong?" he inquired kindly. He planned on showing just how 'gentle' he could be and that there was no need for her to fear him.

Tears rolled down the sides of her face.

"I thought you were the one-" she sobbed, placing a hand over her eyes in embarrassment and woe.

"I still can be-"

"Logan, you drink *blood*. I drink alcopops! You kill *living* things. I kill dead guys. This is fucking ridiculous."

"Forget all that," he said quietly, rubbing the tears away from her skin with his thumb. "And remember the positive things. We both love each other. And we both make each other happy."

She sobbed some more. Her heart was aching.

"I haven't been able to stop thinking about you for so long and now I find out you're dead and live in caves with an army of vampires!"

"Does that matter?" he cried, suppressing the need to unleash his animalistic desire for blood.

"Maybe not," she replied. "But this is all so wrong."

Logan bit his lip. He thought silently for a moment. "I'll move away with you. Where ever you want to go, I'll take you there. We can live in peace. I'll never harm a human soul... again."

She sat up, listening intently and wiping the tears from her eyes.

"And what about your sister, who showed me such *great* kindness earlier?"

Logan gritted his teeth for a moment at her sarcasm. He wasn't angry with her- he was furious with his sister. "I killed her as soon as I heard what happened. Just like I'm going to slaughter Annara when she gets back here, for cutting off your beautiful hair."

Self consciously, Roxy put her hand to her head. Somehow, the loss of her hair didn't seem that important while she was in the company of a vampire king.

"You killed Shannon?"

He nodded curtly. "I just finished what you had started."

Roxy thought about the comb she'd embedded in the girl's chest and shuddered. She'd never even dreamed of attempting to 'dust' an old friend and yet here she was, facing nightmare after nightmare.

"This is all too much for me to process."

"At least grant me one wish-"

She looked into his beautiful eyes and almost melted. "What?"

"Marry me now."

Her brow furrowed. "What do you-"

"Marry me here," he cut her off. "You have a dress. I brought the priest. At least marry me for who I once was. The young man you once knew wanted to put this ring on your finger-" he produced from his pocket a solid gold band of metal. "Do it for him."

Logan wasn't sure if his words had convinced her. She stared at the ring for what felt like an eternity, her eyes moist. There was nothing more he could say.

Slowly, she wrapped her hand around the fist that was grasping the wedding ring and she pushed it towards him.

All hope escaped him.

"I can't marry a man that died God knows how many months ago," she whispered sadly. "But I *can* marry the man who stands before me now, as long as he keeps his word about not harming another human soul and if he *promises* to love me forever."

"I can give you 'forever' quite literally, Sonja," he smiled, and relished the kiss she gave him as she wrapped her arms around his neck to draw him in closer.

"You won't regret this," he assured her. "I love you."

"I love you too."

He grinned like a madman, feeling like dancing in the sunlight, even if it killed him.

"Father Casey!" he bellowed. "We have a wedding to begin!"

The Priest opened the door a crack and entered looking quite petrified.

"Father Casey?" Logan pressed in confusion.

But as the Priest fell to the ground, he realised why the Holy man looked so afraid and speechless.

Roxy screamed as he fell, for there was a small stake sticking out of the Priest's back. His black robes were heavy with his own blood.

Suddenly, Annara stepped out from behind the door and sauntered in. Logan could smell Father Casey's blood on her hands.

"What's going on?" Roxy exclaimed, looking to Logan for answers.

Annara moved forward as she spoke. "My man appears to have been unfaithful to me," she announced, stopping to press the stake deeper into the man's flesh with the base of her foot, as he gulped in mouthfuls of air. The pressure caused his innards to rip and at last his heart and mind gave up trying to sustain him.

Logan couldn't believe what he was seeing. He didn't want this to be happening now. Not when he was finally a happy man.

"I heard everything you just said you lying, *cheating* bastard," she spat ferociously.

Fuck.

Fuck.

Fuck.

Chapter 45

Put To Rest

The Feeder girl led Kieran and his female friend through the underworld for well over half an hour, talking very little to either of them- for she could tell 'stealth' was required- and at last, on a bend, they all heard two males speaking.

They had found what they were hunting for.

"Tristian," Kiya mouthed.

Kieran nodded, mouthing the word, "Zeke," back.

They hid and listened to the pair speaking for five minutes before making their entrance.

When they finally stepped forward, the girl bolted as soon as Tristian raised the dart gun, knowing only too well what a vampire behaved like when he wanted something badly enough. His watery little eyes were focused on the female Slayer, standing behind her, and she could tell by his expression he had been waiting for her arrival.

"I have to go!" the teenager yelled. No one tried to stop her.

Tristian sent a dart Kiya's way, hitting her directly in the stomach. Success! It made him cry out in triumph, but her lack of care confused him to the point of checking his gun over for ammo. He had been sure the dart-gun would work effectively within a minute of it penetrating the victim, and yet Kiya didn't drop.

"I'm sorry," she said blandly, pulling the dart from her bullet-proof vest. "Were you expecting something to happen?"

Tristian's mouth fell open as she threw the needle back at him, where it bounced off his arm and onto the floor at his feet. Again, he shot at her, aiming for her neck, but she was fluid enough with her blade to hit it from the air quite accurately.

"You're just not good enough," she goaded.

The third and final dart hit her in the shoulder and again she pulled it lose without showing any sign of drowsiness.

"Just give it up, Tris,"' she said, watching him as he fumbled in his jeans pockets for another round of the sleeping draughts. Whilst his head was down, she cracked the hilt of her blade against his skull, twice, knocking him into the wall. Expecting a more pained reaction, she was surprised when Tristian growled at her like an animal.

"I don't want to hurt you," he hissed. He eyes flashed the colour of light on water- silvery white and hypnotic.

"Shit," Kiya stood paralysed. "You're a fucking vampire!"

Tristian laughed wickedly, exposing his fangs to her as they grew lengthy in his mouth. "I did it for you, Kiya. I did it to become powerful. I know you like powerful men."

Kiya swung a fist in his direction, but he caught it in his hand and held her there- mid-hit.

"You don't know anything about me!" she shouted contemptuously.

"Oh- but I *do*," Tristian purred, revoltingly licking her knuckles with his pink tongue. "I know quite a bit about you, Kiya."

"Did you know I have a boyfriend?"

That did the trick. His face dropped witheringly.

"You're lying."

Kiya ripped her fist free and managed to get a punch to Tristian's temple, knocking him to the side ever so slightly. He retaliated with speedy blocks as she tried hitting him some more, and with a powerful kick to the abdomen, she grounded him at last.

"I have a man again. A real man-" she teased, standing over the creature she hated more than anything in the world.

"Who?" he demanded.

Kiya nodded her head towards Kieran, who was locked in battle with Zeke further down the corridor.

"One of the greatest Vampire Slayers I know."

Tristian spun his head around to get a good view of the man she was indicating and his eyes flashed so brightly, they were almost beacons of light.

"Even if somehow you managed to kill me tonight," she said collectedly, kneeling in front of him. "I know he'll rip your spine right from your back, and I'll go to Hell a happy woman knowing this."

Tristian's mouth fell open.

"Either way Tristian, you lose."

Kieran could hardly get a word in before Kiya was off, hitting Tristian over the head with her sword. He was aware the pair of them had issues, and it made him feel relieved that Kiya had the opportunity- at last- to let all her pent up anger out on the man that had killed Rycan.

He shifted his gaze to his old friend now.

Zeke was smiling and clicking his knuckles.

Kieran raised the sledgehammer.

"Not your usual weapon of choice," Zeke pointed out, showing no fear.

"I guess I'm Mister Unpredictable," Kieran replied equably.

"Does *Mister Unpredictable* like the idea of killing his best mate?"

Kieran twitched, but stood his ground. "A vampire killed my friend and planted a seed of evil inside of him. I'm here to put my old friend's body to rest."

It took a lot of energy out of him, but Kieran ran at the vampire with the sledgehammer held high, bringing it down where Zeke's head had been milliseconds before he avoided the blow. There was laughter. Kieran swung again, taking a chunk out of the wall and smashing mud all over his boots.

"Perhaps you should have stuck with the shot gun," Zeke suggested sarcastically. "That sledgehammer is making you look unprofessional in this business we call 'slaying.'"

Kieran gritted his teeth at Zeke's remark and threw the tool to the floor, snatching up a stake from his belt. It was smooth to the touch, due to a lot of sanding on warm summer afternoons, and had a deadly sharp point more efficient than any blade he had concealed on his person.

"Have a heart, Dude," Zeke muttered. "You don't want to stake me, do you?"

Kieran answered him with a rapid swish of his wrist, pushing the wooden tip into Zeke's shoulder and pulling it free again. Blood stained the stake and Zeke's snazzy new shirt.

"You missed the heart," he cried mockingly, pressing a hand to the wound. It healed in a matter of seconds.

"I wasn't aiming for the heart."

Zeke frowned. "So you're going to let me go?"

"No," he retorted. "I'm just taking my time."

Zeke ducked as the Slayer tried elbowing him in the nose, and spiralled away only to feel a heavy, metal capped boot smashing against his lower back, knocking him head first into the wall.

Kieran came up behind him quickly and pressed him against the wall using the broad length of his arms to hold him in place. Zeke was wriggling like a worm on a hook, but couldn't prevent the pressure that kept banging his face into the solid surface.

"You knew the code as well as I did," Kieran said crisply in his ear. "If a Slayer gets bitten and 'turned' he has a duty to kill himself before the turn is complete."

Zeke felt his teeth crack against the wall and tried to force his head to the side in order to speak.

"The prospect of disobeying your orders was too satisfying to pass on I'm afraid," he chirped mischievously, as if the force against him was nothing to worry about.

Kieran brought one of his fists back and staked the vampire between his shoulder blades, twisting it around until he screamed out in agony. Blood gushed out as he pulled the wooden tool free once more and mercifully, he let Zeke go, watching him flop to the floor. Like a cornered animal, he cowered in his friends shadow, then threw a dazzling smile his way.

"I smell that bitch all over you."

Kieran kicked Zeke in the face, who took it without flinching.

"You're crotch still has traces of her scent all over it."

He can tell I've had sex? Kieran thought in awe. *What a disgusting talent.*

"I had a feeling she'd fuck you in the end, seeing how desperately upset and in need of company she was."

His voice was angering Kieran now. He wanted to silence him for good.

Aiming for the heart, he brought the stake down fast and felt it fly free from his grasp as Zeke kicked it aside. His hands were empty, but his belt was still full of weaponry. He froze as Zeke shakily worked his way to his feet.

"Was she a good little whore in the bedroom?" he taunted. The stickiness on his back reminded him that his skin and clothes were heavily adorned with blood, and slowly, he unbuttoned his shirt, revealing his new rippling muscles. "Bet she tasted good, didn't she?"

"What are you getting at, Zeke? You jealous or something?"

Zeke laughed wildly. "I've had my fair share of fucks since I've been dead, don't you worry about that. But at least *my* women don't lie to me."

He paused.

"What are you talking about?"

Zeke folded his arms across his bare chest. "Didn't she mention to you she's pregnant?"

Silence followed, in which Kieran's face grew visibly paler.

Zeke was revelling in his effect on the Slayer. He watched in glee as Kieran stole a glance at his woman, mounted on Tristian as she kept punching him in the head repeatedly.

His sweat drenched countenance shuddered.

"She would have told me-"

"No, Kieran," he assured him. "It was only when I was close enough to smell her sweet, perfumed body that I detected another life growing inside of her. And I'm sorry to inform you buddy, but that baby was there before she met you, so don't go getting any ideas that your going to be a Daddy."

He swallowed painfully.

"She must not know herself."

Zeke shrugged. "Believe what you will. But even if she *hadn't* known before she met the two of us, I told her the night I had her alone in my grasp. She's had plenty of time to mention it to you since that night-"

Kieran didn't know what to think. He looked from Kiya to Zeke, then felt the anger flow through him again.

Zeke received a round house kick as Kieran flung himself at him, and his jaw felt as if it were on the brink of shattering as he lost his balance. Again, Kieran picked a stake from his belt and aimed for Zeke's chest.

There was panic in the vampire's silvery eyes. He needed something to throw the slayer off once more. Another mind blower. Something to give the man reason to doubt himself.

"Dude. Did you know we have Roxy?"

Kieran almost managed to embed the stake in Zeke's ribs, before he was able to move behind him and kick the Slayer to the ground. Stumbling like a idiot, his chin hit the dirt and left a burn mark on his skin.

"She's probably a vampire by now."

Kieran's chest rose and fell rapidly as he turned over, using his flat palms and sturdy arms to hold his upper body up.

"I don't believe you."

"When are you going to realise you can't save the day all the time, Kie'?" Zeke jeered. "Look at me. Your best mate. If you hadn't have gone all googly eyed at the new chick in the factory, none of this would have happened."

Kieran looked at the floor. He knew it wasn't true. He knew Zeke was just fucking with his head, but it didn't stop him from feeling terrible.

"You did this to yourself," he implored. "You chose to be a vampire instead of taking your life like you were meant to."

Zeke waved his hand in dismissal.

"Whatever. I'm getting bored now. Are we going to finish this or what?"

"Fed up of stalling me are you?" Kieran replied, flipping his body acrobatically until he was on his feet.

"Let's just say all this talking has made me hungry-"

His fangs glinted in the flickering light and Zeke threw himself at Kieran, gnashing his teeth like a piranha in hope of clasping onto his juicy neck. But Kieran punched him in the throat and used the space between their bodies to bring his hands up, placing them around Zeke's neck.

"I...don't...need...oxygen," he choked, laughing croakily.

"I know," Kieran said. "I'm just holding you still while my girlfriend does this."

Kiya was behind Zeke now, holding her samurai sword aloft and moved it back ready to swing it hard and fast.

"Any last words?" she asked flatly.

Zeke's eyes were wide with horror, then they narrowed with ferocity.

"Yeah," he looked directly at Kieran. "You're...a real...*prick*."

Kieran kept his face serene, trying not to portray his real feelings of gloominess as Kiya sliced the vampire's head clean off his neck- just millimetres from his hands- watching it bounce off the wall with an expression of astonishment still plastered on the vampire's face. The body itself burst into flames that singed the hairs on Kieran's arms, and to the floor it fell, covering his biker boots in a pile of ash.

Chapter 46

Officer Down

Her fingers were moist and grimy with blood and sweat, making it a struggle to reload her gun, as the yells and screams rose around her to a deafening magnitude. She was so absorbed in replenishing her ammunition that Emilia didn't spot the vampire heading towards her until it was too late.

Annara, blonde and bloodthirsty, threw her minions aside with outrageously powerful thrusts into the path of bullets, as she sprinted faster than a feline towards the female officer, whose gaze was stupidly averted from the battle.

Her silver eyes were pinned on her target.

Time slowed.

Annara hit so hard, Emilia was knocked clean off her feet, slamming her into the side of a police car and leaving a dent in its shiny metal frame. For a moment, she thought her back had been broken in two, but as Annara lifted her to her feet by her helmet, she felt her legs and lower body functioning on her command.

There was no time to fear what was happening.

Emilia brought her knee up between the female vampire's legs and cracked the protective knee pad into her bone, throwing her off for a moment. It gave her time to reach into her belt and pull out the bottle of holy water she had stowed away.

"Aren't you a clever little thing," Annara rasped, feeling a dull ache in her privates. She hadn't felt this bad since she'd suffered from her monthly periods- which thankfully ceased after she'd been bitten.

Emilia brought the bottle up with a free hand whilst Annara was digging her nails in the other, yet she felt hope leaving her as her attacker whacked it aside with an unanticipated kick.

The bottle smashed on the floor, spilling its contents uselessly on the pavement, and as Emilia watched, she felt a blow to her stomach, from the base of the vampire's right boot, falling into the side of the car once more.

Annara cocked her head to the side like a curious puppy and gave the female police officer a smile. "Why didn't you just run away when the reports came in of our war?" she asked with quiet alertness to the rest of her surroundings. When Emilia made to get up, she planted her boot against the woman's armoured chest and slammed her into the car for a third time, holding her in place. Annara wagged a finger at her disconcertingly. "Naughty, naughty. Playtime isn't over yet." Bending down, she lifted the woman up and tossed her like a rag doll over the roof of the car, with its flashing blue lights, and onto the concrete road beyond, just as a volley of bullets slammed into the side of the vehicle.

Annara slid over the bonnet and caught Emilia's hand as she lifted a can of liquefied silver out from her invisible bag of tricks.

With a merciless twist, Annara shattered the woman's wrist and relished in her cries of pain as the can fell.

"I don't get it," Annara said. "Why do you insist on hurting me when all I want to do is offer you eternal life?" She forced her fingers under the helmet protecting the officer's head and pried it lose, revealing a blotchy red, sweaty, yet breathtakingly beautiful face underneath, with slightly parted lips that sucked in the air around her in sheer panic. "Well aren't *you* a pretty one?"

Emilia gritted her teeth and then spat in Annara's face.

"Ooh!" she cooed. "Like a cobra when it's threatened! I like you."

Emilia couldn't stop trembling now. Inside she felt broken and her will was waning. The pain from her wrist was excruciating and all she could think about was her impending death.

Be strong, her mind encouraged. *Be strong. You can still win this. And some day, you'll have a home in the mountains and a family just like you've always dreamed of. You just need to get over this final hurdle. Fight back!*

"What's wrong?" the vampire queried, feigning sympathy as Emilia began to cry. "Are you feeling sad? Did the big bad vampire make the police lady break a nail?"

Emilia ignored Annara's insults and sarcasm and thought about her options.

"If I kill you, there's a better chance my people will win this war," Annara snarled gleefully, then trailed her tongue over Emilia's earlobe. "What will people do if their leading lady gets taken out?"

"There's a Slayer on the way," the police officer spoke up, slowly but loudly, so that the vampire could hear her over all the noise. "And when he gets here, he's going to make sure there's not even enough of you to fill my cat's litter tray, *bitch*."

Annara opened her mouth to reveal her fangs as she hissed in discontent.

Emilia forced a grin, knowing that she had touched a nerve.

"What's wrong? You're looking a little pale," she said derisively.

Annara snapped from her daze and returned her attention to the task at hand.

"I don't fear the Slayers. I killed one just a few nights ago as a matter of fact and made him my bitch, so you'll understand that I'm perfectly capable of looking after myself."

Emilia kept her cool. "So *you* were the one that killed Zeke?" She paused. "Well, we always knew he had it coming...being the weakest of the group, and all that. He was only a member of the team because he was good with gadgets and shit. The *real* Slayers will rip your cold dead heart out before you can even blink."

Annara put her hands on her hips and shifted her weight to one leg. "You're just feeding me bullshit in hope of being rescued soon, whilst I stand here and fret over the lame-ass warriors that cut our numbers down every now and again. Well, I've got news for you lady. Your Slayer is too late to save you now."

The light from Emilia's eyes faded as Annara jammed three fingers, with sharp black nails on each long tip, into the officer's jugular, drinking from the flow of blood that pumped out in streams as she pulled them free. With ground-shaking laughter, the vampire did the same to the opposite side of Emilia's neck, until she was bleeding from both sides.

"Delicious!" she declared, licking her fingers and kicking the woman until she was lying flat on the floor. "If only you knew how good this tastes-" She giggled as she smeared some of the blood over Emilia's quavering lips.

"I'm afraid," she continued calmly, "That I've decided to withdraw my offer of immortality to you." Patiently, she unclasped the officer's gear protecting her body and discarded it uncaringly, until she was dressed in nothing but a thin white t-shirt and pale blue knickers. From Emilia's trousers, Annara found a pocket knife and blithely played with the selection of tools it had to offer.

"Hmmm...," she mumbled thoughtfully. "I'd say you have less than two minutes to live, judging by the amount of blood gushing out of you."

Emilia's eyes closed, but not in unconsciousness. She just didn't want to see what the vampire was going to do to her.

Suddenly, she felt a chill across her stomach as the t-shirt was torn from her body and a further bite from the cold as her bra was cut off at the front. All that remained was the knickers, which Annara hacked off with the pocket knife, cutting her sensitive skin at the tops of her thighs.

"There," the vampire exclaimed in triumph. "Now you get to suffer from humiliation as well as a painful death, because I'm pretty sure those male officers that look up to you have often dreamed of seeing you out of your uniform. And who says vampires are cold hearted, hmm?"

Her body was cold. Ice cold.

Emilia couldn't move a muscle.

But in the darkness of her mind, she saw only smiling faces; her parents on the day she was accepted into the police force; her father when he was the first to hear about her promotion; the officer's at work on her thirtieth birthday, cheering and singing boisterously with drinks and a big chocolate cake laid out on her desk. And last of all... Kieran, on the day she'd shared her first kiss with him in high school.

They were all happy thoughts.

Being naked did not affect her final moments whatsoever.

When her life expired, she saw nothing but the love she'd shared with the greatest people she knew.

And now, I'll share the love of the greatest being of all, if He'll have me.

Annara left the woman the second she was sure she'd died.

Chapter 47

The Right Thing

The gate to the city was open and the toll booth deserted, which didn't come as a surprise when Siren passed through, driving the truck at a dangerous speed and braking as little as possible. If anything, it was an advantage not having to get out and speak with Sean to grant him access.

On route to the Stone Table, Siren saw things he had only ever witnessed in his nightmares.

Corpses littered the streets in mangled positions, bloody and torn- a most depressing and sickening sight. Children lay in the gutters beside their once happy homes, convulsing in pain as their life-blood dribbled from wide open gashes in their necks. Women were sprawled across the sidewalks, covered in grotesque wounds and staring blankly up at the stars- many of them missing garments of clothing.

At a glance, Siren deciphered that there were less men dying than children and women and as he moved further into the city, the headlights on his truck illuminated the faces of human males, checking over the bodies of the fallen and carrying away any hopefuls to a safe place.

His heart went out to them, and if he'd had the time, he would have stopped to help.

Some of the men stared at the vehicle with pleading eyes, as if begging Siren for assistance, but most were actually wrapped up in combat with the un-dead.

"Here's one!" a bearded, brute of a man cried as Siren drove by- his truck window rolled down all the way so he could hear the man's cries. The man had a vampire by the scruff of its neck- a young one, very much new to the game- and threw him to the ground. Siren pushed his foot down on the brake to see what the man planned on doing, and it became obvious when three other men sprang out from the shadows bearing wooden baseball bats. Together, they pummelled the vampire until it was a bloody, fleshy smear on the floor.

When at last Siren reached his destination, he parked the truck haphazardly in the middle of the road, behind some police vehicles with flashing lights, and was met by a group of vampires that had been skulking in the shadows. Siren guessed that they had been planning to drag a few officers away from the battle, but had decided to take out the man with the whopping great big sword on his back instead.

Two males. One female.

They circled him like a pack of hungry dogs, licking their lips and laughing menacingly as they pretended to lunge forward, only to retreat again.

Siren didn't blink.

"Are you planning on striking soon, or shall I make the first move?" he asked casually, allowing the moonlight to glint off the deadly edge of his blade.

Without waiting for an answer, he performed a neat three hundred and sixty degree spin, and watched as the head of each vampire slid off their bodies- thudding to the floor.

"You wouldn't have liked how I taste anyway," he said smartly, kicking a severed head from his sight. The bodies burst into flames all around him, alarming some of the officers who were just metres away and he gave them all a reassuring wave.

"How's it looking?" he questioned a random officer, whose helmet was cracked at the front and missing its tinted visor. He was taking the moment to reload his gun with panicked fingers.

"How do you think it's looking, numb nuts? There's too many of them! These suckers just won't fall and when they get past us, we can't go chasing them into the city. This is fucking futile." The man was panting and with a cry of despair, he dropped most of his ammo on the floor. "Ah, shit!"

Siren assisted him by striking his blade at an oncoming attacker, cutting a neat line between his eyes, making his skull split in half like a melon. Seconds later, the flailing beast was a pile of ash at their feet.

"Hey, who are you?" the officer asked in bewilderment as Siren shook some of the blood from his sword.

"Just a man- like you."

The officer managed a smile. "I wish we had more men like you on the force. We'd have slaughtered the lot of these fuckers by now!"

Siren kept an expressionless face. "You are doing well. Don't give up. And about the vampires that get through- I've seen men grouping together in the city to take some of them out. Not all is lost, I promise you. Now tell me, where can I find Emilia?"

The officer's attention was drawn away for a moment as a vampire a few yards ahead felt the agony of his knee caps being blown off, and with a determined furrowing of the brow, he put three silver bullets in its brain.

"What was that?" he yelled over the sound of gunshots.

"Emilia. Where is she?"

The man shrugged. "You're gonna have to make your way around and find her. Everyone looks the fucking same in these stupid fucking police helmets!"

He was right. Siren could hardly tell the difference from one officer to the next, standing at the edge of the ash strewn ground of the Stone Circle. With helmets masking faces, he had no choice but to judge the *bodies* of the humans around him, trying to pick out the curvaceous figures of any females.

"Emilia?" He put a hand on the shoulder of the person he believed was her, and received an uppercut to the nose from a woman who obviously showed no recognition towards him.

"I apologise," Siren spluttered, holding a hand to his aching face. "I didn't mean to alarm you."

"You shouldn't be creeping up on people like that!" she yelled over her shoulder. "Return to your home and secure the doors for your own safety!"

"I assure you, I can take care of myself." Siren bowed and left the woman, moving on as swiftly as his legs would allow.

Just when he was convinced she was no longer present, Siren noticed a woman moving out from behind a police car- tall, blonde and covered in blood. Instead of running away from the Stone Table, she was heading *towards* it- crouching on the side lines in preparation to dart forward.

Something is wrong, Siren thought. He didn't like the way blood was dripping from the woman's lips, as if she had just scored big.

The vampire was gone before he could reach her, but at last, he found Emilia.

"No..."

She was lying on her back, eyes closed and breasts exposed to the world, as well as the bristly feminine hairs between her long legs. Her hair was lying in a scarlet puddle, and her neck was leaking the last of her blood.

Siren gagged. He'd seen death before, but never so full of malice. Emilia's corpse had blatantly been left there as an example to the rest of the human population. Whoever had bitten her wanted the police officers to know there was no hope for them.

Cautiously, he bent down and touched her face. There was no reaction.

I came too late, he thought broken heartedly. *This is really going to rub salt in Kieran's wounds when I tell him.*

Five minutes of silent praying past, in which Siren shed his jacket to place over Emilia's cold skin and wearily, he held his Samurai sword forth.

"I can't be sure if you'll rise again and be one of them, or if you have just past safely on to the kingdom of Heaven," he whispered despairingly. "But even so, I must do this. It is my duty and as a friend, I wouldn't want you to face eternity as a walking corpse. You deserve better than that. I will see to it that you are buried in a grave that speaks of your remarkable bravery in the midst of this Hell."

With a steady hand for precision, he brought his sword down hard against her soft, blood spattered neck, separating the head from the body.

Doing the right thing hurt.

Chapter 48

Bad Mother

Tristian was unconscious, lying with his fangs in the dirt and his greasy black hair covering most of his sweaty face. His head had taken so many blows from Kiya's relentless fists that his mind had decided to shut down, like a computer with a virus, and now, he was at the mercy of the woman he loved unrequitedly.

Kiya was tense. She'd helped Kieran finish Zeke off; he was looking terribly distraught now that it was over-pacing back and forward- glancing at the pile of ash where his best friend had once stood.

She wasn't sure what to say.

It had been a surprise when she'd caught his signal to assist him in the midst of their vendetta and deep down inside, she'd wished there had been a less disturbing way of killing the poor guy. But a sword was all she'd had at the ready, so a sword was what Zeke got.

The air smelt of blood, burning flesh and pungent bodily odours. It clung to Kiya's skin and seeped up into her nostrils until the need for fresh air became stifling and unbearable. Her brow prickled with sweat and the skin around her lips tasted strongly of salt. Getting Tristian under her control had certainly taken a lot of effort- the aches and pains in her arms and lower back proved it.

"We should move," she said, blowing a loose strand of hair out of her eyes. It had been tickling her nose for quite some time.

Kieran was standing still now, leaning against the wall with his head against the top of his right arm and his back arched to take some of the weight off his legs. The luscious long strands of his hair cascaded over his watery eyes as he focused on the darkness that his arm created- a world that was permeated with the sound of his breath and the dim flickering of light from the burning torches on the wall. The pain in his chest gradually subsided as his heart rate began to slow to an almost regular pace.

Kiya stole a look at Tristian, feeling as if she were in the middle of a tug of war, in which *she* was the rope. On one side was her lover- in need of kindness and comforting words by the look of it- and on the other, the man she wanted to tear apart with her bare hands.

Eventually, she moved in the direction of her new captive, pulling the long leather strap from the back of her jacket, which had been designed to tie up at the front when the weather was too much to bare. Now, it acted as the perfect rope to bind Tristian's wrists at the base of his spine.

"You're not getting away this time," she vowed in his unclean ear-hole.

There was nothing more she could do with him. Roxy was still missing, therefore, the mission was far from complete. Torturing the sick bastard would have to wait.

"I think we should start checking rooms-"

"You're...pregnant."

Kiya froze.

Kieran's head turned towards her, his hair parting to reveal a steely gaze.

"How did you-"

"Zeke."

She should have expected this. Zeke had tasted the delights of vampirism, and on discovering she was pregnant, he couldn't wait to tell his old friend that his new love interest was keeping secrets from him- knowing it would bring him as much satisfaction to share the information as it would draining blood from a newborn baby.

Kiya moved her lips as if to say something, then closed her mouth in defeat.

"Were you ever planning on telling me, or were you just going to let me think you were putting on weight as time went by?" he asked stiffly.

Kiya frowned, showing hurt in the lines of her face.

He stood up straight now, facing her directly.

The sword in Kiya's hand felt strangely heavier.

"At first, I didn't think it was your business," she began, finding her voice at last. It was Kieran's turn to look hurt, but she continued before he could think her wicked. "But when I started to fall for you, I realised how much I wanted you to know." His solemn expression morphed into neutral. "I just didn't know how to say the words. This is like...like a foreign experience to me. I've never even missed a period and had a scare, you know? So it's been hard, knowing that I have something growing inside of me. I have no friends to ask for their advice and my mother has decided I'm a criminal. And with so much going on in *your* life, I didn't think now was the time to tell you."

Kieran's face softened.

"I'm not angry because you lied to me," he said, taking a step forward. "I'm angry that you've put yourself in danger of losing your baby."

Kiya was befuddled. She'd expected Kieran to rip into her about being dishonest from day one, but instead, he was showing concern for the baby's well being- almost as if it were his.

"Well, that's just it. I'm not concerned about it getting hurt-" He looked completely in awe at her words, until she finished what she was saying. "But as a Healer, I've been channelling my powers to protect my womb so that the baby doesn't get effected by my unpredictable lifestyle as a Slayer. It's like a cushion to soften the blows."

"Channelling your power? Can you actually do that? I thought you weren't very good at conjuring your healing talents?"

"I'm pretty sure it's working."

Kieran sighed.

"I just wished you'd have told me this before."

Kiya waved a hand in the air. "Can't you understand why I didn't? I've known you for a few days and already I'm crazy about you. I couldn't be sure you'd see this baby as a positive aspect to the relationship we've developed. Do you see what I mean?"

He moved forward until he could feel her breath against his neck and swooped down to capture her lips with his own.

"When I say I love you, I mean I love *everything* about you. That goes for the cluster of cells in your womb that's gonna give you hell for nine months and a further eighteen years until its ready to move out."

Kieran noticed the brightness leaving Kiya's eyes all of a sudden, as a wave of misery ensued.

"Did I say something wrong?" he queried, losing his smile in an instant.

She looked down at her feet. "I don't think I'll make a good mother."

Lovingly, Kieran stroked the leather that coated her arms, keeping the motion consistent. He was nervous and didn't know how to console her. When Zeke had told him she was pregnant, he had been teetering on the edge of devastation. He had spent the evening previously picturing Kiya at his side for many years to come, riding wild through the night on his motorbike and making love to her in as many positions, and at as many different destinations, as possible. But on hearing about the baby, the imagery in his head had congealed into an ugly picture of a tired, unappealing face, clutching a baby to swollen breasts and rocking it as it wailed endlessly in the early hours of the morning. In this picture, Kieran wasn't present.

"How do you know you'll be a bad mother if you haven't even given it a try?"

She shrugged. "Because I'm already making mistakes."

Tenderly, he pressed her head against his chest. "You're not making mistakes. You're trying to make the right choices. If I was in your position, I probably wouldn't have said anything either."

She glanced up at him to inspect if his face held traces of dishonesty.

"Do you hate me for what I've done to you?"

"I could never hate you."

He gently kissed her forehead. Behind them, Tristian mumbled in his unconscious state. It seemed that even in his sleep, he disapproved of Kiya receiving affection from anyone but him.

"Now, are you sure that baby of yours is safe, because if I had my way, you would never have come on this mission if there was a chance of putting its life in jeopardy."

Kiya touched her abdomen and closed her eyes. The prickle of power in her veins reassured her of its safety and she snapped from her trance with a smile.

"Everything is fine."

Suddenly, a scream ripped through the air. It was a name.

Sonja.

Any further thoughts of pregnancy evaporated from their minds and the pair set off at a dead run.

Chapter 49

Jealousy

"I just came back from the Stone Circle."

Logan's eyes were pinned on Annara as he forced himself to keep his composure. If he showed weakness, he may lose everything, and by flitting his gaze back and forward from her face to her hands, he could judge by her movements and expression when she was preparing to strike.

And strike she would.

"As much as it pains me to say it, I'm angry with myself for not realising your potential to betray our kind."

Logan stood in quiet alertness. He had little to say at this point, only a constant nagging in his mind to keep Roxy safe and an unnerving, cold dread kept running up his spine.

"I had to leave," she continued. "Our army was embarrassing me. We should have waited longer to recruit more men and trained them harder, but I guess you couldn't wait to be alone with this skinny piece of trash."

"Fuck you!" Roxy shouted over Logan's shoulder.

Annara grinned cruel naturedly. "I'd keep your mouth shut if I were you little girl, or you might find yourself with no hair at all next time I have a pair of scissors in my hand."

Roxy's nose wrinkled in fury. Her eyes narrowed to slits. She wanted more than anything to go down there and rip large chunks of that bleached blonde mess of a hairstyle off Annara's ugly head, but Logan had a hand pressed against her stomach, convincing her to stay put.

"The army was never really my concern," he informed her, with clearly spoken words. "That's why I left you in charge of it, so you only have *yourself* to blame if things aren't going according to plan."

Annara stamped her foot. "The army isn't the real issue here!"

Logan shrugged nonchalantly, keeping his cool. "You brought it up."

She was getting tetchy, but sucked in oxygen she didn't even need to douse out the fire in the pit of her stomach. Her fangs receded in her mouth, making it less of a chore to speak.

"I went to Shannon's bedroom on the way here."

Logan remained unaffected by her words.

"She wasn't there, but the room reeks of burning flesh and her night gown was absent of a body. Know anything about that?"

"Indeed I do," he replied. "I killed her."

Annara looked dumbstruck. "But you loved your sister-"

"I love Sonja more."

The words stung her like a blade to her heart. Slowly, she raised a hand to her chest. "I *can't* believe what I'm *hearing*."

"You should," he snapped, letting aggression leak into his tone of voice.

Annara was undeterred by the flash of red in Logan's eyes. She wanted him to get angry- wanted him to let his guard down a little so she could reach the waif of a girl that lingered behind him with a stupidly defiant expression she just *couldn't* wait to wipe off her face. The raging anger inside of her stirred hungrily as she watched Roxy slip an arm around Logan's waist, pressing her breasts against his back and peering over his shoulder. He closed his eyes to relish her touch then threw a hostile look Annara's way.

"Leave now and I'll forget you ever existed."

She laughed. "You think it's going to be that easy to get rid of me?"

"I think if you want to stay alive, you'll heed my advice."

"Fuck you. How's that sound?"

Logan didn't answer. He placed a hand over Roxy's, which was resting below his navel. She was trembling, but her face was trained not to betray how frightened she was feeling.

"I love you," she whispered in his ear, loud enough only for him to pick up.

He smiled grimly. It was as if she was saying her goodbyes.

"Tell me why you love him?!" Annara cried up to the two lovers, standing entwined and radiating their affection for one another. It made her ill, seeing Logan touching a human in such a tender way.

Roxy blushed.

"She doesn't have to answer that," Logan spoke for her.

Annara lifted both hands into the air, flattening her palms and bending her arms in a half-shrug. "Why not?

Am I not owed an explanation for your betrayal? If she loves you, I want to know how much, because I'm pretty sure its not even a *fraction* of the amount of feelings *I* have for you."

She was putting her un-beating heart on the line here- speaking from the hollow where her soul once rested.

"You'll never know what it's like for the pair of us. We grew up together. We've suffered heart break when we were torn apart. But our destiny was to be partners. Time never changed the love we felt for each other."

"I asked for an explanation, not a fucking poem you dumb bitch," she said scornfully. "And I'm pretty sure I've read that monologue in a girly magazine I rifled through one night, after cutting a teenage girl's head off in her own bed." She waited for a reaction from the young Slayer, but got nothing. "Don't you find it disgusting at all," she pressed on, "that your boyfriend takes human lives to survive?"

The shine in Roxy's eyes dulled for a moment. She looked down at Logan's polished shoes- at the distorted reflection of her unhappy face.

"I won't be doing that anymore," he told her, squeezing Roxy's hand in reassurance. The light returned to her pretty, rosy cheeked face. Annara gathered that there was enough trust in the Slayer's heart that if her vampire lover said he was going to get a tan on the beach this summer, she'd offer to rub in some lotion unthinkingly. Pathetic.

"I guess I wasn't invited to the wedding after all," Annara said flippantly, gesturing unnecessarily to the dead Father Casey, whose Bible was resting on the floor beside his shoulder. "Maybe it's just as well. When I was made a vampire, I made sure my husband, Mikel, was the first to die a horrible death and didn't feel enough compassion in me to make him a vampire too. I've never been a one-man kind of girl deep down. Who was I to kid myself that we were going to be happy together?"

"My thought's exactly," Logan said. "Everyone knows how much of a whore you are Annara."

Her eyes flashed silver and her teeth grated against each other.

"At least I'm not a virgin to my kind."

"Who wants to fuck a vampire, when all they really care about is a higher status once they've sucked the dick of someone with power? You're the same Annara. You only wanted to fuck me so you could find your place at my side and boss everyone around. Well here's some news for you...I would never dream of having a cock-sucking, bad-haired bitch like you share my throne. In fact, my intention was to have you executed on the sly if you ever came back from the war alive."

"You fucker," she growled, in boiling outrage. "You complete and utter fuck-wit."

Logan could tell she was ready to take this further.

Violence was only to be expected among their kind.

As anticipated, Annara ran at him, focusing on his handsome face and dreamy, natural blonde hair. Everything above the neck had her attention and as she threw her punch, Logan was astounded to discover that she missed her target.

But Annara had never intended to hit Logan.

Behind him, Roxy loosened her grip on his waist. Her mouth opened in puzzlement and fear.

The vampire had made her enemies think she'd been aiming for the Master, but instead, she reached over his shoulder and smashed her knuckles into Roxy's left eye with brutal force, knocking her into the throne with staggering precision.

Logan's eyes flashed red. If he were human, he would have hyperventilated.

As he twisted his head to glance in panic at his missing bride-to-be, Annara kicked him in the balls, followed by a toe-punt to his chin, where he felt the bone fracture agonisingly.

Annara was known for many things, and one of them was her speed. She'd lived for hundreds of years, studying humans and their weaknesses. She'd tested her skill on men- with their delusion of being protectors of the innocent- and had always managed to slaughter the idiotic bastards with ease. Her speed had made it easier for her to destroy lives. Never in her long life time had she come across anyone, human or otherwise, that could match it.

This time was no different.

As Logan screamed in pure despair, Annara was behind him and upon his lover in the blink of an eye.

She allowed her smile to stretch as wide as it would go and made a point of flashing her impressive cleavage as she rained down on the Slayer at the foot of the throne.

Her fingers uncurled from their balled up state and she swiped them down with all the energy she could muster.

Roxy's mouth clamped shut and her eyelids pressed together as she forced the image of Annara out of her head- waiting for the blow to come.

She had only milliseconds to consider how close she'd come to marrying her soul mate and felt a small pang of regret at not getting the chance to whisper the words "I do," to her beloved.

The pain would have made a person insane for life if there was ever a chance at survival.

As an accompaniment to the sound of her heart beating furiously in her chest, Roxy could hear the sound of her name being screamed by Logan.

Sonja.

The name her mother had blessed her with a couple of hours after she had been brought into the world.

She wished she'd had the opportunity to tell Kieran and the other Slayers what her real name was and perhaps shared more of her memories with them. They were good, trustworthy friends after all.

"Sonja!"

That grin. It was full of merriment and ecstasy.

Logan caught a glimpse of it before he could get his hands on the female vampire.

Annara found it to be almost orgasmic as she ripped the soft, pink flesh of Roxy's throat away, leaving a yawning, bloody gash in her neck as her head crashed to the floor with a disturbing 'thud.'

She marvelled as red liquid spurted out in rivulets, splashing against her boots.

"Say I love you now I have your fucking voice box," she laughed, waving the gory mass in her hand at the lifeless body.

Her laughter filled the throne room.

Chapter 50

Denial

No.

No.

This isn't real.

This...isn't...happening.

Vampires have nightmares don't they? I'm sure I woke from a dream once, covered in sweat and smelling faintly of blood from a meal I'd had before taking a nap.

This is like that time.

A nightmare.

It must be.

I'm going to wake up soon.

I'm going to open my eyes and this'll be nothing but a sickening thought in the back of my tired mind.

Sonja is still with me.

We will wed.

We will live happily ever after.

There are many more moments we've yet to share.

Wake up.

Please *wake up.*

I love her too *much.*

Chapter 51

Falling Men

Siren had lost count. Lost count of how many heads he'd lobbed off as he continually pirouetted- dancing with his blade- showering blood all over the grass.

The vampires dropped liked flies in an extermination.

He'd informed the officer's closest to him of Emilia's death and had asked that they clear a space for him in their circle around the stones; a circle that had grown a lot smaller as the hours progressed, slowly but surely.

"You're a mad man!" one of the officer's had bellowed, ceasing fire for a moment. "They'll rush straight at you when they see you aren't one of us. You'll be up to your ears in the fuckers before you can cry your mother's name."

"You underestimate me," Siren replied quickly. "I do not fear these animals."

"Yeah," the man laughed unpleasantly. "And neither do they fear you."

Siren was never one to show his anger. He kept a calm air about him, making him an approachable and likeable character, but seeing the state Emilia had been in on his arrival had made him feel a little testy.

"Clear some space," he barked.

"Whatever asshole," the officer had replied, no longer doing him the honour of speaking to his face. Showing how obligated he felt to do so, the officer eventually shuffled over, urging a fellow 'boy in blue' to move further down the line.

Give me everything you've got.

As well as vampires, werewolves had joined the fray- big and vicious, even out of their wolf-form. They threw officers aside like an ice cream van would a child, racing into the city making howling noises and barking like the dogs they were just a few nights a year.

One werewolf took it upon himself to run at the Vampire Slayer, who had killed more vampires in one hour than any of the officers had killed since the war had begun.

"I see you, you hairy bastard," Siren muttered under his breath, getting his sword at the ready.

When the werewolf came into range, he brought the sword down at a slant, cutting it from right, to left. But he hadn't counted on it getting wedged between flesh and bone, and as he felt the blade fly from his hand, the angry beast swatted him to the ground.

Pain bolted through Siren's head. His ears thrummed and his nose tickled with the moistness of warm blood. Somewhere inside his mouth, a tooth had loosened from its protective gum.

"Fuck me!"

Being a talented fighter, Siren breathed as normal- keeping his cool to the best of his ability- and plucked a knife from his boot, just as the werewolf ripped the Samurai sword from its bleeding chest.

Apparently, the blade had missed his heart.

Ah, nuts.

The werewolf looked far from amused as the stench of his own blood filled his flaring nostrils.

"Painful?" Siren asked it.

The creature howled as the Slayer stabbed the knife into its thigh, using the hilt as support to lift his body from the concrete. But as he found his feet, he felt the beasts hand around his throat.

"I'll crush the life out of you," it cried, making wheezing noises from all the pain.

The blood vessels in Siren's eyes exploded. His veins became ten times more visible.

"This is for our great Master," the creature said, driving Siren's sword into his gut.

Before Siren could black out from lack of oxygen, the werewolf dropped him to the floor.

The pain sent his body into violent convulsions and he almost felt embarrassed as his attacker slinked away into the city, shockingly still alive even after the loss of so much blood.

In the distance, police siren's sounded.

"The Karanthian's!" someone screamed. The word spread like a fire in a field of dry, yellow grass.

The despair in the atmosphere melted to relief.

The Karanthian police force had been alerted to Meridion's predicament well over five hours previous to the assembling of men at the Stone Circle, but due to the distance between the cities, they had had no choice but to arrive fashionably late.

And with the police force, there came the ambulances.

"This one's still alive!"

Siren was faintly aware of a hand against his wrist.

After much effort, his eyes depicted the blurry outline of a man in a green t-shirt and trousers, bearing a yellow 'Paramedic' label, which was sowed smartly in italics on the man's breast pocket.

"You're in good hands mate," he said, his tone bearing a positive attitude that gave injured people the hope they desperately needed. "The blade looks as if its missed your main organs."

Siren managed a sloppy smile and in the strong arms of two ambulance men, he allowed the darkness on the borders of his vision to overwhelm the light.

Chapter 52

Feeling The Burn

It hurt so badly.

He hadn't wanted to believe it, but what he saw was as clear as a sunrise in a cloudless sky.

Roxy was dead.

Gone.

Forever.

A part of him had died all over again as he stared into the lifeless eyes of his true-love. The beautiful prom-dress he'd obtained as a special gift for her was now more of a dark shade of red than its original green colour.

Roxy resembled a china doll. Pale, stiff face and lifeless limbs. It made his heart jolt just to look at her. Knowing she was lost to him now.

Annara was standing with her legs slightly parted and her head dipped low, trying to give her silver eyes an even more satanic touch by showing more white than anything. Her chest rose and fell sharply as she imitated the human need to breathe- her impressive cleavage sparkling with droplets of fresh blood. She held her hands bunched up in fists and her eyes remained transfixed on the Master. Her muscles were rigid and her body poised.

Although she felt giddy from the taste of Roxy's blood- after licking it from her finger tips- she was ready to finish what she had started.

"Whore!" Logan screamed, pouring all his pain and hate into the word.

"Yeah, yeah!" she retorted. "Tell me something new, *asshole*."

Suddenly, he moved towards her at an astonishing rate, throwing the altar into the air and slamming its top into her stomach. Annara fell to the ground under the weight of the wood and she felt her thighs getting crushed as Logan pressed the table into her flesh. She tried to slide her fingers under the edge and lift it, but the vampire Master's weight combined with the heavy table made it impossible for her to move.

"You're going to pay for what you just did you fucking bitch!" he spat, spraying saliva and tears over her blood stained face.

Summoning all the energy he had, Logan punched the altar in its centre, splitting the wood in half. Annara felt the pressure easing instantly against her thighs and she began the awkward process of wriggling free.

"No you don't," he hissed vehemently. His fingers twisted through her hair and dragged her to her feet.

Before Annara could deflect his movement, Logan's arms rose, where he then placed both hands on either side of her face.

For a fleeting moment, she thought he was going to kiss her fiercely.

His eyes bored into hers- watery and full of vampiric fire at the same time.

But instead of a wild and unexpected kiss, she felt his two thumbs slipping over her eyelids.

Panic ensued.

"No!" she screeched, grabbing both of Logan's wrists and trying to pry him off her head.

"*I hate you*," he exclaimed hoarsely, his voice bearing no pity as he pushed Annara's eyes further into the back of her skull, feeling the moistness as they squished beneath his flesh.

She screamed like he'd never heard a creature scream before. Her voice punctuated his earlobes painfully and left them ringing even after he punched her in the neck to silence her.

She fell backwards and hit the floor with a thud, a metre or so away from the dead Father Casey.

I can't see! I can't see! her mind bellowed in the darkness. *This can't be fucking happening!*

The sound of footsteps padding against the soft dirt floor alerted her to Logan's presence. He was moving away from her.

"We were both fools," Logan said, bending down and pulling the wooden stake from the Priest's back. "I trusted you, and *you* trusted me. Now look where it's led us."

Annara was biting back sobs. If she was going to die- *again*- it would be with as much dignity as she could muster. But who was she kidding? She wanted to live! More than anything else in the world she wanted to keep playing her games among the humans- an outcast to God's kingdom and a fearer of Hell's gates.

She didn't want to die. Dear God, she didn't want to die.

"What you have done to me," Logan continued, "hurts more than any wound ever could."

"I loved you, you bastard!" Annara yelled suddenly. She wasn't facing him as she spoke; she couldn't tell where he was now that she had lost the use of both eyes. "I loved you! More than *she* ever did"

"Stop saying that!" Logan replied with a bitter edge to his command. "Stop talking like you know her and listen to the sound of this stake cutting through the air as it falls to meet your chest."

"*Please*!"

Blindly, she reached out.

Logan avoided her flailing hands and screwed his face up in disgust. Annara was a sorry sight to see. Blood caked her cheeks as it had spilled from her mangled eye sockets.

"Burn, bitch," he muttered, forcing the wood between her breasts.

Her mouth opened wide.

The expression on her mutilated face was the last to go up in flames.

Chapter 53

Ashes to Ashes, Dust to Dust

"It came from in there!" Kiya waved her hand at a partially opened door.

"I heard it too," Kieran confirmed, taking a deep breath.

As Kiya made to run forward, he looped his arm around her waist and pulled her in to his chest, obstructing her route to the door.

"Kiss me."

Kiya's surprise faded in a heart beat as she parted her lips and planted a kiss on Kieran's mouth, feeling the rough brush of his stubble against her chin. He tasted delicious.

Kieran said nothing as he released her, leading the way into the room with a pistol in one hand and a wooden stake in the other.

Logan lay beside Roxy's corpse, sobbing quietly to himself as he stroked her lovely face with quivering fingers. He tried not to trail his eyes over the hole in her neck and in a sudden brainwave laced with hope, he bit his hand and dripped scarlet droplets into her mouth, praying emphatically that it might rouse her from an eternity of darkness.

But there was no way she would wake now. Not even as a vampire.

"I failed you," he cried, pressing his forehead against her shoulder. Blood from her dress smeared across his skin where his hand gripped her thigh. "I'm so sorry."

Just as he was about to lean in and kiss her cold lips, there came a disturbance at his door.

The first thing Kieran noticed was the Priest on the floor. The second- a good looking young man bent over a scarily still Roxy.

He raised the gun to the beast bearing strange, red, tearful eyes.

"Step away from her."

Logan sniffed and lifted his hands in obedience, climbing to his feet unsteadily.

"He's got Roxy," Kiya whispered in her lover's ear, although it was unnecessary for her to say so. Kieran could already see her lying against the throne.

He kept his voice firm and steady.

"Come closer."

Logan glanced at Roxy one last time, then edged towards the Slayer holding the shiny gun that was aimed at his heart.

"You don't have to do that," Logan said, lowering his hands. He wiped his nose on the sleeve of his expensive suite, feeling no embarrassment in doing so.

"I'll do what makes me feel comfortable around you, thank you very much."

Kiya could see Kieran's eyes full of wild ferocity. She could tell it was hard for him to keep a straight face- holding back the urge to lash out.

"She dead?"

Logan made a sound of despair, choking on the word "Yes" as more tears started to flood from his relentless ducts.

"You killed her?" His sentences were short and to the point. Kiya could feel her heart sinking with every word and every pause that passed.

"I loved her."

Kieran ignored the declaration. "What are you?"

"Excuse me?" Logan lifted his head in confusion. His eyes were no longer blazing red.

Kieran stepped forward, becoming more aggressive. "I said, what are you? Human or *scum*?"

In the dim light, it was hard to tell if he had fangs.

"You're that guy from the pet shop," Kiya marvelled half heartedly.

"Logan," he replied with a nod. He recognised the Slayer- the one who had disturbed Roxy and him when they were about to get intimate.

"That doesn't answer my question," Kieran snapped. His finger slid against the trigger of his gun impatiently.

"Vampire," the young man informed them both, moments before Kieran's fist connected with the creature's jaw.

Logan fell and didn't get up. He was too weak.

"You killed her didn't you!?"

Repeatedly, with sobs of anger and despair mixed together, Kieran kicked the man on the floor with his metal capped boots, causing more damage than normal shoes would. And like a frightened child, the vampire took the beating.

"Kieran! Kieran," Kiya chimed in, pulling on his arm in an attempt to stop him. "Let him talk! For fuck sake-"

"He's a vampire!"

"He can tell us what happened to her. Don't you want to know how this happened? You're not thinking straight!"

His breath escaped him in ragged gasps. Logan was a bloody, beaten mess at his feet.

"Speak," he rasped. Once again, he lifted the gun and pointed it at the young man's face.

"What is there to say?" the heart broken, night dwelling fiend asked wearily. He felt completely drained of the life force that sustained his half-dead body. "I brought her down here so we could be wed-"

"Wed!?" Kieran interrupted incredulously. "Are you fucking serious? Vampire's are getting married these days? Is this some sort of joke?" He glanced at Kiya, who was showing no sign of amusement at his rant. "I suppose you dragged her here against her will?"

"No. Not quite," Logan responded dryly. He didn't like the way the Slayer lacked in knowledge of his utmost love and devotion to Roxy. "She was brought here by your friend, on my orders, so that I could speak with her."

"But she was kidnapped. Her hair was all over the floor-"

"That was an unfortunate event that I had never given my word to perform. The girl who did it- the girl who killed Sonja- is dead."

"How?"

"I staked her-"

"No," Kieran said firmly. "How did she-" he faltered slightly, "-kill Roxy?"

Logan bowed his head. "You can see for yourself." He gestured miserably to where Roxy lay, then sighed "Is that all?"

Kieran was lost in thought for a moment.

"Is that all?" he cried again, looking at both the Vampire Slayer's in misery.

"Yes," Kieran mumbled. "Accept for one more thing-"

"Yes?"

"I'm afraid I can't let you leave this place alive."

Kiya shot a look at Kieran, who was squeezing the trigger of his gun. To both their surprise, Logan took the bullet in the shoulder, knowing full well he could have dodged the small piece of silver with his vampiric abilities.

He crashed to his knees.

Kiya was trapped in the slowest minute of her life. Her eyes studied the hole in Logan's suit with a vague feeling of sympathy swelling in her chest.

"I...I wasn't planning on staying anyway," Logan wheezed, putting a hand out. Kieran stood in bewilderment, watching as the vampire latched a hand onto his belt. Slowly, the vampire pulled a stake free and gripped it tightly.

Kieran took a step back, unsure of what he was planning.

"I...I loved her," Logan assured them. "I did. And I can't live without her."

Kiya whispered Kieran's name. He was paralysed-caught in the moment.

"I know I won't see her where I'm heading, but maybe my soul, wherever it is, has found hers and they'll be together in that great void where the angels play."

A tear sprung to Kiya's eye. It was all taking its toll on her now.

Rycan was dead. Roxy was dead. Zeke was dead. Siren was off fighting in some war, *alone*. How many more people was she going to lose before the month was up?

"I'm going to make this easy on you, since you both cared enough to come down here and save her from me," Logan said, barely above a whisper.

Kieran suppressed a look of astonishment as he watched, for the first time in his career, as a vampire willingly staked himself; gritting its teeth against the pain as its flesh bubbled and burnt, until their was barely enough of him to hold in the palm of your hand.

Silence followed.

Kiya placed a hand on Kieran's shoulder, and in that moment, he broke down and cried.

Chapter 54

Grave

Kiya allowed Kieran to spend as long as he needed at Roxy's side, watching him from afar as he kissed her goodbye and placed the white cloth from the splintered remains of the altar over her face.

He said nothing as he carried the young Slayer out of the underground labyrinth, feeling a small pang of relief as the sunlight on the horizon met his eyes, illuminating the bottoms of black clouds that were beginning to break up into less threatening grey puffs. The ground was slick with rain and the air smelt strongly of burning flesh. His boots slipped about in the mud, but his solid frame persisted in keeping its balance as he moved between the gravestones.

"I'll walk from here," he said plaintively. "You can take the bike." He forced a grim smile to his perfect lips, encouraging his hesitant girlfriend to take the keys from his hand.

Kiya didn't want to argue, but she also didn't like the idea of Kieran trudging for hours in the wastelands with a dead body in his hands. It could mess up a man's head.

"Maybe you should try and-"

"Please," he stopped her. His eyes were full of pain. "Please do this for me."

She nodded, trying to show understanding, but feeling like she was being tossed into a dark pit- not knowing what lay in wait for her.

"You should call Siren."

"He'll come home when he's ready."

"But what if he's-"

"*He'll come home when he's ready.*"

His tone frightened her and she decided it was probably best for the both of them if she left him to his thoughts. He didn't mean to get angry. He was just a little on the sensitive side right now.

"See you when you get back," she muttered gloomily, dragging Tristian along by the end of the rope tied around his wrists. It was a struggle, now that the ground was uneven with grassy clumps and muddy humps, and eventually, she picked the slimy bastard up, slinging him over her shoulder and gritting her teeth against the touch of his skin on hers.

He fell from the motorbike once during the ride back, scuffing up his face badly and leaving his body caked in sand and mud. Kiya considered it to be only a minor inconvenience and before she knew it, he was balanced on the seat of the bike again, held in place only by the unstable grip of her free hand. They made it to the factory in good time, just before the sun bled over the land.

"Tonight," Kiya said, dumping the heavy waste-of-space onto Zeke's empty bed, "I clear Rycan's name."

Kieran arrived two hours later, exhausted and aching, but before he could rest, he had unfinished business to attend to.

Grabbing a shovel from the storage room, he made his way out to the dead trees, putting the remaining dregs of his energy into digging a hole deep enough and wide enough for Roxy's small frame.

He tried to keep his mind blank as he worked.

Each shovel-full of dirt irritated his hands until pussy blisters formed.

Kiya came to him when he was near completion, showing an absence in grime after a long shower. She was wearing a tight white t-shirt that showed her cream bra through its thin cotton and had dark jeans on- no belt. Her denim jacket was open at the front, parting to reveal her cleavage and her hair was trailing around her shoulders and back, wavy from the dampness of it. The skin on her beautiful face was devoid of make-up.

On approaching, she cleared her throat loud enough to be heard over the scrape of metal against rock and dirt.

Kieran lifted his head, shaking the hair from his eyes and managed a wilting smile.

"You okay?" she asked him, slipping her hands nervously into the back pockets of her trousers. Her eyes clocked onto the body of her female companion. The white cloth over her was rippling in the breeze.

"I'm almost done," Kieran replied, the drowsiness in his voice betraying his determination and strength.

"Come inside."

"In a minute."

Kiya let out an audible sigh, slipped the jacket off her shoulders and took the shovel from Kieran's blistered hands. He stood in awe, unsure whether he should argue with her or thank her as she began to dig deep into the earth, making the grave a couple of inches deeper in preparation for the burial.

He sat and watched tiredly, feeling the wet on the ground seeping through his clothes.

"That'll do," he muttered gruffly, fifteen minutes later.

Kiya wiped her brow and climbed out of the hole with help from her lover. He then settled Roxy's body in the grave, finding Kiya's hand to squeeze. She kissed his arm before resting her head against it.

"She was a good kid." Kieran kept his eyes on the grave, ignoring the trembling of his body against the cold. "She fought well. A true warrior." He reached out for the shovel. "I'll miss her."

"Me too," Kiya agreed softly.

Nothing more was said.

The grave was packed tightly with dirt and the Slayers returned to their dwelling, seeking food and sharing a desire to dive into the oblivion of sleep for a *very* long time.

Chapter 55

Clearing His Name

The Mayor of Meridion paced his study with a glass of scotch in one hand and the half empty bottle in the other. He was fretting over the war that had occurred just one night previous and the carnage that the vampires had left behind. It seemed he owed his life to the Karanthian's for showing up when they did. If it hadn't been for them, the city would have been overrun and in the hands of evil and he, no doubt, would be dead.

But for now, things were quiet. Or at least, as quiet as they could be after the massacre.

There were a *lot* of people dead. The gates around the city had proved useless, after he'd *promised* years ago that they would help keep the bad guys out. How could he have been so stupid as to forget the old mine? A perfect and protective breeding ground for the un-dead?

He downed what was left in his glass and re-filled it hastily. Sleep had eluded him for well over twenty four hours now and he was beginning to feel an unbearable heaviness on his eyelids.

"Lydia," he whispered, slumping into his padded green leather chair. In his hands he clasped a picture frame bearing a relatively recent photo of his deceased daughter. Her smile was full of warmth and beauty- fresh and one might say 'contagious.' She had loved life.

He stared into the oblivion of Lydia's eyes until eventually, his misery took its toll. With tears bleeding from his eyes, he rested his head on the tabletop, no longer able to look at his daughter in case his heart might break in two.

Suddenly, there came a tap on the window pane behind him.

He bolted upright, sniffing back the sadness that was spilling from him and as smoothly as he could, he plucked up the gun that was attached to the underside of his impressively polished desk.

The tapping came once more.

Taking a deep breath, he threw himself from his high-backed chair and aimed the gun at a woman, crouched outside on his windowsill.

The woman seemed unfazed by his display of stealth. She was beautiful; long dark hair, pale skin, with high, rouged cheekbones. Her eyes were narrow slits and her thin brown eyebrows almost met in the middle as she scowled in at him. The weather outside was abysmal as usual, and the wind whipped her long leather coat around her- like an angel flapping its wings.

For a moment, he thought she was a vampire, until her unfriendly smile triggered something in his memory. He had seen her face before.

"Mind if I come in?" she said, steaming up the glass with her breath.

The Mayor's mind went dizzy on him as he glared at her- the effects of the scotch of course. It took a couple of shakes to get the mushy organ scientists called a 'brain' to become coherent.

"I'll call security!" he threatened, slurring his worlds ever so slightly.

"No you won't," she replied, showing a lack of fear, which he found to be quite intimidating.

"Please, leave me in peace. What's done is done." He was referring to the execution of Kiya's boyfriend. He believed she was here, at his window, to avenge her lover's death.

"I'm afraid you're wrong." Kiya could feel her legs cramping up. She was in a most uncomfortable position, but she refused to give up. "Let me in."

"No." He pointed the gun at her head, suddenly more sober than he had been in days.

She sighed, and using her elbow, smashed a hole in the glass. Quickly, she reached through, being careful not to scrape her skin on the jagged shards, and lifted the latch. The window slid upwards with ease and she dived through onto the carpet at the Mayor's feet.

"I'll shoot-" His voice wavered. He wasn't sure where to take this. If he killed her, he'd have a lot of explaining to do, followed by a lot of paperwork.

"But then you'll never hear what I have to say."

"I'm sure I'll sleep easy even if I don't."

"It regards your daughter."

The Mayor showed a flicker of doubt in his eyes as he whispered, "That's over with. The man who killed her is dead-"

"He lives," Kiya persisted, standing before him now. Rain dripped from her clothes in little rivulets. She was trying her hardest not to look at the gun in his shaking hand.

"I saw them cut his head off. Of course he's dead."

"Rycan wasn't a killer."

"Don't come here pestering me with new theories. Just let me mourn my daughter's death so that I can move on."

"I have a signed confession from the man who did this."

The Mayor's mouth dropped open, then closed just as abruptly, as Kiya handed him the note with Tristian's crude poem scrawled on. His eyes became teary as he slowly recited each line.

"Do you believe me now?"

"How do I know this isn't made up? A fake?"

Kiya had a feeling he would say this. "I have him. The man who framed my boyfriend and put the sword in your little girl. He used to obsess over me to the point of doing crazy things, as you can see. And now I have him, secured and at my mercy."

The Mayor handed the paper back to Kiya, looking as pale as a ghost.

"Take me to him."

She nodded. "With pleasure."

The factory was empty when Kiya pulled up on the motorbike, dismounting with a very shaken-up Mayor at her side, his thin grey hair looking terribly wind swept. Kieran had leant her his bike for the evening, while he took the long trek into the city on foot. He had received a phone call from Siren, claiming he was at the hospital suffering from a 'sword in the gut'- as he'd put it. The doctors had sewed him up and given him a blood transfusion. Because of the damage, he was to stay there for five, maybe six days so a nurse could change his dressings.

"I don't know how I'm going to tell him-" Kieran had said, holding Kiya close to his bare chest as they'd laid together on the bed, naked. They had not made love, but had felt the need to touch intimately.

"You'll find a way," she'd assured him, trailing her finger over his muscles.

When the rain had eased off, Kieran had set off, wishing Kiya the best of luck.

"Send Siren my love."

"I will," he'd promised, with a tip of his cowboy hat that he'd found in the bottom of his wardrobe. It helped keep the rain out of his eyes apparently.

In the darkness of the night, the Mayor appeared anxious, glancing around at the unknown territory as if a group of ninjas were about to jump out of the shadows and beat him to a pulp.

"This isn't a trick?"

Kiya put a hand on her hip. "Yes. You're right," she said blandly. "I've brought you here so that I can kill you and post pieces of your corpse to all the people who voted for you as Mayor."

He blinked in astonishment.

Kiya sighed loudly. "Don't be so fucking stupid. I'm not a murderer."

His expression altered. "Didn't you chop a man's arm off recently?"

"He tried raping me first. *I* just saw to it that *Carl* will think twice before approaching an innocent woman in the night again to-" she threw her hands up in the air in disgust. "Well, you know."

The Mayor nodded. He'd had a sneaking suspicion that Carl had left out most of the story when he'd read the interview in the newspaper. "I'll see to it the police are informed and that your name is cleared."

A small weight lifted from Kiya's shoulders. "Thanks. That would be great-"

Inside the factory, strange scratching sounds were coming from within Zeke's bedroom. Before Tristian had come around, Kiya had tied a rag to his mouth to stop his voice from disturbing her 'quiet time' with Kieran a few doors over.

"Is that him?" the Mayor queried, indicating the door.

"There's something you should know."

"Oh God- this isn't going to give me a heart attack is it? I've had enough on my plate this week-"

"He's not human." She opened the door to reveal Tristian trying to gnaw the rag off with his pearl white fangs. "He's a vampire."

Tristian looked up at the pair of them, his eyes displaying fear, which soon melted to anger. He struggled against his bonds like a dolphin caught in a net and made incoherent growling noises.

"This is you're daughter's *real* killer."

More weights lifted from her shoulders as the Mayor took a few nervous steps forward, kneeling before Tristian in order to get a better look at him in the lamplight.

"Did you?" he asked, barely above a whisper.

Tristian looked to Kiya as if urging her to free his mouth. To his surprise, she obliged him by untying the rag.

"She lies!" was his first outcry. "All lies and false accusations. She's lost her mind since her boyfriend was executed- running around calling herself a 'Vampire Slayer.' I'm innocent, I *swear*!"

The Mayor raised his hand. "Is your name Tristian?"

"Yes."

"Are you a vampire?"

Tristian tried concealing his fangs, but knew it was far too late to convince the Mayor he was human. "So what if I am?"

"Did you kill my daughter Lydia?"

"Did she bear bite marks?"

Tristian was playing dumb. Kiya became frustrated.

"He was *human* when he killed Lydia! He's only been a vampire for about a day or two."

His eyes flashed silver. With a long pink tongue, he licked his lips.

A thought flashed through Kiya's mind.

"If you tell the Mayor the truth I'll...," she hesitated, "...kiss you."

The silver disappeared and his face became full of intrigue.

"Kiss me first."

She frowned. "I can't trust you to tell him once I have-"

Tristian sighed.

"If you have information concerning my daughter, I demand that you tell me!" the Mayor exclaimed, trying to rattle the vampire's cage a little. Tristian ignored him with a cool flutter of his eyelids.

"*Tell him.*"

"Kiss me."

She rolled her eyes and swiftly pecked him on his moist, thin lips.

"I want tongue-"

"Tell him first."

The Mayor was looking completely distraught now. His eyes were bulging from his head and his veins were visible at his temples. His fingers were curled up into fists.

"Okay." Tristian bowed his head, avoiding the eyes that were fixed on his pale face. "I wrote the poem. *Yes*- I killed your daughter. *No*, I don't regret it. Getting Rycan out of the picture was the best thing I ever did- next to becoming immortal that is."

With a harsh back-hander, the Mayor smacked Tristian in the side of his head, knocking him to the floor. When the vampire was sat upright again, a trickle of blood spilled from the corner of his mouth.

"I believe I'm owed a snog-" he smiled smugly, pretending like the Mayor's distress was nothing to do with him.

"You fucking bastard!" he screamed.

"Now, now Mayor. What kind of roll model are you to the good people of Meridion using language like that?"

He gave Tristian a good hard kick to the head, breathing heavily in his old age. Kiya allowed him to do so. Who was she to intervene? This man was hurting just as much as she was.

"Tutt, tutt," Tristian said in feigned dismay at his behaviour. "Now kiss me Kiya and pretend like you're enjoying it," he ordered.

She leant forward, inches from his mouth.

"Fuuuuck you."

In a rage, Tristian tried lunging for her neck, but Kiya was already upright and backing away with the Mayor in tow. She closed the door behind them, leaving Tristian to his screaming and bawling. He could yell all he wanted- no one was going to save him from his fate.

"I'm sorry to have put you through all this," she said, now that they were at the open door of the factory, "But it had to be done for Rycan's sake, as well as my own."

"I know," the Mayor replied solemnly. Boldly, he placed a hand on Kiya's shoulder. It was vacant of her Samurai sword- for once. "It's quite understandable. I'm glad you did."

"Then that's it I suppose. You can keep the confession for your own records."

His eyes twinkled in the light. "I'll have the authorities take him away if you wish?"

"No-" she said abruptly, throwing his wearied mind into confusion. "The police have suffered enough losses after the vampire siege. I wouldn't want to drag them out here for this. To be honest, I planned on dealing with Tristian myself."

He stood silently for a while, mulling things over.

"Very well... but I don't want to hear reports of a man with severed limbs on my desk anytime soon."

"You won't. I promise."

There was a pause, in which the Mayor extended his hand for her to shake.

"If you don't mind, I think I'll phone for one of my men to pick me up, if that's okay with you? Bikes were never my kind of thing."

Kiya was glad of this. She had a sunrise to catch and a destination to reach before then, with her disobedient and reluctant captive. The Mayor was just someone she'd been obligated to reach- taking him home would have just slowed her down.

Stone Table, here I come.

The rain she hated the most- the fine, almost fluffy, floating kind- seemed to find its way to her face without any problems as she sped along the dirt road with Tristian perched on the back of the leather seat. It was a miserable night, as usual, but Kiya had grown accustomed to the bad weather after so much exposure.

"I'm slipping!"

"No you're not," she bellowed over her shoulder.

Tristian was still bound at the wrists and was clinging onto the bike with his thighs alone. If he had the guts, he would have jumped off, but Kiya had warned him that if such an event occurred, she would swing the bike around and chop his head off without batting an eyelid.

"You're gonna kill me anyway-" he'd complained.

"That's right. But it's up to you how many more hours you have left to enjoy in my company. You can die now, or later. It's your choice."

At the Stone Table, police tape trailed around the stones haphazardly, yellow and vivid in the street lights. It had been broken in places, but had been wrapped around enough times to at least circle the stones in one unbroken circuit.

In the centre, the Stone Table had been left at a jaunty angle, revealing the hole in the ground, and later, Kiya would discover from her lover that the Karanthian's had gone below to flush the vamps out with flame throwers and silver bullets. It was just as well she and Kieran had left with Roxy's body when they did.

"Well, the great vampire revolution didn't last very long, did it?" she pointed out, propping the bike up and sliding her leg over till it came to meet the other on the pavement.

"I was never particularly interested in it anyway."

"Why, not enough little girls for you to kill?"

"Something like that."

Kiya scowled. "You make me sick."

Grabbing him by the scruff of the neck, she threw him towards the stones, feeling the adrenaline pulsing through her body.

This was it. The moment she'd been waiting for.

Tristian fell into the tape, unable to break his fall with his hands still bound behind his back and he crashed down onto the flattened, boot trodden grass.

"Recognise this place?" she said, becoming angrier with each intake of rancid air.

"How can I not?"

Tristian wriggled onto his knees. Kiya assisted him roughly onto the Stone Table.

"Going to cut my head off like the executioner did to your poor, dear Rycan?"

She grit her teeth and smashed her fist into his nose. It was still flecked with blood from their previous onslaught underground and now bled afresh.

"You are not to say his name."

"But it's so pretty-" he grimaced, making her blood boil even more.

"He's trapped here because of you."

"Do you believe *all* the myths and legends you hear?"

"I'm sitting in front of a vampire. A few years ago they were nothing but fantasy to me. So what do you think?"

"True. True."

Tristian's knees were beginning to hurt against the cool grey stone. He fidgeted, glancing around in hope of spying a vampire companion, who might come and free him.

"You're remarkably calm for a guy who's about to die."

Inside, he was screaming. He'd become a vampire to live forever. Now, his gift was about to expire with the sunrise.

"Gotta make my girl proud of me," he grinned, studying the icy glare on Kiya's face.

She glanced at the sky. Not long now.

"I hate you so much," she whispered, closing her eyes for a moment. Tristian was silent as she reached out to Rycan with her mind.

I hope you're okay baby, she thought. *You'll always be in my heart until the day I die. I promise. I told you I wouldn't let you down.*

Suddenly, Tristian groaned, breaking her inner calm.

In the distance, the sky was being spiked with rays of light.

Her heart sped up.

"Can you live with yourself for doing this?" Tristian asked through the pain. His face was contorted grotesquely as it became patchy in places.

"If you had been human, it may have taken a few days. But since you're already dead, it doesn't really occur to me that you have feelings anymore-"

A tear spilled from one silver eye as Tristian's skin broke apart here and there. Red burn marks appeared all over his arms and face and his hair was prickling and curling up as if being exposed to fire.

"You're a cruel bitch!" he screamed. "A cruel, cruel bitch!"

She stood in a trance, watching the skinny man writhing in pain as the sunlight burnt his flesh. It felt so satisfying, seeing him pay for what he'd done. Revenge was most *definitely* sweet.

"I loved you!"

Her eyes began to spill with tears of hatred.

"*I loved you!*"

Without much thought, she reached out a hand to the back of his head and kissed him hard on the lips- not out of love, or pity, but *spite*- feeling his skin blistering against her touch. It silenced his screams long enough for his bones to crumble to powder and his ashes to blow away with the rain and wind.

The ordeal was over at last.

A new day, full of endless possibilities, had arrived and Kiya found it to be *most* welcoming.

Epilogue

Six Months Later

Since the war, and Kiya's conversation with the Mayor about his daughter's killer, the government had funded Kieran's 'vampire slaying' business, so that it collaborated with the police force and had an easily accessible station- on the map- which citizens could go to when they were in need of well qualified men and women to slaughter bad-guys.

Kieran was appointed highest ranking officer. He worked hard, and he played hard. The pay was astounding and the perks endless. After word had gotten around about the 'Master' destroying himself in Kieran's presence, he'd even been granted a brand new motorbike- minus Zeke's name in the paintwork.

Life was good.

And he'd earned it.

In the kiss of the evening's dwindling warmth, upon the rooftop of the Sun Tower, Kiya clutched the barrier tightly, leaning her weight into the flaking paintwork of the metal so that she could glance over its edge. Below her, the Stone Table peered up at the clouds, ominously surrounded by white lilies that had grown in thick bunches the day after Tristian had gone up in flames.

The silence up high was breath taking.

Meridion had never been so peaceful.

"Hi, beautiful."

Her breath caught in her throat as a hand laced around her swollen stomach. Kieran spread his palm as wide as it would go so that it covered most of her abdomen. He could feel movement instantly.

Kiya smiled broadly, turning to wrap her arms around Kieran's neck and standing on tip-toes to do so. Her scarlet maternity dress billowed around her hypnotically and her hair, cut short and layered, fluttered across her eyes.

They kissed. It was long and passionate. Two lovers feeling the ache for each other after a long day apart.

"I taste beer-"

Kieran scratched the back of his neck sheepishly as they pulled away. "Siren and I stopped off for a couple of drinks."

Kiya punched his arm playfully.

"What?" he laughed, rubbing the place where she'd struck him.

"You know he's not meant to drink when he's covering the night shifts."

"I know, I know. He only had one."

"Good. I don't want him patrolling when he's intoxicated."

Kieran waved his hand in her face to cast her accusations and concerns aside. "Things are slow now anyway. We don't see many un-dead guys and gals around here like the old days."

"But you never know when something might come up."

He pulled her into a hug, feeling her round belly pressing into his flat, muscular stomach. It gave him tingles up his spine.

"Siren knows the score. Don't fret."

She sighed. She was just glad Kieran didn't have to patrol every night like he used to. He had his men working in shifts and spent most of his own time writing and reading reports at the station all day long. Action was thin. The closest he'd gotten to slaying anything in months was the big black spider she'd discovered in the shower.

"How are you feeling?"

"Tired and a little hungry."

"You shouldn't keep coming here in your condition. What if you fainted- or worse- and no one was around to help?"

"Now who's the worrier?" she asked, smiling up at him.

His eyes looked serious all of a sudden.

"I worry about you. I want to take more time off work-"

"Don't be silly. There's still a long way to go yet."

Kieran placed a hand on her face, touching her tenderly and drawing her in for another kiss.

"That was nice," she breathed in pleasure, feeling the brush of his lips lingering on her own.

"Of course it was nice. Look who you're engaged to!"

Kiya rolled her eyes. "I swear, if I hadn't have known you were a Slayer and we'd just met in the street, I would have thought you were an arrogant underwear model or…or a *stripper*."

"Hmmm," he said thoughtfully, "All compliments,"

She groaned, feigning aggravation.

"Enough about me. Let's talk about you."

"Are you sure?" she retorted in mock surprise, as if it was a foreign occurrence.

Kieran grinned and started to tickle her above her hips. She wriggled and laughed, trying to get away from him, crying "Stop! Stop! I'll wet myself! You don't want me to go into labour while we're up here do you?!"

"Okay. Okay." He put his hands up in defeat. "I'll leave you be."

She tried to compose herself by patting the maternity dress down and tucking her hair behind her ears.

"Have you come up with any names yet?" he queried, now that they had calmed down some.

She let out the breath she'd been holding in before speaking. "I was thinking… 'Phoenix.'"

Kieran nodded his approval. "So you've got our son sorted. But what about my little girl?"

Kiya's lips spread in happiness. Kieran had taken the 'twin' thing quite well when they'd seen the results of the ultrasound.

"Your choice. What would you like it to be?"

He looked to the sky in thought, making *hmmm* noises.

"I've always liked the sound of '*Atlanta.*'"

"Atlanta." Kiya repeated. "And Phoenix."

"You feeling it?"

She couldn't stop grinning from ear to ear.

"I love it."

Kieran burst into the biggest grin she'd ever seen and he picked her up off her feet, being careful not to press into her belly too much. Kiya squealed in delight, clamping onto his shoulders for sheer life and feeling the air parting around her as her legs swirled about. When he stopped rotating on the spot, his facial features relaxed ever so slightly.

"I told you I wouldn't let anything hurt you."

Flashes of memory hit Kiya as she thought back to her short-lived occupation as a Vampire Slayer. Now, she was looking into training as a nurse, so that she might put her healing powers to good use.

"I know."

"I love you so much."

She didn't need to reply. Kieran could tell by the look on her face that she felt the same way about him.

"Let's get you into bed," he suggested at last.

Kiya nuzzled her head into his chest and felt a wave of content spill over her as he carried her towards home.

She was the happiest she'd been in a long time.

And as they left the roof, she smiled up at the Heaven's, assuring her lost lover that Kieran would make a brilliant father in his place.

You have nothing to worry about Rycan, she thought, and bid him fare well, one last time.

THE END

About the Author

Karla Brading lives in South Wales, where she currently works as an assistant at Merthyr Tydfil Public Libraries.

She enjoys reading, writing about strong female characters, getting tattooed and wearing fabulous dresses as often as she can.

She was raised single handed by her mum- Denise- and would like to express her gratitude for all the sacrifices she's had to make for both herself and her three sisters, Emily, Nadine and Alice.

Karla believes that no matter how crap life can seem, as long as you have three very interesting, stunningly good looking and insanely hilarious siblings, you'll be just fine. She'd like to thank Emily for all the entertainment she's provided in front of the camera (our Most Haunted episodes blow Derek Acorah's out of the water!); Nadine for all the times she accompanied her to the cinema (carrying Karla's shopping bags because she didn't have any of her own) and little Alice for making the effort to buy really nice birthday and Christmas presents, even though she has very little money to save!

With high school at its end, Karla finds herself missing her friends dearly. She hopes they'll keep in touch and would like to remind them that they are never far from her thoughts.

If you would like to get into contact with Karla, or would like more information on Destiny in Blood and its sequel, Blood of Angels, go to:

www.myspace.com/destinyinblood